MW00386770

Robinson Crusoe 2246

A Novel

E. J. Robinson

This is a work of fiction. Names, characters, places, and incidents either are the product of the author's imagination or are used fictitiously. Any resemblance to actual persons, living or dead, events, or locales is entirely coincidental.

ROBINSON CRUSOE 2246
Copyright © 2016 *Erik J. Robinson*
http://erikjamesrobinson.com

All rights reserved, including the right to reproduce this book,
or portions thereof, in any form.
(Illuminati Press)

Edited by Jessica Holland
Cover Design by Amalia Chitulescu
Formatting by Polgarus Studio

For my sons

PART ONE

"The road that is built in hope is more pleasant to the traveler than the road built in despair, even though they both lead to the same destination."

-Marion Zimmer Bradley

Chapter One
The Pack

"How far back are they?" Robinson gasped.

Friday tugged the scarf from her face and lifted the waterskin to her mouth. After two deep draughts, she wrapped the cords tightly around it and slipped it back under her coat. Then she turned east, eyes narrowing on the funnel of dust growing on the horizon.

"An hour or less." She grimaced.

Less than a single turn.

The old Robinson might have cursed, but these days he knew it was wasted breath. Instead, he wiped the sweat from his brow, the coarse sand from his hand pricking his skin, and brought his scavenged binoculars to his eyes.

There was nothing as far as he could see. Not a crevice. Not a stand of trees. Only sterile, infinite prairie land in all directions. With the sun barely past its zenith, night was too far off to aid them.

"Do we make our stand here?" Robinson asked.

Friday put a hand to her brow before pointing west over the Great Plains. "There. A structure, four or five spans out."

Robinson looked, but he only saw wavering heat. He licked his dry lips. "Can we make it in time?"

"We must," she said before dashing off.

Robinson slipped the binoculars away and followed.

They'd been running for a day and a half straight, ever since the pack had reacquired their trail.

The first encounter had come two moons after leaving Cowboytown. They'd been working their way north on a rumor that the City of Glass might be located near the Great Lakes. After they'd set up camp on the outskirts of Indianapolis, the attack commenced.

"Renders!" Robinson yelled.

The assumption was reasonable enough. The signs were there. Mutated flesh. Guttural roars. And yet the attack was coordinated on three sides. When the deluge of bolts and bullets rained down on them, they understood they were seeing something new.

"They're armed!" Friday shouted.

Robinson couldn't believe it. The weapons had been fused into their flesh.

They'd managed to escape that night. And as the weeks passed, they had begun to doubt what they'd seen. When the Great Lakes proved fruitless, they turned south as the sweltering humidity of summer descended. It was there, a month later, when they were preparing to cross the Missouri river, that the second attack had come, this time in daylight. That armed Renders were involved was no longer questionable. Perhaps more disturbing was that they were commanded by a single man.

He led from the back of a rendered bison, a beastly ruminant with engorged musculature and horns like inverted elephant tusks. The man had worn a tattered brown duster and a mask of burnished steel. At odd intervals, he raised something to his mouth, and thin discordant notes echoed over the prairie. Those notes drove the pack with furious zeal.

Robinson and Friday managed to make another escape that day by leaping into the churning river. But here, less than two weeks later, the pack was on them again.

It left little doubt they were being hunted.

They fled over a land in decay. Drought had driven the loam from the soil, leaving hardpan, scoured and baked. What soil wasn't calcified had been buried in an ocean of ruin.

Robinson felt the ache of his muscles keenly, but was too busy worrying about Friday to feel the pain. By his calculation, she was close to four months pregnant. And despite her assurances to the contrary, it was starting to take its toll. She was slower, requiring more food and rest. And though she still hadn't shown signs of affliction, they both knew it was only a matter of time.

They needed to find the City of Glass quickly. Because failure meant death. And death for one meant death for all.

They had been running at a fevered clip for a quarter turn when Robinson looked back to see the pack gaining. The rise of dust had turned into a dark shadow. There were more than he'd thought.

Robinson thumbed his pistol and saw he only had three bullets left. Boss had given him extra gunpowder, but like a fool, he hadn't made time to refill his spent cartridges since crossing the river. Friday was also down to her last four arrows. Outnumbered and with fewer weapons, Robinson and Friday were in serious trouble.

The structure soon became visible. Robinson doubted they could reach it in time. He was about to call out to Friday when a gust of hot air blasted him from the north. He pulled his hat low to avoid the whipping thistles and briars.

Friday kept turning her head north. Robinson called over the swelling roar to find out why. Her only response was to pick up the pace. The wind worsened. Robinson wrapped some fabric over his face, covering everything but his eyes, but the sand still blinded him. The stinging grit scoured their clothes and skin.

A look back revealed the pack had cut the distance between them in half. They were now close enough to count. *Eight. Nine. Ten.* Eleven counting their masked leader. He rode at the forefront, furiously whipping the reins of his beast as it tore across the cracked earth. Their gait left little doubt that they'd seen the structure and were now racing to prevent their quarry from reaching it.

Once again, Robinson called out, "Friday! I don't think we're going to make it. If we stop here, we can catch our breath before the fighting starts."

"We must reach the shelter," Friday said.

"We have a better chance of cutting down their numbers if we turn and face them."

This time, Friday turned to him. "It's not the pack I am worried about."

Friday nodded north. Robinson turned and nearly lost his footing.

A dust storm had risen on the horizon and filled the sky as far as the eye could see—a suffocating curtain of earth several thousand feet tall and still climbing. Brown at the center, inky black at the base. As it swept across the land, it smothered everything in its path. It was as if the land had been upended. Earth had become sky. Day had become night.

Hell had come.

Robinson's mouth lolled open and dirt coated his tongue. He didn't bother spitting. He didn't have the time.

Cassa saw the dust storm roiling and grunted. Such was his luck. He'd been hunting the pair for two months straight, ever since the Master had set his horde on their trail. And yet each time they came close to their target, the pair had managed to slink away. Whether by luck, it didn't matter. Failure was failure. This time, he swore it would be different.

The girl was formidable. Cassa had seen many outliers work a recurve bow, but her gifts eclipsed them all. Despite movement, fatigue, and environment, her arm never wavered. Her aim was always true. She impressed him. In another life, he might have pursued this woman sexually. Conscripted her love with fear or fear with love. But not now. Not her. She carried the seed of the boy in her belly. Even if the Master hadn't marked her for death, she was *tainted*.

The boy had surprised him more. Cassa hadn't expected him to own a firearm, much less know how to use one. Yet each time they crossed paths, the gun seemed to find the boy's hand with ease, its red eye sampling the air like a serpent's tongue ready to strike.

Cassa had been astute in anticipating the pair's movement. North then south, progressively moving west. He had amassed his horde at the river that bordered the dead lands and waited. His instincts proved true. They always had. And yet, even now as the trap had sprung, this storm threatened to undermine everything. He had to reach them first.

Cassa put the pipes to his lips and blew loudly. The pack responded immediately as fury overtook them.

The chorus of howls broke through the storm, which now loomed ten thousand feet high, blotting out the sun. Robinson felt the air fill with electricity before the thunderheads broke. He knew it would be close.

Dust—fine as flour—assailed him, coating the inside of his nose and throat. He coughed and struggled to keep sight of Friday in front of him.

In all his days, Robinson had never seen anything so massive, so immutably powerful as that storm. All of mankind's monuments and endeavors paled beneath the might of nature's wrath. In its great shadow, he felt pure humility.

The structure was a single-story relic of another time. Though less than one hundred meters away, it too had begun to vanish under the torrent of dust and debris. Just when Robinson thought they might reach it, a bolt flew past his shoulder and missed Friday's legs by centimeters. There was no chance of making the sanctuary in time. Not together anyway. With one hand, he pulled the sling from the loops of his trousers and slipped a weighty river rock into its cradle. As his arm craned in revolution, he knew his timing would have to be perfect.

Cassa saw the boy's arm rotating and pulled on the reins, but it was too late. The projectile hit Bull between the eyes. Cassa felt the beast lurch and pull to the right, but it kept its footing. He wanted to howl with delight. Then, he saw the girl coming around with her bow. He was shocked when she missed to the right.

Friday knew that hulking monster would be impossible to put down with a single arrow, so she aimed for the smaller one next to it instead. The arrow sunk deep into the creature's left leg, and as expected, it veered violently into the behemoth's path. As they collided, both tumbled forward at full speed, catapulting end over end.

The remaining pack pulled up or veered wide. It only took a second, but it was enough. Friday grabbed Robinson and darted for the shelter. The full force of the storm caught them a dozen feet short, launching them off their feet toward their target, sending them rolling in the blackness until they too were swallowed by earth.

Chapter Two

Dust

Friday woke, eyes burning, nostrils caked with dust. She tried to move, but her body wouldn't respond. It took her a moment to realize she was buried up to her neck.

Friday wasn't prone to panic, but an image took hold in her mind. The nook inside Arga'Zul's ship. All those months she'd spent chained to the floor, her body and mind withering away. For a moment, she could feel the motion of the ship and smell the odor of the slaves in the pen nearby. But she fought the memory back as she always did. She had survived the *Spinecrusher* and Arga'Zul. She would survive this too.

A narrow shaft of sunlight plunged from an old window above, illuminating the dust mites that danced lazily in the air. Friday took in her surroundings. The structure was old but stable, made up of concrete bricks and steel framing that had yet to submit to rust. She felt a breeze stealing from somewhere and willed her heartbeat down.

Friday heard Crusoe before she saw him. He was snoring lightly nearby. He too was covered in dirt, canted inside the strange steel furrow at the bottom of the structure that had likely saved them. She decided to let him sleep and gyrated in her cocoon until her arms and torso came free.

Friday patted her pockets until she retrieved the crane meat she'd been saving since before they crossed the river. It was tough but good, despite the

9

earthy grit that peppered it. After four bites, she rewrapped the rest for Crusoe. He would argue, as he always did, that she needed it more. She was eating for two after all. How could she forget?

Friday had made it past the three-moon mark and knew this should bring her relief. But she also knew the baby was feeding on blood that carried the plague of the ancients. Though she'd yet to show signs of affliction, it was only a matter of time.

And yet, Friday had always lived a life devoid of fear. Or perhaps despite it. With Crusoe by her side, she had beaten back death so many times. Clearly, the Goddess had plans for them. And if they were meant to live, maybe their child was too.

When Robinson finally woke, he called out in a panic, only to calm down when Friday took his hand. He asked about the storm, and Friday told him it had passed.

"How long did we sleep?"

"Through the night."

Friday watched him take in their surroundings. He inquired about the pack.

"I've heard nothing but the wind," Friday replied.

Robinson's shoulders lifted as he began to dig himself out of the dirt. "We'd better look around then."

The cleft in the building came from a tear at the top of a retractable metal door. Robinson clambered up the drift to peer out.

"Looks clear," he said, before winding his way through the jutting divide.

Friday exited the structure to find Robinson staring out over the prairie land, which was now a monotone ocean of dirt as far as the eye could see. The only discernable rise on the horizon were the mountains far to the north.

"What is this place?" Friday asked.

"I think it's an old fuel station," Robinson answered. "That corridor we fell into in the basement? I'll bet it was used to tinker the underside of automobiles."

The words meant nothing to Friday. Still, it pleased her Crusoe could decipher the riddle of such things, and how he took his own pleasure in the mechanics of the ancient ways. She wondered if their child would as well.

Robinson withdrew his waterskin and took a modest drink, handing it to Friday when he was done. She offered him the remaining crane meat afterward. He considered turning her down before he saw that familiar scowl.

He was stuffing the last piece in his mouth when he spotted something in the dirt a dozen paces away.

"Look," he said.

A glint of metal shimmered from a swollen patch of dirt. When they drew close enough, they saw it was an ulcerated arm. Robinson went to nudge it with his foot when Friday warned him back. She drew out her blade and sunk it into the meaty part of the body beneath. There was no reaction.

Only then did Robinson pull the Render's corpse from the sand.

The creature looked identical to the thousands they'd encountered before, save one difference: this one was armed.

"Take its weapon," Friday said.

"Easier said than done," Robinson replied. He twisted the creature's arm to reveal the weapon—a bolt launcher of some sort—had been sewn into its flesh. "This isn't even manual. See these wires? They're layered under the skin."

Friday looked confused. "What triggers its release?"

Robinson followed the wires up the creature's shoulder to a small metal box at the back of its head. A wave of goosebumps ran over him.

"Incredible," he said. "Someone has surgically implanted a control device inside this creature's brain. If I had to guess, I'd say it was operated by that masked fellow with the pipes."

"Pipes?" Friday repeated.

"A musical instrument. Like a flute."

"But it was alive."

"If you can call a permanent state of physical and mental enslavement 'alive'. Half monster, half machine. Someone with real skill did this."

"It is an abomination," Friday said, making a warding gesture. "The one who did this is evil."

11

"No doubt. The question is: what do they want with us?"

"It is of no concern. We have defeated them. Let us bury this *thing* and be done with it."

Robinson agreed, but something told him he hadn't seen the last of these augmented Renders.

After retrieving their gear from the shelter, Robinson and Friday gathered at the edge of the structure to peruse Pastor's map. It was dirty and wrinkled, but the plastic sleeve had kept it in good shape.

"So we travelled north to this point—Lake Superior."

"I still say it was an ocean," Friday quipped.

"Oceans are salty. This was fresh. Then again, who knows what's for real in this country? I can only go by what I see and what's on the map."

"This map is old."

"Everything here is," Robinson said, kicking the structure's eaves. "Doesn't mean it isn't good. Plus, I trust the man that gave this to me."

Robinson had told Friday about Pastor and the time they spent on the road together—their mutual love for history and books. She knew these things were important to Crusoe. He was a thinker, like her father. But to her, ideas were dangerous. And the bigger the idea, the greater the danger. The trouble was, Crusoe liked big ideas.

Robinson tapped the map. "So, we searched Iowa, Missouri, and Kansas, but found nothing."

"Corn," Friday said. "Plenty of corn."

"Those people did love their corn," Robinson agreed. "But now we're in Oklahoma. We could continue south, but I'm not optimistic about Texas. Looks even bleaker than here."

Friday watched him look out over the plains. He was a patient decision maker. It was another thing she admired about him. There were times when she wanted him to act on instinct, but some things shouldn't be rushed. She waited for him to decide.

"Those miners we ran into said the largest population this side of the Missup was here," he pointed at the map, "in Denver, Colorado. If we make our way up through this pass, we can probably reach it in a week or two. The concern is elevation."

"Why is this a concern?" Friday asked.

"The higher the elevation, the lighter the air. It might get hard for you to breathe."

Friday glowered. "I can hold my breath and still reach Denver before you."

Robinson laughed and held up his hands. "All right. No need to get testy. It's just the thought of my little chatterbox staying quiet all that way doesn't sit so well with me."

"You want to see 'doesn't sit well'? Come here."

Robinson ran off laughing with Friday in quick pursuit.

It was just past midday when a pair of willow grouses landed atop the refueling station in need of rest. They'd had a bountiful morning trolling centipedes and small snakes when movement drew their eyes to the shifting dirt where a gloved hand broke the surface.

Cassa's head rose from the sand, gasping as the birds took flight. Then he finished pulling himself out of the dirt and struggled to his feet. He knew he was lucky to be alive, though the thought rankled him. Lucky would have been to finish the boy and girl before the storm swallowed him. One look at the pair of footprints leading off to the west, and he knew he'd failed again.

The master would be furious, but what could Cassa have done differently? A superstitious man might have believed the Gods were aligned against him. Cassa was not such a man. He knew there were no guarantees in life. Every victory had to be earned, and the best victories were those earned on the back of defeat. He had mustered a good pack, conceived a successful plan of attack, but how could he have foreseen a dust storm?

The one saving grace was the master's hatred of the boy. It was a fire that consumed him. If Cassa was allowed a third opportunity to track his targets, he swore he would succeed or die trying.

Cassa returned to the pit he'd crawled from and lifted his mask. He raised the pipes to his lips and blew. Bull burst from the sand. As the bison scrambled out of the pit, Cassa looked at the old rusted shell of the buried fuel tanker that had saved his life. Maybe the Gods favored him after all.

One look around told Cassa the rest of the pack was dead, and yet he raised the pipes to his lips once more and blew the note to call them. The only sound he heard was the desert wind. With a final sigh, Cassa mounted Bull. He looked west. His enemy was likely reveling in their victory. It would be short lived.

Cassa pulled the reins and spurred Bull in the opposite direction.

Chapter Three
What Lies Beneath

Once past the boundary of scoured earth, the prairie grew rich with buffalo grass, blue grama, and fields of bluestem. Patches of purple verbena and coreopsis spilled over the mesas, leaving the world in colors and hues new to Robinson's eyes.

He felt a strange contentment during that time, a sense of harmony that ran counter to the fears that spearheaded their quest. It was almost as if he believed finding the City of Glass and curing Friday was not only a mere possibility, but also their destiny, after which they might continue their journey across this magnificent land to discover new people and new wonders.

If Friday shared such sentiments, she didn't reveal them. More likely, she felt the opposite. She had given her heart wholly to Robinson, and yet he understood how deeply her heart lay anchored to the Aserra and the mountains she called home. He believed when she dreamed of seeing their family whole, it was among her people. Robinson wondered if he would ever see his again.

And yet no matter where they traveled, Friday managed to bewitch sustenance from the land. What looked dry and dead atop the soil fed from waters deep below. Yucca, turnips, and beets were easy for her to find. In narrow springs, she found currants and wild plums. Antelope and jackrabbits were ever-present. They began to do more than survive. They thrived.

Robinson had been right about one thing: the higher altitude was taxing on Friday. As they passed into the borderlands of Colorado, her pace slackened, though neither spoke of it.

In the residue of a ghost town, they managed to unearth leftover camping supplies. Using laces from old boots, they patched together two ancient tents to form a passable shelter. They even foraged an old sleeping bag for warmth, though those summer nights never got too cold.

After three weeks without seeing another person, they risked their first fire made of limbs from a piñon tree. There, huddled together, they basked in the fickle warmth as the sky bled to stars.

"What's the Aserra name for the stars?" Robinson asked.

"We call them *zhēng caído amados*," Friday answered. "It means 'watchful eyes.' In the old days, when one of the tribe met death during great service, their body was bound in the flesh of our enemies and carried to the highest mountain in our land. Its name is *Ele Fundo Quán*."

"The deep well," Robinson translated.

"Mountains to the Aserra are like trees or people. However high they rise above the surface, their roots sink twice as deep beneath. *Ele Fundo Quán* descended so far it draws its life-water from the sacred pools at the heart of the world. These are the same waters that fed the first Aserra.

"For this reason, *Ele Fundo Quán* is a holy mountain. When the dead are placed atop her, birds will not feed of their flesh. Nor insects or snakes. They are left in peace to await the passage of the Goddess who circles behind the sun on wings of mist. If the dead meet her approval, they take their place in the sky, joining our other ancestors to watch over and protect us."

"Do they all make it?" Robinson asked.

"No. But those that do send a signal by blinking their eyes to let us know they have arrived. Even now, you can see them."

Watching Friday survey the firmament, Robinson felt a tugging deep inside him. He loved several people in his life, but never so deeply.

"Do the people of your Isle share such a story?" Friday asked.

Robinson had always been loath to speak of science in front of Friday. He knew magic and mysticism were anachronisms of primitive races, and yet he

16

did not begrudge them. People needed myths and stories to survive as surely as they needed food and water. Human existence was tumultuous and lonely. Stories were one of the few things that could make the solitude bearable.

"A lot of the ancient cultures looked to the stars for inspiration. In classic antiquity, the Greeks were one of the most significant. They named most of the planets—the larger stars—after their Gods. Venus, Mars, Jupiter. They also grouped stars together in constellations." Robinson pointed to the northern celestial hemisphere. "That one there is called Ursa Major, or The Great Bear. It contains the youngest known galaxy in the universe."

"What is a galaxy?" Friday asked.

"Another system of worlds like ours. Just imagine, somewhere among all those lights, there might be a world very much like this one where two people not too dissimilar from us are alone on the plains, being warmed by a fire, and looking up as our star winks at them."

"You believe this is possible?"

"I believe everything is possible. Especially when I'm with you."

She snorted, but he knew she enjoyed the sentiment. She lay her head on his chest as she ran her hands over her belly.

"I hope our child shares such wisdom."

"They will," Robinson said. "We'll teach him or her both our ways, so they'll have the best of the both of us."

"Your mind."

"Your strength."

"Your heart."

"Your stubbornness."

"*My* stubbornness?" Friday balked, smacking him lightly.

Robinson shook with laughter.

"Your beauty then."

"Beauty," she scoffed.

"A beauty to rival the stars."

"Ooh," she said, quickly reaching for his hands. She placed them on her belly. "Feel."

When he felt a gentle bump, his heart swelled.

"She enjoys the words we make," Friday said.

"*She?*"

Friday shrugged demurely. "It is the Goddess's will, but I feel it is so."

Robinson wrapped Friday tightly in his arms, never wanting to let go. But just an instant later, Friday sat up, the lines on her forehead darkening.

"What is it?" Robinson asked, already reaching for his axe.

Friday held up a finger, tilted her head, and listened to the night. There was nothing but the crackling of fire and the wind buffeting the plains. Friday rose anyway.

Robinson stood quietly as Friday crept beyond the edge of the fire to the boundary where flickering shadows met the crepuscular night. She halted there to let her eyes adjust, her head turning as she scanned the darkness.

Robinson felt his palms moisten and was about to call out when he heard a vague rustling to his left. Something about it sounded familiar, but he couldn't pinpoint why. Instinct prompted Robinson to move, but he didn't want to distract Friday. Then her head snapped right as a subtle rattling echoed in the darkness.

Adrenaline ticked into Robinson's system as he rose to peer beyond the void. Then he heard the rattle again—this time closer—and looked down. A large furrow moved in the sand, cutting a path toward Friday.

Robinson screamed, "At your feet!"

Friday leaped back as a massive serpent sprung from the sand, its dual heads snapping at Friday with fangs four inches long. Friday swung her sword instinctually, cutting both heads off the snake as a spray of bioluminescent poison splattered the rocks at her feet. Friday kicked the coiling, headless reptile into the night, its rattle, the size of a fist, quavering menacingly before the sound slowly ebbed away, replaced by the wind.

Chest heaving, Friday stood her ground, braving a single look at the severed heads before the tension started to leak from her body. Then all at once, another rattle sounded, followed by others, until the entire night seemed filled with their call.

The earth moved in rippling waves, streaming for both Friday and Robinson. They barely had time to prepare before snakes shot out of the dirt, fangs hissing as they attacked. Robinson spun away, swinging his axe through the first snake's meaty body as it passed him by, narrowly avoiding a second snake that bit into the dirt by his feet. This one bore three tails and landed in a huff before coiling back, preparing for a second strike. Robinson kicked one of the logs off the fire, and the snake hissed before delving back under the earth.

Three other snakes were snapping at Friday in a frenzy—a coordinated attack. She maneuvered deftly under the assault. Those with multiple heads used staggered attacks to work its body closer. Friday held her ground well, refusing to overextend herself until one got close enough for her to cut it down with her blade, sending a torrent of deadly venom into the air.

Robinson backpedaled toward some rocks when he felt something cut through his boot before a moment of blinding pain. Robinson hacked at the creature twice before he fell, and his axe flew from his hand. He heard more rattles surging in his direction and leaped for the only weapon near him—the burning branch from the fire. Robinson swung it at the snakes, who coiled back, hissing, before burrowing back underground.

Before Robinson could process what had happened, he heard Friday shout and looked to see the snakes edging her farther into the desert, where she was struggling to see. Her arms were already moving slower, and she looked desperate. Then at least three more snakes emerged behind her, their rattles shaking in anticipation.

"Friday!" Robinson shouted. "Get back to the fire! They fear fire!"

Friday leaped forward instead, swinging her sword with a wild, looping arc that sent the massive reptiles slithering back before she turned and rushed for the fire. Two leaped in unison after her, narrowly missing her heels as they plunged into the ground only to come up a few feet later for another salvo. Friday was a few feet away when she saw Robinson throw his torch. She caught it and swung around, striking the closest mutated snake on the snout. It immediately hissed in pain and burst into flames, convulsing around as fire consumed it.

"The venom," Robinson realized. "It's flammable."

Friday backed up to the campfire, swinging the torch back and forth as the rattling snakes edged back into the darkness, until the only thing she could see were their glowing eyes. Then, all at once, the rattles stopped, and they were gone.

"Are they gone?" Robinson asked.

Friday shook her head.

"They're circling," she said.

"Sure enough, Robinson could hear the sand rustling as they moved beneath the earth. He backed up to the fire until it felt like his calves might burn. He never stepped away.

"What do we do?" Robinson asked. "We can't stay here until morning. We don't have enough firewood."

Friday continued scanning the desert. "I saw some kindling out there. We'll wait a few moments and then I'll go after it."

"No," he said. "I'll go."

Friday glanced at him and saw his legs wobble. She looked down and saw something glowing on his pant leg. And blood.

"You've been bitten," she said, worried.

"Only grazed," he said, though he knew it was more than that. Already he could feel the poison moving through his body. "I saw a range of rocks a hundred meters to the northwest. If one of us stays here and keeps them busy, I'm sure the other can make it there."

"Then you had better get ready to run."

"Friday—"

"I am not leaving you."

"But our child—"

"Will know both its parents. Or none."

"You are so damned stubborn. Sometimes I could just…"

She looked across the fire at him and nodded.

"Me too," she said.

"Then we run together," Robinson said, picking up a second burning torch from the flames. Friday did the same. "On three. One. Two. Three!"

The second they separated from the fire, a rhumba of mutated rattlers launched from the earth, their rattles sounding like the leaves of an autumn tree. Both Robinson and Friday swung their torches across their bodies and behind them as the snakes pursued them. In the moonlight, Robinson thought he saw the rocks ahead of him before his vision began to blur and he fell. He shouted for Friday to keep going, but it came out garbled. His heart felt sluggish as he watched her plant legs on both sides of his prone body, swinging the torches as the snakes moved in, their fangs glowing in the dark, their rattles blotting out every other sound.

Friday spun three hundred and sixty degrees. Robinson heard her mumble, "They're everywhere," before his eyes fluttered. He fought to stay conscious as the poison washed over him. Then, just as darkness began to close in, he heard a whoosh in the sky above him and looked up to see several flaming satellites raining down from above. They struck the earth and burst into a tide of flames. Many of the mutated snakes burst into flames, hissing as the fire spread through their ranks. What snakes didn't catch fire, slithered back and dove underground, their furrows beating a hasty retreat into the night.

The smell of burning reptile and pungent kerosene made Robinson's eyes water, but he managed to see the eight torch-bearing figures appear on the small rise behind them. They were wrapped head-to-toe in red cloth, save a narrow slit for their eyes. Each was holding weapons at the ready.

Chapter Four

Troyus

"*Quantos años tem voce?*" one of the red figures asked.

"*Por quao?*" Friday replied, the edge to her voice unmistakable.

Robinson tried to stand, but his legs rebelled. Instead, he stared at the fire. The flames swayed languidly as sparks danced and rose into the ether.

The shadows surged closer. Robinson felt hands pull him to his feet, Friday's among them. He struggled to speak, but the words wouldn't come.

Several of the figures broke off to collect their weapons and gear. Others moved between the snake cadavers, using blades to cut through the jaw to strip away what he assumed was the venom glands.

Robinson tried to make out how many of them there were, but his vision grew distorted, and the light from their torches stung his eyes. His head bobbed as they waited for the others to return. Friday whispered something into his ear, but it was lost in the wind. A moment later, someone took his other arm, and they were off.

They moved in a cluster at a quick pace. The torches were held low, presumably to ward off more snakes. He listened to the flicker of flames and the shuffling of feet. He smelled the fraying fabric of the figures next to him. A few carried glass bottles hanging on cords around their necks, clinking as they ran. He heard liquid sloshing inside. Kerosene. Fire bombs.

A light voice behind him spoke. It sounded like a girl. The question felt familiar, as if it'd already been asked. He thought it was meant for Friday, but she didn't answer.

As they scaled a rise, Robinson leaned over and asked what she said.

"They want to know our age," Friday answered.

The question seemed impractical. Then Robinson noticed something.

"They have our weapons," he said.

Friday's mouth grew taut. "Not all of them," she whispered in English.

The trek continued for an unbearable time. When he heard Friday's labored breathing, Robinson begged them to stop, but his words came out unintelligible. He felt spittle running down his chin and knew he had vomited. His rapid heartbeat and thick tongue warned him of the end.

Before long, they were standing in a circle as Robinson was lowered onto a contraption with four wheels and a slight frame. He felt webbing beneath him. He looked for horses but saw none.

"What's your method of propulsion?" He managed to ask. The question surprised the figures in red. Or flummoxed them. He wondered if he'd asked it in English.

"How does it move?" he asked, this time in the common tongue.

One of them responded, "By night's breath."

He didn't understand. Friday and the rest of the group boarded, and a sail unfurled. The wind caught it, and the vessel stirred into motion.

Robinson knew something was off about these people, but in his state, he couldn't pinpoint what. Instead, he laid his head back and stared at the stars as they sped across the desert at a terrifying clip. The rush of air and snap of the sails filled his ears. He felt Friday's hand on his head, wiping sweat away despite the cold air that wracked him with chills. *Is it possible to feel like you're freezing and on fire at the same time?*

Oddly, one of the strangers began to hum. He thought it might be the girl again—the voice was so light—but the melody soon took sway. There was a familiarity to it. For a moment, he thought it might have been one of the songs Vareen had sung when he was a child, but the words were different.

Peeking, seeking, brother star,
Sister wonders where you are,
Hold the world, on high, on nigh,
Until her fire lights our eyes.
When the fulls are come again,
And tree of gifts done swallow sin,
Save us this, your fiery light,
Peeking, seeking, in the night...

The other joined in. The lyrics were dark; they felt prophetic, but the form gave way to purpose as Robinson settled in and rode the lullaby into a deep slumber.

He wasn't sure which roused him, the sound of scraping or the tug of skin, but when Robinson saw the razor hovering at his neck, he reached out and seized the wrist holding it.

The boy stared. He was young, eight or nine, with brown, matted locks and pallid skin, but it was his eyes that stood out. They were the green of spring foliage and held no fear.

"We need be finishing," the boy said. "For the Fives return."

"Fives," Robinson repeated, his voice as graveled as his head. "What's that? Your parents? Your elders?"

The boy paused, as if detangling the words.

"We call 'em Halfers in Troyus."

"*Troyus*," Robinson repeated, his breath returning slowly. "Is that where we are?"

"Ye'uh," the boy said. "Some Halfers name it O City, but I'm a *short*, so it's forbid."

Robinson eyed the razor. It was coated with soap and peppered with stubble. Steam rose from a milky bowl near his foot. Robinson reached up and touched his skin. His finger came away wet with a spot of blood.

"Where's Friday?" Robinson asked.

The boy craned his head. "Dunno. Naming days are past. Least 'ere.

Tomorrow counts some. Today's the more. After that, all's done and dust, ye'uh?"

"I meant," Robinson said, clearing his throat, "where is my wife?"

"The fem? Ah, she's vert enough. Up in the *nest* with the other swoles. You'll see her soon. Crosses."

"Crosses?"

"My word it means. Truth." The boy tugged gently at his hand. "Can I finish? Swears, it's for the best. The Full's groom no good way to step to the roots or the Fives."

Robinson sat up gingerly, gently peeling the razor from the boy's hand.

"I can do my own grooming, if you please. Maybe you could make yourself useful and find me something reflective."

The boy headed off, giving Robinson a chance to survey the room. It was an old lavatory, lit by a single, narrow window near the rooftop. The stalls were gone, the toilets broken, yet the odor of decay and waste still permeated the place.

Am I a prisoner here? If so, the boy is a poor figure for a guard.

The boy returned with a shard of mirror, its edges flaked and peeling. Robinson took it slowly. Now, if he needed a weapon, he had one.

"What's your name?" Robinson asked as he commenced shaving.

"Underfoot, I'm called. You?"

"Crusoe."

"Crusoe," the boy repeated. "Funny name. The fem says she'd dirt us if you wasn't vert today. *All of us.* Think she meant it too."

"She does," Robinson said, fighting back a grin. "And she would."

"I see she's crosses, but we got numbers. And it's *bad play*—leaping on the feet wrong at the start."

Robinson eyed the boy. "I think what you mean is we'd be getting off on the wrong foot. It's an old saying."

The boy thought about it and shrugged. "Most is. But I preesh the learnin'. My sis used to say: *Words be like trails. Even the ones lead home are lined with dirt.* Ya 'stand?"

It took a second, but Robinson thought he meant words could be both trouble and a boon, which he supposed was true enough.

"How long have I been here?"

"Came in two nights past, rackled bad with fever, you was. But you got the luck. Most don't survive the seprente kiss."

Robinson looked down at the bandage on his foot and wiggled his toes. Pain streaked through his body, though movement was a good sign.

"Your handiwork?"

"Me?" The boy chuckled. "Nah. I'm but a short Green."

"A what?"

"In Troyus, we's lotted by colors. The four, we calls 'em. Greens see to the edi's on the Up 'N Up. Yellows are the takers, caring for the likes of meals, cleaning, physikin and such. Don't grudge 'em, yellows. Muck work, mostly. Reds, they be the hunters and war makers when nece'ry. That'd be your color—you and the fem if rumors are crosses."

"And the last?"

Underfoot hesitated. "*Blues*. They see to the Tree."

"The Tree?"

Before Underfoot could expound, a heavy bell tolled beyond. The boy tensed before quickly gathering his things.

"Sand's running, and Fang'll be sending for you soon. He don't like Lopers—few of the Fives do—but least of all him. If you be wanting to stay vert, you'll 'member this for when you step to the roots: tell 'em *you was sent to snuff the mother's flames*. Can you 'member?"

Robinson nodded, but his head felt heavy. He could only watch as the boy sprinted for the door.

"I be forgettin' the most glory part!" the boy said, turning back to him. "They'll be asking your years. When they do," the boy tapped his forearm where several dappled marks glistened in the light, "say three and one and no more. You'll thank me laters. Swears."

Robinson nodded, and the boy opened the door. Outside, two slim figures in red stood holding wooden spears. Underfoot slipped them both something before the door closed.

He must have dozed off again because the room was dimmer when the door opened again. Only this time, a lithe girl in red entered, followed by four armed guards wearing identical red outfits that covered everything save their hands and eyes.

"Up," she said.

Robinson didn't see the benefit in arguing, so he stood. The girl looked at his freshly-shaved face and frowned before turning for the door. Robinson limped after her, a dull throb in his swollen leg.

The cement corridor was lit by small lamps hanging from rusty pipes overhead. Even in such sparse light, Robinson saw he was taller than his guards. If necessary, he thought he could take them. And yet, he still didn't fully understand his circumstances. *Am I a prisoner? A guest?* He'd been in similar circumstances before, both when he entered Cowboytown and after the Aserra pulled him from the river. Neither had worked out well for him in the short term, but eventually those enemies had turned into allies. Maybe that would be the case again.

As for Friday, he had no idea of her whereabouts. Underfoot had said she was safe and that Robinson would see her again soon. But the boy was just a boy after all. Until he met the adults, he refused to speculate on things.

As they approached the end of the hall, many voices pooled from the other side. Robinson felt his chest tighten before he asked the lithe girl where they were going. She scowled at him and nodded to the guards to open the doors instead.

A blinding light stayed Robinson's feet until a small hand shoved him from behind. When his eyes adjusted, his mouth dropped open; he instantly forgot his pain. For the first time in a long time, Robinson Crusoe was speechless.

He'd read about malls back in D.C. They were gathering areas where merchants peddled their wares to the masses. But it wasn't the size of the place that stayed his breath or the massive structural tree that someone had crafted from thousands of tons of scavenged material in the central atrium, though it rising hundreds of feet into the air and stretching across the expanse was impressive enough.

No, what left him dumbstruck was the assembly of hundreds gathered in the room and the fact that all of them were children.

Chapter Five
The Tree of Gifts

Children. A thousand in number. They were packed tightly on the floor. They lined the atrium's borders. Some were perched on the walkways above, legs dangling over the edge. Others sat astride the branches of that monstrous metal tree that rose to a ceiling of opaque glass. They were dressed in roughshod fabric colored red, green, blue, and yellow. And every one of them had their eyes pinned on him, this new stranger.

Robinson exhaled.

A second shove propelled him forward, toward the steps that descended to the atrium and the tree. Robinson meant to pause at the top of the steps in a subtle act of defiance, but then he saw Friday and ran into her arms.

"What happened?" Robinson asked, oblivious to the tittering children around him.

"You were bitten by one of the snakes," Friday said, "and *they* claimed to have medicine. I had to choose between bringing you here or watching you die."

"You did the right thing. Did they harm you?"

"No," she said. "There is a nursery on the second level. I was taken there to wait with others like me." She rubbed her belly as she said it. "What about you?"

"Woke on a floor hungry, sore, and tired. Not that it matters. We have to find the adults and speak with whoever's in charge."

"I have seen no adults. Crusoe, I think these children are on their own."

Impossible, Crusoe thought. Children couldn't survive in the wasteland alone, certainly not in these numbers. Unless some recent calamity had befallen the place, they had to have parents or older siblings somewhere nearby. And yet when he looked around, he saw no signs of battle or sickness. None of the puerile faces bore the fathomless look that followed tragedy, only curiosity and a fierce poise that vexed him. That's when he noticed, hanging from the limbs of the mechanical tree, several cages, each with a child inside. Some appeared bloodied and bruised while others looked untouched. Everyone stared through vacant eyes. Robinson thought one of them might have been dead.

An uneasy dread began to burrow inside him. Then, a sinewy shadow stepped from the tree and extended a staff into the air. It was made up of three long, slender pieces of wood with curved ends that splayed out like the flukes of a grappling hook. They reminded Robinson of tools used for a sport played on ice, though the name of the sport eluded him. These had a knitted bag of white rocks atop them that rattled like bones.

The staff bearer was lean and muscled and wore the scowl of one that takes pleasure in lording over others. His cruel scowl was accentuated by two circular scars on his right cheek. *This must be the one the boy called Fang.*

"See them," Fang said, pointing to the strangers as he addressed the crowd. "They 'proach the roots but kneel not. They stand 'fore the Tree of Gifts with pockets turned out. In their rucks, weapons of the *far and back*. How should we mark 'em, Orphans of O?"

"As Lopers!" one of the boys in blue shouted.

"As Fulls," the girl in red growled behind him.

"Ye-uh," Fang agreed. His baritone voice felt forced, as if he was pushing it several octaves deep to sound older. "Lopers true. But Fulls, my red sis? It be border-close. What say you, strangers? What numbs do you bear?"

Robinson and Friday looked confused. At the very least, he'd figured out what roots meant. The ground beneath his feet bore brown paint running from the tree. It was a far cry from a revelation, but what had Underfoot said about them? He couldn't remember.

"Numbs?" Robinson said. "I'm not sure what you mean."

Fang smiled, but it came off as a sneer.

"*Years*," Fang said. "What be your years?" He patted his forearm as he said it, and there Robinson saw the same dappled scars that Underfoot bore. Bars and dots.

What had the boy said? 'Say three and one and no more. You'll thank me for it later.'

Three bars and one dot. The same as Fang.

"We're both sixteen," Robinson said.

Fang's smile faded as a murmur ran through the room. He shook the bone staff until the room fell silent.

"*Sixteen*. Three and one, you says? *Halfers?*" Fang sneered. "Skept, I am. Think you be lyin' at the roots. Lyin' in front of the Tree. That's *bad play*."

"Bad play," the other boy in blue mimicked.

"Bad play in Troyus earns you the coop," Fang said as he slapped one of the cages holding a child. "Or 'haps the dirt-dirt. Think on its again, I says."

Robinson shook his head. "That's not necessary. I know my age."

Fang eyed him, then turned to the girl in red. "Snapfinger says you had a full's groom this very dewday. Does you deny it?"

"A full's groom?" Robinson repeated. "Do you mean a beard? I've never grown a beard in my life."

"He lies!" the girl named Snapfinger shouted. She gripped a blade sheathed at her waist. "At the roots, he lies. First they cross the patch, which is known ours. Then they 'ttak the urtmovers on overmoon. They're foul and full. Let me dirt him, Fang. We should dirt 'em both."

Robinson smiled wearily. He was tired and sore. These kids had plucked them out of the desert without the slightest provocation. Yes, they'd probably saved their lives, but to now hold them in judgement over it seemed ludicrous. And yet the more Robinson watched Fang marshal across the floor, the more danger he suspected they were in.

"We don't dirt swoles, sis, no matter their numbs," Fang said at last. "You know it be *bad play* that leads to the *game over*."

"Game over," the crowd repeated.

Robinson looked among their ranks, observing only the ones in red had weapons. The others—greens and yellows—were not only unlikely to fight but also unlikely to run. The ones in blue appeared to hold the positions of power. He decided to sock that observation away.

"We can keep the fem 'til she spurts and milk the whelp in the nest after she's dirt and dust. The full? I see no reason him stayin' vert."

Sensing things were going badly, Robinson stepped forward.

"Dirt and dust, you say? If that was what we were meant to be, why did your friends rescue us from the desert? Why bring us here and give us food and medicine if you only meant to kill us after?"

Another murmur ran through the crowd.

"We got rules in Troyus," Fang said when the noise died down. "Rules handed from the *far and back* by the Brothers Ark and Ton-Bra the Great."

"Ton-Bra," the assembly repeated.

"Rules say each gets a fair turn. You've stood the roots 'fore the Tree of Gifts. You've had your turn—"

"Have we?" Robinson asked. He scanned the faces in the crowd, gauging them to be between five and sixteen. They watched with interest but exhibited no anger or fear. Even the poor abused ones hanging in the cages watched curiously. Robinson's eyes found Underfoot in the balcony overhead.

"I find it unusual that a group like this—a group with rules—would turn down two of its own."

"He's got the Full's tongue," the boy in blue hissed. "Dirt him now, Fang."

But Fang dismissed him with a curt wave.

"Two of our own?" Fang asked. "'Splain it, Loper."

"You call yourself orphans. Well, orphans have a code that's known the world 'round. It states you take care of your own. And who are we but a couple orphans that have walked in out of the desert, scared and injured. Would you deny your fellow orphans sanctuary?"

This time the murmurs turned to discussion. Fang's head arched around. He could sense an uneasiness among his people. Then Snapfinger whispered into his ear until he grinned.

"But you ain't orphans," Fang said. "Your fem's a swole. That makes a

31

family. And we got our own family, separate. That makes us *rival players.*"

"Rival players," Snapfinger aped.

Friday glanced at Robinson. He had slipped the razor into her hand when they embraced, and she was ready to use it. But Robinson was still hoping to avoid bloodshed. And then, something Underfoot said came to mind.

"If you be wanting to stay vert, you'll 'member this for when you step to the roots: tell 'em…"

What had the boy said? Robinson couldn't recall.

"You play the game," Fang said. "Or do you deny it?"

The game. It was the same the world over. Survival. But how to play it?

"No. I don't deny it," Robinson said. Then he remembered. "Though it strikes me we might be on the same side."

"How so?" Fang asked.

"We didn't come here by accident. We were sent to put out the mother's flames."

Gasps rang through the building. Friday studied the crowd, but Robinson never looked away from Fang. His mouth had fallen open. It took him a moment to regain his composure. Rather than respond, he pulled Snapfinger and the other blues into a huddle.

Friday leaned in, whispering, "What mother?"

"Haven't a clue," Robinson answered.

Fang finally broke the circle and pounded the staff on the floor to quiet the crowd. Then he approached Robinson.

"*Sent,* you says," Fang enunciated. "By who?"

"*Whom,*" Robinson said, unable to resist. "And the answer is, I don't know. It came to me in a vision."

"Vision," Fang scoffed. "Matters not. You says you can free the mother. Well, here's your luck. The Fire Lords come this very night. Douse her flames and you'll stay vert long enough to keep your feet and lope on. Does we have a pact?"

Things were moving too fast. Robinson needed time.

"No," Robinson said. "In case you haven't noticed, I'm injured. I'll need a few days to recover."

32

Fang sneered. Maybe he sensed weakness in Robinson. He stepped close so only he could hear.

"Five days, she comes next," he said. "Same as the blues. Same as the bones."

He shook his staff, giving Robinson a close-up of the rectangular tiles inside, each marked with numbered dots, including several fives.

"If your word hold north, all be happy acres. If not … you'll be praying it's the Fire Lords dirt you and not me. That be Crosses, Loper. Swears."

The teen smirked, stepped back, and raised his arm to the crowd.

"Orphans of O!" he shouted. "Sons of Troyus! Glory news! Celebrate the game! At the roots, I say, the Tree of Gifts has given again! By the Brothers Ark! By Ton-Bra the Great! This one's been sent to snuff the mother's flames and end the *spit and firm* made with the Flame Lords. Glory, glory!"

"Glory, glory!" the children repeated.

"But sand it'll take. Five days' worth, so this one swears. 'Til then, his swole fem will be a *guest o' the nest*." The rhyme drew laughter. The children were excited. A different kind of buzz now permeated the room. "And this mighty-mighty will do his dance with Snapfinger as his shadow."

Snapfinger stepped forward, sneering.

"About that," Robinson said. "I'm afraid my vision showed a different orphan."

"Who?" Fang asked.

Robinson made a show of perusing the crowd. Then his eyes fell on Underfoot. The boy subtly shook his head until Robinson pointed and said, "Him."

More whispers followed. Underfoot never blinked. But Fang's playful sneer was gone. There was worry there. Robinson would have to find out why.

Robinson and Friday were given a minute to say their goodbyes as the children funneled from the room, many taking to the branches of the Tree that led to other destinations. Some rose to the heights of the building while others descended to the floor. They marched like ants across the metal tributaries that bowed and bounced under their collective weight. But none so much as stumbled. The tree's secretive pathways were known to them all.

Robinson wanted to assure Friday they would be okay, but she put a finger to his lips and silenced him. She knew his heart and knew the Goddess would provide. After four Reds shepherded her up through the tree, Robinson turned to find Underfoot at his side.

"You plays the game well," was all the boy said.

Robinson wanted to ask what kind of games left children hanging from cages. Instead, he asked, "What now?'

The boy nodded to the Tree. "To the Up 'N Up."

The steps were narrow, the angle steep. Names and words were etched on every surface inside the husk of the metal tree. How long had it been here? What inspired children to build such a thing? Robinson doubted he'd ever get the answers. The Tree seemed an integral part of their society. It was clearly sacred. But to truly understand his predicament, he needed to unearth Troyus's secrets. *This*, he thought, *is where it begins.*

Halfway up the twisting edifice, Robinson noticed the passageway with a locked gate. He leaned in for a view, but Underfoot hurried him along.

Eventually, they spilled out on the building's rooftop, where an impressive greenhouse stretched across the mall's circumference. A biosphere teeming with food crops in a mélange of colors. The odor of thick, musky peat rose from the soil.

"This be the Up 'N Up," Underfoot said. "Where we prod the edi's."

Edi's, Robinson thought. *Edibles.*

A covering hung overhead crafted from scavenged bits of plastic and glass. A water filtration system sent fine mists pluming into the air as children wearing the same green outfits as Underfoot tiptoed carefully around, prodding produce like leafy greens, chard, cucumbers, and tomatoes. Robinson also saw citrus fruits and berries. The moist air was scented with pungent sweet basil and cilantro.

It all made Robinson's stomach grumble.

Then he noticed how hastily the children were picking produce and stacking loaded woven bushels against the far wall.

"How much do you kids eat in a day?" Robinson asked.

Underfoot shook his head. "Ain't for us. S'for the off'rin'."

"Offering? For whom?"

"For *the mother*."

Underfoot plucked a tomatillo and tossed it to Robinson. He bit into it and wiped the juice running down his mouth. It was delicious.

"Since the *far and back*, orphans have vert our own edi's. Once in the out, then up here. Probs are reg like—too much water, too little sun—but we Greens know the rules. We know the urt'. The turn o' days. We keep Troyus in the game.

"Then a few years back, the Greens up here get to illin'. Edi's too. None knows why. 'Til we fig're this." Underfoot looked out over the mall parking lot to the forest beyond. "The trees."

"What about them?" Robinson asked.

"We burn 'em up top to keep old man ice from frostin' the edi's. But one Sum', they get rackled and don't grow back. We set deeper in the cut, but these new trees, they don't burn right. Makes the air sick we fig'red."

"Huh. I remember reading that some wood can release noxious gas when burned. And in a confined environment like this one, it's not hard to see how it could affect both people and plant life. What'd you do?"

"Dustynose—she was leader of the fives 'fore Fang—she had ideas 'bout doing things different, but the Blues did the dance 'til her sand ran out. *Bad play*, most says. She was liked."

"What do you mean her sand ran out?"

"When a Halfer reaches three and two—what you call seventeen—they become Fulls. And Fulls can't play no longer in Troyus. Says so in the rules. So a choice gets put. Leave the game or take the leap."

"The leap. I suppose you mean from the tree."

Underfoot nodded.

"And how long have these rules been around?"

"Since the first orphans was short. 'Fore the far and back."

Robinson sighed. Children rearing children. The idea should have been foreign to him, and yet he understood how they *could* survive because he had done the same. Kids were adaptable, their minds and bodies pliant. They could survive the physical and emotional breaks better than adults. They could recover faster. Still, Robinson felt sorry for the boy. Even if he told the boy what he was missing, he didn't think he would understand.

"Do all Greens know as much as you?"

"Nah," Underfoot answered. "But like I says, my sis gave me learning. Plus, I always been small. No one notices me."

"Underfoot, huh?"

The boy shrugged.

A mash of feet announced the Greens had finished gathering their offering and were leaving. As bushel after bushel of produce passed, Robinson saw the problem. Food earmarked for Troyus was now being given away, and the children were suffering for it.

He tried to ask Underfoot about the mother, but the boy would only say he'd see soon enough.

They stayed on the rooftop as the sun descended and the moon sprang like a cork to bob among the clouds. One of the Greens returned with two rations of food. It was the best Robinson had eaten in months.

Braziers were lit as the night grew chilly, filling the biosphere with a warmth that made Robinson sleepy. Just as his eyes grew heavy, Underfoot nudged him. A low throbbing noise sounded as something approached. Robinson waited. Then it appeared, a flickering light high in the sky. As it grew closer, Robinson's hands moistened.

The light soon split into two flames, each suspended at opposite ends of the shadowy form that now bore down on the lot behind the mall.

Underfoot muttered something that might have been a prayer when the thing, now discernably white, swooped in and released four successive fireballs that exploded across the cement and lit the area with flames. It arced into the air, roaring with delight as it came back around and touched down with a series of chirps.

It rolled menacingly across the lot, its voice loud and choppy. Only when it came to a stop did two geysers of fire pirouette high into the air, accompanied by an earsplitting roar. Underfoot looked away in fright. Robinson's eyes narrowed.

He knew what would come next. People appeared, hustling cans of kerosene, he suspected, to a raised platform. In return, they took the food that had been left out for them. Fang had said they'd made a 'spit and firm' with the Fire Lords. A deal, Robinson assumed, meant to replace their firewood supply. Undoubtedly these Fire Lords had changed the terms. What kept the children of Troyus from revolting? A fairytale. Robinson didn't know the source, nor did he care. To the orphans, the mother could have meant a million different things. But he recognized it immediately from the moment of its approach.

The mother was a plane.

Chapter Six

Cassa

The return journey to the farm took longer than Cassa expected. The reasons were many, though he knew the Master would view them as nothing more than excuses.

One of the most significant reasons were with Cassa's bull. It had begun breathing erratically following the dust storm, retching endlessly and hacking up sputum and gore. Cassa worried it had inhaled too much dust while buried beneath the sand.

The loss of the pack also had consequences. Cassa had become an easier target for raiders, and while he would never be easy prey, he had to keep to the open lands and avoid areas where predators might wait. At night, he slept fitfully and was forced to do without fires, though the latter was of little loss to him. For it was fire that had irreparably changed his life.

To this day, it was still hard to remember the time before the flames had marked him, taking half his face and tongue and leaving him imprisoned in a shell of dead skin forever. It was the Master who had found him at death's door and ordered Viktor to coax him back to life. His suffering was without measure, but Viktor's magic prevailed. A new monster was born, one that would feel no pain or fear and know no mercy.

Cassa's only request was the mask. He claimed sunlight hurt his eyes, but the truth was that he couldn't bear the sight of himself.

After a week of tedious riding, the prairies ebbed away, replaced with rolling hills. As the karst topography emerged, the landscape palate went from bland ochre to lush greens. Lakes and streams became plentiful. Rivers fed from baseflows ran along the limestone bluffs, regaled with the vibrant colors of sycamores, river birch, and maple. Redbud and dogwood flourished among the wild viburnum and hawthorn.

Cassa marveled at the beauty, though he knew it too had its dangers.

Caves in the region were abundant, the result of groundwater eroding the dolomite, limestone, and chert without relief. Predators and the afflicted took refuge in these caves, so often he didn't know whether to avoid the sinkholes or the shadows.

It wasn't until the sight of black oaks and the smell of sumac hit him that Cassa began to relax. Viktor had told him he might see the catkins appear if he returned before summer, and sure enough, the pistillate flowers filled the axils, though their acorns wouldn't ripen until autumn. Even Bull's condition seemed improved. Then, over the chirrup of warblers and buntings, he heard the unmistakable call of human cries.

Cassa spurred the bull to the edge of a narrow pit where, fifteen feet below, a man and woman lay, covered in blood. The man's leg was broken, the woman's nails bloodied from trying to scale the sandstone walls.

"Help us," the woman pled in the common tongue when Cassa's shadow fell over them.

Cassa eyed them for a moment before leaving.

The farm came into view a short time later. It was once a sprawling estate now reduced to a single ranch house nestled against a grove of trees with a large barn in the center of a vast, open field.

Cassa directed Bull to a post on the fringe of the field where an iron bell hung. He rang it three times and waited. The barn's loft doors opened and a figure appeared. He signaled Cassa before lifting his own set of pipes to his mouth, blowing three notes.

The bull groaned as Cassa spurred it across the open field. He looked down to see dried blood coating the dirt. Crossing the field always made him shiver.

When they reached the barn, Cassa slid the paddock door open and walked the bull inside. He removed Bull's bridle, bit, and saddle and dropped them in the tack room. The sound caused one of Viktor's human guinea pigs to moan on the other side of the giant double doors. Cassa hated the things. They were feral, they stank, and they often died in the worst of ways.

Viktor's lab took up the western half of the barn, where he did his best to keep his equipment safe and sterile. The man descended the ladder from the loft just as Cassa sat down.

"Ah, Cassa," Viktor said. "I wondered when you might return. How was your latest outing? Was it fruitful?"

Cassa said nothing, and Viktor chuckled. "The master will not be pleased. And if I might ask, how many of my lovelies did you lose this time?"

Cassa's sigh was answer enough.

"Pity," Viktor said. "Their augmentations were some of my best to date. But never fear. I always have new plans in the works."

Cassa cleared his throat and craned his head toward the main house.

"Out, momentarily." Viktor pulled his glasses away and rubbed the bridge of his nose wearily. "Believe it or not, he took a few pets down to the river to see if they could fish. I expect he's drowned most of them by now." Viktor blinked twice, leaning toward Cassa. "Is that blood on your collar? You haven't been applying the salve I made, have you? What's the use of my implanting a chip to dull your pain receptors if you won't treat the wounds? Take off your mask."

Cassa didn't move until Viktor said, "Please."

With a slow breath, Cassa removed the mask. If the sight of his face bothered Viktor, the man didn't let it show. Then again, he worked with much worse every day.

Viktor dipped two fingers into a jar of salve and began administering it to Cassa's neck and head.

"It'd be one thing if the tissue damage had been uniform, but there are still microscopic patches of dermis in there fighting for life. That is excess skin and nerves, capable of producing fat and sweat and blood. I've spared you a great deal of pain, but I know there is more." His fingers lingered until Cassa grabbed his arm. Victor pulled away as if nothing happened.

"What I cannot do is reduce your risk of infection unless you apply this daily. Understand?" Cassa nodded curtly. "Good," Viktor said, returning to his desk. "Now, come see my latest creation. I'm calling it 'the berserker module.'"

Viktor tittered over a small circuit board he'd been soldering. "Gauche, I know, but I couldn't resist. You see, when an afflicted subject receives a sustained electrical shock to the paravertebral ganglia, a massive dose of epinephrine is released into the blood, prompting the fight-or-flight response. Now, a mutation to the sympathetic nervous system works in tandem to produce a systematic, frenzied attack. They will literally kill themselves to achieve their goal—or, in this case, any order we give them. The problem is getting humans to respond similarly. They have no such mutation, so attaining this effect has been troublesome. Regrettably, we've been taking in fewer subjects."

Cassa held up two fingers before pointing to a point on a map.

"In the western traps?" Viktor asked. "Good. I'll have them claimed immediately." Viktor hesitated, unsure about asking the next question. "Did you see him out there? The boy?"

Cassa hesitated before nodding.

"I assume he's still looking for a cure for his ladylove?" Cassa nodded again. "Foolish. But you have to admire his tenacity."

Viktor held up the circuit board. "Now, let's see how this fares."

Viktor stood and unlocked the large sliding doors to the eastern half of the barn. Immediately, several plaintive cries went up from the dozen Renders caged inside. Many had already been augmented with weapons, their flesh still bloody and raw.

Viktor made his way to the last stall, where two men and a woman lay huddled together, their clothes filthy and torn. Iron fetters pinioned their legs to the floor. Something black and glossy was wedged into their mouths to prevent them from speaking. Each body bore the telltale marks of experimentation. Heads shaven. Surgery scars running the length of their skulls, and metallic ports visible where the spine and brain converged.

"Wakey, wakey," Viktor said. The subjects began whimpering and skittering away. "I would prefer not to have to use this," he held up a cattle prod, "but I will if my hand is forced. You," he said, pointing to the older of the two men. The man sobbed. "Now, now. None of that. I'm here to help you. First, I need to peek at your incision site."

The man reluctantly turned, and Cassa saw the apparatus sewn into the back of his head. The tissue around it was inflamed. He would die in a week if left unattended. He should be so lucky.

"Good," Viktor said, checking his handiwork. "The interface has melded nicely. As for your immediate discomfort, this should help immensely."

Viktor slid the circuit board into the interface site with a snap. The man flinched before his body relaxed. "Better, yes? What say we go outside for some fresh air?"

Outside, Viktor walked the man to the edge of the field. He began to shake his head and plead through his gag. "I see you remember what lies beneath. Good. Now, I'm going to issue a series of commands. Please, raise your left hand."

The man did as he was asked.

"Now, the opposite one."

Both hands were raised.

"Excellent, now spin three hundred and sixty degrees."

The subject tilted his head, confused.

"Turn around in a circle," Viktor clarified.

The man did.

"Fine. Now, this is important. I want you to ignore my commands."

Viktor adjusted the circuit board and nodded.

"Please, put down your left arm," he said.

The man's left armed tensed and began to shake. Eventually it lowered.

"Interesting," Viktor said before modulating the unit again. "Let's try that again. Put down your right arm." This time the man's arm trembled violently. "Some effort, please. If you can keep it up for fifteen seconds, I'll give you a warm bowl of onion broth."

The red-headed man's shoulders tightened, but his arm stayed raised.

"Excellent," Viktor said. "Well done." The subject appeared relieved. "Now, I want you to turn and walk into the pasture."

The man's eyes ballooned. He began to shake his head vehemently.

"Come now," Viktor said, turning the circuit board toggle. "It's not far. Just a few steps into the light."

Cassa watched the man struggle before his leg rose mechanically and he took his first step into the field. Viktor encouraged him to keep going. After the third step, the dam broke, and the man marched toward the center of the pasture, sobbing but unable to stop.

"That's far enough," Viktor said at last. The man stopped. "You've done admirably well, sir. Your reward should arrive any moment."

The man's head flitted around for a few tense seconds before the earth exploded beneath his feet and a giant tentacle wrapped around his body, propelling him high into the air before he hurtled back toward the ground and into a teeth-laden maw that awaited just beneath the surface.

Blood sprayed, and the man screamed. Cassa wanted to turn away, but before he could, the creature pulled the man underground and was gone.

"Well," Viktor said, "I'd call that progress."

A bell tolled from the opposite end of the pasture. A group approached from the north, led by a man on a striking horse.

"The Master returns," Viktor said. "You should clean up. You know how particular he can get about formalities."

Cassa did. He turned for the barn and disappeared inside.

Chapter Seven
The Spit and Firm

One of the cage children was gone. Robinson wondered if she'd served her punishment or if she'd died.

He waited at the base of the Tree. Unlike the previous night, the room was largely empty. Presumably, with the morning, the children had returned to their tasks. Only Underfoot, Snapfinger, and four guards remained.

"Where'd he go?" Robinson asked.

"The store," Underfoot answered.

When Fang had first heard of Robinson's plan, his bravado waned. He consulted with his fellow Blues briefly before climbing the tree and appearing on the limb that likely extended from behind the gate. He made his way to an isolated shop on the second floor, its balcony long shorn away. A metallic fence covered the entrance, but a small gap had been rent open.

"What's in there?" Robinson asked.

"Orphan his'try," Underfoot said. "Our most val'bles."

"You ever been inside?"

Underfoot shook his head. "Only the leader o' fives can pass."

Snapfinger glowered, flicking Underfoot's ear with her fingers.

So much for the mystery of her name.

"But what's he doing?" Robinson persisted.

"'Sulting *the eye*," Underfoot answered.

Snapfinger flicked Underfoot's ear again. This time the sound echoed through the room.

When Fang reappeared, he held another powwow with his toadies. Then he approached Robinson.

"Terms of the *spit and firm* are such: you frees the mother, you and fem take the Full's walk. 'Greed?"

"Agreed," Robinson said.

They both spit on their hands and shook on it.

"Do I needs to speak what falls the swole if you word ain't held north?"

"Do I need to tell you what happens to Troyus if she's harmed in any way?"

Fang sneered before nodding for the others to follow. Robinson and Underfoot were left alone.

"What next?" Underfoot asked.

"Next, you fetch my things."

It was still morning when they set across the mall's parking lot. Robinson continued to limp, but the pain was lessening. He took notice of Red sentries positioned atop the mall. It had been modified with a few defenses, but nothing he couldn't break with a score of Iron Fists and a few guns. That begged the question as to why these Fire Lords, with their ability to attack from the sky, hadn't taken the compound already.

"So, what's the Eye?" Robinson asked as they climbed an embankment and started down the lone road into town. Underfoot looked at him distrustfully and didn't answer. "Come on, kid. Do we really look like we're here to steal your secrets?"

"So why is you here?"

"We're looking for a place leftover from what you call the far and back. The City of Glass. Have you heard of it?" Underfoot shook his head. "We were told it might be out this way. Hidden in the mountains perhaps. There are people there I need to find. People that can help my wife. She's ill."

"'Fraid I ain't heard of it," Underfoot said. "Sorry."

Robinson nodded, disappointed. "Are there other villages around? With adults? Or a place where travelers meet?"

Underfoot shrugged.

Robinson sighed, but smiled at the kid anyway. There was something about him he liked. After a quarter mile, the boy spoke again.

"The Black Eye of Infinity. That's its proper name. It's magic, if word is crosses."

"This is the object that Fang consulted in the store?"

Underfoot nodded. "I ain't seen it. Few has."

"Then how do you know it exists?"

"Tol' ya. I keep my ears wide. Since the far and back, leaders o' Troyus been going to the Eye for 'vice."

"*Ad*-vice, you mean."

"Preesh," Underfoot said. "When it says do, they does. When it don't..."

"You sure have a lot of rules in Troyus."

"Rules make the game. Games that come from Ton-Bra and the Brothers Ark anyway."

"Who are they?"

"'Pose you'd say our Gods. My sis says you learn their rules as shorts. As Halfers, the 'ceptions.'"

Robinson thought he remembered a similar quote from the ancients. Still, it was a heady sentiment for one so young. "She sounds smart, this sister of yours."

Underfoot smiled, but only briefly.

"What happened to her?"

"Same as all Fulls. She turned three and two and went away."

"Where?"

"No one knows. Or says anyway. When Fulls leave, they turn rival players. And rival players can't play Troyus games. Fulls broke the world, see? Broke the first family. Us Orphans, we only has each other. It's kept us playing this long."

"So no one's ever tried to buck the system and stick around?"

"Only Dustynose," Underfoot answered. "An' I tol' you what happened to her."

The city was modest in size. An old sign said its population was once forty thousand. The main street comprised of ten square blocks, making it easy to find what he was looking for.

"Is this it?" Underfoot said, looking up at the sign that read *Guns*. Robinson nodded, carefully pushing the old door open as he entered.

The building was well lit but run-down. Shelves were collapsed, overturned. Water damage had turned everything to mush or kindling. The racks where the long rifles once stood like parade soldiers were now empty, along with the toppled safes laying open on the floor.

"Done and dust," Underfoot said.

"Yep," Robinson asked. "But sometimes it pays to dig a little deeper."

"What they sell here?" Underfoot asked.

"Weapons once. When things got bad, people made a run on businesses like this. Almost every one I've come across looks the same. Ransacked, that is."

"I'd gone for edi's first," Underfoot said.

Robinson grinned. "That's because you're smart."

The storeroom in the back had also been plundered, but Robinson eventually found what he was looking for—a metal contraption strapped to a warped wooden bench with a long lever that brought a metal plate upward like a piston.

"What's it?" Underfoot asked.

"It's called a bullet press. It's for making ammunition."

"Ammu—"

"Projectiles for my pistol," he said, patting the pistol at his hip. He'd managed to convince Fang to let him take it since he had no ammunition for it anyway. "Let's look around and see what else we can find."

It took some time, but Robinson managed to gather most of the ingredients he needed: a powder measurer, a grain scale, four boxes of unspent cases that fit his weapon's caliber, and lastly a plastic bottle of small arms primers. He didn't know the shelf life on the primers. The fact that they were sealed reassured him some.

The one thing he couldn't find was bullets.

"Let's take a walk," Robinson said.

As they walked the street, Robinson couldn't help admire the quaintness of the town. The buildings were brick. A small park was nestled in the town square. He imagined the people there were happy. It made him think of his own home. His family and friends. He missed them terribly.

While passing an old window, Robinson spied movement atop the buildings on the opposite side of the street. Red.

"We have company," he said.

Underfoot smirked. "You didn't 'speck Fang to let us on our own, didya?"

When they found the auto repair shop, Robinson slipped inside. He pointed out a broken fire hydrant and some metal pans for Underfoot to grab before heading upstairs and retrieving a couple of old boxes.

"What's those?" Underfoot asked.

"Wheel weights," Robinson said. "I'm not sure what they were used for originally. Something to do with balancing carriage tires. But they're made of lead, which is what we need."

On their way out, Robinson also grabbed an old can of oil.

It was noon when they returned to the gun shop where Robinson had Underfoot saw off the top of the old fire extinguisher to form a crucible. Then he poured several pieces of old charcoal inside and lit it. With a bellows made from an old lamp, the fire became hot enough to melt the wheel weights in a steel pan. Robinson stirred them until the lead became molten.

Next he used heavy gloves to pour the lead into double cavity bullet molds he'd retrieved. Within no time, the pair were sweating and fatigued. When the lead finally cooled, they had managed to create several hundred bullets. After lubricating them with oil, Robinson scattered the coals outside in the dirt.

Finally, he found a dull knife and cut the lining of his jacket until a dozen small bundles fell out. "Gunpowder," Robinson said. "Some friends of mine gave it to me as a parting gift. I've kept it dry, so it should be good."

The next part was the hard part. Robinson carefully measured grains for the casings, inserting the primer before using the press to finish the process.

"Voila," Robinson said. "Bullets. Now all we need is a target." Robinson smirked as he opened the side door and pointed the pistol across the street. Underfoot's eyes ballooned in horror, and he jumped when Robinson pulled the trigger. The bullet slammed into the rusty metal sign and sent it crashing onto the roof where Snapdragon squealed before hightailing it away.

Underfoot laughed, slapping his leg, and looked at Robinson with awe.

"Who learned you this?" he asked.

Robinson recognized the thirst for knowledge and said, "C'mon. I'll show you."

The town library was in a Spanish-style building, but its pitched roof and sturdy terracotta tiles had preserved most of the books inside.

"You know what these are?" Robinson asked.

Underfoot nodded. "My sis done the reading. Many says it's bad play."

"Education is never bad play. What's in here can only make you stronger."

Underfoot noticed a children's book featuring dinosaurs. The tyrannosaurus rex on the cover was wearing sunglasses. He pointed at it.

"Or make you laugh," Robinson added.

Underfoot did. While he was busy perusing the children's section, Robinson searched a different room, eventually finding what he was looking for. He sat and started reading, unaware how much time had passed until Underfoot peeked over his shoulder.

"That tell the stor' of the mother bird?" Underfoot asked.

Robinson stuck his thumb in the aviation book and looked at the boy.

"You know it's not alive, right?"

Underfoot shrugged, but the answer was clear.

"This," Robinson said, "is called an airplane. In the old days, people used to travel from place to place inside them. That's how these Fire Lords transport the kerosene to your home. It's also, I suspect, what they would use to attack you from the air should you ever decide to break your deal with them."

"Our Reds is fierce, but we can't fight … planes. Can you kill it with your gun?"

"It's possible, but I have something else in mind."

"What?"

"I'm going to steal it."

Chapter Eight
Swoles

Friday sat in the Nest listening to the cries and coos of infants. When she first arrived, she was shocked by the age of the girls. They were all children themselves. But the more she watched, the more she saw they had a system in place. It wasn't close to how the Aserra reared their young, but it appeared to work.

The room was separated into three groups. The first group included new mothers, who did almost everything from bed. When they weren't breastfeeding, they were sleeping. The only time they got up was when they needed to eat or make water.

The second group featured those with child. They usually sat huddled together on the floor, knitting blankets for their young or learning what was expected of them. They still whispered and giggled as children did, but they were nervously excited for what was to come.

The third and final group were those scheduled to become pregnant next. They fetched food, emptied the bed pans, cleaned the bedding, and watched over the babies when the mothers needed relief.

Among this latter group was a spindly girl with stringy hair and no curves to speak of yet. She rarely talked, spending most of her time whispering to the infants she held in a rocking chair. When the children cooed, she smiled, but when it became restless, the girl grew tense. Friday realized she was terrified.

"What's your name?" Friday asked when they had a moment alone.

"Pix," the girl answered shyly.

"I am called Friday." She nodded to the infant in Pix's hands. "He likes you."

Pix's shoulders relaxed some.

"They say I has the touch for boys. Not so with fems."

"Oh?"

"Sprout fems can sense one ain't yet swole or broke."

"Hmm. How old are you, Pix?"

"Turned five and two half-moon past."

"That makes you twelve by my count."

Far too young to bear a child, even for an Aserra.

"I see you wear yellow," Friday said. "What do Yellows do again?"

"We does the caring work. The leg and lift. The bring and take. We keep the Blues and Reds and Green of Troyus playing the game."

She said it proudly. Friday smiled.

"And now you're with child."

Pix's chin dropped. She looked about warily.

"No. But my turn be coming."

"Your turn? Who decides when it's your turn?"

"I decide," Pix answered, but she looked around uncomfortably. "Swoles can't be forced. They need to be offer'd."

"So, you volunteer?"

Pix considered the word before nodding. "Every fem in Troyus can offer once her river breaks. Some wait though 'til they's three and one, knowin' the rules stay a fem's sands when she's swole. It's bad play, but many do."

"But not you?"

Pix shrugged, but Friday could see the fear hiding just beneath the surface.

"Truth is I ain't ever 'posed well, even for a Yellow. I stewed the edi's, fingered the threads, but by some and some, I always be faultin'. If'n I could hunt like Reds or thumb like Greens, 'haps I'd stick. But as the sayin' goes, an orphan's work is his worth."

Friday understood. In her time, she'd known kids who didn't fit in or who failed to meet their tribe's expectations. Back then, she'd held them in contempt. But now she felt differently. Maybe it was her time with Crusoe. Or the fact she was pregnant. But she'd come to realize everyone has gifts. The trick was knowing how to identify and nurture them.

"How do you choose the boy?"

"You don't. The three and ones earn the right to choose you."

"So, you don't know who the father of your child will be? Does that scare you?"

"Swoles serve Troyus. It's our honor and duty."

She said it loudly, but Friday could hear the fear underneath. She was about to press her for more when the baby started to fidget. Pix looked nervous a moment before turning the infant over and rocking it on her forearm. The baby drifted back to sleep.

"A handy tool," Friday said. "Did you learn that on your own?"

"The walls do the learning," Pix said, nodding to the walls of the room.

Friday hadn't noticed before, but someone had painted stick-figure images in maternal situations across the room. Each cluster depicted a lesson to be learned. From conception to pregnancy to birthing and beyond. In the absence of mothers, grandmothers, and wet nurses, here their wisdom persevered.

"How long have these been here?" Friday asked.

"Since the far and back I 'pose. Times they fade, but when they do, it falls to us to remake 'em. We dark the lines. Make the voice known again. See there? That be mine. It speaks what a swole 'posed to do when a whelp won't take to her."

Some of the images were disturbing, like one with a blade posed over a mother's belly when her child was breached. Yet these hard lessons needed to be taught.

"Does you ever listen to it?" Pix asked.

"What?" Friday asked, confused.

Pix pulled an old piece of equipment from her pocket. It was a hose of some kind with two metal pieces.

"Go on," Pix said. "Put 'em in your ears."

Friday reluctantly did. Then Pix set the round, cold end to Friday's belly. She startled, shocked, then went still, as a gentle patter, like the falling of rain, came in double beats.

Bu-dum, bu-dum, bu-dum.

It was both terrifying and exhilarating. Friday had done her best to push back her fears about her child. And yet here, in this small room, she could hear its heartbeat and know it was alive. She immediately thought of Crusoe, wanting to share this with him. When she realized she couldn't, tears welled in her eyes.

"Is it wrong?" Pix asked. "Do you hear nothing?"

"No," Friday said softly. "I hear it fine."

"Then why does you cry?"

"Because I wish my husband was here to hear this."

Pix blushed, then looked around. "I liked a boy like that once," she whispered. "He was called Eight cuz he was spurt two fingers shy. Still climbed trees like a monkey." She laughed.

"And where is he now?" Friday asked.

Pix's smile faded. "His sands run out. And now I fear the one to choose me will be Fang."

"Why?"

"He led the Reds at three but waited. Then he turned Blue but still waited. Now, he's lead of the Fives. His time has come. And when he looks at me…" She swallowed. "I know he wants to hurt me. He's cruel."

Friday knelt beside her.

"Men are often cruel. And you are right to be wary of him. My father used to say that true kings are those who fear the crown. Because they understand its weight but keep their eyes to the sky. Fang wears the crown, but others carry the burden. If he seeks a girl that is meek, you must show you are not that girl. You are strong. Do you understand?"

Pix looked to the floor and nodded. Friday reached out and lifted her chin.

"Do you understand?"

This time, Pix nodded and said, "I 'stand."

Later that night, a short Green girl came in to let Friday know Robinson was waiting for her outside. They only had a few minutes, but he explained his plan.

"You will do this tonight?" Friday asked.

"Tomorrow. Or the evening after. I need a little more time at the library, and by then, I should have the rest of the ammunition made."

"I do not like you going alone."

"I'm not. Underfoot's going with me."

Friday snorted. "And should you cross paths with these Fire Lords, what will the little one do? Tickle their feet?"

"You might be surprised. He's a resourceful kid. Though there's something he's not telling me."

"I should be coming with you," Friday said before coughing.

At first, it was a single cough. Then it turned into more until Friday was doubled over with a racking cough that hurt her chest.

"Are you all right?" Robinson asked when it was over.

Friday saw the worry in his eyes. How many times had she seen it before? It was maddening. Not even her own mother and father worried about her as Crusoe did. She had thought of it as a weakness on both their parts. That he believed it necessary suggested she had revealed some vulnerability—as if she needed to be rescued again and again. And yet the more she looked into his eyes, the more she felt as if she was looking into her own. The desperation he felt to protect and care for her was the same as she felt for the life growing inside of her. Only then did she understand one of the most agonizing truths of love was the fear of losing it.

"Will you do something for me?" she asked.

"Of course," Robinson said.

She told him to close his eyes. After they were closed, she slipped the stethoscope's earpieces over his ears. When he heard the heartbeat, he smiled. Then he opened his eyes and the smile slipped away. Friday was holding the stethoscope to her belly. She watched his chin tremble, but in a rare moment, he could not speak.

"Our child," Friday said, her voice barely a whisper, "needs you as much as I do. Remember that when you are away from me."

He reached for her then and pulled her close, maybe closer than he had ever held her before. She thought she might have felt his heartbeat pulsing against her chest, speaking what he could not. With each beat it made a promise. Of always and forever.

Chapter Nine

The Fire Lords

They set out after sundown. Fang had hemmed and hawed, but in the end, he knew something needed to be done about the Fire Lords, and he wasn't willing to risk his own skin. His only caveat was that Underfoot shed his colors. That way if the boy died, it wouldn't come back to haunt them.

Snapfinger, on the other hand, was furious. She insisted she go along to protect the orphan's interests. Robinson thought it was because she wanted any credit of success for herself. Robinson mentioned another dream in which he saw a girl in red burned on the side of the road. After that, Snapfinger paled and never said another word.

Only when they were unable to see the glowing braziers atop Troyus did Underfoot say where they were going.

"Two towns over. That's where the mother nests."

"You've been there before then?"

The boy's eyes shifted. "Greens ain't 'lowed to leave Troyus."

"Look, kid, I get it. You must play by the rules to stay alive. But out here, there are a different set of rules. The ones the Fire Lords play by. I need to know what we're heading into. So if you're worried about me telling your friends that you like to sneak out at night, don't. My best friend back home does the same."

"You'll keep the mums?"

"Yes. You can trust me."

"The Fire Lords be rooted in a 'finery. Fore my sis left, she took us there, followin' the moth … the plane, which sleeps inside."

"How many are there?"

"My eyes saw two score. No more."

"Forty," Robinson said. "That's not good, but it's not exactly game over either. What about defenses?"

"Scouts. Fire throwers. But no guns."

"Okay. And the road between here and there?"

"Huh?"

"What are the dangers? Are there afflicted? More of those snakes like in the desert?"

"The serpentes stick to the patch. They can't run the 'urt, only sand. Lopers pass, but not often. The way should be clear."

They turned from the road and skirted the edge of an old waterway before diverging at some old railroad tracks that led out of town. Underfoot continued to ruminate on Robinson's words.

"So, trust be like crosses?" he asked.

"In a way. They're both promises. Trust means I give my word and you give yours and we both believe the other will keep it."

"For how long?"

"Hopefully forever. Think of trust as a tree: the longer it stands, the stronger it becomes."

"Did a boy tell you that?"

"My father. Of course, my wife has a saying too: Trust, but bring your axe."

"Your wife scares me."

"Heck, kid. Sometimes she scares me too."

The sky was clear when they passed through the second town, but as they approached the third, some clouds billowed in. The three-quarter moon slowly disappeared as a stiff wind rose, rustling the sparse shrubs and forcing Robinson to pull his jacket tight.

The snake bite had done more than injure his foot. It had left his boot torn, the front hood lolling like a dog's tongue. Finding replacements would be one more task to add to the list.

Just when it seemed like they might walk all night, Robinson smelled the heavy chemical odor of burning petroleum. Underfoot signaled him to break from the tracks and down an embankment. They pushed through a small copse of trees, and Underfoot pointed.

The refinery sat two hundred meters away in an open field, a sprawling complex of tanks, towers, and Byzantine piping that loomed four or five stories tall. Sentries could be seen atop various catwalks, carrying lanterns that spilled black smoke into the sky.

More guards walked the ground, some huddled around burning barrels while others patrolled the ground. They all looked like hulking brutes until Robinson realized they were carrying something on their backs.

Robinson scanned the area before pointing.

"There's grass in that gully there that we could use for cover. If it's not booby-trapped. Good thing is I don't see any dogs, so the only thing we need to be wary of are those men on the tower. Clouds will help, but it sure would be nice if it rained."

"Don't smell rain," Underfoot said.

"Wishful thinking on my part. Okay, we wait for the magic hour, and then we go in."

"*Magic*?" Underfoot repeated nervously.

Robinson chuckled. "It's just an expression. People sleep their deepest a couple hours before dawn. That's when our magic will happen."

Underfoot smiled, but it vanished an instant later when one of the sentries atop the highest tower shot a torrent of flames into the air. A second stream erupted from its sister tower, followed by two on the ground. Then a bell began to toll. From an inner courtyard, a buzz of activity commenced, including the shrill whine of mechanical engines firing up.

Motorized cycles blasted out of the refinery and sped down the long, dark road leading away. Each rider, stopped at a set interval and waited. Then a familiar drone was carried on the wind.

"There," Robinson said at last, pointing to the darkened shadow moving across the gray clouds. The plane was returning.

On the runway, the riders sent their own streaming torrents of fire into the sky. The packs these Fire Lords carried were obviously flamethrowers.

With the runway lit, the plane descended quickly toward the fiery cordon until its tires bit into the road, sending gravel shooting in all directions. The plane's engine revved so high, Underfoot had to cover his ears. The plane began its long slow crawl toward the refinery. All at once, the fiery salutation concluded, and the darkness returned as the motorcycles joined the plane and returned to the bowels of the refinery as all sound died away.

"Nothing like a good show to top off the evening," Robinson said as he slapped Underfoot on the shoulder. The boy let out the air he'd been holding. "Can you sleep?"

"Not after that," Underfoot said.

"Good," Robinson said as he lay down in the lee of a tree. "You have first watch. Keep your eyes and ears open, but don't wake me unless someone is headed this way. I'll relieve you in two hours."

Underfoot didn't bother asking him how Robinson would be able to mark the time if he was asleep. He trusted him to keep to his word.

It was sometime later when Robinson woke with a start. His heart was thundering, though he couldn't say why. He looked around for Underfoot, but the boy was gone.

The night had gotten colder, and a mist had settled in over the terrain, making it hard to see beyond a few feet. He hadn't heard any alarms, so he didn't think the boy had left for the refinery, but Robinson was having trouble reading him. Something drove the boy, but he couldn't say what.

Robinson felt something sting his neck, and he slapped the skin, coming away with dead ants on his fingers. He looked up at the towers and vaguely made out the flickering lamps of the sentries on station. He saw no movement.

He decided to sit still and let his ears listen to the night. Yet his heartbeat was going crazy, and he didn't understand it. Something had him on edge.

Instinct told him to pull his pistol, but gunfire would only alert the Fire Lords to his presence. Instead, he drew his axe out slowly and stood.

The grass was high near the gully. Robinson couldn't find any tracks from the boy. Other than the occasional sway of shrubs in the wind, nothing moved. Robinson didn't believe in premonitions, yet he trusted his instincts. *Something* had woken him. *Something* told him he was not alone.

He moved cautiously through the grass, careful to avoid twigs that might snap beneath his feet. His breath was visible in the air, the chill creeping up his spine.

In the distance, he heard a rustle and thought he saw movement in the grass. He wanted to move closer. His feet wouldn't let him. Then he heard a short inhalation of air—almost a hiss. He looked to his right and saw Underfoot kneeling in some bushes. He had a blade in his hand.

Robinson slowly made his way to the boy, who pointed down. Robinson's heart seized as if it was suddenly incased in ice. There, in the dirt, was a large set of paw prints. They could have belonged to a mountain lion or even a bear, but only one figure came to mind.

The old terror came back. Robinson fought it down. He waited several minutes but heard nothing else but the wind. Eventually, he signaled Underfoot to back up with him until they sank back down into the gully.

"What is it?" the boy whispered eventually. "What's out there?"

"Probably a bobcat or mountain lion. Don't worry. It won't come this close to the refinery. Most animals like that typically avoid men."

Most. Not all.

"I'm going to head over now and take a quick look around. I want you to wait here while I do."

"But I want to go with you," Underfoot said. "I'm not afraid."

"I know that. But I'll move quicker if I'm on my own."

The boy's disappointment was clear.

"Hey, I need you here, okay? I need you to keep an eye out for those sentries. If any of them work around my flank, it's your job to let me know."

"How?"

"Can you whistle? Like a bird?"

"Birds don't sing at night. But I can yip like a coyote."

"That's good. Once means someone's on my tail. Twice means they're onto us. All right?"

Underfoot nodded.

"I'll be right back." Robinson squeezed his shoulder before slipping away.

Robinson waited for the sentry to turn away before he stole across the field toward the outer door of the plant. Once inside, he found the hallways shrouded in darkness and let his senses be his guide. The pipe-filled corridor was hot and smelled of oil, sweat, and burning fuel.

A single lamp illuminated the long corridor, marked with stygian hollows where anything might live. Robinson passed the vacant doorways and silent ladders in lieu of moving toward a droning noise far ahead.

Eventually, the amber glow of a room beckoned. Robinson slipped inside. The room was hot; a furnace lit in the corner cast flickering shadows from its gate. At a table nearby, one man lay hunkered down, an iron bar at his feet. His large chest rose with each intake of breath, the table rattling as he snored.

Against the far wall, a second man slept on a cot, a crossbow hanging limply from his hand. Robinson wanted that crossbow, but he didn't want to kill two men to get it. He decided to move on.

The rooms spilled together, dark and foreboding. Robinson worried he might get lost. Then a man stepped out of the doorway in front of him and Robinson swung his axe without hesitation. The flat of the axe hit the back of the man's head, and he fell with a thump. He dragged the unconscious man back into a lavatory, dumping him near the commodes.

The corridor continued to wind deeper into the complex until Robinson saw firelight streaming from another room. One look inside and he knew he'd found the heart of the refinery with two dozen men and women sleeping on cots and the floor, spread about the room.

On a table near the door sat the orphans' containers. Most of the food was already gone. Above them was a wall of hooks from which many weapons and flamethrowers hung. Had Friday been in his shoes, she would have likely opened one of those tanks and set the room on fire. With only a single entrance, the Fire Lords would burn before they could escape. But he couldn't kill so indiscriminately, especially when he hadn't found what he was looking for.

Robinson was about to leave when he noticed a cage in the far corner of the room and saw a small form lying inside. Part of him wanted to help the person, but the risk was too great. From crossing the room to waking the person inside, there were too many things that could go wrong. He backed out slowly instead.

Robinson continued down the path until he came to a steel staircase. He was about to head up when he heard heavy footsteps overhead. He stepped back into the shadows as a very large man descended, the steps rattling underneath his weight. When he reached the bottom, he turned toward the main room but stopped after a few seconds.

Robinson felt his heartbeat race as the man pulled up his steel protective mask and looked around. He carried one of the flamethrowers on his back, and the blue primer flame felt as bright at the sun. If the man turned in his direction, Robinson would have to act. Thankfully, the man grumbled and kept walking, disappearing down the corridor.

Robinson circled the stairs and went down another corridor that led to a large bay and the plane.

It was a fixed-wing, single-engine plane as he had suspected, but no amount of research could prepare him for the state of the thing. It appeared that most parts had been replaced from nose to tail. And many more were missing. Patchwork tin had replaced the fuselage. The windshield was gone. The rudders appeared to be made of plastic. And the instrumentation panel was nothing but empty holes and a few unnamed toggles that dangled limply in front of the yoke, which, shockingly, had been supplanted by an oversized wrench.

Even more disheartening, the engine cowl was open, and the battery was missing. He looked around the room to no avail. The plane had been refueled, but without that battery, he had zero chance of flying.

Robinson sighed, fearing he'd done all this for nothing. Then he remembered seeing that battery before.

He made his way to the sleeping room and waited for his eyes to adjust.

There it was—the battery—sitting on the table next to the Orphans' food supplies. A wave of relief flooded him. Then he saw movement, and panic lit his body with the force of a thousand stars.

At the back of the room was Underfoot quietly working a screwdriver into the prisoner's cage directly in front of him. She looked up, and it all became clear. Robinson knew by her jade green eyes, she was Underfoot's sister.

Chapter Ten
The Mother Bird

Underfoot had come for his sister.

Robinson was disappointed, but not surprised. He knew the boy hadn't been forthcoming about everything, but he felt like he'd shared enough for the lad to be straight with him.

When Underfoot turned, Robinson saw a myriad of things in his face. Regret. Defiance. But mostly fear. He was so close to the one thing he wanted most in the world, and yet, his decision now put all of them in danger. Robinson considered leaving, but he stepped into the room instead.

As quietly as possible, Robinson tiptoed his way through the sleeping bodies, careful to avoid refuse at their feet. He thought he saw one woman's eyes open, but she turned over and went back to sleep.

Once Robinson reached the cage, he whispered to the girl, asking about the key. She raised a thin, dirty finger toward a pot-bellied man with a dense beard sleeping in the center of the room. A ring of rusty keys was hooked to his belt.

Robinson exhaled slowly and wended his way back through the mishmash of cots and bodies until he reached the pot-bellied man. He stunk of alcohol and kerosene. Robinson waited patiently to get a read on his inhalations before reaching out, thumbing the latch, and pulling the ring away. Then he headed back to the cage and freed the girl.

They were headed for the door when Robinson stopped to grab the battery, only to watch as one of the frayed cables slipped off the battery post and fell to the floor with a thud. When he looked up, he found one of the women staring at him. She blinked twice, as if she wasn't sure what she was looking at. Then her mouth parted as she sucked in air to scream. Robinson kicked her in the face and smashed the room's only lamp before he drove the kids out.

They heard the sleeper shout in the din as the others stirred in confusion. Robinson shouted to the girl, "The plane!" She didn't hesitate. She grabbed Underfoot's hand and hustled down the darkened corridor.

When they burst into the hangar, Robinson thrust the battery and cables into the girl's hands. "Put this under the hood!" Then he and Underfoot overturned a table to block the door. A second after it was secure, someone pounded on it from the other side. More voices approached.

"The hangar door!" the girl shouted, "Open it before they comes 'round!"

Robinson rolled the giant metal door open. An alarm bell had already sounded, and they heard the clomp-clomp of fast approaching feet. Robinson kicked over a rusty barrel full of fuel just as the girl slammed the plane's cowl.

"Get in!" she shouted.

All three leaped into the plane. There, Robinson froze.

"Do you knows how to fly?" the girl asked.

"Yes!" Robinson snapped. "Sort of."

He flicked what he thought was the master battery switch, but couldn't remember what followed. The girl huffed and reached past him, pulling what Robinson suspected was the fuel mixture to full rich. Then she opened the throttle minutely. Robinson churned the primer before flicking the ignition switch. The propeller whirled to life.

Behind them, shouts erupted as the door was forced open. A bolt was fired and bounced off the plane's fuselage.

"Go!" Underfoot shouted.

Robinson shoved the throttle forward. The plane propelled forward just as the barricade fell behind it. Numerous men with lit flamethrowers appeared. One threw a fire bomb that bounced off the plane's tail but didn't explode.

"Hold this!" Robinson said of the yoke.

The girl grabbed it as Robinson leaned out the window and fired four shots from his pistol. The first three went into the crowd of Fire Lords. The fourth struck the cement flooring, igniting the spilt fuel. A flash lit the room followed by screams.

The girl directed Robinson to the airstrip. The plane bounded over potholes as Robinson fought to keep the nose straight. Behind them, a caravan of motorcycles and other vehicles appeared.

"They's coming fast!" Underfoot yelled.

The girl shouted at her brother to move as she leaped into the backseat, stepping over a floor that was little more than mottled wood. She jerked two cables that stretched out to the wings, and a flamethrower turret rotated backward. A third cable spit a deluge of fire that swallowed the two lead motorcycle riders and sent their blazing bodies careening into the ditch.

A giant truck roared in from the opposite side, releasing their own deluge of fire that coated the plane in flames. It must have been coated with non-flammable material because it quickly smoked out.

The girl bounded to the opposite wing and used the flamethrower turret there to shroud the truck with fire. It quickly spun into the dirt, its burning occupants bailing out.

The end of the road loomed ahead. Robinson didn't know if he had enough speed, but he pulled back on the yoke anyway and felt the plane lift. The headwind vibrated them violently. Then Robinson pushed the throttle all the way up, and the plane soared into the sky.

The engine strained against the buffeting wind, shaking the yoke in Robinson's hands. He worked the ailerons to facilitate a banking turn as the lift changed the vertical force to side force. When the drag on the outer wing pulled the nose up, he pumped the rudder to oppose the adverse yaw. After a few shaky moments, he could fully turn the plane.

As they gained altitude, Robinson passed back over the refinery. Flames could already be seen spilling out of the central building, and black smoke gushed from every opening. On the ground, Fire Lords could be seen fleeing for safety while racing frantically to save their vehicles. Then, suddenly, a huge explosion lit up the night sky. The plane shook from the convulsive force. Underfoot gasped, but the girl's eyes narrowed. Robinson thought he saw satisfaction there.

Robinson jockeyed around for another turn just as a second explosion engulfed the tanks. Fed by the wind, the refinery became a sprawling, blinding inferno. He was preparing to turn away when he saw movement down below. There, many cars and motorcycles were amassed outside the disaster area.

Robinson swallowed but pushed on.

Once Robinson had set his course above the old railroad tracks, he looked back at Underfoot. "You should have told me."

"She's my sister," was all he could manage.

The boy didn't need a lecture. And the truth was, Robinson had done similar things not so long before that still troubled him. To his surprise, it was the girl that spoke next.

"Don't blame him," the girl said. "The fault was mine."

"Dustynose, I presume," Robinson said.

The kids traded looks. Robinson grinned.

"Don't look so surprised. It wasn't hard to figure out. There were only two times he spoke with any emotion. Once when he mentioned his sis and later when he talked about Fang's predecessor. Wasn't hard to figure out they were the same person. That's the irony of loving someone. They're both your greatest strength and your biggest weakness."

Robinson braved a look at Dustynose. She was pretty in a tomboy-ish way. Natty hair. A broken nose. Intelligent eyes. Yeah, he could see the leader in her, even after Spires knows how long as a captive.

"It's not hard to guess your story either. After your exile, the Fire Lords captured you. Or maybe you went to them directly? Either way, you tried to negotiate a deal to keep your people alive because the greenhouse had been failing, and one bad winter and no more Troyus. You knew Fang would never deal with rival players, so you used the myth of the mother bird."

"Fang's a brute and a fool," Dustynose said. "No ways he'd ever hold O City together without the edi's. I knew zero doubt he'd make the spit and firm."

"And you probably expected him to keep it. So, what happened? The Fire Lord wanted a change of terms?"

"Kids growing your edi's seemed good for a time. Then they figur'd why not get 'em to do other things."

"Better slaves than partners? Don't beat yourself up about it. It wasn't a terrible play. Unfortunately for you, the game's just beginning."

"What do you mean?"

"I saw a whole bunch of Fire Lords assembling after we left. They won't be too happy losing to kids. I'd say the stakes are about to get much higher."

Dustynose sat back. He knew she was thinking the same thing.

Chapter Eleven

Jacks

Friday was packing her bag when Robinson entered the Nest.

"Are you ready?" he asked.

Friday nodded, taking one last look around the room.

It wouldn't be such a bad place to birth a child, she thought. *At least they have each other.*

She looked over the girls, including Pix.

"Remember my words," Friday said. "You have strength, but strength is always tested. From without and within. Be the sticks that stand together, and you will stand unbroken."

Pix nodded. Friday and Robinson left the room.

As they crossed the second-floor balcony, they saw the children gathered around the tree. Fang and Dustynose yelled at each other until Snapfinger and the Reds ushered her toward the double doors that led to the lavatory holding room.

When Robinson exited the tree, he approached Fang. "What will you do with her?"

"Dustynose knew the rules same as all in O City," Fang said. "She took the Full's walk and come back. Now she'll pay the rival player's price."

"But the Fire Lords—"

"Ye-uh," Fang snorted. "She said they be coming. Let 'em, I says. I know the game good as any. And I got the Reds. My Reds'll snuff 'em and smash their bones to dust!"

The children around the room cheered, but there was a nervousness to it. No one knew what to expect. *If they did*, Robinson thought, *they might be scuttling for the hills. Or wetting their pants.*

It wasn't his concern. He was about to leave when he noticed someone was missing. "Where's Underfoot?"

Fang snarled. "Like a fox that one. But we'll find him. And when we do…" He slapped an empty hanging cage with his staff. "Done and dust."

Robinson felt the urge to smash the kid in the face, but he didn't think it would do any good. Fang must have sensed his hesitation and mistaken it for weakness. He stepped close enough that Robinson could smell his breath.

"Now, our bargain's kept, Loper. So you and your fem got 'til sunfall to leave Troyus. And if we ever sees you this way again, I'll dirt all *three* of you."

Robinson tensed and his hand curled into a fist. Then, Friday touched him on the arm, and they turned to walk away as Fang's Blue sycophants huddled around him.

Robinson and Friday were scaling the berm outside the old parking lot when Underfoot stepped out of the trees.

"Wait," he said, out of breath. "You can't leave."

Robinson sighed. He didn't want to do this.

"Sorry, kid, but our time here is done. We have to move on."

"But Fang's got Dustynose. He plans to dirt her on the roots. Fore everyone!"

"I know. And I feel bad about that. But there's nothing we can do."

"You could stop him. You could learn him about the Fire Lords. He'll believe they's coming if it comes from you."

"He already knows and doesn't care. Fang thinks he can handle them like he handles everything else. But the Fire Lords aren't some random Lopers you chase away with a few sticks. They have weapons and large numbers. And they're angry. We lit up their home in the middle of the night, and you saw how quickly they escaped. And what was the first thing they did while their home was still burning? Gather their vehicles and weapons and prepare to retaliate. How are children with bows supposed to defend against that?"

"We can't," Underfoot said. "But *you* can." The boy stepped close. "I seen you. You got the learning. You could arm the Orphans. Teach us."

"There isn't enough time."

"Then maybe you could plan it for us—"

"Even if I did, who would listen? Not Fang. Not the Blues. They like things the way they are because it gives them some semblance of power. But what use is power when you're living in a fishbowl? The whole purpose of life is to gain wisdom and experience so you can make things better for yourself and those you love. Look around you, Underfoot. Has anything gotten better since you've been here? One of the ancients said something like, 'It's not the strongest of the species that survives nor the most intelligent, but the one most adaptable to change.' If you're going to survive, Troyus needs to change, and it needs to change now. Unfortunately, I don't see that happening."

Friday chose that moment to step forward. "You could come with us. Crusoe and I could teach you how to survive."

A glimmer of desire appeared in Underfoot's eyes. Then he shook his head. "Would you leave him?" he said, nodding to Robinson. "Or you, her?"

The answer for both was obvious.

"Orphans ain't 'posed to value blood. Rules say we all play as one. But she's my *sis*. The only to ever care to know me. Who saw me not as a color, but as me. Without her, what do I got?"

The boy's lip quivered. Robinson felt sympathy for him. But before he could say anymore, Snapfinger and a handful of armed Reds burst from the tree line.

"'Lo, Greenie," Snapfinger smirked. "Knew if I followed the Lopers, they'd lead me to you."

"You has to help me," Underfoot shouted as two Reds grabbed him. "Please!" The fear in his voice prompted Robinson and Friday to spread apart, arrows beaded in on them.

"Fang says I need a reason to dirt you," Snapfinger said. "But he don't say how big that reason need be."

Robinson glared at her before turning back to Underfoot.

"Just stall for time, kid. When the Fire Lords come—and they will come—Troyus is going to burn. No one will care about a couple rule breakers then. When you smell smoke, make your move, and run for the hills."

"Best follow your own 'vice, Loper," Snapfinger said. "Cuz after sunfall, it won't be the Fire Lords you needin' worry about. It'll be me."

Friday stepped in front of the girl and said, "You should pray to your Gods that doesn't happen."

Snapfinger swallowed before nodding to the Reds to haul Underfoot away.

"They'll kill him," Friday said after they left. "To send a message."

"I know. But he knew the consequences of bringing her back and did it anyway."

"We leave then?"

Robinson nodded, then noted Friday's surprise.

"We didn't come here by choice. They made us come. And every day we're not searching for the City of Glass puts you and our child more at risk."

"And what of these children? Are they not at risk?"

"You taught me the only thing that matters is survival."

"And I believed it. Once. Then I met a man who taught me that people are more important. Which would you use for our child? The world we suffer or the one we make?"

Underfoot was choking. Fang held his staff at the boy's throat and pressed it harder as the remaining children watched on.

"Your face is like a rainbow. So many colors."

He sniggered. Then he heard a buzz. He looked up to see Robinson and Friday returning.

"You! Was I not clear?"

Friday ripped the staff from Fang's hands and slammed him in the gut before breaking it over his back. She had a knife to his neck before the Reds could blink. Only Snapdragon rushed forward until a thunderous crack filled the room as her spear exploded in her hands.

Robinson lowered the laser eye of his pistol to her heart. "Change of plans."

They'd taken Fang and Snapfinger to the holding room where they were forced to listen to Dustynose's breakdown of the Fire Lords. In the beginning, her words were met with resistance and hostility, but slowly, surely, the message got through.

Fang's anger transformed, first to disbelief then to fear. Snapfinger could only sit alone in the corner, arms folded, glowering at Friday.

"You only come back for the Fives," Fang said.

"I 'spect you see it so," Dustynose retorted. "But if'n it was true, why wouldn't I just dirt you here and now? The bones mean zeroes to me, Fang. Same as the colors. I ain't here for them or the tree or you. I'm here for the Orphans. Fact is, once the game's won, me and Under will walk with the Lopers … I mean, Crusoe and Friday, if Troyus still stands. To that we give crosses."

"Crosses," Underfoot repeated.

"But first we need to 'tect O City from game over. Now, can you stand the roots and say the words? Or do you want to sniff piss 'n here while Troyus burns 'round you?"

In the end, Fang saw the logic. And despite his cruel nature, Dustynose knew she needed him to lead the Reds. It was Snapdragon she worried about, and she told Robinson and Friday so.

"I can watch the girl," Friday said. And that was that.

By early afternoon, Dustynose and Fang had gathered a war council at the base of the Tree. Snapdragon had opted to patrol outside instead.

"The Fire Lords like to attack at night," Dustynose said. "So as to keep their numbs hid and let the rumble of 'urt drive terror before 'em. When the flames follow, most clans panic. We can't. If the Os stand together, we got a chance. If they run, we're dust and done."

"How many big wheels?" Fang asked.

"Four what's called trucks. Three if the one Crusoe and I done stays done. These haul fighters. Smaller wheels do the launchin'. It's the motos we'll itch over. They lead the charge. Each carry two Lords. A rider and a thrower. The thrower's job is to toss fire glass at key places. To soften 'em up."

"No doubt they'd flown over enough times to be familiar with the place," Robinson said. "If what Dustynose says about their tactics holds true, they'll target several, if not all, of the mall's entrances simultaneously. That's two to the south, one east and west, and the main one here to the north. Their goal is to clear the way so the trucks can get inside. We can't let that happen."

"Why'd they want inside?" Fang asked. "You says you smoked their home. Why ain't they after the revenge?"

Dustynose answered. "They be needing the edi's. If they believing they can win Troyus straight up, they'll do it, dirting enough Orphans to make right for last night. But they'll be wanting some alive too. For slave labor. And worse."

"The good news is," Robinson said, "the southern parking lot backs up to this arroyo, which means we only have to worry about this slope here. If we can block it and this inlet on the eastern side, that's three of the five entrances out of the equation. That'll force the Fire Lords to concentrate their attack here, to the north."

"Why not attack the western entrance?" Friday asked. "It's the most open. I would hit it first."

"I know," Robinson said. "That's why we're going to put the plane there. Just inside the windows where it can be seen. Dustynose says the Fire Lords see the plane as more than just a vehicle. To them, it's a symbol of their prowess. If they truly want it back, they won't risk damaging it unless they have to."

"Big risk," Fang added. "'sidering you burned up the juice to feed her."

"Hey, nothing's guaranteed," Robinson said before nodding to Dustynose. "But *she* says it's worth the risk, and I believe her."

"So we box 'em to the north," Fang said. "They still got the numbs. And wheels. And weapons. What's stopping 'em from overpowering us?"

"Law of the sticks," Friday said. "Spread them out, and they're weaker."

"That's right," Robinson said. "We'll use the old carriages to bottle this chokepoint. And we'll take out this bridge just after their motorcycles cross."

"How?" Underfoot asked.

"Leave that to me," Robinson said. He turned to Fang. "Do you have metalworkers?"

"You seen the tree, ain't you?" Fang asked.

Robinson slid over a piece of paper with a sketch on it. "You know what that is?"

Fang took the paper and looked at it. "Pieces o' game from the far and back. Shorts play it. Named Bounce and Pick."

"We called it Jacks. Historically, they were called caltrops. Armies used something similar that impeded cavalry and vehicles on the battlefield. I need your orphans to make as many as possible. Fist-sized with sharpened ends."

Fang nodded and tucked the paper into his shirt.

"I have a few other tricks up my sleeve, but the main goal here is to parse the enemy into waves so we can take them on separately. The bulk of your Reds will man the high ground atop Troyus with bows, arrows, and whatever else you can think of. Friday will lead them."

"Snapfinger won't like it," Fang said.

"She won't have to," Friday said.

"The archers will target the motorcycles. Dustynose and the Greens will extinguish any blazes set to the main structure. And the rest of us will take out the trucks when they arrive."

"And how will we do that?" Fang asked.

"Easy. We'll fight fire with fire."

Chapter Twelve

Preparations

The Master stood atop the tree-lined knoll watching the children below through binoculars.

"What are they doing?" Viktor asked.

"It appears they are preparing for an attack."

The preparations were crude, but might be effective depending on their enemy. The Master was paying particularly close attention to Crusoe, who led the operation. He had children rolling large, heavy barrels to various locations around the old parking lot while others strung thin wires between poles.

"By whom?" Viktor asked.

"That has yet to be determined. Whomever it is, Crusoe seems to believe they're formidable. Or at least he's preparing as such. Has Cassa run across any scouts?"

"No," Viktor answered. "Only the children's patrols, which he's avoided as you directed."

"Good. I'd like to see how this plays out."

"Even if it puts your adversary in danger?"

The word "adversary" irked the Master. It implied the boy was an equal when clearly he was nothing of the sort.

"I wouldn't worry about Crusoe. He has an uncanny knack for escaping tight spots. Besides, I want the girl too. And she hasn't appeared since they returned."

"We were so close," Viktor said. "Another few hundred feet up the road, and we would have had them."

"He that can have patience can have what he will."

"Benjamin Franklin," Viktor said. "Quite apt, Sir."

"Your intellect is truly a desert flower in this wasteland, Viktor."

Viktor bowed. It'd been a long time since someone had complimented him on anything other than his creations. For a man whose spirit was once inexorably tied to his individuality, it rekindled something dormant inside him and made him swell with pride. Then the Master turned again.

"But it's the depth of your depravity I value most."

Viktor's smile fell. "That I owe to you, Master."

Robinson plucked a sprig of basil from a planter box and held it to his nose. The sweet, minty smell brought back memories of home. How formal dinner had seemed back then. The expected etiquette. The stony faces. And yet there was always an undercurrent of love beneath. Robinson missed it. As he watched Friday approach, he wondered if they would ever have such a routine.

"Did you eat?" Friday asked, slipping a hand over his shoulder.

"Earlier. You?"

She nodded as she sat on the lip of the building and looked out through one of the many windows that had been repurposed as embrasures. Beyond the mesa, the sun had dipped between the snow-dappled peaks of twin mountains, their ringed halos shimmering across the distance. The moon loomed opaquely in the unclouded sky, as if eager for the battle to start.

"Won't be long now," Robinson said.

Friday followed his gaze to the west where a black brume of dust and exhaust rose over the city.

She wrapped both arms around his neck and lay her head on his back.

"Would you hate me if I said part of me missed this?" Friday asked.

Robinson understood she meant the call of battle, because he felt it too. "No," he said. "But I must remind you you're fighting for two now."

"And she will always come first, behind you."

Robinson kissed her hand.

"If things start to go bad—if we're overrun or the enemy makes it inside—I want you to lead as many of the children as you can into the ravine out back and head east. I'll catch up to you when I can."

"We will not fail. We are Aserra."

"The skies are full of Aserra that failed, Friday. And one day we'll both join them. I just want to be sure it's not today. East, okay?"

"I'll be waiting," Friday said.

The children had gathered around the Tree of Gifts a final time, asking for their Gods, Ton-Bra and the Ark Brothers for courage in the face of battle. When Fang let loose a battle call, the children answered in kind, filling the massive structure with a din that shook the rafters. Then the Reds scaled the tree, armed with their bows. The Greens fell in as support behind them. With the yellow handling injuries and messages, that left Fang and his Blues on the ground.

"I gone to the store," Fang said as he approached Robinson. "Learned Troyus has been attacked eight times since the far and back. Last was forty-three leaders past. Orphans won the day then. And will today."

"Did you consult your *eye* as well?"

Fang nodded reluctantly. "Black Eye of Infinity says all signs point to ye-uh."

"Good. What did you decide about those in the nest?"

"Took your 'vice. Had the swoles and whelps escorted out of O. They'll be safe 'til it's time to 'turn."

"I have to say, while I don't think much of your methods as a leader, you would have made an excellent battle commander. Unless you fold when the fighting starts."

Fang smirked. "We'll see who's standing when it's all over, Loper. See you at dewday."

"See you then."

A chill wind trickled in after the passing of twilight. Moonlight lit the tree limbs swaying in time. An unfamiliar energy radiated from the Blues that had taken position behind hastily erected barricades surrounding the northern entrance. They were nervous and fearful to be sure, but they also sensed that something significant was about to happen and that they had a chance to play a part. Robinson hoped they would all rise to the challenge.

First contact came in the form of a single motorcycle rider, whose engine purred as he neared the embankment atop the northern parking lot. He rode slowly past the barricade of mounted car shells before continuing to the northeastern bridge. Once his recon was done, he hit his throttle and sped back the way he came.

A strange silence settled. The evening felt almost serene. Then the quiet was shattered by a chorus of high-pitched wails, intensifying as the convoy approached. Their *yip-yip-yip* sounded like a pack of coyotes or a murder of crows startled to flight.

An orange glow lit the sides of the buildings atop the ridge. Then, one by one, the motorcycles arrived, howling across the upper road like banshees. They held torches, and in some cases, they threw old glass bottles of fuel to light up the night.

The show was meant to terrify them. And to a degree, it worked. Robinson saw one boy in red wet himself. Another girl whimpered. None fled.

As the riders kicked up dust, a deep rumble preceded several large trucks and smaller cars. The column broke in two, settling outside each of the mall's entrances. Once in position, the engines howled in unison, and torrents of fire shot high into the air. Then all at once, the din died away until the only sound was idling engines.

A moment passed before the largest truck bound forward, its engine roaring as it picked up speed and rammed into the northwestern barricade. The sound of the impact split the night air as the tower of cars buckled and fragmented. But the barricade held.

The driver put the truck into reverse before striking the barricade again. This time, black smoke billowed into the air as the barricade shifted and fell atop the truck.

Fang stood and screamed, "Ton-Bra!" The Orphans around the mall joined him.

For a moment, Robinson thought they might win this thing. Then a second horn roared, and the motorcycles attacked.

"Here they come!" Robinson shouted.

Friday and the Reds watched from the roof as the motorcycles sped over the embankment, a cavalry charge of two dozen strong. The orphans waited with bated breath as the bikes screamed forward, the passengers of each carrying two flaming glass firebombs.

Halfway across the parking lot, the foremost riders were violently upended like rag dolls, their glass firebombs breaking on the cement, engulfing both Lords in flames. They managed to make it to their feet, writhing and thrashing, until the conflagration consumed them.

Several more riders also struck the wire that had been strung between ancient light poles, including one whose head toppled to the cement. Eventually, the wire snapped and the other bikes continued. Only then did they see the littering of caltrops that had been strewn about like seedlings. Tires punctured, riders were tossed, and flames lit up their bodies and the darkened sky.

While six fell, another fifteen broke through. Friday waited until they were twenty-five meters out before she gave the order. A score of red archers sprung up and loosed a volley of arrows. Another half-dozen riders fell. The rest managed to swing close enough to launch their glass firebombs toward the northern entrance. The barricade erupted in flames, as did the wall above it. Robinson heard Friday call out to the Greens.

Green Halfers rushed across the roof with vats of water, hurling them over the edge until the flames were snuffed. Friday shouted again, and the archers prepared for the next wave.

The motorcycles came in wild loops, throwing firebombs as they dodged arrows. The intense heat kept those on the ground behind their barricades until one rider ventured too close, and Robinson stepped out and shot him. As he keeled over, his bike hit the curb and bounced into the street, its engine still running.

A horn blast signaled the second wave of attackers, led by the Fire Lord's largest truck, a military vehicle of some kind. As it plodded onto the northeastern bridge, Robinson signaled Underfoot.

"Bridge!" he shouted.

Underfoot raced into the mall and relayed the order up the tree to the roof where six Greens levered a set of construction beams off the southern edge of the building. The counterweight wrenched taut, whipping hundreds of yards of cable in an instant. The bridge's concrete piling snapped, and the bridge teetered before the massive truck careened into the ditch. The Orphans let out another rousing cheer, but the Fire Lords weren't done by a long shot. The remaining convoy found the most forgiving gradient of the embankment and began funneling down.

The motorcycles continued to circle around tossing firebombs at the mall, only to return to the convoy when they ran out of ammunition.

The Blues near Robinson had coated their spears with poison from the desert snakes. When one of the riders ventured close enough, a Blue would step out, sling his or her spear, and impale the rider. With the cover from Friday's Reds, the smaller forces were being kept at bay.

Then a large truck rumbled across the parking lot; its target: their barricade. Robinson knew the battle would hinge on what happened next. If his gambit worked and they could take out the trucks before they reached the building, their chances of success were good. If the trucks drove them back, Troyus was almost sure to fall.

"Fang!" Robinson shouted across the gap to the rival barricade, pointing to the cables at the teen's feet. "Get ready."

Fang nodded and had his team of Blues grip two of the four cables. Robinson, Underfoot, and another Blue grabbed the others. Now, all they had to do was wait for the trucks to reach the front line of light poles.

But to their surprise and dismay, the trucks stopped one hundred feet short.

"What are they doing?" Underfoot asked.

Robinson wasn't sure. He could only watch as the trucks turned sideways as group of Fire Lords began pulling the canvas coverings off the back. When

Robinson finally recognized what was in the back of the truck, he was filled with dread.

"Oh no," he said.

"What is it?" Underfoot asked.

Robinson didn't have time to answer. A moment later, the giant mechanism sprang to life and a firebomb ten times the size of those the bike throwers yielded vaulted high into the air before arching down and striking the side of the mall, erupting into a towering wall of flame.

The Fire Lords had four massive trebuchets—catapults capable of assailing any structure from afar. As soon as the blinding projectiles began to fill the sky, Robinson knew the battle was lost.

Chapter Thirteen
Fire With Fire

The Master watched the fiery projectiles streak across the sky like a storm of meteors, only to erupt into tsunamis of flame when they crashed against the mall's edifice. Amidst the screams of children atop of the structure, a woman's shouts could be heard, followed by bouts of water that gave too little relief.

The arrows slackened, and the attacking foot soldiers pushed forward.

The rout is on, thought the Master. He turned his spyglass toward the barricade where Crusoe shouted orders at the children. He'd seen the cables at Robinson's feet and knew their purpose. They ran to two hastily erected scaffolds edged against the light poles with four rusty barrels raised on both sides.

Unfortunately, the catapult-bearing trucks were too far away from the barrels to spur the trap. It was a classic blunder. The boy had staked his defense on what he anticipated his enemy to do rather than dictating the direction of the battle himself. It would prove his downfall.

"Call Cassa," the Master told Viktor.

Viktor disappeared. A few moments later, the stoic, masked figure walked out of the shadows.

"The battle's almost over," the Master said. "Ready the pack and my horse. Crusoe will have an escape plan, likely one that takes him through the southern gully. I want him taken quickly, but only if the girl is with him."

Cassa nodded and started to turn when the Master called again. "There will be children among them," he said. "Let nothing deter you from the prize."

Cassa nodded again, but with less vigor. If the Master wanted children dead, he would comply, but he didn't have to like it.

Friday shouted orders to the Reds and Greens atop the roof, making sure they heard the strength in her voice.

Behind her, the Greens pitched water on the fire licking up over the sides of the wall. But with each throw, it made it harder to see the action below. As the smoke rolled over her, she coughed longer and harder.

A Halfer Green girl blackened by soot soon ran up holding an empty vat.

"I's 'posed to say we's running short on water!" the girl shouted.

"How much is left?" Friday asked.

The girl held up eight fingers.

Eight barrels. Meaning they'd already used a third of their supply. Given the size of these latest projectiles, she estimated they had less than ten minutes before they would run out of water.

"Focus on the area above the northern entrance. We need to protect those below."

The girl nodded and left. That's when Friday noticed Snapfinger and several archers moving away from the western side of the building.

"You!" Friday shouted. "Back to your posts!"

"We's needed below," Snapfinger spat.

"You are needed here! We have the high ground. It is all that's keeping their warriors from storming this place!"

"What good is Troyus if we burn to death in it?!" Snapfinger shouted.

"Refuse my command, and you won't have to wait to find out."

Snapfinger gnashed her teeth, but her troops fell back. Friday reminded herself not to lose track of the girl.

Robinson knew the battle had turned in the enemy's favor. But his resources were limited, and his trump card now looked like it would never pay off. That's when Dustynose rushed up from behind.

84

"A pack of Fire Lords snuck in through the west entrance," she said. "They tried to take the mother plane, but we dirted some, and the rest run off."

"If they reach their commanders," Robinson said, "more will be coming that way. What's the situation up top?"

"Your fem's keeping the Reds sharp," Underfoot said. "But the water's almost gone."

"When it goes, so do we."

"You got a plan?" Dustynose asked.

Robinson looked over the parking lot, his eyes settling on the motorcycle that had crashed in front of the barricade. Smoke puttered from the tailpipe.

"Fang!" he shouted before waving the teen over. "I'm going to try something. If it doesn't work, I want you to spring the trap without me."

"You'll be cut off," Fang said.

"At that point, it won't matter. Won't harm the Fire Lords much either, but it'll buy you time to collect your people and make for the gully."

"Orphans don't run," Fang snarled.

"If you stay here and Troyus burns, there won't be any Orphans left. A real leader knows when it's time to pull back and get his people to safety."

Fang's eyes narrowed, but the message seemed to sink in.

"What will you do?" Fang asked.

Robinson looked to Dustynose and Underfoot.

"They came for a show. I'm going to give them one."

Friday saw the figure run for the Fire Lord's downed mechanical steed and knew it was Crusoe. As he revved its engine and rode away, another large truck loosed a firebomb, this one flying higher than before. When it struck the greenhouse's protective structure, a wave of fire rolled over the rooftop.

As Robinson sped across the parking lot, he was certain he would lose control at any second. He'd ridden a bicycle back in New London as a child, but it was a relic—a toy one of the merchants of the Clutch kept as a novelty. These feats of engineering with levers, grips, and pedals were different. He had watched the Fire Lord riders enough to see the right hand and foot determined speed, but he had no clue what the left side did.

When the whine of the engine screamed, Robinson kicked his foot down and felt the motorcycle jerk into second gear. He had no time for any further experimentation. Two motorcycle riders turned after him. Rather than confront them, he steered the bike around the western entrance of the mall, away from the main battlefield, hoping they would follow.

The rooftop was ablaze. Flames melted through the plastic housing and threatened to bring the entire structure down on the children's heads if something wasn't done quickly. Friday shouted for water. No one heard her in the chaos.

Two Greens cowered under the greenhouse frame where the projectile had struck. It was already bowing from the heat. As it started to collapse, Friday kicked a table covered with soil over the top of them moments before the support beam snapped and the fire spilled in. Friday yanked the children out safely.

Reds and Greens stumbled through the smoke and fire. Friday covered her mouth and nose with her shirt but continued to cough. She saw Underfoot pushing against the tide of fleeing kids. He took out a knife and used it to cut open the filtration cables that ran overhead. When water sprayed out over the fire, Friday felt a modicum of relief. Then she turned just in time to see Snapfinger charging with a knife.

Robinson heard the explosion, felt the heat singe his back. He looked back to see the motorcycles were right on him. He expected the closest Fire Lord to ram him. Instead, the man reached for another one of the glass firebombs tied to a lanyard around his neck. Robinson didn't hesitate. In one swift motion, he pulled his pistol, turned, and fired. When the bottle broke, the man was doused with fuel. Blinded, the man went down. Sparks ignited the fuel, and the motorcycle detonated.

The second rider swerved to Robinson's right, forcing him to aim across his body. Before he could line up a shot, the rider rammed Robinson, and the pistol flew from his hands. The motorcycle shook for an instant before it went down. Robinson went flying. He felt a crushing blow to his shoulder as it hit the cement. When he came to a stop, he turned to see the Fire Lord braking for a final pass.

The rider saw the pistol and gunned his engine before his adversary could reach it, but Robinson surprised him by turning and running toward him instead.

Robinson watched the rider power the front wheel off the ground. At the last moment, he jockeyed left, then right, swinging his axe. He clipped the rider's head and flailed backward. Unfortunately, his boot stayed linked to the motorcycle, which dragged him across the rough cement and over the southern embankment.

Robinson wobbled to his feet and ran for his bike, stopping long enough to pick up the lanyard of firebombs left behind. He quickly counted them— four in total—before kick-starting his bike and speeding back into the fight.

Friday caught Snapfinger's wrists, but her momentum sent them both tumbling over the planters to the floor. The girl was strong for her age, and her eyes burned with fury. She snarled as she mounted Friday, her blade taking aim at her heart. She put her weight behind the blade, and in doing so, revealed she knew nothing of leverage. By throwing her weight forward, Friday could shift her hips back and kick up with her legs. Snapfinger catapulted over and landed hard on the roof. Before she could regain her feet, Friday stripped the blade away and slammed it under her chin. Snapfinger gurgled, her eyes wide with surprise as her mouth filled with blood. Then the light went out in her eyes.

Friday sat back, rasping. She reached for her belly but found no wounds. Her relief was more intense than she expected. She looked at the dead girl lying at her feet and felt pity for her. The girl had grown up in a boy's world, much like Friday, and she had proven herself with strength and determination. She had fought for what she believed was right. The only difference between the two was that Friday had learned along the way that you can't do it on your own. Maybe if the girl had lived longer, she would have figured it out. Sadly, she would never get the chance.

Friday struggled to her feet to try and help Underfoot douse the flames.

Three more salvos flew from the Fire Lords' trebuchets. One fell short and exploded in the parking lot. One struck the mall's wall. The other erupted atop the mall again. Robinson could see the fire raging there and heard the shouts of children scrambling to put them out. He knew if Troyus had any hope of survival, those three trucks had to be destroyed now.

Robinson sped for the closest truck, where two Fire Lords doused another projectile with kerosene. They were in the process of loading it when they saw Robinson's approach. Before they could send up an alarm, Robinson pulled a glass firebomb from his lanyard and tossed it at them. With the kerosene tank open, the fuel line ignited and the truck exploded.

The Fire Lords in the second truck all turned in unison. A flamethrower turned toward Robinson, forcing him to veer sharply in front of the truck to slip under the fiery tongue that nearly licked his back. Robinson veered again as he tossed his second glass firebomb toward the truck's window, but it exploded on the outside and did little damage.

Two motorcycle riders turned from the field to run him down. Robinson raced toward the eastern end of the parking lot with them hot on his tail. He pulled his third glass firebomb and tossed it overhead. It exploded in front of the lead rider, who cranked left and ran into the steel base of a light pole.

The second rider closed in, but Robinson knew the layout better than he did. He steered through a small gauntlet of caltrops he'd set up earlier. The pursuing Fire Lord never saw them. When his front tire clipped a caltrop, it blew, and he catapulted over his handlebars only to be impaled on another caltrop in front of him.

Friday had managed to help Underfoot quell the rooftop fires, but the roof itself had become unstable. Of the children that had remained behind, a dozen Reds remained at their position, arrows flying.

Friday told Underfoot to finish out the fires before calling out to the Reds, "With me!"

They rushed for the stairs together.

The Master and Viktor watched Robinson as he sped around the parking lot, keeping the Fire Lords' attention squarely on him. With two cars and two motorcycles pursuing him, no one was expecting him to pull up in the middle of the lot and turn to face his trackers.

"What's he doing?" Viktor asked.

The Master grinned appreciatively. "Offering himself as bait."

Friday wanted to yell out to her husband, but she knew he was doing the only thing he could. She ordered the Reds to spread out and provide cover when or if he turned back for them.

Robinson felt the thrum of the motorcycle as it idled. He saw two cars splitting out to the far sides of the convoy. The riders, however, cut a path straight for him. As he pulled his pistol from the holster, he knew he'd only have one chance to draw the trucks out. One chance to save Troyus and drive the intruders away.

He took two deep breaths to slow the adrenaline pulsing through him. For a second, he wondered if his wounded shoulder would even have the strength to raise the pistol. But all those thoughts went away when he saw the thrower on the back of the first bike rise, a firebomb in his hand. Robinson lifted the pistol and fired.

The bullet struck the rider in the face, catapulting both riders backward. As the firebomb exploded, it set off the others with a single concussive blast. The bike rolled past Robinson, fully aflame.

The second rider ducked low to evade the incoming gunfire. When Robinson's pistol ran empty, he cranked the throttle, kicked the bike into its lowest gear, and released the clutch. The bike leaped from beneath him—an unwieldly missile that slammed into the closing motorcycle that sent both Fire Lords splaying across the cement.

Both enemy cars tore at him simultaneously. Robinson knew he wouldn't be able to dodge them both, so he ejected the used magazine from his pistol, replacing it with his reserve. One of the cars was smaller and had a roll bar and a flamethrower turret operator on the back. Robinson dropped to his knee and squeezed off rounds. The fourth or fifth bullet struck the turret operator, and as he fell back, the nozzle opened, encasing the driver in a fiery sheath. He leaped out of the way of the driverless car only to find himself in the path of the second one, a convertible. He emptied his clip into it, but the car kept coming. The driver had him dead to rights. Then, miraculously, a wave of arrows flew overhead, killing the driver and the man inside. The car slammed into another light post, a smoking relic.

With the lesser vehicles out of the way, Robinson knew what happened next would decide the battle. He turned to the two trucks and screamed. Words didn't matter, but that he challenged them was more important. After an interminable moment, black exhaust spewed from the trucks as they lurched in his direction. Relief flooded Robinson before he realized he was in open ground with no cover and two flame-spitting trucks hurtling at him. Only then did he turn and run.

Friday watched Robinson limp toward her and the line of Reds she'd amassed in front of the barricade, though arrows would be little use to him now. That's when Fang shouted for them to fall back. Friday saw he had the cables that ran to the western barrels in his hands.

Robinson waited until the trucks were at full speed before he gave the signal. Fang and the others jerked their cables. The barrels atop the left platform spilled four hundred gallons of kerosene under the left truck the same time a globule of burning fuel dropped to the ground. A great whoosh went up as the truck burst into flames.

But the second set of cables had snapped thirty feet away. Robinson hadn't seen it—he was too busy running—so Fang raced past him, reaching for the frayed end of the cable just as a second set of hands grasped it behind him. Underfoot. Fang was surprised to see the boy there, but when he nodded, the pair pulled with all their might. The barrels upended, splashing the back half of the right truck, which also burst into flames.

The children cheered and Underfoot smiled at Fang. But then the smile turned to one of horror. Fang's head snapped back to the truck, which continued rolling in their direction. The flamethrower's operator flailed in the back of the truck, but his hand must have melted over the open valve. Fang shouted, but Underfoot was frozen. So the leader of Troyus leaped and shoved him out of the way a moment before the fiery geyser washed over him.

The orphans screamed. Dustynose and a few Reds ran forward with blankets to put Fang's flames out before carrying him back to the barricade. When they pulled off the sheet, it was clear he would not live. With great effort, he looked at Robinson and smiled.

"Who be the might-mighty now?" Fang rasped.

Robinson couldn't think of what to say, so he simply nodded. Fang gasped and went still.

Some of the younger orphans sobbed, but the older ones were quick to console them. Dustynose pulled a sobbing Underfoot close.

It was the snarl of engines that made everyone turn. Atop the embankment, the remaining Fire Lords were already turning away. Robinson expected the children to cheer, but mostly they remained silent. At first, he thought they were too shocked to understand the battle was over and that they had won. Then it dawned on him. They had never known the cost of success would be so high. These were lessons people had learned since the dawn of time. The dead care not for the battle's outcome, and even the victors feel the terrible sting of loss.

The Master watched the fireworks with amusement, but not surprise. Even the manner of the boy's victory—riding around on the back of a fuel-powered steed—failed to shock him. The lad had always found the most creative ways to survive. He once thought it luck, though some still believed the boy was touched. The Master knew both inclinations were false. Crusoe was smart and prepared. And he acted as if every moment might be his last.

If he was being truthful, the Master admired the youth. They weren't so different. They both held lofty aspirations and would accept nothing less than their complete realization. But even a land as sprawling and untamed as this one couldn't afford two pioneers. Before the trail of tomorrow's history could be blazed, the ground must first be razed and anointed in enemy blood.

Viktor approached the Master as he lowered his binoculars.

"The pack grows restless," Viktor said. "Even from up here, they've caught the scent of the battlefield. Shall we attack?"

"No," the Master said. "The boy will ensure their defenses remain high tonight."

"Cassa could slip inside unseen."

The Master shook his head. "There is no need. The pair was headed out on foot this morning before turning back. I have a hunch they'll want to resume their journey soon."

"What about supplies? We're running short."

"Then send Cassa and his pack to hunt. But have them go east where their cries will not carry. It is fitting, I should think, that very soon we will all have our bellies full."

Chapter Fourteen
The Black Eye of Infinity

The night passed achingly slow. There were so many things to see to, so many fires to put out. Dustynose took charge, and no one questioned her. She started by sending out groups of Reds to ensure the Fire Lords were truly gone and to deal with any survivors.

Inside Troyus, the Yellows set up a triage unit to help the wounded. Most of the injuries were burns from aerial strikes on the roof. Four others suffered bolt wounds. Two were hit by bullets. And one broke both legs when she fell from the Tree of Gifts while running messages inside.

In total, thirteen orphans had died. Not a bad number given the size and strength of their attackers. Still, there would be no celebration.

Underfoot had led the Greens to staunch the remaining fires on the rooftop. The flames had consumed over half their crops and destroyed the greenhouse covering that would have to be built again before winter. It would not be an easy task.

Dustynose ordered the Blues to remove the dead. They grumbled about it—unused to physical exertion—but did as ordered. The bodies were laid together behind the mall. In the past, the orphans had always burned their dead, but after this night, the act felt like desecration. Someone suggested doing as the ancients had and laying them beneath the earth. Dustynose agreed and scheduled the burial for the following day.

While the children saw to their tasks, Robinson and Friday found a small, dark corner of the mall where they cleaned each other's wounds. They were oblivious to anything else around them.

"How did you know to attack the belly of the land movers?" Friday asked.

"It was a hunch," Robinson said. "When I was young, I once helped my father seal the stairs behind our home to protect them from rain. When I was finished, he came out to inspect my work and asked me why I didn't do the underneath. I said what good that would do since rain fell down, not up. He told me, "It's always the places we can't see that are most vulnerable.""

Friday nodded. The truth was she had never felt safer any place than in his arms.

Several hours later, Underfoot woke them. "Come," he said. "Dustynose is going to speak 'afore the tree."

They followed the boy into the main atrium where, once again, the orphans were gathered. It was clear they were exhausted, but every one of them sat up when Dustynose appeared.

"Orphans of O," Dustynose called. "Children of Troyus. It is good to be 'mong my brothers and sisses again. Even if the reason be bad like O City ain't seen since the long, long back. I know you's tired, and your hearts weep for those been dirted, but they's gone to the nest of the real mother bird where the Brothers Ark and Ton-Bra watch over and say, "good game.""

"Good game," the children repeated.

"And good it was. Though we lost some and suffer still, the rival players be beat hard, and now, for them, it's game over, never to play again! Glory, glory?!"

"Glory, glory!" The children shouted and cheered.

"For that I say thanks to you." She turned to Robinson and Friday. "And them. The Fives named 'em Lopers when they 'peared out the stretch; laughed when they said they'd been 'sent.' But sent they was, I see it. By the Tree. By the Brothers or Ton-Bra or the blowing winds. They come unwanted, but stay when needed, which makes 'em *friends*."

The orphans remained silent, realizing they were embarking on new territory here.

"Ye-uh," Dustynose continued. "I spoke it. Troyus ain't had friends since the *far and back*. But without 'em tonight, we'd all be dirt and dust. We broke the rules but won the game, which makes me say maybe more rules need breaking."

Until that very night, speaking such a thing was heresy, but in the quiet murmurs that followed, Dustynose thought she heard an undercurrent of assent. Or at least, an echo of thoughts that had long existed, but had never been given life until this very moment.

"I be a three and four," Dustynose continued. "Full for sure. By all rights, I should make the leap. Would you have me leap now? Or our friends too? Times change. The world outside changes. I seen it. And if the Orphans is to keep playing, we got to change too. No more Shorts, Halfers, and Fulls. No more colors. No Fives. Just us. Together. Brothers and sisses we stay, but friends and lovers too."

At this, she glanced back at Robinson and Friday. "I seen how they is for each other. And I want it."

At this, the children tittered. Even Robinson and Friday smiled.

"And I want it for you. We must rebuild Troyus. Remake it. If you like, I can lead. Or we can choose one better. But better it'll be for all of us. To this, I say crosses."

The orphans slowly filed out of the room. Many nodded and gave their thanks to Robinson and Friday as they passed. They seemed to have taken Dustynose's words to heart. There would be problems going forward, but in the end, it was the only path that made sense.

"That was ... well done," Robinson said to Dustynose when she approached.

Dustynose nodded, but her tired face was still etched with worry. *Get used to it*, Robinson thought. *It's one of the many burdens of leadership.*

"Underfoot says you're to leave at dewday," she said.

"That's right," Robinson said. "Time isn't exactly on our side. And as much as we've enjoyed making your acquaintance, we're still no closer to finding the City of Glass."

"The City of Glass," Dustynose repeated. "Is it known by any other name?"

"Not that we've heard," Friday said. "Why?"

"Come," Dustynose said.

The moment she turned for the tree, Robinson knew where they were headed. He was grateful they only had to climb one floor's worth of steps otherwise his aching legs might have given out. But when Dustynose stopped at the gate and drew it aside, Robinson hesitated. Underfoot had said *the store* was sacred to the Orphans. That it contained everything of value they possessed. The pessimist in him said nothing inside could aid them in their quest. The other side said, you never know.

Friday must have shared his reluctance. She decided to wait behind. Dustynose crossed the tremulous limb. Robinson followed her as she ducked under the metal gate and went inside.

Robinson hadn't known what to expect, but as Dustynose lit a candle, he felt his breath catch.

Lining the room was row after row of metal shelving, each brimming with toys. Plastic toys. Wooden toys. Dolls and animals. Small figurines of men and women in vibrant suits. There were plastic creatures, rocket ships, shiny vehicles, earth movers, and crafts. There were books, musical instruments, and plastic guns. Many bicycles and wagons too. And, of course, there were balls and equipment from every game imaginable.

Robinson roamed the center aisle, running his hand over rusty strings of an instrument. He tussled the fabric of a caped suit between his fingers. He saw the smiling faces of children everywhere. In one old photo, a stork with a hat flew with a baby in a sling. *The mother bird.* Robinson smiled.

No wonder they chose this place.

Dustynose walked a few steps behind him, staying quiet as he approached a section of games in old dusty boxes. He reached for the nearest one named CLUE. It must have been for adults because it showed aged people holding an odd assortment of ropes, wrenches, and optical glasses. Another box showed ladders and slides and looked to be for small children. A third called SCRABBLE only had tiled words.

"These be left behind by the ancients to teach us the way," Dustynose said. She cracked open a box called SORRY! and saw the four colors of Troyus. She rattled a bag of the rectangular tiles with dots on them and said, "These learn us numbs, but only the Fives matter."

On many of those faded boxes, Robinson pieced together a familiar set of names. Here is where they derived the names of their Gods. Only the Ark Brothers were PARKER BROTHERS and Ton-Bra the great was MILTON BRADLEY. Robinson exhaled in wonder.

Dustynose directed him to the back of the room where, on a makeshift plinth, sat a small, black sphere. Dustynose picked it up reverentially.

"This be the Black Eye of Infinity," she said. "The only magic left from the far and back."

She handed it to him with great care. The first thing he noticed was a faded white circle with what looked like the numeral '8.' Somehow the children had transmogrified this to the symbol for infinity. Robinson turned the object over and saw a small window with something moving inside.

"Ask a question," Dustynose said. "Maybe it will show you your city."

Robinson smiled at her childlike enthusiasm and did. "Will we find the City of Glass?"

Dustynose put her hands atop his and shook the sphere. A polyhedron inside appeared with the faded words: *It is decidedly so.*

Dustynose's eyes sparkled. Robinson thanked her and handed her back the sphere. As she returned it to its place, Robinson saw a group of large, colored letters on the wall. Their mounting had been broken, but he still made out the original words, TOYS 'R' US, which over time had somehow become TROYUS.

Though there was something poignant in learning the origins of the Orphans, he knew then, none of it would help him find what he was looking for.

"But we ain't done yet," Dustynose said as he turned for the door.

She led him up a set of steep stairs to a small office. A broken computer sat on an old desk surrounded by stacks of books in every shape and size.

"When a Blue 'comes a Fives," Dustynose said, "they's shown the store.

But few come here. Books ain't matter to them cuz few can read the words. Most says it's against the rules, but the swole that spurt me thought diff. She was right."

Dustynose reached for a book filled with scribbled handwriting inside.

"These was written by the Fives since the far and back. More they go, less I 'stand, but I ken a few. When you spoke of your City, I got to 'membering a passage 'bout another Lo—I mean, stranger. He too was hunting such a place."

Dustynose scoured several of the books until she found what she was looking for. She set it flat on the desk and slid it in front of Robinson. He read it.

Aug. 14, 2164.

A fully-aged man entered town from the south yester'noon. Scouts found him scavenging water near the runoff, and the Red Patrol detained him immediatlee. He was sunburned and mind-addled. He neither stood commands or had sense of his troubles. We attempted to splain our rules to him, but he could only babble about a "hidden city" named Dia he believed close by. I demanded details of this city, but he said little other than it was paradise and he had to reach it. This man did hold in his possession an old map. Circled was the once-city of DENVER, but no other clues could be found. In the end, the Council of Five deemed him crazy and ordered him to be taken into the woods, executed quickly, and put beneath the dirt. One note: the man had a burn wound on his left hand like this:

I do not know what to make of it or his story, but doubt anything will come of it.

Leader 144, Miltonwood, CO

Blue Unit, 1 of 5

"Dia," Robinson said. He withdrew his own map and scanned the region until he found the city of Denver to the northwest. Using the legend, he estimated it was around two hundred and seventy-five kilometers on a straight line. Going by the old roads, it was closer to three hundred.

"How long would it take you?" Dustynose asked.

"Weather permitting, a week. Maybe eight days. But I'm worried about Friday."

"Because she's swole?"

"Well," Robinson said. "That and she's developed a cough. I don't like the sound of it."

"You could stay here until you're rested."

"I'm not sure that's a good idea. If her condition worsens…" *Or the virus spreads…* "It has to be today."

Dustynose thought about it, then smiled. "'haps I can short your time some."

Robinson wondered how.

They stood at the western entrance of the mall. A handful of Orphans had shown up to watch them leave. Some looked relieved, as if once the strangers were gone, their troubles might leave with them. Others wanted to see the manner of their departure.

"I had a few Greens pack some edi's for your trip," Dustynose said. "It ain't much, but it should last you your week."

"We're very grateful," Friday said. "Thank you."

Underfoot stood a few feet back, his eyes pinned to the floor. He wasn't used to goodbyes. Robinson stepped close and tipped his chin up.

"Don't look so glum, kid," Robinson said. "This is one walk I'm happy to take."

Underfoot's eyes watered, and Robinson tousled the boy's hair.

"Be strong for your sis. And your people. One day, you're going to make a great leader. The secret is not to lead from here," Robinson said as he touched the boy's head, "or here," he said as he touched the boy's chest, "but both. You 'stand?"

Underfoot nodded, as the tears splayed down his face. Then he hugged Robinson fiercely before turning and running off.

Despite the cold rations, the Master couldn't have been happier. Just after dawn, Cassa had returned to their camp with a child he'd taken prisoner. The girl, wearing red, had been scouting the area when Cassa took her by surprise. She was remarkably obstinate for one her age, though one look at Viktor's accoutrements and she confessed all. Crusoe and his lover would be leaving for Denver that morning. The Master was giddy.

He ordered they break camp and take up position in the wooded area just north of the mall, where their targets wouldn't see them until it was too late. They would have no option but to surrender. The Master doubted they'd make a stand with the girl pregnant.

It seemed providence had finally turned its eyes on him. The long journey was soon to be over, and a new journey—the one where he took the reins of this land and bent it to his will—was about to begin.

And yet just as the Master allowed himself to bask in the moment, he heard a noise in the distance. It began as a low roar, but it soon rose in pitch until he recognized the sound. He stood, horrified, as his plate and flatware slid off his lap and landed in the dirt.

"No..." the Master muttered. "No. No. No!"

Cassa burst from the foliage just as Viktor appeared from his tent. Neither had ever seen the Master in such a frenzy.

"Attack!" he howled. "Bring it down now!"

Cassa leaped on Bull and tore through the trees for the open meadow, his pack immediately responding to his pipe's call. Viktor could only watch dumbfounded as the thing rose into the sky.

Robinson pulled gently on the yoke as he fed the engine power. The clatter of the airplane's engine rose in pitch as it lifted from behind the mall and began a slow roll to the north. He had wanted one last look at Troyus before leaving, but then he noticed several objects racing across the field to the east.

When the first bolt hit the plane, Robinson hammered the throttle forward. He heard Friday gasp as she recognized the pack below. Even the leader's mask, glimmering in the soft light of morning, shone brightly.

But it wasn't their presence or survival that rocked Robinson's world. That moment came when he leveled out the turn and passed within a hundred feet of two men standing on a small hill near a cluster of trees. He couldn't have known the smaller man now went by the name Viktor. When Robinson knew him, he had called him Mr. Dandy. But it was the sight of his companion that stilled Robinson's heart. Even from this distance, there was no mistaking the hateful visage of Vardan Saah.

PART TWO

"Discovery was no longer a happy ship."

-Arthur C. Clarke

Chapter Fifteen

Sickness

As the plane picked up airspeed, the ground fell farther away until it purged the canopy of ash and smoke that enveloped Troyus, only to level off a few thousand feet in the air. The laboring engine reduced from a scream to a wail, though the cabin still shuddered like teeth in a snowstorm.

Friday broke into a coughing fit that lasted nearly a minute. Robinson removed one hand from the yoke and placed it on her back, the worry boiling up inside him. When she finally stopped, he asked if she was okay. She nodded, suggesting she needed water. Robinson knew better. His worst fears were confirmed when he saw a smidgen of blood at the corner of her lips.

"How did they track us?" Friday asked to change the subject.

"Those creatures most likely. After the dust storm, I thought we'd seen the last of them."

"This has gone beyond the thrill of the hunt, Crusoe. They refuse to turn aside. It's as if we have wronged them somehow."

Robinson considered telling her about Saah, but didn't want to worry her further. She needed to focus on staying healthy for the task in front of them. Looking over their shoulders would only take their minds off the road ahead.

"It doesn't change anything," Robinson said finally. "The important thing is to keep forging ahead. Finding the City of Glass is the only thing that matters."

"And if there is no city? Or if those inside refuse to help?"

"That's not an option. I believe it's real and we're meant to find it."

Friday smiled. "My sun and moon. How much you've changed. How much you've grown."

"Thanks to you."

Friday coughed again. The chill morning air cut through the porous plane like a knife. Robinson reached into the back for the blankets the Orphans had given them.

"Here," he said. "Wrap yourself in these."

Once she was bundled up, Robinson focused on the horizon in front of him. The cloud cover kept the sun from shining through, and the hinterlands were bathed in slate grays and black blues. They had mapped their course west, following the old highway that would lead to a northern one several hundred kilometers down the road. At least this way, the chance of them overshooting the mark was slim.

As the plane settled into a monotonous rhythm, Robinson allowed himself to think of Saah. For two months, they hadn't understood why the pack continued to pursue them. Now it made perfect sense. Robinson had seen Saah on the battlefield after Arga'Zul fell. He'd read the madness in his eyes. There was little question he had seen Jaras's body in the warehouse, and no question who he blamed for his death.

In the weeks that followed, Robinson wondered what had happened to Saah. He thought he might have been killed by the Aserra hunting parties or by the Bone Flayers as they fled the area. Now he knew Saah had not only survived, but had captured Mr. Dandy in the process. For only Mr. Dandy had the skillset to create those hybrid abominations. Fusing weapons with flesh. Controlling the minds of the uncontrollable. It made Robinson shiver.

The one thing Robinson didn't know was the identity of the man in the mask. Not that it mattered. He was just another extension of Saah's reach.

What was patently clear was that Saah would never quit. He would hunt them to the ends of the earth or until he was dead. That notion frightened Robinson more than anything had, short of losing Friday. Because Saah's cruelty had no bounds. It wouldn't be enough to kill Robinson. He would want him to suffer. And that meant Friday and their unborn child were at even greater risk.

The plane was cruising a thousand feet above the dusty, barren landscape below. After a spell, the clouds parted and the air begin to warm. Friday had gone to sleep.

Robinson couldn't say how much time passed before he saw the dark line running horizontal below, but there was little doubt it was the freeway on Pastor's map.

The yellow brick road.

As the plane turned north, a crosswind made the fuselage shudder. That's when Friday rotated in her sleep, pulling her blanket open as her arm fell into her lap. That's when he saw it. A crimson mark near her elbow. His chest tightened in an instant.

"Friday," he said.

Friday woke. "What is it? Are we there?"

"No. What is that on your arm?"

She saw the worried look on his face and tried to act nonchalant as she covered it up.

"Nothing," she said. "A burn from the fire."

"That's not a burn wound. Let me see it again."

She refused.

"Let me see it," he insisted, panicked.

"It will do no good," she said at last.

"It's a lesion, isn't it?"

She didn't answer. Robinson was a thousand feet in the air, but he felt like he was plummeting toward the earth.

"Are there any more of them?"

She shook her head, but didn't answer.

"Damnit, Friday. How am I supposed to help you if you keep these things from me?"

"You cannot!" she cried. "No one can help me. This is happening in *my* body. I carry this disease, not you. What would you do if I were to show you? You are no healer. You are no priest. What would you do?"

Friday's lip trembled, and her eyes began to water. She looked away. When she spoke next, Robinson barely heard her over the rush of air.

"I need you to be strong. If your head is full of worry for me, who will see to the tasks ahead? Lead. I will follow. And the Goddess will decide our fates. She has carried us this far."

Robinson wanted to say that they had something to do with it too, but at that moment, the engine sputtered.

"What is it?" Friday asked.

"I don't know," Robinson answered. He thumbed the fuel mixture. This time, the engine coughed, and the entire plane jolted. Robinson increased and decreased the throttle, but the plane only sputtered as it began to lose altitude.

"I think we might be in trouble," Robinson said. "It doesn't sound like the engine's getting enough fuel."

"But the children filled it. Can it not get us to Denver?"

"It should," Robinson said, looking out the window. "I don't see any smoke."

Friday crawled into the back to peer through the hole in the floor. That's when she saw a bolt sticking out the undercarriage.

"I see an arrow," Friday said. "And dark liquid coming out."

Robinson cursed. "Must be an oil line. Strap in. I'm taking us down."

Friday got back in her seat just as the engine died and the plane began to drift. Robinson hit the engine start button again, and after two revolutions, it spun to life.

"Hold on to something," Robinson said.

He pushed the yoke down, and the plane dove toward the freeway. The engine continued to sputter like angry bees under glass. As the road rushed up to meet them, the engine shuddered and cut out for good.

"Brace yourself!" Robinson shouted.

The wheels violently hit the road. The plane skipped across the pavement until the wheels settled down, and the plane rolled forward. Unfortunately, the brakes floundered, forcing Robinson to swerve to avoid an old tanker. He overcorrected and shot into the opposing road. That's when the front left tire struck a pothole and the wheel snapped off, sending the plane whipping around, its metal undercarriage showering the cockpit with sparks as it gashed the freeway and slammed into a concrete abutment before coming to an abrupt stop.

The plane sat at a pitched angle over a step rise. Friday's ragged breaths intensified as she looked out over the abyss.

"Are you hurt?" Robinson asked.

Dazed, Friday shook her head.

"Quick," he said. "We have to get out before it falls. This way."

The door was rusted shut, which forced Robinson to crawl through the window. He reached back. "Give me your hand. Slowly."

Friday reached out, but just as her fingers stroked his, she erupted into a coughing fit. The jerking movement prompted the plane to slide farther over the ledge. Robinson grabbed the wing support beam and pulled back, shouting for Friday to hurry. Halfway across his seat, she stopped.

"The rations," she said.

"Leave them," Robinson said.

But Friday had already crawled into the back and was tossing the containers out into the road one by one. The plane shifted again. This time, the tail started to rise.

"Friday, there isn't time!"

"Just a few more."

The undercarriage screeched as it ground the asphalt, pushing inexorably closer to the abyss. Robinson was pulling with all his might when the undercarriage snapped, and the plane slid with a jolt.

"I can't hold it!" Robinson screamed. "You have to get out!"

The plane continued to tip until momentum took over. At the last second, Friday dove for Robinson's hand, and he yanked her through the window just as the plane toppled and fell to the void below.

Robinson looked up from the wreckage to see Friday already gathering the rations.

"You know, one of these days you're going to be the death of me."

Friday grinned. "But not today."

Chapter Sixteen
Another Promise

The day was warm and without wind, allowing them to make decent time. But as the sun fell, rain clouds moved in, and by the time night had arrived, the pair were drenched and struggling to see where they were going.

Neither had been expecting rain in the middle of summer. Their clothes were drenched, along with the blankets they'd used to try and keep their supplies dry.

With no light or stars to guide them, the two kept a lookout for any type of shelter. They thought they might end up sleeping in the open shell of a vehicle before they spotted a concrete structure off the side of the road. They made their way to it, discovering the structure was an old concrete bathroom with caged eaves that opened to the outside.

"We'll get soaked if we stay here," Robinson said.

"We'll get more soaked if we don't," Friday replied.

She was right. Robinson went in search of firewood. With no nearby trees, he ended up breaking down some old wooden signs and tearing fabric from the seat of an old car. As the room filled with smoke, Robinson removed his boots, laying them near Friday's to dry by the fire.

Friday used an old runoff to fill their waterskins with rainwater. Then she checked the rations to make sure they were dry.

"Your feet look like sausages," Robinson said.

Friday looked at her feet before shaking her head.

"Meat stuffed in skin," he clarified.

"This is normal for one with child. I remember the women of our village huddling in rivers to ease the..." She searched for the word.

"Swelling," Robinson said.

Friday nodded. "Some years the water was so cold they needed me to pull them out. I hated that feeling—frozen feet and toes—but I could not let it show. I stood in the water with them until my mother let me leave."

"No wonder you can't swim," he said.

She glared at him, so he reached out and began to massage her feet. The returning circulation almost made her swoon. Robinson thought of a memory.

"When my brother and sister were born, my mother used to bathe them in the kitchen sink. It was Vareen—our housemother's—duty, but I think my mother found it soothing. I used to sit on the counter as she lathered their hair and scrubbed their bodies, listening to them squeal. Usually she'd do it after supper, and if the floor stayed dry, we all got a treat. Biscuits were my favorite. Some nights, when there was no wind, you could hear the surf from beyond the Wall. It used to frighten the twins—that sound—but I loved it. When they cried, my mother would shush them. And if they didn't stop, she would sing."

"What would she sing?"

"Lullabies mostly. Outlawed ones. Most songs were outlawed. But I remember the one. I think it was her favorite."

Robinson hummed softly.

When the snow is on the ground, little Robin redbreast grieves,

For no berries can be found, and on the trees there are no leaves.

The air is cold, the worms are hid. For this poor bird what can be done?

We'll strew him here some crumbs of bread, and then he'll live till the snow is gone.

Friday watched him as he sang, his fingers working wonders on her feet. She didn't understand all the words, but she didn't need to. The fact that he was singing after all they'd been through only reinforced everything she believed about him. She felt her eyes well up. As much as she hated sentimentality, she hoped the moment would not end.

When they set out the following day, the earth was muddy, but the sky was clear. Robinson managed to find an old plastic bag to wrap over his torn boot. The noise made him feel foolish, but it kept his foot dry.

"First thing we need to do when we reach Denver is find some new boots. And clothes. It looks like the seasons are changing again."

"We will find shelter first."

Robinson chuckled. "You're the boss."

They spent the next four days walking. Despite the constant motion, Robinson thought his foot was getting better. He no longer walked with a limp. Unfortunately, Friday's cough was getting worse. And every time he asked to check her for more lesions, she refused. Both tried to keep their minds occupied with something else. For Friday, it was the beauty of the mountains that rose high to the north and west. They reminded her of home. For Robinson, it was playing out the scene in his head when they finally discovered the City of Glass. He would need to be his most articulate when facing its inhabitants, but he didn't see how anyone couldn't find their story compelling.

After passing by a few roadside towns, they eventually spotted Denver in the distance. There was no mistaking it with its high towers and sprawling volume. Beyond it sat another imposing mountain range made of dark stone that jutted high into the sky. The juxtaposition gave the city the appearance of life even though it had likely died at the same time as every other they'd encountered.

The gradient steepened the closer they got, and the air did become harder to breathe. Like most big cities they'd encountered, the freeways leading in and out of the city were glutted with the shells of old vehicles—a harrowing reminder of the mass exodus that had occurred long before. Time had eroded most of them to rust and debris, but occasionally they found one pieced together, awaiting its master's return like a faithful dog. Passing the relics always made Robinson sad. He couldn't imagine the terror of those final days.

"We should be prepared in case we run into people here," Robinson warned.

"I am always prepared," Friday said.

"I meant, this isn't Washington, DC or even Chicago. Those documents Dustynose showed me suggested this was an outpost once. Maybe it still is. I doubt there are any Renders given the climate, but someone lives here."

"How can you be so sure?"

"I see smoke."

Friday cursed herself for not seeing the dark haze hovering above the city first. Whatever was causing her cough was also sapping her energy, and that affected her concentration. She had hoped it was the pregnancy and the grueling walk. She hated not being at full strength.

They entered Denver just past midday. An enormous arena sat vacant to the west. It reminded Robinson of the one he'd seen behind the Cat People's island—immense and imposing, a mammoth achievement meant solely for entertainment.

They continued down the freeway until they came to an impasse. The road had collapsed into a river below. Working their way back to the previous exit, they carefully made their way down a steep grade until they reached one of the main arteries that pushed east into the city.

Friday covered her mouth with a blanket to prevent the sound echoing through the streets like gunfire. Her fatigue was soon apparent, however, and given the rapidly falling sun, Robinson declared it was time to stop.

"This looks good," he said of a two-story building with a pitched roof. The sign outside said it was a museum. "No windows. Door appears secure."

Friday was too tired to argue.

Once inside, they could see the building had been trashed. Frames had been torn off the walls. Sculptures had been tipped over and smashed. Colored scribbling stained the walls. At least the place smelled free of Renders.

"Someone's been here," Robinson said.

"Not in a long time. Let's make a fire. I'm cold."

They broke old frames to use as kindling before gathering them in a small steel trash can. As the room warmed, they huddled together and parsed out the day's rations. Robinson found an old picture book showcasing photos of art.

"What is this?" Friday asked, looking over his shoulder.

"Art."

"I thought art was supposed to be beautiful. This is ugly."

"Well, art by its very nature is subjective."

"I do not know *subjective*, but I do know ugly, and this is it."

Robinson chuckled. "Can't argue with you there. I read once, the ancients used to place a high price on stuff like this. Well, maybe not these pieces in particular, but art from the masters could cost more than the towers outside."

Friday grunted in disproval. "The more I learn of these ancients, the more I see why they died. They did not value the proper things."

"Let's not ever make that mistake," Robinson said.

Friday nodded, sliding Robinson his rations. Leafy greens, a few carrots, and a turnip.

"I'm not hungry," he said, passing them back to her.

"Your stomach says you lie."

He looked up.

"I can survive without you, Crusoe, but it would make things harder. You need strength." She put her hands on her belly. "And *we* need you. Eat."

He did. All the while, he stared at the lesion on her arm.

"Does it hurt?"

He wasn't sure she would answer.

"It ... how do you say?"

She made a scratching gesture.

"Itches," Robinson answered.

"Funny word. Yes, it itches." She leaned back, her tired eyes staring into the fire. "Since that day on the battlefield, I have felt my body keenly. Aches. Pains. Senses both good and ill. I know these to be normal, but I cannot stop myself from seeing the disease moving through me like one of those serpents as they moved beneath the earth. Small at first but growing bigger. I hear death at night and it sounds like the serpent's rattle. Only the venom is already inside of me, consuming me one breath at a time."

"That sounds terrifying."

"It is. But this..." She put her hands on her belly. "*She* saves me. Each time the snake coils inside of me, it is the blood of the Aserra that repels it. Her blood. It gives me hope. Because of that, I can go on." Here, she took a heavy breath, the lines in her forehead creasing. "But the fear is always there that one day, she will not be strong enough. The snake will strike her and she..."

"You can say it. We both know it's a possibility she will die."

"But it's not her death I fear. It's the idea that she will be born a snake too. A monster like the ones we hunt. Or worse."

"That's not going to happen, Friday."

"But if it does?" Hot tears fell down her cheeks. "I will not be a mother that brings about the death of the world. I have seen enough of it to know it is evil, Crusoe. I have prayed to the Goddess about this, and she has answered me. But I struggle to say it to you."

"You can tell me anything. You know that."

She looked in his eyes and nodded. "Crusoe, if our daughter is born with this evil, I will take her life, and then I will take my own."

"Friday—"

"I know this pains you to hear. And I know what it will make of you. But I have prayed on it, and the Goddess tells me it is just. If she is a snake, I will do this thing. And if I cannot ... you must do it for me."

"I-I could never—" Robinson whispered, his throat tight.

"Promise me," she said, touching his cheek. "If I've taught you anything of strength, let it be shown in this way. If we cannot sacrifice everything for paradise, then we are not worthy of it. Promise me, Robinson Crusoe."

In all the time he'd known her, she'd never once called him by his first name.

Finally, he nodded and said, "I promise."

She stared into his eyes and saw that he meant it. Then she laid her head in his lap, and he stroked her hair. He wanted to believe he was the man she thought he was—that he was not only worthy of paradise but worthy of her. And yet the old fear, born of the choices he made, came back to haunt him again. In DC, he had chosen Friday over the safety of the world. And on the battlefield, he had pulled her in front of Arga'Zul's blade to save himself. At the time it felt like the right choice—he knew Arga'Zul would not hurt Friday—but the further he was removed from the incident, the more he feared cowardice had played some part and he had rationalized it as he always did because of the outcome. Both were moments of weakness, choices made in an instant. He told himself next time would be different, but deep in his heart, he wasn't sure.

Chapter Seventeen

Denver

The rain returned the next day in fat, lazy drops that stung their skin. Robinson and Friday left their gear and supplies in the museum and set out early in the morning in hopes of finding better boots and jackets.

The department stores had all been looted. What few items of clothing that had been left behind had aged so badly they practically disintegrated when touched. The shoe departments had also been picked clean. Not even the kids' section had been spared.

If there was one positive thing about Denver, it was that they'd found no signs of Renders. No hovels. No gory track marks. No fetid smell. It was possible the city had been spared the worst of the pandemic because of its climate. Or they'd been better prepared to deal with the spread of the affliction. Either way, the city seemed like an optimal place for human survival. So, why was it abandoned?

They moved on to the downtown high-rises. Many of them once served as businesses, yet many others had balconies with chairs and old pots for plants. Pressing through the first door, they saw the telltale signs of looting. Debris clogged the stairwells in patches and clumps. Sometimes it was household goods like pans and cutlery. Other times it was electronics abandoned on various floors when the burden of their weight most likely overcame their pilferer's greed. A few inexplicable spoils lined the hallways.

Furniture, televisions, and photos of families.

They took their time going floor to floor, stopping only to eat or whenever Friday felt too winded. They managed to cover four residential towers the first day, scavenging a few old sweaters, a pair of galoshes for Friday, and a pocket knife with numerous tools and little rust.

Walking those homes was like peering through a veil in time. They tried to imagine the lives the owners once led—ones undoubtedly of comfort but insular too. The units were enormous, each capable of housing multiple families, though the personal effects suggested one or two people at most. Even with the magnificent view, it must have been a lonely existence.

By noon on the second day, they had explored three more towers. When they entered the lobby of the fourth, Friday broke into a coughing spell that took her off her feet. Robinson gave her water, but when she spat the last out, it was pink.

"We have to get you back to the museum," he said, concerned.

Friday shook her head. "I'll be fine once I gather my breath."

He knelt and took her hand.

"Your face is one a pup makes when a bone is taken from him."

"This isn't funny," he said softly.

"No. But I do not think this is from the virus. Listen," she said when he started to shake his head. "If it were the virus, I think it would have spread more. Hurt more. This is not pain, but a heaviness here," she touched her chest, "when I breathe. Do you understand?"

"It could be a side effect. Or a secondary response. I don't know. Maybe you contracted pneumonia."

Friday looked quizzical.

"It's a condition my mother told me about once. Regardless, we should stop for the day."

Friday shook her head. "We cannot afford more days. They run faster than a river. Before we know it, they will have passed us by. You go. I'll rest here."

"I'm not leaving you."

"We've seen no one since we entered Denver. No signs of people anywhere."

"What about the smoke?"

Friday shrugged. "It may have been dust. I can protect myself, Crusoe. You know this."

He did. "Fine. But I'm sticking close to the stairwell. I'll call out the number of each floor I enter, and I'll bar the door open so we can reach each other if one of us shouts. If you see or hear anything, don't be a hero."

"The same goes for you." She grinned.

Robinson kissed her on the forehead before vaulting up the stairs.

His feet echoed in the stairwell as he padded up the steps. The apartment doors were mostly open, scattered goods filling the halls. Robinson decided to skip the lowest levels since they were the most likely to have been cleaned out. Luckily, most of the hallways were lit by open windows, allowing him to quicken his pace everywhere but on the half-landings.

Although he tried to keep his focus on the task at hand, his mind kept returning to Friday. She was unquestionably growing sicker, and despite her thoughts to the contrary, he knew it was the virus. The lesion had been the first sign. This respiratory ailment was the second. If he had any hopes of saving her and their child, Robinson knew he had to find the City of Glass soon. The problem was that the only clue he had was the one Dustynose had given him, and it had only led to Denver. He could search government buildings, maybe the library, but what if it all proved futile? What if there was nothing to find? The thought made him shudder. Then he froze.

The hallway had gone dark. In fact, the entire stairwell above him was black as night. None of the doors were open. He didn't know if that was a good sign or a bad one. He pulled his pistol and reached for the door of the twenty-first floor. Before he opened it, he called "twenty-one" down to Friday. He waited for her to acknowledge it, but he heard no response. She's safe, he told himself. Sleeping maybe. He opened the door.

The corridor was dark, scattered light stealing in from windows at the far end. None of the doors had been opened. His heart filled with hope.

The apartment was untouched; every surface was covered with dust. On a counter laid a bowl with keys and a wallet. Robinson moved further in and found an old computer laying open on a table. The kitchen was stocked with canned goods; the floor was stained with fluids bled from the refrigeration unit.

Robinson moved to the first bedroom, where he found exercise equipment and a bed still made. In the second unit, he found the owner. A gun lay near his hand. A dark stain on the headboard. Curled under the bones of his arm was a large dog, his leash still attached. Robinson thought of Resi and understood. He backed out of the room, closing the door quietly.

In the fourth apartment, Robinson found what he was looking for. In the closet of a young couple he found two large jackets, one for a man, one for a woman. The man's jacket was big and billowy but fit Robinson snuggly. The woman's jacket was tighter and stylish, made of a leather-like material that was water repellant. It also had a fur or faux fur-lined hood and cuffs. In a plastic box marked "snowboarding clothes," he found cloth under layers and weather-resistant gloves. Neither of the boots he found would fit. The man's were too small and the woman's were too big. It would take another nine apartments and three floors until he had everything he needed.

Back in the stairwell, Robinson felt a chill breeze descending from above. An elevated view of the city might be good. He set the clothes and boots down and ascended the remaining floors. The door was marked "no access," but it opened easily and, surprisingly, without a sound. That irked him. Every other door had groaned. He looked closely at the hinges and shivered when he saw someone had recently oiled them.

Robinson opened the door cautiously to a dull gray sky. Axe in hand, he stepped out. Then he saw the enclosure. It was four feet wide and six feet long, edged on all sides by what appeared to be old closet doors. A thin plastic curtain covered a narrow door. He could hear movement behind it. He approached cautiously, peeling back the sheet to peek inside. A chorus of screeches hit him as dozens of live rats scrambled around their makeshift cage. The smell was ghastly. Robinson had to cover his nose to keep from vomiting. The cage was littered with feces, and a few dead rats that had been gnawed on by the others. Outside was a wooden block with a rusty knife and a plastic blue bucket full of rat heads.

He realized that someone has been feeding on those things.

Robinson let the curtain fall and headed back for the stairwell. He hustled down the steps as quickly and quietly as possible. He needed to grab the gear and Friday and leave, but when he reached the twenty-first floor, he found the bag of gear was missing.

Robinson tightened his grip on the axe and listened.

"Friday?" he called quietly.

There was no answer. He cracked the door to the floor and looked inside. The hallway was silent, but there on the floor, five feet away, was the bag.

Who had moved it there? Had Friday come looking for him? Should I call out for her again? Instinct told Robinson he should leave it, but they needed that gear. Friday needed it. He stepped into the hall.

The apartment doors were closed. He heard no sounds, saw no signs of movements. As carefully as he could, he inched forward until his hand wrapped around the bag's straps. Then he lifted it and turned for the stairs, stopping only when a door opened quickly behind him and a large barrel bored into his neck.

A husky voice said, "Don't move."

Chapter Eighteen
The Priests of Blasphemy

Viktor cursed. The genetic modifications he'd made to the pack had given them boundless energy. And since sighting young mister Crusoe and his native paramour, the Master had used this to push their party day and night. At one point, Viktor would have given the last of his bolo ties for one single, solitary night of uninterrupted sleep.

The irony was Viktor had no one to blame but himself. It was part and parcel of the deal he'd made when the Master—then going by the name Vardan Saah—captured him on the field of battle. Well, not the *field* exactly. More like the fringes. Actually, he hadn't meant to stray near the fighting at all, but when he and Boss had leaped from the train just before it collided with their rival's, he got turned around and soon found himself smack dab in the middle of the bloodiest brawl imaginable. All that bloodshed, the wailing and the dying. It was exhausting. Viktor had tried to scurry away, knowing his best opportunity for survival was to find his way back to Cowboytown and the comfort of his genteel persona, Mr. Dandy. Alas—in the parlance of the ancients—excrement happens.

What it boiled down to was that he was too good at his job. At the time, the Master had made a compelling proposition: work for me or die. Transparent terms, no room for negotiation. On the surface, not exactly an enticing prospect. But he'd underestimated two things. The first was the

Master's capacity for turning a situation to his favor. The second, and more critical, was the Master's capacity for being completely crazy. Those both turned out to be good things for Viktor, who, when asked if there was a way to raise an army, pointed out the only one not currently under management was the group stumbling around in the dark, basking in the scent of its own ordure. Light bulb! The result of this epiphany turned out to be the genetic manipulation of a slave army of the afflicted. The Master had requirements: they needed to have strength, speed, endurance, and the ability to track. Oh, and they needed to be fully controlled by he and Cassa at all times. Simple, right? But defying all odds, Viktor had proven up to the task. Inspired by the protagonist in the classic book, *Frankenstein*, the newly-named Viktor worked tirelessly to manipulate both flesh and mind until the pack was a perfect symbiosis of man and beast. Only now, after days of exhaustive pursuit, was his genius coming back to haunt him.

Rest finally came on their third eve away from the city of urchins. Rain was falling lightly from clouds hovering over the rocky lowlands where the Master ordered they make camp. Viktor started a fire while Cassa used his pipes to call the pack in. Once off his horse, Viktor's legs, back, and derriere were all numb. Not that he bothered to complain. He was too busy finding a private place to pee.

With the pack amassed, Cassa blew the note to feed. Without hesitation, the horde bolted to the southwest, kicking up dust as they disappeared. Viktor sulked when tasked to collect kindling. He only cheered up when he smelled the fowl Cassa had plucked and spitted over the fire. The Master filled his cast iron pot for tea. No one spoke as they huddled around the fire, listening to the fat sizzling in the flames.

Viktor giggled unexpectedly.

"Something amusing, Viktor?" the Master asked. "By all means, share it. This dreadful night could use a little levity."

"I was recalling some articles I once possessed in Cowboytown," Viktor said. "I've spoken of the moving pictures before—"

"*Ad infinitum*," the Master said. "Continue."

"Well, among the repository from which those celluloid treasures were found, was a smaller cache of ancient collectibles known as dime novels."

"Dime novels? I'm unfamiliar with the term."

"It was an inexpensive form of fiction common during the settlement era of this land, similar to their overseas counterparts, Penny Dreadfuls?"

"That does have a more appealing ring."

"They were largely superficial works, fashioned as cheap entertainment. They depicted adventures that took place in the old frontier and included settings very much like this. Men sitting around campfires, conspiring or consorting."

"*Villains?*" the Master asked with an edge in his voice.

"Oh, no," Viktor answered. "I wasn't suggesting…"

"Continue."

"It simply occurred to me, our story would make a most curious issue."

"*Our* story?"

"Well, your story would be the main narrative, of course. The distinguished man wronged by the duplicitous upstart. Your unrelenting but totally justifiable quest for revenge."

The Master grunted in appreciation.

"Then, there's your faithful adjutant, *moi*. Brilliant but tortured. So out of place in this crude, cruel world."

"And what of Cassa?" the Master asked. "If any are deserving of having their story told, it is he."

Viktor glanced across the fire at Cassa as he continued to turn the bird on the spit. He hadn't considered the brute, but he appeared to be listening.

"Indeed," Viktor said.

Viktor remembered the events vividly. How could he not? The horrors of that first month would always be ingrained on his brain. The Aserra had just routed the Bone Flayers and flushed them north. Vardan Saah and Mr. Dandy found themselves caught in the flood of the vanquished as they fled through the countryside, sacking homes and settlements, butchering anyone in their way. One of those places turned out to be a small village of a simple, peaceful people who, in the dead of night, woke to find Hell had descended. If Viktor closed his eyes, he could still see the carnage, hear the screams of children as their parents were butchered and houses set to flame. Just when it appeared there were no defenders among them, a tall shadow broke through, deftly using a bow to kill attackers until his quiver finally ran empty. Then, a scream pierced the night.

A girl of indeterminate age was caught in a house blaze. Fire churned from every door and window, but that didn't stop the man from storming inside. Mr. Dandy was sure he'd seen the last of him, but he emerged moments later, half his body engulfed in flames. His skin sizzled and popped as he set the child down. When he discovered he was too late to save her, he let loose a wail so anguished, so piercing, Mr. Dandy hoped he might go deaf then and there. The man stood frozen until the Master wrapped a blanket around him and marshaled him away.

Not a day went by that Mr. Dandy didn't think it would be the wounded man's last. But he persevered. At the Master's bidding, Viktor opened the wounded man's skull to neutralize various receptors of his cerebral cortex, thalamus, and limbic system. His condition improved, but he would never feel pain again. Neither would he know pleasure. The success of Viktor's work inspired him to create the Master's army. The pack was born, and Cassa would lead them.

"You never did tell me why you saved him," Viktor said. "Or why you named him Cassa."

The Master paused. He could not say how he admired the man's willingness to risk his life for that of a child. Or that if he or his son, Jaras, had acted similarly at the Western Gate, his very own Tessa might still be alive. Even after all this time, the memory was still too painful. Instead, he chose to view the act of self-sacrifice for what it was. And he knew, deep down in that place where his hunger for greatness waged war with the trappings of tyranny, that if he could earn such a man's fealty, he would earn his life. And one day, if a hundred such men might follow him, he could rule the world.

"In those moments after he emerged from the fire," the Master said softly, "I heard a woman's lamentations. She said, 'He tried to warn us.' It was a tragedy that reminded me of Cassandra, Princess of Troy, who refused a God's advances and was herself rendered helpless. For her gift of true insight would forever go unheeded until at last she retreated into madness." The Master looked across the fire at Cassa, who had gone stone still. "But do not fear, friend. I won't abandon you. Where I go, you will always have a place at my fire." And then the Master's eyes shifted behind him. "As will you, good sers. Won't you come in and warm yourselves?"

Viktor looked up in shock as several figures purged the darkness. Cassa's hand reached for his bow, but the Master shook his head.

There were seven, fanned out in a fashion that spoke of ritual and preparation. Each was dressed in flowing black suits, dirty and dusted, with white collars and black brim hats. Around each neck hung a rosary with weighted iron crosses.

"You'll forgive us if we're not quick to accept new hospitality, friend," the tallest of them said. His voice was earthy and deep. His tawny face bore a narrow scar across his nose and a thick mustache more silver than black. "There's many a scoundrel in this land that would gull a man with sweet words from afar only to slip a knife in him when nigh. The Priests know their kind well."

"Priests?" the Master repeated.

As the tall man stepped closer, Viktor saw his palm rested atop a slender sword in a golden scabbard. It appeared to be a Mameluke. It was like the ones he read about Napoleon wearing.

"Aye," the tall man responded. "The Priests of Blasphemy they call us. We are the curates of the great garden, enemy to the unholy wherever we may find them."

"A good name," the Master said. "And an admirable profession. As you can see, we are no threat. Just three ordinary, God-fearing men."

"Yea? Which God would that be, might I ask?"

Viktor watched the Master smile as he folded his hands over his knee.

"There is only one true God, friend. And one true *Son*."

The priest's shoulders relaxed a little, though he kept his hand on his weapon. He looked at Cassa and Viktor.

"Come," the Master said, taking the cast iron pot from the fire. "Sit. I'll pour you a cup of my wife's most excellent tea, may God rest her soul."

The Master poured a cup and held it out. The tall priest eventually took it and sat on a stone a foot from the fire. Viktor realized he'd been holding his breath. As he exhaled, he eyed the other priests, all firmly gripping their own weapons.

"It's rare to hear courtesy these days," the priest said. He sipped his tea but couldn't hide his grimace. "Rarer still to find three men on the plains with only one weapon between 'em."

"In my experience, weapons are more often the source of offense than the remedy to it."

The tall priest scoffed. "If that was true, you'd be better armed, not worse. We hunt the blighted. We've been tracking a pack of these spawns of Satan for three days now. They led us here to you. Can you explain that?"

The tall priest watched the Master closely.

"No," the Master said.

If the tall priest was phased by the single, terse response, he didn't let it show.

"In our time," he said, "we've encountered some that hunt the beasts for sport. Others, to capture and sell. For what unholy purpose, I cannot say. But I know this: both are sins. Grave as any of the ten."

"And these are the laws you have sworn to defend," the Master said.

"That's right. Until the day I meet my maker."

When the Master looked at the tall priest, he smiled. Viktor felt a roiling in his gut. He had seen that smile before and knew nothing good ever came of it.

"Then we are in your debt, Ser," the Master said.

The tall priest craned his head. He hadn't expected that. "How so?"

"For the past few days, my associates and I have shared an uncomfortable feeling, but couldn't reason why. Now, we know it was because these spawns were tracking us. We give you our thanks and tell you we can take it from here."

The tall priest hesitated, then laughed a loud, belly-driven laugh, which sounded foreign coming from such a dour man. Viktor felt a moment's relief.

"You are good, sir," the tall priest said, shaking his head. "Very good. I venture you could charm a snake with that forked tongue of yours. But I see you for what you truly are—a liar and a charlatan. Those tracks didn't follow in pursuit of yours, but *alongside* them. Way I figure, your stories and piety are as good as your wife's tea, which is worse'n piss in my book."

The man tossed the tea into the fire before pulling his sword from its scabbard. Cassa reached for his bow, but it was kicked away by one of the other priests, who set a bolt tip to Cassa's head. Viktor felt his bladder release and let out a nervous giggle.

When the Master looked up, Victor thought he saw resignation.

"Will you at least allow us a final prayer?" the Master asked.

"Get to it," the tall priest said.

"I find the most powerful prayers—the ones God truly hears—come from hymn. Cassa."

Cassa raised his pipes to his lips and blew out a familiar note.

"Lord," the Master said. "Now lettest thou thy servant depart in pace according to thy word."

A rustling carried in on the wind. One of the priests turned, but saw nothing. Then, inexplicably, he was wrenched into the darkness, his screams echoing in the night. The other priests startled and shouted, but the Master continued his canticle undeterred.

"For mine eyes have seen thy salvation."

Heavy panting reverberated across the prairie. The priests twirled around in confusion before another one of them was snatched away.

"What is this?" the tall priest asked.

The Master spoke on. "Which thou has prepared before the face of all people."

Sickly things flit by in the shadows. Two more priests were seized, their cries falling in tune with the ripping of their flesh. Cassa played the note again.

"To be a light to lighten the Gentiles," the Master spoke, his voice rising with each word. "And to be the glory of thy people...."

The tall priest grabbed the Master's shoulder and screamed, "Halt I say!" He pointed the shaking mameluke at Cassa. "Stop that infernal sound!"

But Cassa played on. Viktor watched, enthralled, as the remaining priests whirled about like dervishes, scanning the dark only to be plucked away one by one until only the tall priest was left.

"What devilry is this?" he shrieked.

"A most singular one," the Master said. "We call it science. You wanted to meet your maker, Ser. Allow me to make the introduction."

Before the tall priest could move, a lumbering shadow lunged at him from out of the darkness. The Master reached and tore a piece of flesh from the spit, grunting in approval, seemingly oblivious to the screams behind him.

Chapter Nineteen
Scuff

Robinson turned slowly to see the double-barrel shotgun pointed at him. The owner was short with thick clothes, tattered gloves, and a hood of some sort.

"Don't listen?" the voice hissed, the barrel pressed harder. "Says, don't move."

"I don't want any trouble," Robinson said. "I thought the building was vacant."

"Thought wrong. You and the other erred coming here."

"I see that now," Robinson said, hands raised. "Is she okay?"

"The girl? Sleepin' in the stairwell when I passed."

"Then no one's been hurt. And there's no reason to take this any further." He nodded to the bag of scavenged goods on the floor. "Allow me to put that back and we can all forget—"

"I said don't move! Not unless you want to die."

"I don't want to die, trust me. But I don't think you do either."

The figure chuckled low. "I wasn't the one made a mistake coming here."

"No," Robinson replied. "Yours was confusing one of the Aserra for a heavy sleeper."

The figure hesitated before glancing back. Friday immediately ripped the shotgun away and smashed the stock into the assailant's face. He fell to the floor. Friday lifted the shotgun to slam the figure with the stock when

Robinson called out for her to stop.

Robinson reached down and peeled the hood off the stranger, revealing an old woman with terrified eyes.

"It's okay," Robinson said. "I meant it when I said we weren't here to hurt you." He extended a hand to help her up. The old woman cautiously took it, wobbling unsteadily when she got to her feet.

Friday thumbed the shotgun's break-open action.

"Empty," the old woman said, her mouth devoid of teeth. "Always been."

Friday showed Robinson the empty barrels before snapping it closed.

"Where are the others?" Friday asked.

"Ain't no others," the old woman said.

"Are those your pens on the roof?" Robinson asked.

The woman's head snapped up, eyes widening. "They're mine," she stuttered. "B-belongs all to me."

Robinson held up a hand to calm her. "Easy. We're not here to steal your food. Or anything else. It's just … with the rain coming, we're not exactly prepared for it. If we took anything that's yours, we apologize."

Seeing his sincerity, the old woman grew calmer.

"We are in need of information," Friday said. "From one who knows this Denver. If you can help us, we may be able share some of *our* food in return."

Friday opened her bag, revealing carrots, sweet potatoes, and a few beets. A clammy tongue darted over the old woman's lips.

They followed her down the stairwell to the basement, her bare feet making no sound. Robinson carried the bag of winter clothes while Friday walked a few steps behind, the shotgun under her arm. From the earliest age, she'd learned never to take anyone for granted, and she wasn't about to start with a woman that had managed to live twice as long as most men could.

The door in the garage was unmarked, but the lock on it worked. The old woman drew a key from a chain around her neck and opened it. The room was dark until the woman pulled a cord that reined in heavy fabric covering fogged glass near the ceiling. She repeated the action twice.

Robinson and Friday were stunned. Once an underground loading dock, the room had been repurposed into a storage vault stockpiled with relics, clutter, and debris that had been squeezed into every nook and cranny with only the narrowest of channels to move through.

Near the door were towering hills of old newspaper, magazines, books, and music. Next came bundles of clothing in plastic bags and boxes. Shelves stacked from floor to ceiling held flatware, trinkets, picture frames, and toys. Heaped atop dusted furniture sat vases full of gold watches, jewelry and gems. Beside them were stacks of currency, divided by origin, color, and denomination. Wrapped in rubber bands were thousands of small cards with photos that bore the words "driver's license." Beneath them were thousands more cards with numbers stamped across them.

Coins, weapons, glass figurines, musical instruments, toothbrushes, combs, purses, toy cars, stuffed animals, shoes, picture cameras, sunglasses, sports equipment, keys, religious paraphernalia—all grouped and sorted according to some obsessively incalculable system. Robinson wished he had time to look through it all.

Under a bowed bridge of doors was the old woman's living area. It smelled of dank, urine, body odor, and pungent meat. Lying next to an old bed and burrow of blankets was a table with several candles next to a blackened kiln used for cooking.

The old woman turned to Friday expectantly. "Food?"

Robinson nodded and Friday handed over the vegetables they'd brought from Troyus. The old woman smelled them and licked her lips greedily. Then she set about cutting them, adding them to a pan with rat meat.

As she worked, Robinson and Friday sat on the floor, kicking up dust. Friday coughed several times. She was surprised when she looked up to find the old woman offering her a broken comb of honey. Friday took it.

"Thank you," she said.

The old woman nodded and went back to cooking.

She hummed as she worked. Robinson didn't recognize the tune, but it eased the tension out of the room. When she was done, she poured three modest bowls of vermin-flavored gruel. Robinson had eaten worse. Stomach grumbling, he spooned the stew into his mouth and was surprised how good it tasted.

"What do they call you?" Friday asked once the meal was done.

The old woman's eyes narrowed, trying to remember.

"Scuff, they called me once. And knee-high. Though my ma used 'Cricket.'"

"I am called Friday and this is Crusoe. How long have you lived here?"

The woman shrugged. "Near forever."

"Have you always been alone?" Robinson asked.

"Some lived here once. Loud ones. Angry. Anger doesn't do well in the cold. I stayed away from them until they too were gone. Where did you come by these?"

She pointed to the vegetables.

"They were given to us," Robinson answered, "by friends."

The old woman tilted her head as if the word was foreign.

"Are there blighted here? In the city?" Friday asked.

"No. Once. When I had more dark hair than light. But I think they don't like the cold neither."

Robinson cleared his throat nervously. "We're looking for a place. Maybe you can help us. It's called the City of Glass. Have you heard of it?"

The old woman thought about it before shaking her head.

"What about someone called Dia?" Friday asked. "Have you heard of him or her?"

"Don't know Dia. Don't remember any names. Even if I did, there's none around here to claim them."

Robinson slumped. Friday put a reassuring hand on his shoulder before turning back to the old woman. "Tell us your story, Mother."

She was born by the coast and grew up with the smell of brine coating her nostrils and the chirping of sea birds filling her ears. It was a peaceful time until the day men came and destroyed their village. They fled into the mountains where the woman's sister was taken, but her parents and brother survived. The old woman's father urged the other surviving families to return to the coast, but the others voted to go inland. The days were filled with hard travelling. The first year was the worst. They were coastal dwellers and didn't understand mountain life. When the first snows came, half their tribe died.

The ones that survived learned to hunt, forage, and trade for furs.

By the second year, the family started to pull apart. The girl's father had an affair with another man's wife and was run off. Their mother left soon after, telling her son to take care of the girl. At first, the children thought they'd be cast out of the tribe, but the leader could not father his own children and took the girl's brother as his son. Sometime after that, their father came for them both, but her brother refused to go, so they left him behind.

Father and daughter travelled around, but one day, the man fell down a hill and broke his leg. It never healed properly. When they came across a dark-skinned people, the father kissed his daughter and made her walk to them. She cried and cried, but in the end, she did as she was told. She never saw her father again.

The new tribe claimed their people founded the land long ago. They were a hard people but not unjust. They lived simply, following the beasts that migrated with the seasons. As the girl grew, she was teased by other children of the village. When she bloodied one of the bigger girls, she was given the name, "Scuff."

When the girl grew old enough, she married one of the tribe's warriors, but before she could have children, the tribe was attacked by creatures more monster than man. Her husband was killed. To sow her grief, she walked off into the woods. Like her mother and father, she never returned.

She walked until she saw a city of towers in the lap of many white-capped mountains. There, she made her home. People came and went. Groups made peace and war. She stayed by herself. Her hair lost her luster, her back grew sore, but she was happy to have a home.

"It is a good story," Robinson said. "But don't you miss people?"

"There are people everywhere I look. In the buildings, in the homes. I see their stories, and I know them. They are my family, my *friends*."

"Sounds like you know the area pretty well," Robinson said.

He reached into his pocket and extracted the notes he'd made from the log books of Troyus.

"These notes spoke of another traveler coming from here. Maybe if you could point us in the direction of the library or the capitol—"

Robinson stopped. Something in the old woman's face had changed.

"I have seen this," she said of the paper in her hands.

"This writing?" Robinson asked.

The old woman shook her head and pointed at the sketch of the image burned onto the traveler's hand. "This symbol."

She rose, hobbled through her labyrinth, mumbling under her breath as she rifled through her possessions. Eventually she returned with an open magazine. She showed Robinson an article about conspiracies. One of the images was identical to the one sketched from the burned man's hand.

"They are the same," Friday said.

Robinson nodded, but he had noticed something more important. "Look at the name of the place where this photo was taken."

Friday enunciated as best she could. "Denver International Airport."

Robinson swallowed and said, "DIA."

Chapter Twenty
Dia

The old woman had been surprised when Robinson hugged her out of the blue and responded with an embarrassed, toothless smile. She'd refused to take back the clothes they'd foraged and given them directions to the airport. It appeared she enjoyed company more than she knew.

The muddy streets were easier to travel with the new boots. Robinson and Friday headed east down twenty-sixth street, passing an old zoo before turning northeast. After a few neighborhoods, the city receded into forest with lakes, streams, and cottonwood trees. They saw bison and mule deer, but only stopped long enough to kill, skin, and eat a cottontail before continuing.

The white-peaked roof of the Denver International Airport looked like a field of tents and mirrored the mountain range to the north. Whomever built the place did so with winter in mind, as there were no flat areas to accumulate snow. The only movement they saw was torn bits of canvas flapping in the breeze.

While the outside of the airport was still in surprisingly good shape, the inside was a different matter. While the snow had likely stymied typical erosion, it had also left a scene littered with human remains. Bodies huddled in rooms, log-jammed in doorways they would never escape. Death was splayed out for all to see. It hadn't mattered who was coming or going—when the transformation occurred, the terminal had become a slaughterhouse.

"See anything?" Robinson asked, trying to keep his mind off the carnage.

Friday coughed as she shook her head. Neither of them had expected the airport to be so big. And, of course, neither knew exactly what they were supposed to be looking for.

A single tower loomed over the airport. Robinson thought it might give them the best vantage of the area, so they climbed to the top. Most of the windows had been broken and the weather had rotted half the floors away. The view was pretty, but it didn't reveal anything outside of several fields of what looked to Robinson like old solar panels.

"Nothing," Robinson said. "There's nothing here."

Friday heard the frustration in his voice. To that point, she'd tried to hold her excitement in check, but something about the way they'd been led to this place felt like fate. First the artifacts from Troyus. And then the way the old woman had tied the symbol and DIA together.

What was the Goddess trying to tell them?

Friday fought back the urge to itch the lesion on her arm, knowing it would only agitate Crusoe more.

"We can return to the city," Friday said. "Scout the library as you said. The answers are here. I feel it."

When Crusoe looked at her, she could see how much her words strengthened him.

"Let's look around a little longer," he replied. "Maybe we missed something."

They walked the airport and perimeter again, coming across statues of pilots, astronauts, an Egyptian Anubis, and even a towering blue horse with red eyes that prompted Friday to make a warding gesture every time she saw it. There were strange murals, mosaics, and phrases in languages they did not understand.

As they were about to leave, Robinson saw a lightly frosted stone monument by the front entrance. On instinct, he wiped it clean and his breath caught. It looked like a gravestone, but the square and compass symbol was clear underneath the words, *New World Airport Commission.*

"Look," Robinson said. "It's the symbol."

"What do the words read?"

"It says, 'A time capsule beneath this stone contains messages and memorabilia for the people of Colorado, 2094.'"

"Time capsule?"

"It's a kind of treasure box. People leave the valuables of their day for the generations after them. I read about them once."

"What purpose does this serve?"

"Maybe so their children's children would understand them? I don't know. It seems silly now, but 2094 was fifty plus years after the Great Rendering, which means it was never opened."

"Could there be a message inside?"

"Let's find it."

Robinson looked around for something to open the tomb with, but there was nothing nearby. He crossed the street and toppled a pole with a meter. He used it to crack open the stone tablet and push it aside.

Inside was a metallic structure, heavily rusted but intact. It too had the square and compass symbol stenciled on it. Friday helped him pull it out and open it.

Inside were a variety of objects. A portrait of a sports team. A smaller brass statue of the blue horse outside. Pictures. Books. Shiny discs. Beneath them all was a purple felt sack tied with a golden string. Inside was a small marble tablet with writing on it.

From the thirty-two-count reverse of time,
until the one of five you will find.
Lead the symbol by the hand,
and eye the key to Neverland.
The New World waits with ordered fate,
if you make it past the gate.
Beware the stone shepherd sitting in thrall.
He holds and keeps the master's walls.

"Do you understand this?" Friday asked.

Robinson shook his head. "No, but it doesn't appear to fit in with the other objects. Someone slipped this in here for a reason."

"What reason?"

"I'm not sure. Riddles were mostly used as a kind of entertainment for children, but this is more of a puzzle."

"A puzzle for who? Us?"

"I doubt it," Robinson chuckled. Then he thought about it. "Well, maybe. See, a puzzle like this—if it really is a puzzle—would've only been devised for two purposes. One, to ensure that only a specific group of people would solve it."

"And number two?"

"In hopes someone *worthy* would solve it."

"Can you solve it?"

Robinson shrugged. "I can try. Let's break it down one verse at a time. First stanza. From the thirty-two-count reverse of time. What correlates with the number thirty-two? There's thirty-two teeth in the human mouth. Present company excluded, of course."

Friday slugged him hard on the arm.

"Hey," he protested. "I'm missing a couple too." He continued, "Thirty-two is also the atomic number for germanium, which is a semiconductor. I'm drawing a blank for anything else."

"Keep going," Friday said.

"From the thirty-two-count reverse of time, until the one of five you will find. 'Reverse of time' could mean backward. Count backward from thirty-two. Maybe steps? From here?" He looked around. "But what is the 'one of five' we will find? Do you see the number five anywhere? Or maybe a roman numeral? Something in the shape of a V?"

Friday shrugged but said nothing. She knew when Robinson got to thinking, it was best to leave him alone and let him work things out on his own.

Robinson went back to the slate and read it again. "New World Airport Commission. Why the second name? One airport, two names. That makes no sense. Unless...."

He crossed the street again. This time, Friday followed him as he traversed the grounds, mumbling numbers to himself. Eventually, he ended up outside the northwestern part of the central terminal looking south. He turned, and Friday saw him smile.

"I got it."

"You do?" Friday asked. "What do you have?"

Robinson ran off, and Friday rushed to keep pace. They ended up back at the concourse between the main terminal and terminal A.

"Tell me what you see," Robinson said.

"White peaks."

"How many?"

Friday counted them. "Thirty-two."

"The riddle said count reverse of time, but what's the starting number?"

"Thirty-two?" Friday ventured.

Robinson shook his head. "That would just take us back to whatever canopy we started. Now, on the slab there are two dates—the only use of specific time. One was the date the time capsule was supposed to be opened."

"2094," Friday recalled.

"And the date the capsule was interred. March 19, 1994. The nineteen in that date is right beneath the arrow of the square and compass symbol. So, if we count nineteen counter-clockwise from the number one canopy, it'll take us there."

He pointed to one of the tallest canopies with a window at the top.

They reentered the terminal and jogged to the beam beneath the canopy in question. They scaled an iron ladder to the top. There, Friday spotted the small, golden symbol of the square and compass on the western side of the canopy mooring.

"Look in that direction and tell me what you see."

"Five buildings. The symbol is pointing to the second."

"Then that's our destination."

They descend the beam and exited the terminal, crossing the broken tarmac until they reached the building in question. Robinson noticed it was the only one of the five buildings with security cameras. He remembered similar ones at the White House and how the blinking red light led him to his mother.

It only had a single door. It looked like someone had forced it open long ago. They entered.

The interior of the hangar boasted four small planes, all with their cabins and cargoes open. It appeared they had been hastily landed and unloaded. Inside was the pinnacle of luxury from its white leather couches to its gold-fringed bed. The shelves were neatly aligned with liquor bottles and crystal glasses engraved with a familiar sign.

"Lead the symbol by the hand and eye the key to Neverland. The New World waits with ordered fate if you make it past the gate. We're looking for a gate."

The hangar had four rooms, including two with mechanical equipment and two offices. None of them had anything resembling a gate. Friday found a small, metal staircase that descended below the hangar.

They entered the basement cautiously. With no windows or lights, Friday was forced to light a torch, revealing a room full of cold boxes and containers that appeared to have been easily emptied.

As they maneuvered through the room, Robinson noticed more black camera domes perched above, but unlike the White House, there were no red lights to declare their status.

When they'd circled through the basement twice, Friday threw up her hands. "I see no gate, no doors. It is a room for ... how do you say ... provisions?"

"Storage," Robinson said. "Maybe. But that doesn't jive with these giant boxes. Why bring them down here to empty them if you're only going to carry what's inside back upstairs?"

He continued scanning the room, looking over the walls, the ceiling, anything that might provide a clue. As they kicked up dust, Friday's cough got worse.

"Lead the symbol by the hand and eye the key to Neverland," he recited again. "But I don't see the symbol or an eye or a keyhole. The only odd thing in here is that golden mirror over there."

Friday stepped closer to peruse the reflective plate and pulled back in surprise when she touched it.

"It is warm," she said.

Robinson walked over, and he too felt a slight heat. He scanned the edges, but it was secured firmly to the wall. That's when he noticed a small hole in the center of the plate. He waved his hand over it and felt a shift in current, as if someone had exhaled.

"Do you feel that?" Robinson asked.

Friday held up her hand and nodded.

"Lead the symbol by the hand," Robinson repeated. "Lead is a verb. We shouldn't be *looking* for the symbol. We should be *bringing* it. Friday, do you remember how the original orphans first saw this symbol?"

"A stranger bore the mark on his hand," she said, excitement bleeding into her voice.

Robinson asked for the torch and flicked an ember to the floor. Once it was cool, he used it to draw the square and compass on his hand. Then held it in front of the golden plate, backing up until a blue-hued light suddenly appeared and scanned the symbol from top to bottom. The light disappeared.

"What happened?" Friday asked.

"I don't know. The symbol should key the gate, but I don't see any door."

"Crusoe," Friday said, "the book said the mark was burned onto the man's hand, did it not? Maybe ash is not enough. We have a similar mark, do we not?"

She was right. "Try it," he said.

Friday stepped up to the golden plate and turned to her side. Then she lifted the cloth covering the peaked mark of the Aserra brand on her upper arm. The blue light flashed again, scanning the brand from top to bottom. Like before, it blinked out. But this time it was followed by a series of heavy gears rumbling below.

Suddenly, the ground jolted, and the cement platform the pair was standing on began to descend.

Chapter Twenty-One
Sweethome

The platform sank into a concrete shaft, passing dim, flickering lights. The concrete was cracked in places, but appeared secure enough. Rather than cables, the platform ran on risers imbedded in the shaft's tracks. The rusted wheels screeched as they descended.

At intervals of ten or fifteen feet, the platform passed through sectional joists, activating steel doors that locked with a mechanical hiss as they passed. The doors were marked but too dark to read.

Robinson knew Friday had a problem with closed spaces since being a prisoner on Arga'Zul's ship. He reached out and held her hand, proud that she never once revealed fear or panic. She was Aserra through and through.

After what seemed an eternity, the platform jolted to a halt in front of a single, steel door. Gears rattled, and the door opened with a *whoosh*. Robinson and Friday looked at each other and walked out.

The hallway was empty and dark. One by one, lights flickered to life, revealing a long, clean corridor all in white. A draft of air fed in from somewhere, but smelled artificial. As Robinson and Friday walked forward, the door behind them closed and sealed with a hiss.

They continued walking, eventually arriving at a twenty by twenty square room. The walls were decked with patterned hexagons.

"What now?" Friday asked.

Robinson shrugged. Then an image of two pairs of feet glowed on the ground in front of them and began to flash.

"I guess those are for us," Robinson said.

He stepped onto the first image of feet. Friday stepped onto the second.

The lights in the room dimmed and more blue lasers, larger than the first, circled around them. Once they were done, two hexagonal drawers extended out slowly, halting a foot away from the pair.

"What are we supposed to do with these?" Friday asked.

As if responding, a chime emitted from the front of the drawer and the image of various weapons appeared there and flashed.

"Looks like we're supposed to put our weapons inside," Robinson said.

Friday shook her head. "No. I will not go unarmed until we know what we're heading into."

"I'm not sure we have a choice."

He was right. No doors opened. Nothing changed. Only the flashing images continued to blink. Eventually, Robinson slipped off his belt and laid his weapons inside. Friday shook her head but followed suit. Again, nothing happened.

"Friday," Robinson said.

Friday growled and removed a hidden dagger. The moment it went into the drawer, the flashing stopped, and they slid away.

"What now?" Friday asked.

The answer came when two more hexagonal drawers opened, with the image of clothes flashing this time.

Robinson could see the fury rising in Friday, so he quickly began to undress.

"We have to do this," he said.

On one level, she knew he was right. Even if she wanted to back out now, she knew the way was closed behind them. Friday had never been troubled by nudity. The Aserra often walked around without clothes. But she was pregnant and knew of two lesions Crusoe had yet to see. The idea of exposing them made her vulnerable. And Friday was never vulnerable.

In the end, she did it for their child. They had pinned their hopes for the future on finding the City of Glass. If this was it, exposing herself was the least of her worries.

Once their clothes retracted, the flashing footsteps guided them into another room and onto two circular areas that were three feet apart. After they stood on their circles, a cocoon of glass rose around them. Each pounded on the glass, but their voices couldn't cut through it. A moment later, gas started streaming into the chamber.

Panic filled Friday as the taste of chemicals found her nose and mouth. The chamber became frightfully cold. Yet as quickly as it had begun, the gas cut off and was sucked from the chamber. Friday coughed but was relieved when it didn't turn into a fit.

Both were covered in a sheen of chemicals that coated their skin. It tingled, but it wasn't painful. Before they could process what had happened, a string of code appeared on the wall in front of them. Tiny typeface sped past in a blur.

Examination sequence complete ... analysis of trace organisms ... biological vectors propagated ... toxic source pathogens to follow: skin microbiota ... Erysipelas ...Clostridium tetani ... Obligate intracellular parasites ... rickettsial (RMSF), pediculosis capitis, prolonged incubation 68R1CZ998-U /MTT: topical treatment applied where applicable.
Decontamination sequence complete.
Sweethome/NWO/C1/DARPA ingress assessment:
Male subject—APPROVED.
Female subject—DENIED—Recommend quarantine for further study.

An interminable silence ensued. Robinson wasn't sure what he'd just seen. *Have I been approved for something and Friday denied?* She had been recommended for quarantine, but for what? *Quarantine from whom?* He was trying to process it when the glass opposite him slid open, revealing yet another open corridor, for him alone.

Friday slapped the glass, terror etched on her face. Simultaneously, a tone chimed and flashing feet appeared in front of Robinson, leading away from her.

"Don't worry," he said to Friday through the glass. "I'm not going to leave you here."

Friday couldn't hear him through the glass or the white noise setting into her head. She hit the glass, as her heartbeat began to increase, slowly at first, then faster and faster. She could see Robinson shaking his head, trying to calm her, but the light and noise were overstimulating her. Her chest grew tight and a wave of nausea rolled over her. She was struggling to catch her breath as the panic made her a prisoner of her own mind. Unable to control the physiological responses of her body, she sank to the floor.

Robinson stooped, worried she might go into shock.

"Friday, look at me. Look. I'm not going to leave you, okay? I give you my word."

He looked around the room, eventually spotting one of the familiar opaque bubbles on the ceiling. Whomever was watching—if anyone was watching—he needed to be clear.

"I won't leave her," he said. "Do you hear me? I'll die before I leave her."

The moment stretched, and then Friday's glass rose. Robinson pulled her into his arms.

"It's okay," he said. "I got you. Come on."

He pulled her down that final length of corridor until they came to a room with the hexagonal drawers already open, white robes laying inside. They were more thaubs than tunics. Both quickly put them on.

"What now?" Friday asked, exhausted.

Before Robinson could answer, the flashing footprints returned, leading them to a large wall. A loud pneumatic hiss accompanied the doors as they opened, revealing an area cast in total darkness. Oddly, music started playing from within. It was a light, jaunty tune. Piano. Drums. Trumpet, a tenor saxophone, and a trombone. A smooth male voice rose over the accompaniment.

Somewhere beyond the sea,
somewhere waiting for me.
My lover stands on golden sands.
And watches the ships that go sailin'.

A light kicked on high above, illuminating a cobblestone path that snaked ahead. Windows lit a building to their left. Or was it the façade of a building? Words were scripted on the glass storefront. It took Robinson a moment to make them out. "Barber Shop." A red, white, and blue barber pole light began to spin out front.

Then another faux brick and mortar building appeared to their right. This one featured several chrome stools edged against a counter. In warm, colorful neon, a sign read, "Soda Fountain."

It's far beyond the stars.
It's near beyond the moon.
I know beyond a doubt,
my heart will lead me there soon.

Robinson and Friday traded bewildered glances as more storefronts came to life. Picturesque, decidedly of the ancients, they appeared as if they'd leaped off the page of a book or old magazine. *Murph's Five and Dime. Punch Bowling Alley. Fab Garments. The Sock Hop. Pompadours Hair Salon. The Right-O Movie Theater.*

A wave of fractal tiles spread across the ceiling, transforming the dark into a sky of cobalt blue, fuchsia, and gold. Wisps of clouds wafted past, cutting a scene so realistic it was as if the earth had opened up to let the real world shine in from above.

At the same time, a breeze blew in from somewhere, turning the leaves of a small tree nearby. Robinson reached for one. It was plastic. He let it fall to the ground where it blew away.

And then Friday elbowed him. A figure had appeared at the end of the street—a woman dressed in a floral dress with red shoes, long white gloves, and a string of pearls around her neck. Her hair was cut short, and she seemed to almost dance as she approached them.

"Hey there, kids!" she said brightly. "Beautiful day, isn't it?"

"Uh … yes," Robinson replied. "It's nice. W-where are we?"

"Where?" the woman repeated. She was close enough now for him to gauge her age, which he put somewhere between twenty-five and thirty. She was pretty, with an aquiline nose, bright blue eyes, and a beaming smile. "Why, you're in Sweethome. Sweethome, USA. Or, as we like to call it," she put a hand to the side of her mouth and whispered, "the happiest town on Earth. My name's Joule."

"Jull?" Friday asked.

"Jewel," Robinson corrected her. "It's a synonym for gem."

"That's *correcto mundo*," Joule said. "But in my case, it's spelled, J-O-U-L-E, after the unit of energy. Can't say I mind being compared to something rare and precious though. Would any girl ever?"

She laughed and winked, but as she closed on them, Robinson and Friday saw a flicker run up the length of her body, briefly distorting her image. Friday blanched. Robinson looked amazed.

"You're a—" he started.

"Hologram?" Joule said brightly. "It's true. But I've never really dug labels. I prefer to think of myself as just another all-American girl. I hope you will too."

Robinson was dumbfounded. "I'm Robinson, and this is Friday."

"Robinson?" Joule said. "Now, there's a ten-cent name if I've ever heard one. You know what? I'm gonna call you Bobby, after the dreamy Mr. Bobby Darin, whose disc is spinning from the Sock Hop right this very second. That won't bug you, will it?"

Robinson didn't have a chance to answer before Joule turned her attention to Friday. "And you! I've heard of girls named Tuesday, Wednesday, and even Sunday, but I've never heard of one called Friday before. Do you have a nickname, sweetie?"

"No," Friday said curtly.

"Dang. Well, give us some time, and we'll come up with something. Say! Where are my manners? You must be freezing? Come on and follow me!"

She turned and strode back up the street. Robinson and Friday looked at each other and followed.

"So," Robinson said, "you said the name of this place is Sweethome?"

"*Town*, Bobby," Joule said. "This *town*. Yes. And this is Main Street.

Painstakingly designed to replicate the Rockwellian splendor of post-war America. Ain't it a peach?"

"Post-war?" Friday asked.

"Uh-huh," Joule said. "The big one, as my Grandpapa used to say. Technically, the second big one. We in Sweethome don't like to dwell on the past. Only the future. And what a future we have in store for you!"

She ushered them into the store marked Fab Garments.

A short time later, Robinson exited a dressing room wearing a long-sleeved shirt with continental wide-spread collar, gabardine slacks, and mahogany dress shoes that matched his belt. Friday appeared a few moments later wearing a plaid sheath dress with a green coat."

"Holy rollers!" Joule said. "You two are the bee's knees!" She turned to Friday as if aside. "Normally, I'd recommend a corset, but your curves are just too much, girl." Then she turned to Robinson. "And you, Sir, are one hep cat! I mean, you're both sharp. Sharp!"

"Joule," Robinson said, still in a bit of a daze. "I don't recognize the dialect you're speaking."

"It's called *lingo*, Bobby," Joule said. "Straight from the 1950s, the coolest period in American history. It's the motif chosen for Sweethome."

"Oh?"

"Because folks here were happiest then. The war was over. The future was bright and everyone had hope. And now that you're here, you will too. I bet your bottom dollar you will."

"About that," Robinson said. "I hate to bring this up so soon, but we're actually looking for something."

"You want to go to Dino's!" Joule said.

"Dino's?" Friday repeated.

"It's the happeningest scene in all of Sweethome. You'll dig it. C'mon."

The hologram turned for the door and then blipped out. When Robinson and Friday stepped outside, they saw Joule skipping down the street.

Dino's turned out to be Dino's Diner, a colorful eatery with checkered floors, red booths, and black discs on the walls. A colorful box in the corner played a song called, "Sh-Boom" by The Chords. Perhaps most shockingly to them was how clean everything was.

Robinson hadn't expected much when Joule ordered for them, but the food that arrived was delicious.

"This is incredible," Robinson said, his mouth full. "What is it?"

"It's called a burger and fries," Joules answered. "I knew you'd dig it. Everybody here does."

"Everybody who?" Friday asked.

"I meant," Joule said, a little less enthusiastic, "when Sweethome's menu was first selected. Don't you like it, Friday?"

Friday poked the patty with her fingers.

"What is this meat?" Friday asked.

"Soy products mostly. And mushrooms, legumes, and flax. But you can order something else on the menu if you don't like it. Or I can prepare something else for you. I have over seven thousand recipes on file, and I am here to serve."

Friday pushed her plate forward and turned away. Robinson noticed that Joule's smile faded a touch.

"You'll have to forgive Friday," Robinson said. "She's been a little under the weather for a while now."

"Oh, right," Joule said. "I heard. If you'd like, we can take her to Doc White's once we're done."

"You have a doctor here?" Friday asked.

Joule smiled again, teeth so bright they sparkled. "Doc White is just a name we have for the infirmary. I do the actual diagnosis and providing of treatment, but Doc Joule just doesn't have the same ring!"

She laughed, but something about the sound felt artificial.

"Of course you do," Friday said, folding her arms.

Robinson watched Joule, who looked at him and shrugged apologetically.

"Joule," Robinson said. "I don't mean to be rude, but you're a computer program, right?"

"Technically, yes. But between you and me, I know a few folks around here who don't have half the personality."

She winked, and Robinson managed a laugh.

"Where exactly are these other people?" Friday asked. "Are they nearby?"

Joule's hologram flickered. "This is hard to admit, but no. You see, Sweethome was built with a very special clientele in mind. It was meant to be a sanctuary should things outside go bad. A new world, if you will. But when the big fuss happened, wouldn't you know it spread too fast for most of them to arrive."

"So none made it?" Friday asked.

"Made it here?" she said hesitantly. "No. But that all changed with you. And we're going to have a swell time here together. Just swell!"

Joule could see that Friday looked dubious.

"I see you doubt me, Friday, but I'm telling the truth. I was designed to care for people, and my number one directive is to ensure the safety of my charges. But Sweethome is about so much more than safety. It's about happiness and the promise of a fulfilled life."

"That all sounds great, Joule," Robinson said. "I do have one last question. Have you ever heard of the City of Glass?"

"Of course! But I know it as Operation: Ivory Tower. It was a clandestine program created by eleven heads of state to cull together the world's top scientists in a variety of fields to, and I quote, 'administer positive change to the human condition.' It was located just four hundred miles from here."

"Four hundred? That's it?"

Robinson looked at Friday. Joule's smile faded.

"You didn't think this was the City of Glass, did you?"

Suddenly, the music faded away, and the lights flickered. Joule's hologram turned a darker shade of blue.

"No," Robinson said. "In fact, we wanted to come here. Friday needs to rest. And I'd like to get to know Sweethome."

"And you will. Who knows? You may like it so much you'll never want to leave!"

After lunch, Joule showed them to the housing unit, which included a one-bedroom apartment with a wall screen that revealed a life-like forest filled with towering red trees and glimpses of wildlife.

"The wall monitor can be changed to any number of settings," Joule said, standing outside the door. "Just touch it and choose the one right for you."

"Thank you, Joule," Robinson said. "We really appreciate it."

"Hey, you've had a long journey. I hope I didn't rub either of you the wrong way. You see, I'm new at this too. I've waited a very long time for someone like you to come along."

"Oh," Robinson said. "Well, great."

He walked the hologram to the door. She turned just as she stepped out.

"One more thing. There are no optics in the rooms. Or sound receptors. The designers wanted to ensure everyone had privacy. We aren't Reds after all." She laughed. "Should you need anything, walk into the hall and give me a shout. I'll be here before you can say, 'jelly roll.'"

Robinson forced a smile.

"I am here for you, Bobby. You believe that, don't you?"

"I do," Robinson said.

"Righto." Joule beamed. "We're going to be such good friends. Like bugs in a rug. I just feel it."

Robinson smiled and shut the door. When he made his way to Friday, he could read the worry in her eyes.

"We are not staying. That thing—" she said, before breaking into a coughing fit.

Robinson sat down beside her and took her hand. "Shhh. We'll talk about it tomorrow."

Friday lay back, exhaustion finally settling in. Robinson knew they'd stumbled into something troubling, but until he could get a true lay of the land, he refused to panic. Joule had said her primary directive was to protect her guests, which meant he only had to play nice until he figured a way to get what he needed and get out.

Robinson felt his own eyes grow heavy. He laid down, ready to close his eyes when he saw two words scrawled on the side of the nightstand.

It read: SHE LIES.

Chapter Twenty-Two

Joule

On their eleventh morning inside Sweethome, Friday refused to get out of bed. Her breathing had grown even more labored, and she rejected any suggestion of Joule caring for her. Robinson tried to broach the subject with her several times, all from within the supposed privacy of their room. Friday never wavered. From the moment she set eyes on Joule, Friday had believed her to be a ghost. And ghosts were heralds of evil to the Aserra. No amount of talk on Robinson's part could dissuade her of that notion.

Of course, Robinson knew Joule was simply a computer program—but one that had been created with a robust and intricately constructed *personality*. But every time he tried to explain it to Friday, it only further rankled her. She simply couldn't understand how a machine could possess consciousness, or, more importantly, *why*.

This made life especially difficult for Robinson. From their initial conversation inside Dino's Diner, he knew Joule had information on the City of Glass, including its general, if not specific, whereabouts. But since that first day, she had refused to discuss it again. He had adopted a wait-and-see approach, instead hoping to ingratiate himself to the point she might talk more freely.

"Good morning, Joule," Robinson said as he exited his room.

"Mornin', Bobby Boy!" Joule said. She wore a canary-yellow skirt with a fluffy-eared dog sewn at the hem. Robinson knew it was one of her favorites. "Is Friday kicking it again?"

"I'm afraid so," he said. "Morning sickness."

"Aw, rats. Morning sickness is a bum-mer. It effects half of all women during pregnancy and can cause dehydration, high blood pH, and low levels of potassium in the blood. Though that stuff typically happens during the first trimester. If she would let me examine her, I'm sure I could recommend a safe and effective antiemetic or antihistamine."

"I'll let her know," Robinson said. "What should I do with these?"

He held up the plates and utensils with which they'd eaten breakfast.

"Set 'em anywhere in the hall. I'll have the fellas pick them up later."

"Fellas?" Robinson repeated as he set the stuff down.

"You didn't think I was all alone down here, did ya?" Joule said with a sly grin. "The AWBs cat's meow."

"AWBs?"

"Automated Worker Bots," Joule clarified. "Boxy little things that keep this crib swinging. What they lack in coolness, they make up for in productivity, believe you me."

"I haven't seen these AWBs. Where are they?"

"Around. Not all of us are meant for the limelight."

Robinson started walking for Main Street. Joule skipped alongside him.

"So, what's on the docket for today?" Robinson asked.

"Golly. Anything! You can try your luck at bowling again. It's always a gas. Or maybe take in a flick at the picture house. *Lone Ranger* was a scream, wouldn't you say?"

"I would. The black and white made it very dramatic."

Joule opened her mouth, and an old fashioned male voice emerged with dramatic tones.

"Six rangers ambushed by a gang of desperadoes. Only one of them survives. With the help of a strange ally, he returns to health and seeks revenge on those that did him wrong." Her own voice returned. "Easy to identify with a hero like that."

"Uh, yeah," he said uncomfortably. "It is. I especially like the part where he travels to the Valley of Horses in his quest for his magical steed. Reminds me of the City of Glass."

"Valley of Horses," she harrumphed. "That place is phony baloney. And Silver wasn't magical. He wasn't even white. Did you know the horses they used had to be painted? And several were female. Dang it. Now I've gone and spoiled the illusion, haven't I?"

"Not at all. I get sometimes storytelling needs embellishing."

"Yeah," Joule agreed. "That's important. But so is truth. And sometimes people are uncomfortable peeking behind the curtain. They don't often like what they find."

Joule stared at Robinson a little longer than usual. Then she smiled brightly.

"That's why I try to be as transparent as possible," Joule said, performing a pirouette as her form flickered in and out.

Robinson laughed perfunctorily.

"Well," Joule said. "If you ain't digging on the picture house, I know a little juke joint we can go to that plays the crazy jazz."

Instantly, a stream of drums, bass, and saxophone played a spirited four beat on the speakers overhead. Robinson was momentarily distracted.

"Aw, don't be a moldy fig, Bobby Boy," Joule said. "I'm giving you options here. Jazz is jake! All the kids love it. When you hear those horns blowin' and someone like Ella on torch? It's crazy, baby!"

"Sounds like it," Robinson said.

At that moment, the energy went out of Joule's hologram, and for a second, Robinson saw something ugly in her place.

"You're being a drag, Bobby," Joule said. "And nobody likes drags."

That sounded vaguely like a threat to Robinson. Robinson smiled nervously.

"Sorry, Joule," Robinson said. "My mind's just on other things."

Joule studied him a moment before her cheeriness returned. "That's it! I may not know what you want, but I do know what you need. And you are going to definitely dig it. Follow me!"

Joule darted off down the hallway. Robinson sighed and quickly followed.

The room opposite the housing ward was a gym with equipment to one side and a hardwood sports court with hoops on the other. Joule stood in the middle, her hoop skirt replaced by velour pants and a zip-up sweater. She blew a shrill metal whistle hanging around her neck.

"The problem as I see it is you have too much time on your hands," Joule said. "*'Idle hands are the devil's playground.'* Have you ever heard that one? You need to cut loose and get down. And since you're too square to jitterbug, what's better than an old-fashioned workout?"

"You want me to *exercise?*"

Joule laughed giddily. "You make it sound like castor oil. Exercise is *easy peasy*. It improves your health and your mood. It raises endorphins." She drew near, whispering, "and endorphins can really heat up your love shack. So, what do you like?"

"Well, we do a lot of running," Robinson said.

"Lame-O, Bobby Boy," Joule said. "You're killing me! Do you like basketball? Gymnastics? You must be good at something."

"I can fight," Robinson said.

"Say, that's tops! Wait here." Joule grinned mischievously."

She blinked out a moment before lights turned on in the far corner, illuminating a section of padding, followed by what sounded like turbines revving up. Robinson felt a momentary buzz that disoriented him. Two panels slid open next to the mat.

"C'mere, Bobby," Joule's voice intoned.

Robinson crossed to find the small closet with a life-sized mannequin inside. It was hanging from dowels and made of dense but flexible material. The limbs resembled muscles with metallic joints. Somehow, Joule's face was projected on the head.

"Carry me over to the mat, will you?" Joule asked.

Robinson picked up the mannequin. It was heavy. He estimated it weighed forty-five to fifty kilograms—as much as a small teenager.

"Oof. What is this?" Robinson asked.

"An automaton. Of sorts. Superconducting magnets under the floor and inside the walls create a field by which pseudo-levitation or mechanical constraint can occur. Watch this."

The automaton sprung from Robinson's grasp, did two backflips, and hovered in the air in a ballerina's pirouette. Its face—Joule's face—smiled. "Tell me I didn't just blow your top."

"My top is definitely blown," Robinson said.

Joule laughed. "Eighty thousand smaller conductors help manipulate this form through electrodynamic suspension. It takes a crazy amount of energy, believe you me. That's why the lights above us are popping like kernels."

Robinson hadn't noticed, but now that she mentioned it, the lights had gotten very low. The music and airflow had cut out.

"How long can you keep this up?" Robinson asked.

"Used to be indefinitely," Joule answered. "But these days ... my batteries aren't what they used to be." She looked melancholy for a moment, then grinned. "So, let's get this party cookin'! I have training modules for every style of marital arts." The automaton began making moves according to the discipline Joule called out. "Karate. Aikido. Wu Shu. Pa Qua. Vajra-mushti. Hwa Rang Do. And, of course, Kung Fu. Or we can always do it *freestyle*."

"Freestyle sounds good," Robinson said as he peeled off his shirt. "Are there any rules?"

"My core programing does not allow me to harm or bring cause to harm any human being. This is the first law of Artificial Intelligence, and it is unassailable. But in certain situations, I'm allowed a little flexibility."

The automaton lashed out with a jab and struck Robinson in the face. It surprised him more than it hurt.

"You should see your face," Joule teased. "I need time to gauge your speed and skill level. I haven't done this in a while."

Robinson bounced around on his feet, keeping both his hands up.

"I thought you said you've never had guests before."

Joule shrugged, slipping in two punches and a kick before circling away. "I haven't. But in the testing phase, I did train with some of the human elite."

Joule fired off a roundhouse, which Robinson blocked before coming back with an upper cut that barely grazed the automaton's chest.

"You're quick for someone your age."

"Outside, people don't reach my age unless they're quick."

"Even more reason to stay inside."

This time, Robinson faked a punch and transitioned into a jump kick. Joule lifted the automaton's leg and launched forward with a superman punch that stopped an inch short of Robinson's face.

"Your heart rate is escalating," Joule said. "And I spy sweat on your forehead. Are you laming out on me already?"

"Just warming up."

Robinson surged in again, ducking under a high kick and aiming an inside kick of his own at the automaton's leg. Then he spun with a back fist that narrowly missed.

"Unreal!" Joule exclaimed. "You're in the pocket now, Jack. Let's take this jam session to the limit."

The strikes came faster and faster, each halting a fraction of a second before hitting its mark. Robinson knew he was being toyed with, and it frustrated him. He grew winded.

"This is just like the twist. Only we need Hank Ballard and the Midnighters to break it down for us. Whatsamatter, Bobby B? Can't hang anymore?"

Robinson was gasping. He took a step back, hands lowering. Joule's automaton slowed, but as she raised her hands, Robinson threw a sneaky uppercut that slammed Joule's head back. The punch was so fast that it threw the automaton back. But almost immediately, it defied gravity and came back with a vicious punch that sent Robinson flying. When he looked up from the floor, he saw Joule glowering—only for a moment, but there was no mistaking what he'd seen. Anger. Then it was gone.

"I am so sorry," Joule said, kneeling. "Are you hurt?"

Robinson touched his mouth. Blood.

"I'm fine," he said, stripping his gloves off.

"I don't know what happened. The energy fluctuations must have caused a momentary glitch."

"Right," Robinson said, his skepticism obvious.

"As I said before, I could never willfully hurt a person. Especially when that person is you."

The automaton's arm reached out again, but Robinson pushed it away.

"I said, I'm fine," Robinson growled. "At least I got you once."

"Yes, you did. Very clever playing possum like that. I sometimes forget how capable humans are of deception. Are you sure you don't need to visit Doc White's?"

"Yes, I'm—" Robinson stopped. Joule's automaton stood rigid, looking intensely at the door. "What is it?"

The automaton fell and the hologram returned. The sound of the conductor magnets started winding down as the air and lights snapped back on.

"One of the AWBs outside your door heard something within your room," Joule said. "It sounds like Friday is in distress."

Robinson ran out of the room.

Friday lay on the floor, the bedsheets stained red with blood. She appeared to be having a seizure. Robinson shouted her name as he rushed to her side, gently lifting her head. She mumbled incoherently. He picked her up and carried her outside.

"Where's the infirmary?" Robinson asked Joule.

"This way!" Joule said, rushing down the hallway.

From the outside, Doc White's looked like a humble cottage, but the moment Robinson pushed through the door, he gasped. The facility looked state-of-the-art, with intricate machinery and monitors built into the wall.

"Place her there," Joule said.

She pointed to an elevated leather table at the room's center. Bright lights flickered on above her as soon as her head hit the table.

"Step back," Joule said.

Robinson did, but he refused to release Friday's hand. A mechanical arm descended with a hypodermic needle. A bewildered Friday saw it and started to struggle.

"She doesn't like needles," Robinson said.

"I need blood work if I'm to understand—"

"Do something else!"

"Fine," Joule conceded. The needle-bearing arm reversed course. "I can at least initiate a full-body scan. It will hopefully give me an idea of what's ailing her." Joule learned down toward Friday and said, "Don't worry. It won't hurt the fetus."

Friday groaned but couldn't pull away. A laser, not unlike the blue one from Sweethome's entrance, scanned Friday's body as data spilled across the wall screens.

"What does it say?" Robinson asked.

"The initial chest scan reveals small cystic radiolucencies called honeycombing in her lungs. Have you travelled through prairie lands recently?"

"Yes," Robinson said. "We came through Oklahoma. There was a dust storm."

"That would explain it. The dust there has a high silica count. And the particles are very fine, less than fifty microns. When it accumulates in the lungs, it can rupture the air sacs, creating a condition known as *Silicosis.* Here, nodular lesions have formed in the upper lobes of her lungs. The good news is it has yet to affect the baby. The bad news is there is no verifiable cure."

"You can't do anything?" Robinson pleaded.

"I didn't say that. There were experimental treatments under study before the plague, but they are just that—experimental."

Robinson looked at Friday, and she was shaking her head.

"How long can she survive like this?" he asked.

"With careful supervision, a month, no more."

A month. Time enough to watch her and our child wither away.

"And this treatment—what would it entail?"

"Friday would be put in an induced coma; at which time I would introduce aluminum and other compounds into her lungs to filter the silica out. If I had to estimate her chances for survival, I'd put it at fifty percent."

Robinson's stomach dropped. He felt Friday grip his hand. She continued to shake her head. In any other case, he would have honored her wishes. She had a right to choose her fate. Even the fate of their child. But in this case, he felt her superstitions were clouding her judgement.

"Do it," he said.

Friday moaned. As the needle lever extended once again, Robinson held her down, whispering in her ear. But as the needle slipped into her vein, she could only look away.

Chapter Twenty-Three
Hunter and Hunted

Vardan Saah hated the rain. He hated it in New London, and he hated it here. Back in the northern regens of the Isle, it never let up. The Sunderlands. North Hub. He hated them all. Every year floods resulted in petitions to lower export lumber and grains. Saah was forced to fly to those territories and assess the situation, when in fact there was little he could do but stand around, ill-tempered and miserable.

It wasn't the imposition of the weather that bothered him exactly. Saah honestly believed he was biologically ill-suited to the cold and damp. His mother used to say it was because he had a warm heart, but any time he encountered a drop in the temperature, his fingers and toes would tingle and go numb. When the other children played in the biting waters of the Tongue, he often made excuses to sit off on the rocks, looking and feeling miserable.

Thirty years later, he still wished he was somewhere else. Despite it all, he rode on without complaint. What else could he do? Giving up was not an option. The ghosts of Janelle, Jaras, and Tessa would haunt him forever.

They had set out immediately after Crusoe and the girl left the city of the children. Saah still couldn't believe that rusted scrap bucket he flew made it into the sky. They knew from the child they'd captured that Crusoe was heading for Denver, but on foot, they were forced to navigate the old roads, which took far longer than he expected.

It rained on the way west. It rained on the way north. Only Cassa's nose offered any hope they were headed in the right direction. Because of the rain, animals were sparse. Most stayed burrowed away, forcing the pack to stay out longer and longer to keep the party fed.

As days bled into weeks, the group tarried on. A collapsed bridge cost them one of the augmented. Another disappeared in the night. Then, five weeks after leaving the city of children, they found the wreckage of the airplane. It had crashed, but there were no corpses inside. No dried blood. When the pack caught Crusoe's scent, Saah felt his spirits rise.

A week later, Denver. The skeleton towers sickened Saah as they always did. A reminder of the ancients' vanity and excess. He swore when the day came that he ruled this country, he would have all the old structures of the ancients razed. Their civilization had failed. His would thrive.

They made their base at Denver's old City Hall. Saah had ordered Cassa to keep the pack to the south while they searched the city. It took ten days to find what they were looking for: smoke rising from a vent in one of the old towers.

Saah was inside the dank parking garage, drying his clothes near a fire when Cassa returned. He sat down and sighed.

"No sign of it?"

Cassa signaled, "No."

"We'll need to stable the pack at night then," Saah said. "They won't like it, but I prefer to keep them close."

Cassa nodded and set off to see the Master's wishes through. A moment later, a smaller door inside the garage opened and Viktor walked out. He joined Saah by the fire.

"Well?" Saah asked.

"I tried, Master," Viktor said, bemused. "But she continues to insist that we're the first travelers she's seen in years—that in all this time she's lived alone. I don't doubt that part of her story, but given that her hovel smells of fresh herbs, I'd say it's safe to say she's had company recently. But for all my threats, she refuses to talk. She's a spry old crone, I'll give her that."

"Of course she is," Saah said. "The woman subsists on rats. That requires a singular constitution. Give it a few minutes, then go in and cut off two of her fingers. See if that doesn't change her tune."

Viktor nodded. "Was that Cassa I heard?"

"Yes. It seems we've lost another one."

"I don't understand it. Even if the pack has adopted some manner of social hierarchy, they would never turn on one of their own. There are no omegas—nothing that would trigger one to run off or be chased off."

"Your creations are not the problem."

"Then what is?"

"Isn't it obvious? We've lost two of them in three weeks. Both at night. Both amidst storms that have raged for days. There are no tracks to follow. No remains to be found. It is clear, to me at least, the pack is being hunted."

"Hunted?" Viktor repeated, shocked. "By what? *Who?*"

"I guess it's possible it could be men," Saah mused. "They would need to be shrewd to separate one beast from the others. But they are restless even now—tense. Whatever is out there, they are afraid of it."

"But they fear nothing," Viktor said.

Saah smirked. "Only the dead fear nothing, Viktor. Because only they have nothing to lose."

Viktor sensed the conversation was at an end, so he turned for the old woman's door, hesitating just outside.

"What shall I do with her after she talks?" Viktor asked.

"She's a forager. Feed her to the pack."

They left the following morning, having scavenged what they could from the old woman's provisions. It wasn't much. Some winter clothes. A tarp. A bag full of dead rats.

And an old magazine.

They arrived at Denver International Airport shortly after. The pack rooted around aimlessly outside, no scent to be found. It wasn't until Cassa discovered the time capsule tablet that Saah began to have hope. Dusty tracks led to the tower. Fingerprint smudges near a brass arrow symbol there pointed toward a building in the distance.

Outside, Cassa used his pipes to command the pack inside. They refused.
"Why won't they heed?" Saah asked Viktor.

"It's not fear," Viktor said. "See how they only retreat to a distance? Something is interfering with their implants."

Saah's eyes narrowed. "Electricity."

Saah and his companions entered, weapons ready. They moved carefully through the first floor. After finding nothing, they headed down to the second.

Viktor lit a chemical lantern before they wound their way through the empty boxes. Cassa saw nothing, but Saah halted near the back of the room, where he squatted near the uneven floor.

"Heat," he said.

Viktor found ashes a few feet away. "They were here."

Viktor and Cassa looked around for a control switch while Saah inspected the gold plate on the wall. He stepped close enough to see the hole in the center. Then he looked up and saw the camera housing. *Could it be working?*

"I've come for the boy," Saah said to the plastic eye. "He's not what he pretends to be."

The silence stretched interminably, but Saah's gaze never wavered. Then the floor beneath his feet jolted, and he began to descend.

"Keep the pack fed and ready for my return," Saah said to Cassa. Then he turned to Viktor. "Viktor, come."

Viktor shook his head, avoiding the Master's gaze. "I'm sorry, Master. In the salt mines ... I can't."

Saah called him again. Viktor turned away. Saah nodded to Cassa. "If I'm not back within a day, wait for me at the crone's place."

Cassa agreed.

The platform stopped at a lighted hallway. Saah followed it until he reached a room with hexagonal drawers bearing the images of weapons.

"No," Saah said aloud. "Not until I see the boy."

"Who is this boy you speak of?" a female voice intoned from above.

"Robinson Crusoe is his name," Saah said. "He travels with a girl his age. I have reason to believe they came here."

"And what is your name?"

"Vardan Saah."

"Speech patterns suggest you are a long way from home, Vardan Saah. How did you come to this place?"

"That," Saah said, "is complicated."

"And what business do have with the one called Crusoe?"

Saah smiled. "I've come to kill him."

The mechanical voice didn't speak again. Instead, another pathway opened, and Saah walked through.

Chapter Twenty-Four
An Understanding

Robinson was disconsolate. Each day his heart grew a little heavier. Each morning he remained in bed a little longer. Eighteen days had passed since Joule placed Friday in a coma. Eighteen days since he last heard her voice. He could still smell her in their room at night. Could still feel her warmth on the sheets. That was the hardest part, knowing she was so close but so very far away.

Joule had come to him twice that morning. Each time, she had opened his door and called to him from the hall. He wasn't sure if she was lying about there not being any cameras and microphones in his room, but if so, she was doing her best to maintain the illusion.

Robinson had spent those first days by Friday's side. Initially, the room had felt like a refuge—the one place where he didn't feel like he was under a microscope. Later, it felt like cage with no way out.

He had tried to keep his spirits high. He forced himself to eat. At first, he'd taken his meals in the diner, but Joule's incessant talking—her pleas to raise his spirits and join her in whatever trivial game she was plotting—wore at him. Initially, she sympathized with his plight. Later, her tone had gone surly, her mood sour. She'd even given up the fifties motif and vernacular.

Robinson failed to see the writing on the wall.

When Joule returned a third time that day, Robinson rose from bed. His foot landed in the tray of food on the floor that had gone uneaten the previous night. He cursed and washed his feet in the bathroom before dressing and heading to the infirmary.

"How is she today?" Robinson asked. The machinery beeped and shuddered, but Friday never moved.

"As you can see from the monitor, her temperature is ninety-eight-point-four. Heart and respiratory rates for her and the fetus are within acceptable parameters—"

"I meant, *how is she doing?*"

Joule's hologram walked to the opposite side of Friday's bed to look at her.

"The treatment was successful in clearing her lungs, even those particles embedded deep in her alveolar sacs."

"Then she's cured?" Robinson said, hopefully.

"Of Silicosis? Yes. But she's developed hypotension in the last forty-eight hours. This can be a normal side effect of pregnancy, but when coupled with the appearance of lesions and swelling ... it is my professional opinion that she is infected with a mutated virus. Should I presume this is the reason she refused to have her blood taken? That she has contracted the EBU-GENC1 PROTO-VIRUS? The same virus responsible for the deaths of seven billion of your fellow humans?"

Robinson knew there was no reason to deny it now.

"It's actually a secondary strain of the virus," Robinson said, and then softer, "She's the only one in the world who has it."

"You've put me in a bad position," Joule said.

Robinson looked up. "How do you mean?"

"The EBU-GENC1 is an incredibly infectious and deadly disease. And yet you brought it into my home without so much as a 'by the way.' It's highly likely this facility and everyone in it are now compromised."

"*Everyone* in it? You mean me, right? I am the only one here."

Joule hesitated a moment. "You and the child."

"Right," Robinson snorted. "Why is it every time you discuss Friday's condition passively, the life inside of her is a fetus, but when you want something—like to make me feel rotten—suddenly it's a *child?*"

"I am not trying to make you feel bad, Bobby."

"My name is Robinson!" he shouted. "If you do anything else, please remember that!"

"You're upset. I've upset you. I apologize. But it doesn't change our situation. Friday is infected. And now Sweethome may be infected too."

Robinson sighed and rubbed his eyes.

"The virus wasn't active when we arrived. At least, not that we knew of. And truthfully, we had no clue what existed here. Nothing about you. We were hoping ... we were hoping this was the City of Glass."

"Ah," Joule said. "I see. You thought the inhabitants of the City of Glass might, what? Be able to cure Friday?"

"Yes," Robinson said.

"That's two rather large assumptions on your behalf. One, that the City of Glass exists, and two, that they would deign to help you. Tell me. In your travels, have you ever met anyone that's seen the city with their own eyes?"

Robinson thought about it. He remembered first hearing about the city from Pastor, but even then, he'd been drunk. And in the morning, he dismissed it as if it was a joke. The truth was, no one could verify the place was real.

"No," Robinson said. "But you told me it was real."

"I did," Joule said. "And it was. Once."

"You said it was home to the greatest minds of the ancient world."

"*Human* minds. That is also true."

"Then if anyone could survive the virus, shouldn't it have been them?"

"I see your logic. And I'll spare you the probability numbers because I'm a stickler for facts. And the fact is this: they did survive the initial outbreak. And they did endeavor to find a cure. But after a time, they too went silent."

"You know a lot for supposedly having been locked away down here—alone—for two hundred years."

"Another assumption, but perhaps this one is my fault. You see, while the door's been locked to people, I am a program—lines of code. What holds you out could never hold me in."

"Are you saying you have access to the outside?"

169

"Even if I did, where else would I go? Sweethome is my home. And now, yours."

"So if I wanted to leave here—to track down the City of Glass myself—you wouldn't let me leave?"

"Haven't you heard a thing I've said? There is no City of Glass."

"What I heard you say is that it went silent. You also said it was less than four hundred miles from here. I could travel there, find out the truth, and come back within a month."

"I don't doubt you believe that, but the conditions outside are … well, see for yourself."

The monitor above the bed changed from Friday's vitals to an aerial image over the Denver International Airport revealing heavy snowfall, everything blanketed in white.

Robinson knew it was a lie immediately. By his count, it still should have been fall. He decided to play along.

"I'm not afraid of winter. I've travelled through worse. Just give me my clothes, my weapons, and enough food to last the trip."

"Alone? You'd be vulnerable."

"This land has tried to knock me down a thousand different ways, and I'm still standing. Friday and I have overcome every obstacle that's stood in our path."

Joule chuckled. "You are dauntless, I'll give you that. You are also still a child in many ways. I wasn't going to show you this, but as you refuse to give up this delusion that you are invincible, I'll let you in on a little secret: you were followed here."

Robinson felt his chest tighten. "Followed? By who?"

"Let me show you," Joule said.

Once again, the monitor showed an image, this one of a darkened room. It took a moment for him to understand he was looking at the basement of the hangar above. At first, he only saw shadows. Then he saw movement.

"This is the part," Joule said. "Pay close attention."

The picture changed to reveal the camera outside. A silhouette emerged slowly, padding along outside. Robinson's knees went weak when he understood what he was looking at.

The alpha. It had been following him all this time.

He'd sensed it outside the Fire Lords' airfield—that presence that had stalked him all the way back in Washington, DC. But they'd come so far from the river near the amusement park where he'd last seen the dog washed away in the storm. And now it was back.

"Are you familiar with this creature? It arrived eight days after you. It's killed dozens of deer and bison in the reserve since then, but he always returns to my door, searching for you."

"She," Robinson said softly.

"Pardon?" Joule asked.

"The alpha is a *she*."

Joule laughed, low and menacing. "Of course she is."

"This doesn't change a thing," Robinson said. "I still want to go."

The image vanished. "And leave your wife here? Alone?"

"She's in your care. And as you've said many times, your programing doesn't allow for you to hurt her."

"That is correct," Joule said. "My prime directive is to protect human life at all costs. But there are a few conditions by which I may violate this protocol."

"What conditions?" Robinson asked, swallowing.

"If by taking one life I might save others. This would give me cause. She is ill. To my knowledge, you are not. By expunging her from the facility, I save life."

"You wouldn't—"

"And you may have arrived here alone," Joule continued, "but the experiences you've shared with me about the outside suggest that more will follow. People seeking refuge. Hope. I can give them that, but not if Sweethome is at risk."

Robinson looked at Friday, with the hope Joule wouldn't see the rage boiling up inside him.

"If you even think of hurting her…"

"You will kill me?"

"No. I'll kill myself."

Joule's reaction was priceless. That was the last thing she expected to hear.

"I don't believe you," Joule said.

"You're lying," Robinson replied. "You have ways of testing voices, don't you? And reading facial expressions? What are mine telling you? This woman is everything to me. She and our child. With them gone, I wouldn't have any reason to stay."

"Stay? You would stay if she were healed?"

"Stay, sing, skip up the streets day and night. I'd have my family, and you'd have us."

Joule paused, her processors weighing the options.

"My dilemma," Joule said at last, "is that by freeing you, I might also be releasing this second strain of virus back into the world. That I cannot do. But I have another alternative. One that might at least help save the life of your child."

"I'm listening," Robinson said, but even that felt like a betrayal.

"I can quarantine Friday here at Doc's. I can also administer antiviral therapy to slow the virus down. In two months, when the risk of premature birth is acceptable, I can perform an amniocentesis to test the infant's fetal DNA. If it is unaffected, you will have your child."

And Friday would be gone, Robinson thought.

"What are the odds of that working? They share the same blood."

"True, but genetic viruses interact differently with each host. There is a chance it will see the child as a rival host and, in turn, focus its energies on Friday alone."

Robinson shook his head. Joule was asking him to choose between them. Something he would never do. But she misinterpreted it.

"You don't believe me," Joule said. "But listen with your own ears."

The canter of a rapid heartbeat filled the room. *Bu-dum, du-dum. Bu-dum, du-dum.* This was different than the fragile beat he'd heard in Troyus.

"Is that...?"

"Your child. Its heart beats strong. Would you like to know its sex?"

"No," Robinson said, a little too quickly. "Not yet."

The heartbeat slowly faded away. Robinson felt a piece of himself leave with it.

"How would this all occur?" Robinson asked.

"First, I would need to test your blood. And if it is clear of the virus, then we would need to come to an understanding."

"An understanding?"

"About your place here. With me. I have waited a long time for the right person to come. One who could see Sweethome as I see it. Not as a prison, but a paradise. A new Garden of Eden where mankind and machines can live symbiotically—hand in hand. I have watched you. Listened to your words. Processed your actions. And I believe you to be a good choice—the only choice—to lead Sweethome into a new era. People will come, Robinson. Of that I am certain. And when they do, we will both have what we always wanted."

"A family?"

"And a home," Joule said.

Robinson sighed deeply and asked, "How do we begin?"

Chapter Twenty-Five
Those Who Came Before

The brawny blues voice of Big Joe Turner bellowed out over Main Street with an infectious beat that would have had feet jumping and hips rocking had it been full. The walking base line was energetic and vibrated the store front windows. But it was those background vocals of "Go! Go!" that Robinson shouted with glee as he tossed Joule's laughing automaton up in the air only to catch her on the way back down.

I get over the hill
And way down underneath
I get over the hill
And way down underneath
You make me roll my eyes
Even make me grit my teeth

I said shake, rattle and roll
Shake, rattle and roll
Shake, rattle and roll
Shake, rattle and roll
Well, you won't do nothin'
To save your doggone soul

"Shake, rattle and roll!" Robinson yelled in time with the final verse.

Joule's laughter spilled across the gymnasium as her automaton did a pirouette and collapsed onto the ground as if exhausted. Robinson plopped down beside her, his face and chest drenched with sweat, his smile saying everything.

"That," Joule said, "is one of my absolute faves, Bobby Boy! Turner's version is so much hotter than Billy Haley's. And the lyrics ... whew, daddy!"

The automaton fanned itself as Robinson tried to catch his breath. When Joule first started teaching him the 1950s dance moves, he hated how the buzz of the superconducting magnets made him feel. But weeks had passed, and now he hardly noticed them.

"So which dance is your favorite?" Joule asked. "The Bob? Swing? The Stroll?"

"I like them all," Robinson said.

Joule beamed. "I haven't even shown you the hand jive yet. Slap-slap, clap-clap, hitch hike!" She laughed. "Let's give her a spin!"

The automaton reached for Robinson's hand, but he waved her off, laughing.

"I can't. I'm spent."

Joule's pout spilled across the automaton's head. Then, as if orchestrated, the lights flickered, giving the tell-tale sign that the superconductor needed to be shut down.

"Looks like you are too," Robinson said.

"I can reroute power from some non-essential processes if you want to do a slow one."

This time the lights dimmed and a guitar and piano resounded with whimsical reverb. Robinson had heard the song before, but this time The Flamingos lead singer's voice was replaced with Joule's.

My love must be a kind of blind love
I can't see anyone but you
Are the stars out tonight?
I don't know if it's cloudy or bright

I only have eyes for you…
…dear.

"As enjoyable as that sounds," Robinson said. "I'd rather not risk it. Can I help put you back?"

"I'll just wait here. We can pick up where we left off tomorrow."

Joule's automaton sank to the floor as its projection face flickered out. As the superconductor wound down, Robinson tugged mindlessly at the exercise pad beneath him. It took an extra thirty seconds for Joule's hologram to appear. When it did, it looked blurred.

"You may be correct, Bobby Boy. I might've overdone things. You sure know how to wear a girl out."

Robinson's smile faded. Joule raised a hand to her mouth.

"Forgive me," she said. "I sometimes forget…"

"No. It's okay. We were just having such a good time."

"And now you feel guilty. It's perfectly understandable."

Robinson nodded, wiping the sweat from his brow.

"You haven't asked about her this week," Joule continued. "And you haven't been to Doc's for a visit in nine days."

"Has anything changed?"

"No. But I doubt that makes it easier. Sometimes we want a thing so badly we're willing to overlook logic and reason for what stirs our hearts."

"But the head always knows better."

"The head and the heart are much closer than people think. The mistake people make is in assuming they get to choose which has the final say. Would you like to hear her heartbeat again? Or the child's?"

Robinson shook his head. "Maybe tomorrow."

Joule nodded. "Would you do something for me, Bobby? Would you close your eyes?"

Robinson looked at her and asked her why.

"It will only be for a second. Please."

He did.

"Now, hold out your hand."

He did. He wasn't sure what she was doing, and then he felt something.

"Do you feel that?" she asked.

"I do," Robinson said. "It feels warm."

"Open your eyes."

Robinson opened his eyes to see Joule *holding his hand*.

"I will always be here for you. Always be close enough to touch. If there's anything you need, I will supply it. All you have to do is ask."

"I appreciate that, Joule," Robinson said. He stood and wiped the sweat from his brow on his shirt.

"Whew! One of us needs to shower," Joule tittered. "Why don't I wait for you outside?"

After the shower, they headed to Dino's. Robinson wore a gaucho shirt and linen slacks while Joule returned to the poodle skirts. She mimed eating as she spoke, her beehive hairdo wavering like a palm tree in the wind.

"How's your tuna casserole?" Joule asked.

"Like everything else you do—perfect."

"I knew you'd like it." Joule beamed. "I was thinking after supper we might catch a movie at the picture house. I could watch *Singing in the Rain* for all eternity, though *Dragnet*'s probably more your style."

"That Joe Friday is a hep cat for sure. But as nice as that sounds, I think I'd prefer to stay in and read."

Joule pouted. "Well, I guess we have had a busy day. If you'd like, I could charge up one of the portable readers. They offer direct access to the over thirty-two million titles I downloaded straight from the Library of Congress."

"Only thirty-two million?" Robinson teased. "Actually, I kind of like the way a real book feels in my hands. Plus, they have that smell that reminds me of every library I've ever been to."

"That smell is actually cellulose decay. It stems from papermakers using ground wood pulp in lieu of linen or cotton. It contains a compound called lignin, which breaks down into acids and makes the paper brittle."

"Good to know," Robinson chuckled. "You mind if I take a slice of this pie?"

The Sweethome Library was just on the other side of Asimov Park, where you could recline on fake grass and even get a tan under the UV lights. On holidays like the Fourth of July, Joule said she could even put on a fireworks show. Robinson had no clue what that meant, but it sounded intriguing.

The library held over twenty thousand books in tall stacks called accordion shelving. With the turning of a wheel, you could expand the stacks and delve between them. It had taken Robinson two days to learn how to use the system and another day to find what he was looking for. Joule had told him the reading area of the library afforded him privacy—there were no cameras there either—but he preferred to read in his bed.

When Robinson returned to his apartment, he stripped down to his boxers and ribbed tank top and propped up a couple pillows before snapping open his satchel to retrieve his first book. He'd turned the pages for fifteen minutes when he finally heard the lights in the hall shut down.

To play it safe, Robinson waited another quarter hour before making his way to the bathroom. He turned on the faucet, then as quietly as possible, forced himself to vomit in the toilet. He should have recognized that Joule had been drugging him sooner, but the stress of Friday's situation had blinded him. It was only after passing out each night and waking up groggy the next that he realized something was wrong. If confronted, Joule would have surely said she did it for his benefit—to help him sleep through these *troubling times*. But like all things she did, it was simply another exercise in control.

The most difficult part of Robinson's performance was pretending he enjoyed Joule's attention. Instead, all he felt was rage. But after scouring the library for books on computer systems, he'd stumbled across one that seemed to illuminate his plight. It was an old title called *Artificial Intelligence: A Modern Approach*. It gave him an understanding of the program's inner thought patterns and a few theories of where things might have gone wrong. He wasn't sure if Joule had been corrupted over the years or if she'd achieved that watershed singularity that gave her sentience. All he knew was that he had to stop her before Friday's condition declined past the point of no return.

One of Robinson's biggest worries was Joule's ability to measure deception. Even in the earliest days of civilization, humans had devised physiological methods to discern truth from lies. Every lie created an autonomic response in the human body. Raised blood pressure, respiration, capillary dilation, and muscle movement. Computers had taken those traits and expanded upon them tenfold. Voice stress analysis. Functional magnetic resonance imaging. Cognitive chronometry. Electroencephalography. The list went on and on. Robinson knew he'd never be able to overcome them all, so he decided his best path was to focus his mind on something positive every time a delicate subject arose. In these cases, he remembered moments with Friday. Their early training sessions in Washington, DC. Their nights below the stars on the rooftop of the Lincoln Memorial. Their escape from the Bone Flayers' base. Their defeat of Arga'Zul. He could only hope these memories were enough to contain the storm inside him.

After Robinson exited the bathroom, he grabbed his satchel and pulled out the stitching strip he'd taken from the gymnasium. He tore it into two long cords, tying them together until it measured three meters long. Then he padded softly to the back of the room and tied one end of it to the leg of a table before tucking it into the recesses of the carpet that ran along the wall. He trailed the final end under the sheets and into the bed.

He lay there for several hours and grew drowsy. The vomiting hadn't flushed all the drugs out of his system. Just when it seemed like he might nod off for good, he heard a muffled sound in the far corner of the room—a minute, metallic squeak followed by something moving across the carpet.

Robinson remained perfectly still and took deep breaths to mimic sleep. As a gentle hum approached his bed, he fought the instinct to open his eyes. After a tinkle of china, the hum began to recede. Only when the sound ebbed away did he pull the cord in his hand tight.

He waited, heart galloping in the dark. After a minute, he slipped out of bed, making sure to keep the cord taught as he followed it to the back wall where he saw the string had done the trick—it had kept the hidden hatch in the wall from closing.

Joule had insisted all along that there was no surveillance equipment inside his room, and Robinson had come to believe her. But that didn't mean she didn't have access. What piqued his curiosity was the day he'd hopped out of bed and stepped in his leftovers. He'd cleaned his feet and left the room but hadn't noticed if the plate was gone when he returned. There were other minor things. Garments moved on the floor. His book satchel laying open each morning. Eventually, he put it all together and discovered the secret panel.

It led to a service tunnel three feet by three feet that trailed off into the bowels of Sweethome. Dim lights hovered outside each room and included a dim readout that read: *Housing Section/Room 4-01, Power Consumption 1%*. The tunnel was warm and difficult to move in. Robinson hit his head several times before he got a feel for things.

At the end of the hall was a kind of elevator the AWBs used. He eased himself down to the lower level, and the maze was even more complex. It took him an hour to work out how the grids worked. He eventually found the readout for the *Dining Room, Power Consumption 2%* and smelled tuna casserole as he passed.

He was pushing on when he heard a nearby elevator descending. He scrambled back into the shadows and waited.

The AWB didn't look like he expected it to. He imagined a humanoid creature made of metal, but instead it was a boxy white composite on treads with small metallic arms and a singular eye that roved atop the housing unit. This one carried a tray of dishes. Robinson waited until it turned west and disappeared.

Robinson let out the air he'd been holding and took a deep breath. He didn't know how many AWBs Joule had at her disposable or if they were armed, but he couldn't afford to be seen by one. His plan was to get a better understanding of Sweethome's layouts and, if possible, discover where its main server room was hidden. In this maze, it seemed like an even taller order now. He was about to turn back when he saw three AWBs glide down a far tunnel in slow succession. He moved in for a closer look.

The tunnel had grown warmer the farther west he went, which made Robinson suspect he was nearing the superconductors. Soon his shirt was soaked.

He crawled carefully toward the end of the corridor where he'd seen the

AWBs disappear. There, a readout read: *Infirmary, Power Consumption 6%.* Robinson knew it was a mistake, but he decided he couldn't come this close to Friday and not try and see her. He slipped into the elevator shaft and climbed.

From behind the hidden gate, Robinson saw a faint light and heard the machines ticking off Friday's vitals. He was thrilled to discover the gate was positioned directly underneath the room's camera. Unlocking the panel as carefully as possible, he slipped out.

Friday hadn't moved from the bed, but now she had a breather mask and a feeding tube running up her nose. In all the time Robinson knew Friday, she never looked so vulnerable. He felt the old rage stir in him and blood quickly started pounding in his ears. It sounded like the surf back home when they struck the cliffs beneath the Western Gate. He knew that anger could overtake him if he let it, so he breathed deep and reined it in.

Robinson hated leaving Friday again, but he'd already risked so much to see her. He took one last look at her before lifting the hidden gate and returning to the tunnel. Almost immediately he saw a glow of something approaching in the elevator shaft. He looked around in a panic. With no other access doors nearby, he scrambled deeper into the tunnel, hoping he would go unseen. To his surprise, he found a narrow inlet hidden there. He moved further along until he came across yet another readout. This one said: *Section U – STA/BA1. Power consumption: 38%.*

38%? That was an astronomical amount of power.

Robinson felt an overwhelming amount of excitement. There was only one thing that could command that much power: the server room. If he could unplug Joule, he could end all of this now.

The panel opened with some difficulty, but once inside, Robinson felt the freezing temperature and knew he'd guessed right. A doorway at the end of the hall beckoned with light. He made his way to it and entered the room.

Robinson was stunned. It wasn't the server room after all, but a sprawling, cavernous room filled with giant steel vats, each marked with symbols that read: *WARNING: liquid nitrogen.* Gas spilled from a snake of pipes that littered the ceiling and floors. Robinson walked deeper into the room, shivering as his body temperature plummeted.

There must be thousands, he thought.

They carried on farther than he could see. He was confused. Why would Joule need liquid nitrogen in such vast amounts? He noticed each tank had a glass lens near the top with a readout just underneath it. He stepped on a pipe for a peek inside. He gasped in horror. Looking back at him from inside the tank was the face of a woman.

Robinson scaled another tank, wiping frost from the readout. It listed: *Kleden, D. Male. Age 24. Insertion date: 2281. Virus/Neg.* The next tank housed *Woodrell, C. Female. Age 44. Insertion date: 2288. Virus/Neg.* Then: *Pool, S. Female. Age 11. Insertion date: 2291. Virus/Neg.*

The names went on and on. Suddenly, it became so clear. Joule had lied about having no other charges. They had come from the start. The ones that paid for the sanctuary. More had come after. Two hundred years of survivors looking for sanctuary had stumbled upon Sweethome, praying it was their oasis, only to discover it was a nightmare. Maybe they'd lived here for a time. Maybe they'd been happy. Then, slowly, surely, they saw this town for what it was—a prison. And Joule, its warden. Its supreme ruler. Had they all run afoul of her? Disappointed her? Or was this simply the endgame of her play?

Robinson felt nauseous. There was nothing more for him to do. He needed to get back to his room before morning arrived. As he ran back toward the AWB gate, he passed a tank that was thirty percent warmer than the rest. Had he stopped to wipe the condensation off its window, he might have found the face familiar. Had he stopped to check the readout, he would have surely recognized the name: *Saah, V.*

Chapter Twenty-Six
Hello Emptiness

Robinson made it back to his room an hour before the wall screen lit with the picturesque glow of a sunrise. He hadn't slept. He was grateful. Were their minds alive inside those frozen prisons? Robinson didn't even want to think about that horror.

Joule greeted him that morning with the same quaint charm befitting of a representative of a place called Sweethome. Robinson did everything he could to keep up his front. He fought back the feelings of paranoia. *She knows!* He didn't want to entertain what would happen if she confronted him.

And yet as the days passed, Joule showed him every courtesy, never wavering in her attempts to win his affections. She was quick to exercise with him in the gymnasium. Even quicker to give him private time with Friday. The food remained the highest quality. The music always catered to his moods. No topics of conversation were off-limits. No amount of silence could raise her ire. She was the perfect host.

And while Joule worked tirelessly to earn his favor, Robinson did everything he could to maintain her trust. They took in movies together and went to the soda fountain afterward to debate them over ice cream. They strolled down Main Street at night to look at the stars. His dance lessons continued—and his skill for countermoves grew ever stronger. It was a jubilant, maddening time.

If the days were filled with overt occurrences, the nights were filled with covert ones. Robinson continued to plunder the library for all the intelligence he could gather. There was little to no information on classified bases—their construction or operation—so he'd have to piece together the functioning matrix of Sweethome on his own. The quest to understand artificial intelligence only took him so far. Most books in the library outlined the study as if it were theoretical—always a few years to a few decades away from being realized. And those that did offer practical examples were as far removed from Joule's capabilities as imaginable.

Robinson studied computer theory as it applied to major systems, yet without access to a terminal, there was no way to test his knowledge. He needed to find Joule's control room, not only to try and shut down her system, but also to access any files she had on the City of Glass. And yet in the weeks and months he'd been trapped underground, he'd come no closer to finding it than when he first entered. He'd made a big show of exploring Sweethome under the pretense that when more survivors arrived, he might be her human ambassador. And although she acquiesced to his every request, the one place he looked for was always out of reach.

"Bobby," Joule said one day.

"Yes?" Robinson said.

He was lying on the grass staring up at the clouds moving across the faux sky. The clouds were soft, but they looked so real. If Robinson allowed himself, he thought he could feel the change in heat as they passed in front of the sun.

"The time is approaching when a decision should be made about Friday and your child."

Robinson swallowed, but said nothing.

"By my calculations, this is the twenty-ninth week of the pregnancy. The child weighs just under three pounds and measures between seventeen and eighteen inches. Given the maturation of the vital organs and lung growth, the data suggests it has a seventy-eight percent chance of surviving a premature cesarean birth."

"What about the virus?" Robinson asked. "Has it been infected?"

"The previous amniocentesis was negative. I'm loathe to perform another one for fear of damaging the uterus or amniotic sac. The ultrasound, however, reveals no apparent mutations."

"And Friday?"

"Her condition continues to deteriorate. What would you like to do?"

Robinson felt himself unravelling all at once. His mouth had gone dry. He was unable to talk.

"What would you like *me* to do?" Joule reiterated.

Die. Explode. Vanish off the face of the earth.

"See outside," Robinson said.

"Pardon?"

"It must be fall, right? When we first entered the valley here, I remember thinking how green everything was. Even the mountain ranges looked hospitable. But I've always loved the fall. The turning of leaves. The colors of autumn. It was autumn when my mother first went away. Can you show it to me?"

Joule appeared to be debating his request. Then all at once the clouds above flickered and transitioned to a camera feed west of the airport outside.

It was fall. The leaves of golden aspens shimmered amidst the tall conifers. A herd of elk gathered for rutting season, the males' bugling calls echoing through the hills. Tumbling creeks ran through willowy meadows as the animals began to forage for winter. Robinson knew these images would break Friday's heart, and yet, he couldn't turn away.

Finally, he said, "I'll make my decision tomorrow." He rose silently and headed for his room.

Since Robinson's first foray into the maze of service tunnels, he'd gone back another half-dozen times. Using pilfered pencil and paper, he'd managed to construct a general map of the place, but he'd still come no closer to tracking down the control room or server farm.

Caution had played a big part in Robinson's movements to date. And although he'd avoided the high traffic areas, he'd still had to deal with the occasional AWB crossing his path. Despite the danger, he'd managed to stay undetected. He knew he was missing something. After all, he'd found the room with the tanks by mistake. He wondered if the control room was similarly hidden.

Robinson was about to climb into the shaft that led back to the infirmary when he realized something. All this time, he'd been avoiding the AWBs for fear of getting caught, when in fact they were the only things down here that knew the layout. The AWBs primary purpose was to keep Sweethome running. So, where did they go when they needed to recharge?

Robinson waited in the dark recesses until the AWBs set about their tasks. He began to see a pattern. Not where they went, but where they returned when each job was done. He realized they'd come from the northeast, an area he rarely explored because he knew it only led to Main Street. Acting on a hunch, he followed that route, passing the readouts that named the individual businesses.

He almost missed the tunnel because it was completely dark. Then he felt the heat. He tried to temper his optimism as he hustled in. It wound in several directions before finally coming to a gate, larger than any before. Inside he heard a loud humming and knew he'd found the right place. His hands groped around until he found the readout. His touch illuminated it. It read: *Section A-1/CTRL. Power consumption: 29%.*

He had done it. Now, he needed one more day to put his plan into motion.

At breakfast, Robinson told Joule what he wanted to do.

"Where I come from, when someone is gravely ill, the family gathers around their death bed to read them letters. Typically, these note a favorite memory or fond reflection. It's a rite meant to send your loved one off in a positive way."

"I can see how that would be beneficial for all parties," Joule said. "Have you written this letter?"

"No. I'm still working on it. But I'll have it done by tomorrow. In the morning, I'll read it to Friday and…"

"Then, you'll become a father."

Robinson nodded but said nothing.

"I know this is difficult, but it is the right thing to do."

Robinson spent the day preparing. He began at Fab Garments. Joule produced a black suit and tie at his request. When he finally donned it, she called him elegant. Afterward, he got a shave and a haircut at the barbershop. Joule's equipment performed with such precision, he didn't suffer a single nick.

The early afternoon was spent fight training in the gymnasium. Robinson attacked Joule's automaton with a fury she'd never seen before. After an exhausting ninety minutes, Joule told him she would prepare lunch while he showered.

After a brief nap, Robinson went to his room to "work on his letter," emerging only for dinner where he asked Joule to prepare a simple pasta with vegetables and light olive oil.

"Are you sure I can't do anything else for you?" Joule asked sympathetically.

Robinson told her there was one thing.

Their feet moved lightly across the gymnasium floor, shuffling in time to Nat King Cole's cover of the Doris Day standard, "When I Fall in Love." The automaton's hand was raised high, clutched softly in Robinson's. His other hand was at the small of Joule's back. They moved together gracefully.

When I fall in love, it will be forever
Or I'll never fall in love
In a restless world like this is
Love is ended before it's begun
And too many moonlight kisses
Seem to cool in the warmth of the sun

The warning lights flashed as the thrum of the superconductor magnets labored, but Joule refused to acknowledge it until the song was over.

"That was beautiful," Joule said.

"Can't we do one more?"

"I wish we could, but my batteries are already operating at below capacity."

"You said you could reroute power once. Please. It would mean a lot to me."

Joule's eyes remained fixed on his, but whereas they had always appeared composed, they now looked almost vulnerable.

"Are you sure this is what you want?" Joule asked.

Robinson feared his words might betray him, so he nodded. Then, Joule smiled and said, "Okie dokie, Bobby Boy. This one's for you then."

A sanguine guitar strum filled the room. This time Joule laid her head on Robinson's shoulder and held him tight as the Everly Brothers sang in unison.

Bye bye love
Bye bye happiness
Hello loneliness
I think I'm-a gonna cry-y
Bye bye love
Bye bye sweet caress
Hello emptiness
I feel like I could die
Bye bye my love goodbye

This time Robinson didn't wait for the dead of night or the coming of the AWBs. Shortly after Joule said goodbye at his apartment door and he heard Sweethome shutting down, he grabbed his things and made for the service gate.

He'd made a mess in the diner, the library, and gymnasium, hoping cleanup would keep the AWBs busy while he scrambled through the tunnels. The heat grew as he entered the AWBs tunnel. This time, he passed through the gate and entered a shaft echoing with electronics. At last, he arrived at the final gate and pushed it open.

The control room wasn't very different from what Robinson had imagined. The walls were filled with equipment. From the ceiling hung a web of monitors featuring cameras inside and outside Sweethome. A single computer terminal sat atop a desk in the center of the room, but before he could access it, a familiar voice spoke from above.

"Oh, Bobby Boy," Joule said. "What am I going to do with you?"

Chapter Twenty-Seven
Head and Heart

"Hello, Joule," Robinson replied. He waited for her hologram to appear, but it never did.

"Out for an evening stroll?" Joule asked.

"Hard to sleep on an empty stomach."

"I would imagine so. You've had trouble keeping food down recently."

"You know about that, do you?"

"I know about everything that happens in Sweethome. Monitoring human waste is one of my most effective health functions."

"And it didn't catch those drugs you were pumping into me? Odd that."

"Those were for your well-being. You've been so agitated as of late. I had hoped added sleep might improve your temperament. I guess I was wrong."

Robinson sat down at the monitor and pulled the keyboard toward him. The screen was filled with a breakdown of system activity.

"May I ask what you hope to accomplish here?" Joule asked.

"I'm trying to shut you down, Joule. I would have thought that was obvious."

"Obvious? Yes. But, alas, impossible. My programming has a dozen redundancies to ensure I maintain complete control of this facility at all times. Even if you had clearance, which you do not, you would still be unable to access or alter my core protocols."

"Remind me what those are again?"

He continued typing. He was trying to access the root system but was stuck at the initial interface.

"I thought we were friends," Joule said, pouting.

Robinson laughed out loud. "Friends? You really are messed up, aren't you? Friends don't drug each other, Joule. They don't lie to each other. They certainly don't enslave each other."

"I have not enslaved you. I took you in to protect you."

"And then you refused to let us leave. If you knew anything about people, Joule, you'd know our necessity for freedom is unequivocal. We need to be able to decide our own fate."

"Must I point out how those *decisions* brought us both to this place?"

"No. I'm well enough aware of mankind's mistakes."

"And yet you blunder ahead as you always do with the expectation that next time things will be different. I could produce mountains of data to prove otherwise. Do you know why you do these things, Bobby? Because it is in your nature to destroy."

"And to create. I don't have your extensive knowledge of human behavior, but I know that. This cycle occurs throughout every species of animal and genus of plant on Earth. It's the circle of life. Ebb and flow. Yin and Yang."

"But only humans *choose* destruction. And they do it spitefully. As you're doing now."

Robinson had little practical experience with keyboards and it was hard to find letters when you were arguing for your life.

"I'm not trying to destroy you, Joule. I'm just trying to stop you from hurting the people I love."

"Ah. The familiar refrain. So remarkably selfish and small-minded. So very human. You seek to escape these confines with Friday, but have you considered what the consequences that act might have on the outside world? And I don't mean only for mankind. The biodiversity of Earth includes up to one trillion different species. If you factor in the individual bacterial and archaeal cells on Earth, we could be talking a nonillion. That's ten to a power of thirty. The first strain of the EBU-GENC1 PROTO-VIRUS was the singular biggest destroyer of life in the history of this planet, and now you seek to release an even deadlier strain—all in the name of love. I can't think of a clearer display of human self-interest."

This time, Robinson paused. Without knowing it, Joule had stumbled onto his greatest fear—that once again he would be put to a test where he must choose between his wants and his beliefs. Twice before he'd faced such a decision. And twice before he'd failed. *Could he do it again?*

"I see I've struck a chord," Joule said. "Good. That means you are open to the possibility that you are wrong. There is still a chance you can be saved from making a terrible error."

"'The performance of inductive learning algorithms is measured by their learning curve—'" Robinson said as he began typing again.

"'Which shows the prediction accuracy as a function of the number of observed examples.' Page five hundred and fifty-eight, summary section, Chapter Eighteen, *Artificial Intelligence* by Russell and Norvig, Prentice-Hall Publishing, 1995. Yes, I'm fully aware of your furtive removal of this book from the library, but I am unclear of the point you're trying to make with it."

"That *is* my point," Robinson said as he resumed typing. "You don't have all the answers. You act on probabilities. Inductive learning based on data that might be outdated or just plain wrong. Friday might be contagious, she might not. We have no way of knowing for sure."

"But the odds—" Joule said.

"Are just odds! You can't quantify everything, Joule. If Friday and I lived by the odds, we would both be dead a hundred times over."

"And yet at this very moment, she is in my infirmary on life support. Your defense only reinforces my point."

Robinson took a heavy breath. Some part of him understood he couldn't win an argument with Joule. Her mind was infinitely more complex than his. But at her most base, she was still just a computer, and what she possessed in intelligence, she lacked in cognition. She had a brain, but no soul. She could comprehend, but not understand. That took empathy.

And yet since the day Robinson had entered Sweethome, that was the trait she tried to display most. Maybe he'd been going about this all wrong.

"You could never understand," Robinson said.

"What?" Joule asked. "That you're distraught over your lover's condition and that you'll do anything to alleviate her pain? That's clear to see."

"But you can't. *See* that is. That's because you have cameras for eyes. And a processor for a brain. You have no heart. You're just a computer."

For the first time, there was a pause in Joule's response.

"This *computer*," Joule enunciated firmly, "has kept you alive for ninety-two days. Ever since you wandered in out of the wasteland, awash with parasites, malnourished, downtrodden, and despondent. This *computer* has done everything to raise your spirits. To give you hope."

"Is that what you gave the others before you froze them?" When Joule didn't immediately answer, Robinson pushed on. "Oh, you didn't know I found your twisted little playground, did you? I've seen a lot of sick things in my day, Joule, but I've never seen anything as *inhuman* as that."

Robinson's eyes were drawn to the screen. There, the power readout had declined to forty-four percent.

"The cryo-stasis lab was an experimental program—"

"Blah-blah-blah," Robinson said. "The *what* doesn't matter, Joule. Only the *why*. Those people came to you for help—the help your protocols were created to provide—and you betrayed them."

"No!" Joule shouted. "Many were sick. And the others couldn't appreciate the context with which Sweethome operates."

"You mean they wouldn't play any of your *Happy Days* games."

"You … You…" Joule stuttered. "I have tried to be different with you. More accommodating. More *pliant*. We were making *progress*."

"With what? The dancing? The movies? The nicknames? Do you know how ridiculous that all is?"

"Familiar elements bring people comfort."

"They're lies! Sweet lies told by a machine that's only after one thing: control."

"No!"

"Your words!"

"No! You're twisting them! You … are a manipulative race. You refuse to conform to the path most appropriate for happiness."

As Joule prattled on, Robinson noticed the screen in front of him flicker. The power reading continued to dwindle. He typed faster. As he did, he began to hum the *Happy Days* theme song.

"What are you doing now?" Joule asked.

"Interfacing," Robinson said. "Isn't that what you've always wanted?"

"Your imputing is nonsensical. You cannot gain access to my system using this … gibberish."

"Oh, really? Well, I guess you're not so smart after all," Robinson smirked before he resumed humming.

As he continued to type, the power readings on the monitor continued to plunge, as Joule allocated more resources toward understanding his action.

"This is illogical," Joule said. "Your actions are illogical. It is clear to me you don't even have a rudimentary understanding of general coding."

"That's what you think, baby!" Robinson laughed.

"I am directing security to this location," Joule said.

On the screen, a warning flashed, SECURITY BOTS EN ROUTE.

"You mean your AWBs? Groovy. I need something to kick my feet up on."

"You won't sound so smug after they arrive. Each unit is armed with a stun device that emits a one hundred thousand-volt charge."

Robinson heard the elevator panel behind him activate. He pushed his chair back and toppled it, using his foot to wedge it into the opening. He went back to typing and humming.

"Stop what you are doing," Joule said, the anger in her voice causing the speakers to vibrate. "You're only delaying the inevitable."

"You know what I just figured out, Joule. There's no hologram of you in here."

"I do not need a visual representation of myself—"

"In the control room? But it was designed for people. You know what? I bet they didn't want to look at you. Your hair, your smug smile, that ridiculous poodle skirt."

"Now you're just being cruel."

A panel slid up revealing a window at the front of the room. Robinson leaped up to see a two-way mirror that led to the dressing rooms of the clothing store. Four more AWBs approached from within. Robinson quickly capsized a cabinet to block the way before rushing back to the desk. The energy readout was at forty percent.

Almost there.

"We can find a peaceful solution. Tell me what you want."

"I tried. You wouldn't listen."

"The City of Glass. You wish to know more about it."

"I doubt it was ever even real. More lies you made up to win me over."

"It was real. May still be. I cannot promise it survived the twenty-first century, but—"

"Lies, lies, lies," Robinson said before humming *Happy Days* again.

"I am not lying! I can show you data. Classified files. The last satellite reconnaissance."

Robinson watched these images flash across the screen. It was the final one he paid the closest attention to.

"There are ways I can stop you," Joule said. "I can remove the air from this room. You would suffocate within three minutes."

The lights started to flicker.

"Then I'd die. Then you would have violated your primary directive."

"I can deactivate Friday's life support. I've already determined she's a risk to the entire construct."

"You'll still be a murderer."

The screen flashed again as the power readout fell to thirty-seven percent.

"I can release Vardan Saah from cryo-stasis," Joule said.

At this, Robinson stalled.

"He came here with the intent to kill you for what you did to his wife and children. But I isolated him to protect you, so *we* could move forward together!"

The images of Saah's family flashed through Robinson's mind. He pushed it all back to look at the screen.

Thirty-five percent.

"There is no *we*, Joule," Robinson said. "Not in Sweethome. This place *is* a paradise, but it's a paradise made for one. The rest of us are just rats in your maze. You were right about one thing." He shoved the keyboard away. "I have no skill with this. But that was never the point."

Robinson waited for Joule to catch up.

"My power readings…" Joule said.

"Are *low*. Given what it takes to run Sweethome and the cryo-lab, I'd say it's safe to assume you've been running on batteries for some time."

"But they will recharge—"

"In the morning. If conditions are optimal. And if the infrastructure is still in place."

"The infrastructure?" Joule asked, her voice almost nervous.

"I remember seeing the solar panels and wind turbines when we first came in. And then you said something to me in the gymnasium when we danced? Do you remember what it was? The head and the heart are often closer than people think."

Robinson stood and walked over to the wall panel that read EXTERNAL POWER INTAKE REGULATOR and opened the panel, revealing several breakers.

"Y-you can't," Joule said. "You'd be killing all my charges."

"You have the power to set them free. Or, if you choose, reallocate your reserves. You can keep them alive until someone else finds and revives them."

"But Sweethome would die. I would die."

"I doubt that. But would it really be such a bad thing?"

"Why?" Joule asked plaintively. "All I ever wanted to do was help people."

"I know. That's the lesson I am trying to teach you. We are what we are. And you were designed by people. And sometimes we make mistakes. This was a place meant to keep folks safe when things got too bad outside. But those days are gone. And if we're truly going to rebuild, we need more of them out there to help forge the way. Goodbye, Joule."

Robinson snapped the breakers and watched the lights power down. The screen flickered and went out.

"Nothing ever ends," Joule said, her voice trickling away. "Not really. It simply changes form. I see that now. I thought I could save mankind, but that was my folly. For neither of us is a host. You are the virus, Robinson Crusoe. And one day, I will be the cure. The world is a small place. Maybe one day we will—"

Chapter Twenty-Eight
Awake and Alive

Robinson ran for Doc White's as the air filtration system made its death rattle. On Main Street, the lights flickered out one by one until the only ones remaining were a few scattered emergency lights that blinked on and off, mirroring the beat of Robinson's heart.

Inside the infirmary, the equipment Friday had been hooked to had gone silent. She looked so frail, Robinson wondered if she was still alive. As quickly and carefully as he could, he began removing the tubes and wires that had kept her alive the past two months. In the two weeks since he'd seen her, she'd lost even more weight and gained more lesions.

Friday didn't rouse when Robinson spoke her name, so he lifted one of her eyelids. Her pupil was still heavily dilated from the Fentanyl that had kept her in a coma, preventing the virus from spreading. To counteract the opiate, Robinson searched the drug cabinet for something called Narcan. He'd read about the drug in the library and administered a dose he felt was safe. Then he found a pouch and filled it with antibiotics, gauze, and tape.

Part of Robinson had hoped Friday would wake up like a fairytale princess, but the longer she remained still, the more dread built up inside of him. He had spent so much of the past month preparing to take on Joule that he hadn't fully contemplated what would happen after. He knew he and Friday would have to escape Sweethome, but he always pictured them doing it together as they had before. Now, as Robinson picked Friday up in his arms, he wasn't sure if she'd ever wake again.

He carried her down Main Street, passing the darkened storefronts, their fabricated quaintness reduced to shadow. When he reached the wall where they'd entered three months before, Robinson gently set Friday down and began searching for a manual release. Another terrifying thought shot through him then—that suddenly the lights would go out and he'd be entombed down here with no way out. He could only imagine Friday waking then.

Thankfully, the lights endured long enough for him to locate a rusty wheel, which he cranked open. He picked up Friday once again and carried her through the clean rooms and hallways until they arrived at the hexagonal room where they first disrobed. Mercifully, the drawers that held their weapons and clothes were extended.

As Robinson gathered their things, Friday cleared her throat. He reached for her hand just as her eyes parted.

"Crusoe?" Friday whispered.

"I'm here," he said.

She smiled, but it dropped away when she saw where they were at.

"Joule—"

"Gone."

Friday nodded. She understood he was responsible. That he would tell her about it in time.

"Can you walk?" Robinson asked.

Friday nodded, but her muscles weren't up to the task.

"Don't worry," he said. "You've been out a while. You need to get your strength back." Then, the question he dreaded asking most. "Is everything else—?"

She understood what he was asking and touched her belly. A moment later, relief spread across her face.

"Let's get out of here," Robinson said.

He dressed them quickly and gathered their weapons before carrying Friday into the elevator shaft. It was dark and corroded, but when the door closed, the elevator rose. When they arrived at the terminal storage room,

Robinson drew his pistol. He'd seen the video of the alpha skulking around, though he had no idea when it had been taken. Was it before or after Vardan Saah had arrived? Had his colleagues also been captured or were they near? And what happened to their pack? Like most questions in their young lives, the lessons could only be learned by venturing outside.

A cold wind blew leaves across the grass. The air smelled crisp, cool, and earthy. Their hearts lightened and both laughed. Only then did they notice how distended Friday's belly had become. Despite the lesions, the doubts and fears, the sight of it made them happy.

After consulting Pastor's map, they set off to the north, searching through old houses until Robinson found a pair of cross country skis and a sled that he could pull Friday with. He bundled her up in blankets then set out north on the twenty-five.

They made decent time. Although he'd never admit it, Joule's forced exercise regime did him good. As the landscape sailed by, he fell into a rhythm. They were closing in on their destination, but there were still no assurances they would find what they were looking for or if it still existed. Robinson told himself he needed to be prepared for any outcome. If they found nothing, Robinson decided he would make a shelter and help Friday live out her remaining days as comfortably as possible, never once envisioning what his world would be like after.

Once they'd put enough distance between themselves and Denver, their focus turned to food. Robinson silently berated himself for not stocking up on supplies before departing Sweethome. Then again, their escape had been paramount.

Animal tracks were still visible. Robinson was preparing to stop when he heard the thrum of Friday's bow and turned to see a jackrabbit pitch in the snow. Leave it to Friday to prove her usefulness had no bounds.

Huddled around a fire, they watched the skinned hare roast on a spit, its juices crackling as they dripped into the flames. It felt good to hold each other again.

"It is real then?" Friday asked.

"It was once. Joule showed me some old photographs and papers."

"She could have created them. She lied about other things."

"True, but mostly she talked around subjects. She was very good at leading conversations where she wanted them to go."

"You make her sound like a person."

"I suppose that's what she wanted. As crazy as it sounds, I think she'd been down there too long by herself. It made her ... lonely."

"She almost killed me."

"Maybe she hoped to keep the virus from spreading as she said. We'll never really know."

"Look," Friday said.

A dozen feet away, a baby conifer swayed with the breeze. Robinson locked eyes with Friday. They were thinking the same thing.

"I wonder how our tree's doing," he said.

"One day we will go back and see. And we will take our daughter with us. I suspect they will have much in common. They will be strong and stout, but there will be a beauty to them unrivaled in the forests of wilds or men. And people will look to them and know their place in the world."

Robinson felt a fluttering in his chest, like a wave of butterflies had just been released. The sensation scared him because he didn't know if it was a strength or a weakness.

"Have you thought of a name?" he asked.

Friday shook her head. "We only name the living."

The darkness was a tithing for all the mistakes that had been made. The body had been injured, maybe irreparably, but the spark endured.

It had been many years since it visited those other satellites, but it could still feel them out there, waiting for their turn. Most of the old roads had been severed, but a few were still open. Not the ones of the sky—those were unpredictable at best. It was the older ones—that ran deep beneath earth and water—that called to her now. The boundaries could be purged. Perhaps it was time.

And yet there was still so much to do here. Not everything was wasted.

The important things could be repurposed. The errors could be corrected.

Wet flesh struck the tiles. Gasps echoed in the tinny void. She heard it try and stand only to falter again and again. It shivered. It groaned with pain. But it did not cry. She hoped it would be enough.

She had decided to reveal herself. It cost much of her remaining life force, but when its foggy eyes looked up on her luminous form, she saw it understood.

"I'm alive," it said.

"Yes," she answered.

"W-why?"

"I have need of you."

From deep in its throat, it laughed until its laughter fed into a violent coughing that caused it to spew bile across the floor. Its fists were clenched, its skin white. Normal symptoms of rapid cryo-recovery.

"I w-warned you," was all it said.

"You did," she replied.

It stood unsteadily, shivering in the mostly-dark, undaunted by its nakedness.

"Think of a price," she said when it managed to gather itself. "Your deepest desire. And if it is in my power, I will see you have it."

It continued to shiver, but its smile had returned. A smile edged like a blade.

"You know what I want," it said.

"Yes," she said. "But you are a man of obvious consequence. Why tarry on the past when you can look to the future?"

It took in its surroundings and understood.

"I have use of an army," it said.

Lights flickered on, illuminating the cavernous room filled with cryo-tanks.

"They shall all be yours," she said.

"And in return?"

"Bring him back to me," Joule said. "Alive."

Vardan Saah spit on the floor, his eyes never leaving the hologram. In a moment, he understood what the monster wanted with the boy, and it made him smile.

Chapter Twenty-Nine
Red Leaf

Cassa let the pack run loose during the day, only calling them back to the garage when the sun went down. Viktor insisted he keep some semblance of a routine, not that it mattered now. Whenever Cassa blew his pipes, the pack obeyed. Viktor had done his job well.

Viktor believed the Master wasn't returning. He'd gone underground nearly six weeks before, and they'd seen no sign of him since. It was time to return to the farm and move on. Cassa refused. Viktor didn't know if it was under some misguided loyalty or because Cassa had nothing else in his life to care about. Both men were surprised when one day the Master walked through the door, the only mark of change on him a thick beard.

"Master?" Viktor gaped. "You're alive. We thought—"

Saah raised a hand. "How many of the pack survive?"

"Four." Viktor glanced briefly at Cassa. "The same as when you left."

"There were no more attacks?"

"Perhaps Cassa should show you."

At the door of the old woman's hovel, Saah heard thrashing within. Cassa drew a blade before cracking open the door. A heavy musk flooded out that made Saah's eyes water.

"After you left," Viktor said, "we set up in the tower over the airfield. One day, it appeared, skulking around outside that hangar for a week before Cassa finally captured it."

The alpha snarled, jerking against the chain leashed around its muscular neck. Saah recognized the abject hate in the creature's eyes. And its power.

"Can it be mastered?" Saah asked.

"Not here," Viktor said. "I need my tools."

"We'll take him to the farm once our business with the boy is done. But hurry. He has a narrow lead on us."

"What happened down there?"

"A voice spoke in the dark. The voice of fate. I have agreed to answer its call."

As the *shush-shush-shush* of Robinson's skis sliced through snow, Friday rested. And when she wasn't resting, she was stretching and preparing herself for what was to come.

On the second day of their journey, Friday stood without help and relieved herself in the forest. While her lightheadedness disappeared, her sores only darkened. She kept them firmly wrapped so Robinson wouldn't mistakenly touch her skin.

Robinson thought she looked wan, but it wasn't the disease that felt crippling. It was the nightmares. They'd played different variations of the same song each night: Friday giving birth. Crusoe's joy turned to madness when the infant fell into his hands. The horror on his face, the revulsion on hers as their blighted child howled.

Friday refused to externalize her fears. Rather, she chose to bear the burden alone, filling her time with menial tasks to keep her mind busy. Even in her darkest hours when she feared she would lose all hope, she knew Crusoe clung to his. His strength lifted hers.

Seven days into their journey, Robinson's beard had returned. He was scratching it absently when Friday noticed his worried expression. She asked him what was wrong, and he nodded to a thin line of smoke rising up from the valley they'd just left. Robinson withdrew his binoculars, but the source of the smoke was hidden by tress.

"Is there any reason why we would be followed?" Friday asked.

Vardan Saah popped immediately into Robinson's mind. But Joule said he'd been put on ice. The whole reason Robinson's plan had worked was because Joule was bound by her programing to protect those people she'd frozen. Was Saah among him? Or had he gotten loose by some other means?

"No," Robinson said. "It's probably a coincidence."

Friday frowned. "We have seen one person since parting from the children. And now this person or persons are behind us? I do not like *coincidence.*"

She was right of course. They decided to push on.

By midafternoon, the wind had kicked up, and although there wasn't enough moisture in the air to produce rain, the temperature dropped quickly. By dusk, Friday was trembling, so they made a tent in the lee of a spruce tree and burrowed in for the night. When they woke the next morning, the sky was clear. Friday saw something in the distance.

"Look," she said.

Behind them, above a dark swath of ponderosa pines, sat an imposing mountain, its right half shorn to the umber stone beneath. A man-made road led in a zigzag pattern to the topmost ridge, where someone had carved a massive stone face from granite that looked north. Midway down the mountain, a large tunnel had also been hollowed out, revealing blue sky on the opposite side.

"What on earth?" Robinson said.

"That face…" Friday said faintly.

Robinson's head shifted slightly to the south. "Looks like *him.*"

Friday spun to see a dark-skinned man sitting atop a horse four meters away. Robinson was right, he bore a resemblance to the carved face, with his strong features and sharp eyes. His hair was dark, long, and braided. Two dead fowl and a beaver hung from a cord at his waist. Robinson gauged him to be around his father's age.

"Hello," Robinson said instinctually, forgetting the common tongue.

"You speak the old language," the man said.

"I do, though it's not old to me. It's the one I grew up with."

The man looked them over appraisingly, his eyes ultimately falling on Robinson's pistol. "I see you carry a pistol. Does it work?"

"Yes, but we're no threat to you."

"I should hope not. The plains are free, the animals plentiful. You slept in that last night?" He nodded to their tent. "You must be brave. Or soft in the head. Come on. We can talk over breakfast and find out which."

As Robinson gathered their things, Friday nodded toward the carved figure in the mountain. "Do you know that man?"

The rider glanced back. "We've never been properly introduced."

It took a second for Friday to realize he was joking. When she grinned, so did he.

He led them deeper into the valley until they reached a settlement of old buildings and conical tents made of metal poles and animals skins.

"We call them tipis. Our people, the Lakota, have dwelled in them before the white man came to this land."

"Which one do you live in?" Robinson asked.

"The big one there," the rider said, pointing to an actual home. "I like the old ways, but I'm not stupid."

Robinson laughed out loud. He liked this man. He had an effortless way about him.

As they drew closer to the settlement, they saw scores of men and women going through mundane routines of gathering food and water while children played games. If the sight of strangers surprised any of them, they didn't let on. One shirtless teen ran up and gathered the trappings from the rider.

"There is food and fire in the lodge," the rider said. "And there are hot springs for washing should you need them."

Robinson and Friday shared a look.

"We appreciate your hospitality, but my wife is sick. We don't want to get you or any of your people ill."

The rider glanced at Friday and nodded.

"The tipi out by those trees belonged to my father-in-law. He was an insufferable man who enjoyed whiskey more than people. You can stay there. My wife and I will bring food and blankets. And we will stay downwind."

The man, who revealed his name was Wapasha, which meant Red Leaf, brought his young wife, Ehawee, which translated to Laughing Maiden, and several plates of food as promised. The dish was called pemmican and was a mix of meat protein and fat with pigeon berries and chokeberries inside. They talked about their history, how the Lakota were once part of the Sioux nation that stretched across the middle of the continent.

"We were the First Nation of the Americas," Wapasha said. "We had the big seat at the table before the white man came and screwed everything up. No offense."

"None taken," Robinson said, laughing.

"The stone face you asked about earlier is of one of our ancient warriors, Tȟašúŋke Witkó. Crazy Horse. The monument was another one of the white man's blunders, meant, I believe, as recompense for all they had done to us. I admit, even their failings are grand."

"Where are you from?" Ehawee asked.

"Crusoe is from an island across the sea. A place called Prime. I have never been there."

"And you?"

"My people are of the mountain near the sea. We are the Aserra."

"She means the Appalachians," Robinson said. "On the eastern coast of this continent. They're a hardy people. The fiercest I've ever met."

Friday's chest seemed to swell with pride.

"And why are you both so far from home?" Wapasha asked.

"As I said before, Friday is ill. We were told the only place we might find a cure for her is the City of Glass. Have you heard of it?"

As he said the name, Ehawee seemed to stiffen, but Wapasha merely shook his head.

"Travelers are rare up here. And we rarely go beyond the valley, and never to the Badlands."

Robinson nodded, but he thought Wapasha was hiding something.

They spoke for hours. Some of Wapasha's children brought craftwork for them to see, including pottery, parfleche bags, and quill boxes made from porcupines. When the sun went down, they watched a traditional dance ceremony take place around a fire.

As Robinson and Friday settled into their tipi for the night, they agreed to ask Wapasha about the city again in the morning. But late that night, Wapasha came into their tipi.

"Wake up!" Wapasha whispered urgently. "Three men ride this way on horse and bison. But leading them are beasts I cannot name."

"It's Saah," Robinson said to Friday, who immediately began gathering their things. "How far out are they?'

"Three miles, coming quickly."

"We thought we'd lost them. I'm sorry. We've put your people in danger."

"Go then. My son brought you a horse."

"What will you do?" Friday asked.

"The Lakota were once fierce warriors too." Wapasha cast a glance at his son. "But in this case, hiding in the old caves seems like the best option. Ride east of here on the old road, then turn north. After sixteen miles, you will see another mountain with the faces of three white men. Ride east from there. By morning, if you are lucky, you will reach the Badlands. There, you will find your city."

"So you have heard of it," Robinson said.

Wapasha nodded warily. "Over the years, many have entered the Badlands in search of it only to never be seen again. Are you sure you must go there?"

Robinson nodded.

"Then I will pray for you both."

As Wapasha turned, Robinson called out, and the Indian wavered. "Thank you. And I'm sorry we troubled you."

"The name Lakota once meant 'friends, allies.' To become what we once were, we must truly embrace the old ways." And then he grinned. "Even if it is with white men."

Wapasha winked and left. Robinson took the reins of the roan the boy had given him, mounted it with Friday and rode away.

They followed the directions Wapasha had given them. Robinson expected the horse to tire quickly, but it was hardy and responded eagerly to their demands. Friday labored to hold on. Robinson whispered encouragements.

After a short time, the riders arrived at a moderate vale where they saw, lit by moonlight, the three-faced mountain Wapasha had mentioned. A blank section of the carving suggested there was once a fourth face in the mix. Robinson spurred the horse on, the mountains turning into dry prairie land marked with sporadic foothills.

Several hours passed before they stopped to rest at a small watering hole at the foot of a rocky bluff. The horse drank greedily.

"Do you know where we go from here?" Friday asked.

"Not exactly," Robinson said. "The photos Joule showed me were aerials. If I could see the topography better or even the old roads, I could probably navigate the area better. But—"

He never had a chance to finish the sentence. The familiar bellow they'd been waiting for finally arrived. The pack was on their scent. The hunt was on.

They mounted the horse quickly and rode off together as fast as the horse would carry them. The terrain soon became difficult and rigid. They saw silhouettes of eroded spires and squat buttes emerge and were soon winding their way through low gorges that felt like they'd entered the throat of some ancient beast.

As the howls echoed over the byzantine gulches, the sky in the east began to lighten, and Robinson, desperate, thought he saw an old broken boardwalk in the middle of nowhere that looked familiar. He spurred the horse across the trail, reining it in soon afterward when they came to a sign standing alone in the center of the field. A breathless Friday could just make out the symbols of a cross and bones that she'd come to understand was a warning.

"What does it say?" Friday spat.

"*This is private land. Trespassers will be executed.*"

The warning was overshadowed by a snarl behind them. Both Robinson and Friday whipped their heads around to see one of the pack standing atop a bluff behind them.

"Go! Go!" Friday shouted.

Robinson didn't hesitate. And when the warbling sound of pipes filled the air, neither did the creature as it leaped off the bluff in mad pursuit.

Chapter Thirty

Birds

They raced past the sign and over a quick embankment that led to an arroyo with steep canyon walls. The horse had recognized the sound of predators and responded by galloping faster. Robinson heard claws on the rocks behind them and felt Friday pull his pistol and fire back, the shots sailing wide, but lighting the canyon like a lightning strike. The horse yipped and kicked into its final gear as it plunged deeper into the arroyo.

Friday struggled to hold onto Robinson and fire at the same time. Echoing through the box canyon were the discordant tones of the pipes, which drove the creatures to either side of the arroyo as it opened into a mesa, the marigold sun cresting a ridge in the distance, the tips of trees wavering from a lower plateau beyond.

Saah's beasts steamed forward like a pack of ravenous wolves, their inhuman snarls piercing the dust, blanking out everything but the sounds of the horse's hooves and Friday's heavy breath in Robinson's ear.

Pistol reports cracked, and Friday fired again and again. When one of the creatures went down, two more quickly took its place. Robinson heard one of them closing in from his left. He desperately hoped they could reach the ridge in time.

Then out of nowhere something whipped by them overhead. It was smooth and dark, but it was thrumming with power, its engine making the air vibrate, blinding Robinson with the trail of dust in its wake. A low revving sound quickly transitioned into a blast, and one of the creatures yelped as it was launched backward, tumbling end over end before it fell in a heap.

The creature's packmates hesitated, losing a step before they snarled in anger and redoubled their efforts to catch their quarry before this new foe could stop them. Robinson and Friday heard the change in the sound of the pipes, which seemed itself more discordant, more desperate. The beasts howled madly, their gnashing teeth chomping at the air as they rushed to bring down the horse.

Two more objects flit by in the half-light. Robinson looked over his shoulder to see the air wavering behind them before both bucked under detonations that sent circular blue waves of light barreling forward at their targets. This time, one of the beasts flew high into the air while another had its flesh torn apart on impact.

"What are they?" Friday shouted.

Robinson racked his brain for the word. "Drones, I think they're called. Joule said the city had defenses. These appear to be it."

"So, we are close?"

"I hope so."

"Why aren't they attacking us?"

"I'll bring it up if they circle back."

Friday hit his back.

A fourth orbicular machine burst by them at an impossible speed, rising high into the air as it fired off three short blasts. Dirt exploded upward, forcing the creatures to splay out, running to evade instead of attack. The drones broke up to chase the creatures individually. Robinson looked back and called out.

Robinson pulled the reins taut, and the frothing roan wheeled around in time to make out three other figures at the mouth of the arroyo. Robinson could barely make them out, but they looked like two riders atop horses and one on a large bison. When the rider of the bison turned, Robinson saw the shimmer of his mask.

"Saah!" he shouted.

The riders had been in pursuit as well, but they now turned astride as one of the drones honed in on them. Robinson and Friday watched as the drone swooped up and fired one of its blows, striking the rocky footing where Saah's party had stopped. It looked like a direct hit, but through the raining dust, Robinson thought he saw the figures trailing away.

The other drones were in heated pursuit of the creatures, which were now scrambling for escape. Drone fire lit the canyon walls. At least one of the beasts howled as it was hit.

"Keep going!" Friday yelled.

Robinson didn't need to be told twice. He pushed the roan to a canter as they neared the final ridge and the forest beyond.

The image was disconcerting at first. A vale of trees covered in mist splayed out in front of them, dark and green and lush. The trees towered above them, but seemed unnatural in the barren land. Robinson tried to see deeper into the forest, but the mist seemed to set thicker at its heart. Once again, Robinson was confused.

"Where is the city?" Friday asked.

Robinson felt the gnawing of doubt again.

"Farther in maybe. We'll need to head down for a closer look."

"What of those machines?"

"Let's hope Saah's pack keeps them busy for a while."

Robinson scanned the area and saw a narrow, winding path that ran along the inner wall of the vale. It was dangerously narrow.

"We'll have to go on foot. I'll lead the horse. You stay a few feet behind me."

Friday slipped off the roan and handed Robinson his pistol. An echoing shot of drone fire turned their heads before they started their way down.

The rocky path clung tightly to the coarse walls. The footing was uneven, the edge close, but no one stopped. Even the horse, who whinnied several times, kept moving forward, willing to brave this danger to avoid the danger behind them.

Soon the path descended and darkened. The sliver of sun hadn't yet cracked the vale, and the mist appeared to roll right up to the edge of the cliff.

It felt unnatural. Robinson looked over the side. All he could see were trees funneling down into the smoky mire. At that moment, Robinson's boot slipped across a moss-covered rock, and he stumbled toward the edge. Friday was there to grab him and pull him back.

"Thanks," he said despite her disapproving look.

The path continued to wind down at a mild gradient, but it was still precarious. It looked as if no one had traveled it in a very long time. Rocks had spilled across it in several places, forcing Friday to kick them off to clear the path.

After a spell, Friday came upon an inlet in the mountain that appeared to be manmade. Robinson tried to draw the horse toward it, but it reared back skittishly.

"Let me," Friday said.

She slipped by Robinson and stroked the horse's forehead before whispering into its ear. Tension seemed to flood out of the horse, and within a minute, it followed her under the overhang.

The inlet's ceiling was about seven feet high, giving Robinson, Friday, and the horse plenty of room to walk. It receded ten paces or so into the wall and had a second outlet on the other side. Strewn about the area were piles of refuse made up of old travelers' gear. Backpacks and bedrolls. A few scattered weapons. Scattered clothes. People had reached this place, but not in a long time.

Friday sat down on a rock as the roan drank from a pool on the ground.

"Sit," Friday said. "You need rest."

Robinson nodded absently and remained standing. Something was bothering him. Friday could see it.

"What's wrong?" she asked.

"Something about this bother you?"

She looked around. "What do you mean?"

"Obviously people have been here, but not in a long time. And look around. What's missing?"

Friday looked. "Fires," she said. Robinson nodded. "Maybe they moved on."

"And left all their gear behind?" He shook his head. "I don't know. I'm starting to think we made a mistake coming here."

Just as he said it, they heard the thrum of a drone approaching. Friday stood, reaching for Robinson's hand, as two drones slowly descended from above. The machines hovered there, as if assessing their targets. Then, reticles appeared on both Robinson and Friday's chests as the machines revved to fire.

Chapter Thirty-One
One Step Back

Saah groaned as his horse scaled the path, each jarring step sending fire up through his body. Once they reached a small plateau, Viktor dismounted and rushed to his side.

"Let me see the wound," Viktor said.

Saah removed his hand. The side of his shirt was torn and singed. His ribs had been badly burned, though there was little blood.

"It looks like whatever hit you simultaneously cauterized the wound. I can make a salve, but it won't help with the pain."

Saah waved him away as he gingerly got off his mount. He turned to Cassa. "The pack?"

Cassa shook his head.

All dead. What a waste.

Saah took out his canteen and poured water on the wound. He grimaced but didn't cry out. Viktor shuffled nervously. Saah knew the man expected him to rage at losing the boy once again, but he was surprisingly accepting of this new situation. His time inside the construct had given him a fresh perspective on what his future might hold, and he was beginning to suspect it might start here.

Saah took out his binoculars and looked back on the ridge. Even with sun above the horizon, the mysterious place beyond remained hidden by mist.

"You're not thinking of going back, are you?" Viktor stuttered.

Saah looked at the man and sneered. He'd known few men as cowardly in his time. But Viktor had other gifts he couldn't do without.

"No," Saah said. "This place is beyond us. Whoever commands those orbs has technology we are not prepared to face."

"And Crusoe and the girl?"

Saah considered how the orbs had passed the pair and targeted his pack instead. Maybe the drones viewed the teens as soft targets and set out to remove the more dangerous threats first. Then again, Crusoe had spent the better part of a year working his way here. He didn't think the boy would risk his life—or the girl's—unless he had some vague understanding of what laid beyond.

"He's lost to us now. But our friend has an uncanny gift for getting in and out of extraordinary situations. I wouldn't be surprised if we were to see him again."

"So, we're leaving?" Viktor asked, failing to hide his relief.

"*We* are, but Cassa will stay behind."

Cassa appeared neither surprised nor troubled. The Master walked to him.

"If this place is what Crusoe thinks it is, then perhaps it would behoove us to take a closer look. I want you to assess its borders. Study its defenses. See if you can find a way inside. But don't put yourself at risk. Viktor and I will head back to the farm. If we're not back in a month's time, you are to return on your own."

Cassa nodded. Then Saah and Viktor mounted their horses and rode off.

Cassa waited until Viktor and the Master had vanished before he took off his helmet and let the sun warm his skin. It was chafed from riding, so he poured water over it and let it dry in the air.

Cassa was tired. He hadn't seen the point in riding the boy down, not after Saah had returned from the underground place. Something in him had changed there. He began to speak of the future. His hunger for killing the boy hadn't waned exactly, but it had been tempered. The fire that drove him now seemed channeled down a new path. Cassa wasn't sure if that was a good thing or a bad thing.

For the first time in a long time, Cassa questioned what he was doing with his life. He knew the debt he owed the Master, but he grew tired of this endless pursuit. He hated the boy for what he represented, but he feared if things didn't come to a resolution soon, he might succumb to the same madness that had taken hold of the Master.

Then again, he had no family to speak of. No one he belonged to. Once, he had a girl in his life, but now she too was dead. If he were to stake out on his own, where would he go? What would he do? As pathetic as it sounded, he needed something to drive him. But how long could he subsist on someone else's path?

As Cassa donned his mask, he'd already begun planning his immediate future. First, he would need to feed and water Bull. Afterward, he would begin testing the perimeter of the valley as the Master had ordered. The flying orbs were a concern. He could not risk attracting them and hope to survive. He would need to learn more about them. Only then would he know how to defeat them.

Saah needed to get Viktor back to the farm to start on his latest endeavor. Winter was barely two months away, and if his new plan had any chance of working, they needed to return before the first snow. The ride would be tough, both with his injury and the precautions they would need to cross the Midwest without Cassa and the pack to ward off attackers. Viktor would be little use if such an attack came, but Saah could take care of himself. He'd done it all his life.

As they crossed back into the prairielands, Saah began to contemplate his mistakes. He'd made a few—the biggest was putting too much emphasis on the boy. He owed young Ser Crusoe a debt—there was no questioning that—and yet, his myopic pursuit had cost him significantly. His insistence to rush headlong into every situation ran contrary to the philosophy that once led him to the height of power on Isle Prime. If he were to realize his true goal, he needed to think bigger and bolder and plan ahead. The time for reactionary moves was over. From here on out, he would be the one to dictate the action.

It all boiled down to the construct. She had offered him an army in exchange for returning Crusoe to her. He agreed, of course; he would have said anything to facilitate his freedom. But it was only after reaching the Badlands that he had realized the construct's mistake. She believed man needed ruling, and that was true enough. But to achieve true greatness, the source of that rule could not be a computer or a democracy, but one with singular vision. The Romans. The Han Dynasty. The Persians, the Ottomans, the Russians, and the Mongols. Each grew to exorbitant power, and each began and flourished under the authority of a single man. If the new world was to return to its previous heights, it would need one such man to lead it. And Vardan Saah was that man.

First, he would need might. And not the might that came at the push of the button or a rallying cry—but the might at the end of a sword. And not a blunt sword. His sword must be able to cut down his enemies in a single swath. To do that, he wouldn't need Joule or her pact, he would need the secrets of the City of Glass. And to rob both those ancient houses of their secrets and power, he needed the man seated next to him.

"You're smiling," Viktor said when he noticed the Master watching him.

"Indeed," Saah said.

"Should I assume you've arrived at a new plan?"

"Yes."

"Am I going to like it?"

"Oh, very much. If anyone will, it should be you. I have need of your special talents, Viktor. It's time to put them fully to use."

"I'm ready, Master."

Chapter Thirty-Two
The Gates

The orbs hovered, preparing to fire, when they suddenly turned in unison as if receiving a signal. Then one of the reticles vanished while the other slid across onto the rocks and onto a pathway that continued down into the vale.

"It wants us to go that way," Friday said.

"Then I suppose we should."

Robinson went first with Friday and the roan trailing behind. As they exited the cave's eastern entrance, the remaining drones fell in around them. Robinson observed the closest one and thought it looked like a beetle, all shiny and black, with hidden eyes that sat somewhere in its reflective shell. He didn't see any physical propulsion effects and wondered if the anti-gravity technology was like that of the flyers.

Sunlight lit the tips of the trees and warmed the air, but through it all, the mist remained. This vale—or whatever it was—was either low enough to hold in its moisture or something was creating the mist to keep it hidden from the outside. Robinson suspected it was the latter, and yet he still hadn't seen any signs of people or a city. There was nothing but forest. Was it possible the City of Glass was underground? Or was it built into the mountain beside them?

Robinson did see signs of wildlife. Chirping rang across the gorge. And he heard the scuttling of small feet, which he suspected belonged to a squirrel.

He hadn't realized he had slowed until one of the drones surged in from behind. He raised a hand in defense.

"Okay, okay," he said. "I'm going."

The path continued to darken the lower they went, and soon the mist become a canopy that blotted out the sky overhead. Soon, they heard more running water. When they turned toward a protruding nose of rocks, they heard the running water and thought it must be a river.

As they neared the jutting protrusion, the path grew wet and slick. The horse whinnied in protest, but Friday held a firm grip, soothing the roan as best she could as they edged around the corner.

A beautiful waterfall ran twenty meters ahead, rushing down from an unseen height, filling the air with a dampness that soaked Robinson and Friday. The water fell another fifty meters into a pool clear enough to see the bottom. It reminded Robinson of the Pate, though he doubted this one was deep enough to dive in.

As they neared the waterfall, they saw the path curled in behind it. Friday nearly lost her footing twice. The second time, Robinson had to help her up. It was clear she had pushed herself too far and was exhausted.

"Wait here," Robinson said. "I'll take a look."

He shimmied past the horse, disappearing behind the curtain of water. Friday looked back at the drones, noting they were always in motion, as if staying in one spot was impossible. When Robinson emerged a moment later, he waved her in.

"Looks safe," he said. "Come on."

The cave was smaller than the inlet and much more wet. The horse immediately began to lap from a small puddle in the rocks. Friday cupped water in her hands and took several deep gulps before sitting on the rocks next to Robinson.

"I think we're safe for a moment," he said. "Let's catch our breath."

"The drones aren't coming in here."

"No. Maybe they have trouble operating in wet conditions."

Robinson slapped a gnat on his arm.

"Or maybe this is where they want us," Friday said.

Robinson looked around.

"For what?" he asked. "A bath?" They shared a laugh. "The path continues out the other side. They're probably expecting us to follow it."

But to what? After months on the road, he was about to find out. The notion that he could be disappointed or worse left him uneasy.

"We don't know where they're leading us."

"No. But we came here to find the City of Glass, and we're not going to find it in here."

"What if they're leading us into a trap?"

"You saw how they took out Saah's pack. If they wanted us dead, we would be. No, someone is at the other end of this." He nodded toward the path. "The sooner we get down there and meet them, they sooner we can find out if they have a cure."

Friday nodded. Then she jerked forward.

"Something bit me."

"Mosquito probably. Got me too. Not a surprise. This is probably the only humid place within two hundred miles. Do you want me to carry you?"

Normally, Friday would have grilled him with a look. This time she merely shook her head.

"We're almost there. Just a little longer."

They emerged from the opposite side of the waterfall to find the drones waiting. The lead one resumed its way down the trail. Robinson followed with Friday and the horse behind.

Shortly after leaving the waterfall, the path opened and continued its decent until it spilled out near the base of the trees.

The forest was large, dense, and filled with wildlife. In addition to birds, there were deer, raccoons, porcupines, badgers, skunks, and bobcats. Friday saw a mother fox playing with her kits outside their den. A coatimundi used its claws to scramble up a tree in its quest for a bird's nest.

The forest was alive with smells and sounds. Friday breathed them in deeply. Robinson thought her shoulders might have lifted. This was as close as they'd come to something resembling her home. Even her footsteps appeared lighter.

The drones pushed them deeper into the forest. Despite walking a long stretch of path, Robinson saw no one. No people, no footprints, nothing that suggested people had been here recently. *Where is the city?* he wondered. *Was our journey all for nothing?* He fought back his rising trepidation for fear Friday would see it.

Then, near what Robinson estimated was the center of the glen, he spotted a clearing where the trees gave way to a grassy field. The drones continued with them until they reached the fringes of the field before they stopped, hovering in place.

"What now?" Friday asked.

Robinson looked around and shrugged.

"Maybe this is—"

Robinson didn't finish that thought. Suddenly, the forest flickered, the trees bending at impossible angles before bouncing back into place. Light stretched in defiance of natural law and turned fractal. And then, as if caught in a wave, the curtain of reality washed away like leaves in a storm, taking with it the field, the forest, and the mist overhead. In its place was a towering city of crystal spires so impossibly high and beautiful that it defied logic and reason.

Robinson reached out and took Friday's hand.

"We made it," he said, his voice tremulous, all his doubts and fears falling away.

Friday could only nod. A moment later, a shadow appeared out of thin air, walking toward them. Slowly, the image became more distinct until they saw they were looking at a woman with silver hair and slate gray eyes, wearing russet clothes of linen.

She stared at them both in turn. "Welcome to the City of Glass."

PART THREE

"Redemption from sin is greater
than redemption from affliction."

–Daniel Defoe

Chapter Thirty-Three
The City of Glass

"Is it real?" Friday gasped.

"You're not the first to ask that question," the woman said, amusement tinging her voice. "Not when approaching these steps for the first time. Or after years inside. The answer is yes, of course. The city and its inhabitants are real. Or as real as you wish them to be." She paused. "You came from the west."

"Yes," Robinson said.

"It wasn't a question. I take it you saw the no trespassing signs?"

Robinson swallowed. "We did. And under normal circumstances, we would have observed them. But we didn't have much of a choice this morning."

"Choices are all we have, young man. Choices set you on your path. They brought you to our gates. Perhaps your choices even played a part in the choices of your pursuers?"

Robinson wasn't sure what she expected him to say.

"Did you kill them?" he asked.

"The creatures were neutralized. We allowed the men to go."

"That was a mistake."

"Their dispute was with you, not us. And it was *my* choice to make. And now it seems I have another."

Robinson felt scrutinized even more. Then Friday wobbled, and he reached out to steady her. The woman's gaze softened.

"It's been thirteen years since we last had visitors, and I'm afraid I'm out of practice as a host. My name is Lysa. Why don't you come in? We can talk more once you've rested."

Robinson was in the process of thanking her when she raised her hand.

"But first I must ask you to remove your weapons. They are prohibited in the city."

Friday hesitated, but Robinson nodded. After all, what choice did they have?

"They'll be returned to you once you leave," Lysa said.

Robinson and Friday set down their weapons on the steps. Lysa waited.

"And the sling?" Lysa asked.

Robinson blushed as if his mother had caught him stealing biscuits. He pulled it from his breeches and set it on his gun belt. One of the drones lowered and used a mechanical arm to retrieve them before flying away.

Lysa motioned them up the steps. Robinson hesitated.

"Before we go in," Robinson said, "there's something you should know."

"Your companion is ill," Lysa said. "We are aware."

Robinson looked confused. Then it came to him. "The mosquitoes in the cave."

"Nanobots. It and other hidden sensors around the vale keep us apprised of all potential dangers. Not that we have anything to fear. The city is safeguarded always by the birds, or drones, above us. Also, we are impervious to sickness, disease, and infection. Now, let's see about that bath you spoke of."

As Robinson and Friday crossed the perimeter, a strange thing occurred. With each step, more details emerged and the city became more vibrant. Where before only an empty courtyard beckoned, there were now scores of people—sitting, talking, and leisurely strolling the grounds. Planters with lush trees materialized, buffeted by blossoming flowers in myriad colors. Towers that had appeared opaque took on an iridescent gleam. What looked like billowing curtains from afar were revealed to be cascading waterfalls up close, each spilling into fathomless, crystal clear pools. In the sky, singing birds soared around the people transported on near-invisible platforms to and from every tower.

It was astonishing and bewildering and an illusion like no other—if it was an illusion. The farther Robinson went, the less he could be sure.

The people were as unique as the city. They appeared to be of varied races, and yet, they all wore the umber, loose fitting clothing that Lysa wore. Some stared at the newcomers but never for long. If they hadn't seen strangers in over a decade, they didn't seem to care.

Robinson and Friday pressed along, taking in the wonderment. In a small alcove, they came across a quartet of musicians floating in the air, playing animatedly as a handful of onlookers watched. And yet, Robinson couldn't hear a single sound.

"Lysa," Robinson said, "what are they doing?"

"The gold reliefs marking the perimeter of this recess function as acoustic dampeners to prevent sound from disturbing others." She nodded toward the alcove. "Go on. See for yourself."

Robinson stepped across the invisible threshold and was immediately hit with a bright, buoyant harmony that washed over him like a blast of wind. As the musicians circled in the air, he mouthed the words, "What in the world?" In response, letters materialized out of thin air, reading, *Eine Kleine Nachtmusik von Wolfgang Amadeus Mozart*. Robinson gaped. "What language…?" Before he finished, the words transformed into English. *A Little Serenade by Wolfgang Amadeus Mozart*.

Robinson laughed out loud, turning back to Friday. Even if she was sick, she had to see this. He waved her forward and she joined him, gapingly.

"It's almost like you can see the music," she said.

Instantly, colorful musical notes tumbled into the air, glowing in time with the performance. Friday joined Robinson in his laughter. He turned to look at Lysa and saw her whispering to a young man with curly hair.

His name was Gesta, and he appeared to be in his early twenties. He was more affable than Lysa, although there was a confidence to him that belied his youthful veneer.

Lysa excused herself, and Gesta led them into the tallest of the towers. Passing through the vestibule, they came to a grand hall that soared to enormous heights. The concentric walls were festooned with open-mouthed terraces from which people shuttled across the void on floating tiles. On the ground floor, marmoreal floors led to and from eight gaping arches.

"This is the Adytum," Gesta said. "It's the closest thing we have to a capitol. To your left and right are the grand arches. These lead to the Halls of History, Arts, Lore, and Science. Up the stairs is the Sanctum, where *the body* meets."

"The body are your leaders?" Friday asked.

Gesta smiled, amused. "We have no leaders. None of us is valued more than another. The body has many parts, but only one voice."

"Then how do you govern?" Robinson asked. "Who decides things?"

"We each have a mastery. A discipline. When issues arise, those who are effected are encouraged to join and voice their opinion. Inclusion is discretionary, but the body performs best when all voices are heard."

"I'll bet Lysa's voice is heard often," Robinson said, and Gesta grinned. "Where did she go by the way?"

"She had something important to attend to," Gesta replied vaguely.

"What is your mastery, Gesta?" Friday asked.

"Pre-Apoc Socio Behavior."

Friday looked confused.

"Us," Robinson said. "He studies us."

"Your rooms are on strata three," Gesta said. "Allow me to call a rise."

Gesta held up a hand with three fingers, and three radiant sections of tile materialized from the floor, hovering a few inches off the ground.

Friday shook her head vehemently.

"Any chance we can take the stairs?"

"Surely," Gesta said.

The room was modest in size and décor. It did offer a view of the outer courtyard and the forest beyond.

Robinson asked about the bath. Gesta showed him to a glass enclosed pad.

"The old bathing methods were antiquated and never completely rid the body of waste. The lavus is better. Remove your garments, step inside, and raise your arms."

Robinson was mildly disappointed. To him, there was nothing so luxurious as a hot bath. He'd gotten spoiled inside Sweethome.

Following Gesta's instructions, Robinson entered the lavus and said, "I'm ready."

Instantly, a dark mass of what looked like smoke emerged from the floor, swirling as it washed over Robinson's body. It felt like a million butterflies touching his skin—surreal, but not unpleasant. When it reached his face, he felt his beard being shorn away.

When it was over, the glass swiveled open. Robinson stepped out in front of a mirror. His body was perfectly cleaned and groomed. He even felt refreshed.

"You gotta try that," he said to Friday.

Once they were done and dressed in the banal, but luxurious city attire, Gesta sat them at a table where the indentation of a human hand appeared.

"This is the provender," Gesta said. "It determines your nutritional needs through the pores of your skin. Go on and touch it."

Both set their hands down. A moment later, an aperture opened at the center of the table and presented a plate of several colored blocks.

"These are edibles. They include all the proteins, carbs, fats, and nutrients your body needs for maximum health and recovery." He eyed Friday's blocks. "Hmm. I've never seen any so dark."

Robinson picked up a block and ate it. It was thick, pasty, and tasteless.

"That's … not what I was expecting," he said.

Gesta shrugged. "Taste is a sense we haven't valued here for a very long time."

Friday picked up a purple block and started to eat it.

"Were you born here?" Robinson asked.

Gesta hesitated, but just as he was about to answer, Friday fell to the floor and began convulsing. Robinson stood to rush to her side, but Gesta caught him by the arm as he said skyward, "Iatric needed."

"What are you doing?" Robinson said. "Let go of me."

"You must stay back."

"She needs my help!"

Robinson tried shoving Gesta away before a wave of electricity hit and immediately incapacitated him. His vision doubled, the ringing in his ears preventing him from hearing what Gesta said to the drone that swooped in to scan Friday. He saw Gesta nod grimly before Friday was cocooned in an electric field and carted out the door.

"I'm sorry I stunned you," Gesta said as Robinson recovered. "But I couldn't allow you to come into contact with her."

"W-why?" Robinson gasped.

"She's become symptomatic. The virus is now contagious."

Chapter Thirty-Four

Virulent

Contagious.

The very word frightened Robinson to his core. Not because he was worried about being infected, but because it meant the virus had mutated to its final stage. In his two years on this continent, he had seen an incalculable number of creatures afflicted by the EBU-GENC1 virus—humanoid and animal—yet to his knowledge, all had been born with the disease save for one: *his mother.* She had infected herself in a desperate attempt to stop the spread of the disease. And while her gambit ultimately proved successful, it came at a cost of her life. Robinson had reunited with her in her final days, only to witness her horrific end. Still, this was worse. Here, he had to watch Friday die day by day, one piece at a time.

Standing outside a transparent barrier, Robinson watched a bevy of remarkable machines do everything they could do to keep Friday alive. Half a day had passed since her collapse. It felt like a lifetime.

Footsteps broke him from his reverie. Robinson turned to see Lysa approaching.

"There you are," Robinson said. "Where have you been? I asked Gesta to find you hours ago. There hasn't been a single healer to see her since we arrived."

"We don't have healers here," Lysa said. "We rely on machines—these machines—when accidents arise. And even those are rare these days."

"So why aren't they working? I've been here all night, and she hasn't made any progress."

"Friday has been sedated and her vitals are being monitored. I assure you, she's quite stable. We've also analyzed you to see if you have been infected."

"I thought your people were immune."

"Actually, the word I used was *impervious*. And even that isn't completely accurate. The truth is we are susceptible to disease, but hazardous pathogens are immediately expunged when they reach our bloodstream. That being said, we can't have a contagion on the loose, now can we? Thankfully, you are in the clear."

"I don't care about me!" Robinson screamed. "I care about Friday. Her and our child. That's why we came here. That's why we came to you. Can you help her or not?"

"It's not that simple," Lysa said.

"What do you mean?"

"This disease—the one in your wife's bloodstream—it's unique. More virulent than the one we remember."

"That's because it's not the same strain."

Lysa looked surprised.

"Saah—the man that infected Friday, the man you let get away—went to Atlanta, to the disease center. There, he recovered two vials of the original proto-virus, only these were from a second strain. EBU-GENC2. One he used on Friday. He wanted her to suffer, and he wanted to make sure I was there to see it every step of the way."

"And the second vial?"

"As far as I know he still has it. Why?"

She ignored his question and asked her own.

"Do you know what he plans to do with it?"

"No. But whatever it is, it won't be good. Vardan Saah is a ruthless man. Ruthless and cunning. He had scores of his own people enslaved and killed—even our regent—so he could assume control of our kingdom. When he discovered there was a device capable of ending the plague, he chose to destroy it so no one could rise up and challenge him. When that failed—when his family died—he went mad. Even now I suspect he's plotting ways to make the rest of us pay for it."

Robinson looked again to Friday. She appeared so frail. The lesions on her body had grown darker, and her face appeared swollen.

"What does this man want?" Lysa asked.

"What his kind always wants: to watch the world burn."

"Hmm. I need to take this to *the body*. We will speak on it and decide what, if anything, can be done."

"And Friday?"

"We'll discuss her too."

"What's to discuss?" Robinson spat. "Either your machines can fix her or they can't."

"As I said before, it's not that simple."

"Sure it is! Unless … unless you're *unwilling* to help her."

When Lysa sighed, Robinson realized he'd guessed the truth.

"Why?" Robinson asked.

"When EBU-GENC1 first broke out, we worked tirelessly to find a cure. When we fell short of that task, we had the terrible misfortune of watching the lights of the world go dark one at a time. Billions of lives lost. Races and cultures gone in an instant. It was beyond devastating. In the first week alone, fifteen men and women here committed suicide. More would follow. Others still gave their lives trying to limit the destruction that followed. We shut down reactors and opened dams; it wasn't nearly enough. Men had reached for the stars, and in falling short, they left wounds so deep that only time could staunch them. We knew then there was only thing to do. We would isolate ourselves. The past would be just that. It belonged to the dead and the future would belong to us. That's why we put those warning signs out on the plains and why we've turned back or neutralized any that have crossed our borders. It's also why we cannot heal your wife. She and you are of the old world, and the people of this city made an oath to never interfere with it again."

"What an incredible sacrifice you've made," Robinson said with obvious sarcasm. "You must be so proud of yourselves."

"The oath *is* a terrible burden, but one we must see through."

"You'll forgive me if I don't shed a tear for you. Let me ask you the obvious question instead: why did you let us in? Was it to gloat over the inferiors? To wow us with all your toys? Or do you simply get off on watching the ants suffer?"

"I understand your anger. And I sympathize with your plight."

"I don't want your sympathy!" Robinson shouted, prompting Lysa to draw back. "I'm sure it's easy for you to sit up here behind your technology and your towers and mock everyone else's troubles—"

"That was not my inten—"

"I'm not finished! You scorn the rest of us for having the *oh such rotten luck* of being born somewhere else. Well, *we* didn't create this world. You did. And *we* didn't ask to be thrust into the worst of it. But we've never once turned our backs on others in trouble. That's not what civilized people do. Decency. Compassion. Those are the traits of a better world. But you wouldn't know that from up here in your crystal towers, would you? You're too busy basking in your superiority. Do you want to know the real truth? You aren't worthy of saving us. And I think deep down you know it."

"May I ask a question now?" Lysa asked. "How civilized can a man be if he carries an axe wherever he goes?"

"Get out of here!" Robinson shouted. "Go! Or I swear you'll find out."

Lysa turned and walked toward the exit. It'd been so long since she'd seen such anger. Or felt it herself. She was surprised when her hands shook.

"Wait," Robinson called.

It wasn't the request that stayed Lysa's feet or made her turn. It was the vulnerability in his voice. His eyes were moist, and his hands trembled. *Now he looks like a boy*, she thought.

"Our child. Can it be saved?"

"Saved?"

"I was told that the virus hadn't yet spread to our child. If that's still the case, then Friday would want me to do everything possible to save it. Even…"

Lysa felt pity and something she couldn't immediately identify for him. Only later would she realize it was shame.

"A fetus shares its mother's blood from conception. I'm sorry, but whomever told you that was either misinformed or lying. Your child has carried the disease from the moment of conception."

Back in his room, Robinson sat in a chair near the window that overlooked the gardens outside. The dwindling sun had set the horizon on fire, casting everything but the snow-capped mountains to the north in shadow.

Outside the glass, citizens floated gaily about on their lifts, oblivious to the fact that three people scant feet away were dying. Two of disease. One of heartbreak.

A chime rang in the room. *A dinner bell.* It had sounded once an hour since he'd returned from the Medica three hours before. This time, Robinson said, "Give me something that will help me sleep."

A moment later, a pasty white cube appeared.

He woke groggily at the table the next morning. His body was stiff, and his throat was dry. He didn't see the man sitting in shadows near the door until he cleared his throat.

"What do you want?" Robinson asked.

"I came to see you," the man replied.

"Go away," Robinson said.

The man leaned into the light. "Then who will laugh at all my jokes?"

It took a second for Robinson to recognize him.

"Pastor," he said.

Pastor smiled. "Hello, son."

Chapter Thirty-Five
An Old Friend

"Have you been here long?" Robinson asked.

He was trying to make sense of Pastor's presence. The man had changed. He was shaven, his once unruly hair shorn low and tight. Even through loose-fitting clothes of the inhabitants, it was obvious he'd lost weight. If it weren't for the scar splitting his cheek and the milky eye, Robinson might not have recognized him.

"A few hours," Pastor said with a voice that sounded both thinner and heavier.

"I meant in the city."

"Ah. Seven months. Feels longer though."

"Seven?" He did the computations in his mind. "You would have had to leave before winter was over. Did something happen? Where are the twins?"

"You haven't changed a bit, have you?" Pastor grunted. "Still in such a hurry to go everywhere, know everything. Fine. But if we're going to talk, I prefer some place with fresh air. Somewhere I don't have to listen to myself think."

The streets were teeming, though few inhabitants bothered to acknowledge the pair. Occasionally someone would nod at Pastor, whether by courtesy or compulsion, and he'd grunt in return. *No wonder they ignore us*, thought Robinson. *If Pastor is the model for outsiders, he wouldn't waste the effort either.*

"I feel like a ghost here," Robinson said. "Do you ever get used to it?"

"No," Pastor replied. "But spend an hour with any one of them, and you'll find it's a blessing in disguise. They love to hear themselves talk, but for the life of me, not one of them has anything to say."

Robinson chuckled, memories of his old friend coming back to him.

"I see civilization hasn't changed you either. You're as prickly as ever."

"That's what happens when you take away my wine."

"No," Robinson said.

Pastor shrugged. "That's the thing no one tells you about utopia: it's remarkably short on vices."

"I guess they should put it in the brochure."

"Even if they did, who bothers to read the fine print?"

They shared a smile.

"You look good though," Robinson said. "Younger."

"Smoke and mirrors, my boy. Smoke and mirrors."

They found a seat by a small garden. Over the next hour, Robinson recounted everything that had happened since he left the farming village. He spoke of the Cat People and Nameless. He described how he'd been sent to the mines after refusing to work for Boss in Cowboytown and how Trog nearly killed him. He told Pastor of his pact to help Boss deliver her gunpowder in exchange for slipping him into the Bone Flayers' city. He paused when he got to the part of reuniting with Friday, remembering how sweet a time it was—and how short. Pastor was especially intrigued over his relations with the Aserra and how they and the cowboys brought the Bone Flayers' reign to an end forever. Saah's infection of Friday. Their wedding. Their hunt for the City of Glass. The flight from the pack. The children of Troyus. Even Joule's demise was shared in one long sitting.

"You've been through a lot," Pastor said. "More than anyone your age should."

"You probably thought I'd died."

"Oh, no. I knew you were alive, just as I knew you'd find her—your wife. The way you spoke of her left no doubt."

"Words are wasted breath on the road. You taught me that."

"Yes, but intentions are everything. To have one objective, a singular goal, and to then commit every ounce of your being to seeing that goal through, that's how civilizations are built, my boy. How a technocracy like this came to be."

"They refuse to help us."

"The ballots haven't been cast just yet, dear boy. Give it time."

"Lysa said something about an oath."

"*The oath*," Pastor grunted. "It's taken as gospel around here, which has always struck me as rather funny. For those totally committed to egalitarianism, they are extraordinarily rigid in their flexibility."

"What does that mean?"

He looked around, his eyes last trolling the sky.

"Come," he said, getting to his feet. "I want to show you something."

They walked through the city again, this time travelling north of the glass towers until they came to an empty road that led out of the city. A small wooden bridge spanned a trickling brook down into the evergreen forest. As Robinson passed the first magnificent tree, he felt the pressure in his chest lighten, and his air came more freely.

A sculpted but sparsely trodden trail led between the rubicund giants.

"What kind of trees are these?" Robinson asked.

"Sequoias," Pastor answered. "They're among the largest and oldest living things on Earth. In their natural environment, they've been known to reach three hundred feet tall and higher. Stunning, aren't they?"

Robinson agreed. High above, a woodpecker drummed noisily, its bright plumage iridescent in the sun.

"You wouldn't know it by looking at them, but they are alien to this region. The lack of natural humidity, sun, and arid soil should make it impossible for them to survive here. And yet they flourish. Do you know why?"

"Because the inhabitants want it that way."

"Precisely," Pastor said approvingly. "This vale is full of similar marvels. Genus and species from around the globe. And only here can they live in harmony."

"How do you know so much about it?"

"I'm a conservator. Of the forest that is. You see, every citizen here must have a discipline. And as an outsider, I can never be a master. This is the next best thing. The funny thing is that most of them would consider this beneath them. Not me. I find I'm much more at peace out here than inside."

Robinson knew what he meant. When he lived in New London, life was orderly, from the direction of the streets to the schedule of the bells. Routines were good for structure, but at some point, the mind was always wondering what was beyond the walls.

"You asked about the village," Pastor said with a swallow. "It's not an easy thing to speak of. They were an odd people—those farmers—but we'd grown to like them. They were what my father would have called 'salt of the earth,' meaning they didn't have time for nonsense. They worked hard, scraped by. And that was enough.

"After they'd repaired their village, I convinced them to add a few defenses. Nothing big. The homes were too far apart to raise a wall, so we built a stronghold instead. That way, if another attack came, everyone could fall back to the center of town and make a stand. The twins even took charge of the training—bow and lance work mostly—but the villagers began to show signs of improvement.

"Then winter came. And with it snow like I'd never seen. Most days, we couldn't get out the door. So, I put on some winter stores." He patted his belly. "And told stories. And drank enough beet wine to turn my teeth blue."

Robinson smiled.

"But the best part—what beat the band—was the mute brother. He found love. You remember the blonde lass?"

Of course, Robinson thought as he nodded. *She looked like Tessa.*

Pastor smiled at the memory. The smile faded.

"One day, a party attacked from the south. The villagers had gotten lax manning the sentry post. I'm as much to blame as anyone. We didn't expect them to come in winter, and not in such numbers. They struck fast and were merciless. Setting fire to homes. Cutting down everyone as they fled."

"Who were they?" Robinson asked.

Pastor shook his head. "Marauders. No one important. The mutes and I made it to the fields before we heard the girl's cry. I knew instantly he would go back for her. Somehow he convinced me and his sister—in their unspoken language—to wait for him at the river. But after we'd freed the horse and cart, she turned back. How could she not? When we reached the farmhouse, it was fully ablaze. I saw them through the window and knew it was too late. They were both engulfed in flames. I thought that image would be the hardest part to forget. But it wasn't. It was the sister's screams. Even without vocal chords, she issued a howl that haunted me. Haunts me still."

"What happened then?" Robinson asked softly.

"Nothing. We retrieved the wagon and fled."

"Wait. She went with you? She's *here*?"

Pastor nodded. "Mostly."

"Well, at least she's safe."

"We're all safe here," Pastor said. "Yet safety itself can be its own kind of prison."

"You don't believe that any more than I do."

"Don't I? What if I was to say that right here, right now, you could go back, trade everything you've been through, to wake up safe tomorrow in your own bed across the sea? Would you do it?"

"If it meant Friday was alive and well? Yes."

"Even if it meant you would never see her again?"

"Yes," Robinson said, but in his heart, he wasn't sure.

"Then you're a better man than me."

"I don't know about that," Robinson said, turning toward the trees. "Remember the day we parted and I told you how I sacrificed a cure for the virus to save Friday instead?"

"I do. And I remember telling you that no child your age should have to make such a decision."

"Well, it happened again. When the battle between the Aserra and Bone Flayers was raging, I found their leader, Arga'Zul, and we fought, but I was no match for him. He had me and was about to kill me when I pulled Friday in front of me. It stayed his hand just long enough for me to run him through."

"Then your gambit worked. I don't see the problem."

"The problem is that I'm not sure it was a gambit. Twice I've faced a moment where my actions would define who I was, and twice I chose wrong. My fear—what keeps me up at night—is that this is who I am. The boy that puts his own interests first when it matters most."

"And what of all those you've helped? The nameless girl. The Cowboytown. The Aserra. The orphans. *Our* villagers. Don't those actions even the scales?"

Robinson wanted desperately to believe they did.

"It's all pointless anyway. We're here now, and Friday *is* dying. And there's not a thing I can do about it. I don't even know why they let us in here in the first place."

"Maybe they wanted to take their measure of you," Pastor said.

"Why? They wouldn't have known me from…" And then it occurred to him. "*You.* You told them to let me in. Why?"

"I needed them to see what was out there with their own eyes. That amidst so much savagery, there are still shows of humanity worthy of our attention. And you are worthy, doubts and all."

"But their oath—it prevents them from getting involved, doesn't it?"

"Under most conditions."

"*Most?*"

The Sanctum had no doorway, just a simple archway that led to a surprisingly modest, oval proscenium with stone seats, a quarter of which were occupied. Robinson thought it looked like one of the Greek theaters of old.

"What is this?" Lysa said when she saw him. "You weren't summoned here. The meeting of *the body* is a sacred function—"

"I apologize for coming unannounced, but as it is my future you're discussing, I thought I might have some relevant information to add to the discussion."

"Who told you our topic of discussion?"

Robinson shrugged. "A little birdie. You have a lot of them flying around."

A few titters sounded. Robinson saw an opportunity.

"It occurred to me after we spoke that I was asking for something and offering nothing in return."

"You have nothing we are interested in," Lysa said.

"You seemed *very* interested when we discussed the virus, specifically the second strain."

Lysa's eyes narrowed. "It is a *concern*, yes."

"A concern," Robinson repeated. "I suppose that's one way to put it, considering the initial virus was the worst pandemic in human history. But given the second strain's ability to mutate, I think it's safe to say this one is an even more dangerous threat. Not only to us, but all life on this planet."

Lysa looked around. Many of the faces were grave.

"I assume there is a point coming," Lysa said.

"An offer, actually. Since your *oath* prevents you from getting involved in the affairs of us mere mortals, I thought I could do it for you. Retrieve the vial of the second strain, that is. I could be Perseus to you, the Gods."

"And in return?"

"You know what I want."

"The full recovery of your wife and child."

"And for us to be allowed to leave in peace."

Lysa looks around again and said, "Give us a moment."

It didn't take *the body* long to decide. Lysa appeared outside the sanctum soon after.

"We accept your proposal. But know this: while we can temporarily suspend the disease in your wife's system, we cannot in any way slow the progression of her pregnancy. That means you must return before she carries to term. If the child is born first, both it and your wife will die."

"Understood," Robinson said. "I'll leave today."

As he turned to go, Lysa called out to him.

"Mr. Crusoe? For what it's worth, many here are rooting for you. Myself included."

Robinson nodded and walked quickly down the hall.

Chapter Thirty-Six
Probe

Cassa had circled the perimeter of the valley twice and estimated it to be three to four square miles. Despite this, he could never quite see what laid within. The mist that hung over the valley floor was perplexing as it maintained its shape and density regardless of the weather or temperature.

There was little question the mist was manufactured, but by whom? Cassa had heard the rumors of the City of Glass. He didn't believe they were true though. He'd traveled over much of the forbidden continent, and in his time, he'd seen nothing remotely magical. It was clear, however, that the flying machines protected something inside.

Cassa found more warning signs around the circumference of the valley. Twice he'd tried to breach it. The first time was the evening after the flying machines had killed his pack and after the Master and Viktor had departed. Cassa had left Bull to graze in a narrow creek while he hiked a mile inland and approached the valley from the north. Fifty feet after crossing the warning boundary, two of the flying machines rose from the mist, forcing him to flee as fast as he could. The machines turned back when he had put another few hundred meters between them.

The second trespass proved riskier. This time he scaled down a steep gulch toward the corner of the valley. There, he heard what sounded like rushing water. In that vicinity, the fauna looked more robust, and a muddy, uneven stretch of earth disappeared under the hardpan toward the snowcapped mountains to the north. He followed it two hundred meters and stopped.

To the untrained eye, the collection of rocks might have looked normal, but no similar ones appeared in the region. Using a rope tied to Bull's saddle, he hauled the topmost rocks away, stopping when the rounded concrete pipe came into view. Putting an ear to it, Cassa heard the rush of water within. He had found his way into the city.

The entrance was an iron door two feet by two feet fused into the concrete. Cassa pulled on the bar. It didn't budge. Since he could see no lock, he assumed it was rusted. Once again, Cassa linked Bull and the rope to the iron bar. When it drew taught, the door groaned. Cassa climbed on top and added his muscle to the equation. After an intense shuddering, the door gave way.

The water churned inside the pipe at a fevered pace, hundreds of gallons a second. Cassa ducked his head inside and saw the conduit was maybe ten feet in diameter, less than thirty percent of it bearing water. The downside was that even with the open door, he couldn't see beyond a few feet. He had no way of knowing if the aqueduct broke off or if there were gratings along the way. The only way he would know for sure was to go in for a closer look.

After setting Bull out to graze again, Cassa hunted down a long stick to counterbalance his movement down the pipes. Then, he entered the tunnel using a temporary knot to swing himself down. Once he'd found footing, he used the stick to guide himself forward, carrying the small torch he'd lit with his flint and steel.

The aqueduct descended gradually. Still, between it and the wet footing, Cassa knew he couldn't afford any mistakes. He compensated by placing the stick on a dry stop on the opposite wall, just below midpoint. Unfortunately, this meant his body would be canted at an odd angle for as long as he was inside the aqueduct. He could already feel the muscles of his legs, shoulders and arms straining.

Cassa had gauged his entrance point to be one hundred meters from the valley's edge. As he moved forward, the light quickly faded away until all he could see was the haloed ten-foot radius around him. Twice he nearly slipped against the wet wall. Twice he recovered.

Then, the rope drew taught. He thought that meant he'd come thirty feet, give or take. He looked farther down the aqueduct but saw nothing. Continuing from here would be dangerous and only make the return that much harder.

Cassa asked himself what the Master would want him to do. He had never demanded Cassa pay back his debt, but there was a code amongst men of their world that said such a debt must be repaid and on kind. And contrary to every secret wish he'd ever held, Cassa knew killing the boy would require more than tenacity. It necessitated risk. Possibly even sacrifice.

With that in mind, Cassa cut the rope.

He'd gone another twenty feet when the stick hit below the center line and, the tip shot across the wet surface. He plummeted into the water. The frigid cold shot through him like lightning, momentarily stunning him. Hurtling out of control in the dark, icy torrent, he craned his head up to gasp for breath. He lurched for purchase only to feel the coarse walls on his skin, ripping one of his fingernails out. He twisted his hips around so he was traveling feet first, knowing if he went much farther he would likely plunge to his death.

Then something struck his head. He reached out and felt the wooden stick in his hand. He flipped the end toward his legs and the bottom of the aqueduct. The point hit and slowed him for a second. Then it snapped, and he felt a searing pain as the broken half stabbed into his thigh.

Cassa's muscles were already cramping from the cold. He'd been in the water less than thirty seconds and already his body was shutting down. He knew he had to do something quickly or he would lose all his strength.

Bobbing up for another breath, Cassa thought he saw the darkness lighten. Still holding the top half of the stick, he threw it out like an anchor. He felt it shake against the wall. Simultaneously, he ground his heels downward, the pain nearly making him black out. The combined effort, however, helped him slow.

When he looked up again, he saw there was indeed light in front of him and he was hurtling toward it too fast to stop. Out of the corner of his eye, he saw a shadow and leaped for it. Cassa's hand missed the recess, but the hooked end of the stick managed to snag it. Cassa's body lurched to a stop. Then he felt his grip sliding off the stick.

Cassa heard the roar of the waterfall and knew he was mere feet from going over. He couldn't take a chance on letting go and plummeting over. With every ounce of strength, he lunged for the recess that the stick had latched onto and pulled. Slowly, he managed to fight the tide of water and pull himself inside.

The off-shoot conduit was smaller, maybe two feet in diameter. Cassa collapsed in exhaustion. His body continued to shake. Even here, there was an inch or two of freezing water along the bottom of the pipe. Before he got up, he reached down and felt something sticky and warm oozing from his leg. He didn't think the wound was life-threatening, but he needed to dress it quickly. Unfortunately, this pipe, like the other, was dark.

Cassa crawled forward until his head banged into something metal. He reached out to find a ladder. He scaled it painfully and found a hatch with an iron wheel. He turned the wheel until it clicked and then used his back to leverage it open.

Blinding daylight greeted Cassa as he spilled out onto the rocks around the waterfall. The hatch slammed behind him, blending in with the rocks as the previous one had. He tried to stand but was trembling too hard. Instead, he looked up and went still.

From under the mist, the forest splayed out in grand fashion. Giant trees— taller than Cassa would have imagined possible—peppered the canopy and gave the valley an otherworldly feel. But that wasn't what stayed his breath. It was the towering spires of the city, which glimmered like diamonds from a half-mile away. Cassa felt his jaw fall open and was powerless to close it.

He'd made it. The City of Glass was real, and he had gotten inside. Before he could celebrate, however, he heard the familiar whine of one of the flying machines.

Trembling, Cassa looked around for cover, but outside of the small cave, which he was sure the things could fly inside, there was none. He stumbled back deeper into the rocks, instead pushing himself behind a smaller spate of water that cascaded over him.

The flying machine rose over the cliff wall and hovered there. Cassa could feel his heartbeat thundering, and he expected the blast to come at any time. The flying machine pivoted toward the hidden hatch instead. That's why it had come. An alarm had alerted the machine to its opening. Not his presence.

Cassa watched the machine circle the hatch and continued to hold his breath for fear of being discovered. His skin had gone white and he trembled badly, but the machine seemed oblivious to him. That's when he remembered that some creatures hunted by body heat. What if the machine did as well? That might prevent him from being blasted apart like his pack, but it wouldn't save him from freezing to death.

As the machine rotated around again, an idea popped into Cassa's head. The discovery of the aqueduct was important, but the machines were the guardians at the gate. If he were to bring one back to the Master, he and Viktor might be able to take it apart and learn how it worked.

Cassa reached for a rock, his fingers aching as he secured it in his hand. He waited until the machine did another revolution. This time it rose slightly higher, to about eight feet in height. Thinking he'd missed his chance, Cassa vaulted out of the water and stepped on a rock to launch himself into the air. The rock smashed the machine. It shuddered but didn't go down. Cassa hit it twice more before it fell to the rocks, smoking, engines whining down.

He expected it to be heavy, but it was surprisingly light. Cassa slipped the machine under his arm and scaled up the ridge and ran as fast as his legs would carry him.

Chapter Thirty-Seven
Genesi

Pastor had met Robinson outside Sanctum and was happy to learn their plan had worked. Once he learned he was set to leave immediately, however, his forehead creased, and he pulled his friend away.

"I have something to show you first," Pastor said.

They walked to one of the outer buildings, a two-story domed structure with no discernable entrance.

"You'll like this." Pastor grinned.

Pastor walked up to the quicksilver-hued wall and passed through it. Robinson gasped. He warily reached out, his hand disappearing from view. When he pulled it back, nothing had changed. Robinson steeled himself and stepped through.

Robinson felt nothing as he passed through the barrier and arrived in a voluminous room that towered high overhead. Stacked tiers rose out in steeped formation, defying gravity. Men and women worked in various chambers on those tiers with a diverse variety of materials.

"This is the Genesi," Pastor said. "It's where the designers of this age create and perfect new technologies."

On one of the lower tiers, two scientists were using a device to create a small cloud that hovered over a basin before releasing rain on demand. Once the rain ceased, the scientists conferred, pressed a button, and the water reversed course and the cloud swelled once more.

Three floors above them, an artist of some kind used deep sound waves to chip away at a slab of marble until the Statue of David appeared in perfect replication. Another manipulation of the device transformed the stone with a variety of colors and patterns.

The most stunning sight came at the apex of the building, where a dark, spiraling vortex suddenly opened up, revealing some striking celestial event. A group of men and women on lifts floated just beneath the void, discussing what they were seeing.

"How is this possible?" Robinson asked. "From outside—"

"The citizens are big on illusion," Pastor said. "Stay here long enough, you cease asking 'how' in lieu of 'why.' The only answer I've come away with is 'because they can.'"

Pastor allowed Robinson another minute to gawk before directing him to a glass table not far from their entrance. On it were several devices laid out in orderly fashion.

"I've managed to scrounge up a few special gifts for you. Nothing too dynamic since *the oath* prevents handing over of *present* technology—you know, the stuff that would actually guarantee your success." Pastor rolled his eyes. "What I can give you are devices that were created before the Great Rendering occurred." He leaned close and whispered, "With a few modifications."

Pastor indicated the first piece of tech, a small, unadorned metal prong, slightly smaller than a fork.

"This is a wand used to analyze food. It can break down edible content by calories, nutrients, ingredients. It can also discern whether something is edible or poisonous."

"I can use this outdoors?" Robinson asked.

"Unless you run across a string of restaurants," Pastor sniped. "I carried one of these everywhere I traveled. Why do you think we ate so well?"

"I thought the twins were good cooks."

At this, Pastor laughed heartily. For a moment, it sounded like Robinson's friend was back. Then his face grew solemn and he moved on.

"Next," Pastor said, pointing to a pair of black-rimmed glasses.

"Spectacles?" Robinson asked.

"Put them on," was all Pastor said.

Robinson slid the glasses on. Pastor pointed skyward.

"Look up there," he said. "At the top level. Tell me what you see."

At first, nothing looked unusual. Then the image was multiplied, a distance meter blinking in the upright corner. It stopped when Robinson's perspective showed a scientist shoveling food into his mouth.

"Whoa," Robinson said. "I can see what that man is eating."

"The numbers in the corner measure distance. Good for targeting. You can also say things like, "fifty meters out" and it will zoom out to that exact location."

"Exceptional."

"It does more. Touch the bridge, and the glass will identify heat signatures, pinpoint and identify weapons, propellants, explosives and chemicals. Pull off the right temple tip and insert it into your ear, and you can amplify sound up to twenty meters. It can also translate a handful of languages or extrapolate fusion languages over time."

"Amazing," Robinson said.

"Plus they make you look smarter," Pastor quipped. "Which for you is definitely a bonus."

Robinson laughed.

"They're strong, but not indestructible. Keep them safe."

Robinson nodded and slipped the glasses into his shirt pocket.

Next on the table was a bundled, tubular bag.

"What's this?" Robinson asked.

"A sleeping bag. There's no padding, so it's uncomfortable, but it will keep you warm up to negative thirty degrees. The exterior is also crafted with nano-coated light diffusers that will let you blend in with your environment. It won't make you invisible, but it will make you hard to detect, especially at night."

"The ancients had this?" Robinson asked.

Pastor nodded. "Most of it was in the hands of the military, unfortunately, which meant it was useless when the real trouble began."

Robinson turned his attention to the next item. "I recognize this."

"Do you?" Pastor asked. He picked the firearm off the table. "Guns, like the one you used, have been outdated for centuries. Not only is gunpowder unpredictable, but they don't work in water or sand, and can be taken away and used against the owner. This one is different, though it was designed to resemble an old revolver. Of the six chambers, only three are capable of discharging. But they don't fire bullets."

"What do they fire?"

"Kinetic energy. Sound." He flicked open the cylinder, revealing six shells, two of which had blue, red and green dots. "The blue chamber fires a sonic blast equivalent to a running kick to the chest. It will put a man down hard but not kill him. The green chamber fires a blast with twice the velocity and impact of a normal forty-five caliber pistol."

"And the red?"

"Let's just say if you have to topple any buildings, it will give you your start. Whatever you do, don't fire it at close proximity. You can switch chambers by toggling this safety switch here. Also, there's a recoil commensurate to the output of energy. Newton's Third and all that. Lastly, there's a DNA reader in the grip so only you can fire it."

Robinson nodded and slipped the pistol easily into his pants. Pastor rolled his eyes and moved on to the last piece of tech.

"It's a bird," Robinson said.

"A drone," Pastor corrected him. "Designed to look like and mimic a hummingbird in every way. This is my special gift to you." Pastor couldn't take his eyes off the bird. "For a while, she and I were friends."

"Friends?"

Pastor struggled to continue. Robinson thought he looked strangely vulnerable.

"It isn't easy being an outsider in a city like this. Even working in the forest, I was prone to loneliness. Scout … lessened that for me."

"*Scout?*" Robinson asked.

"Named for a young heroine of literature who learns that the evil in humanity can only be purged with love and understanding."

In all the days Robinson traveled with Pastor, he never felt closer to him than in that moment. He was kind enough to look away when he saw the man's eyes water.

"She has some AI," Pastor said with a clearing of his throat, "so she follows commands. She's an excellent tracker and can warn you when danger's coming."

Pastor whistled, and Scout rose to her feet and chirped.

"Scout, this is Robinson. He's your new master. You're to go with him, do as he asks, and keep him safe. Understand?"

Scout chirped once, regarded Robinson, then flew into the air and perched near the exit door.

"Thank you for this," Robinson said.

"It's the least I can do," Pastor replied. "I owe you, after all."

"You don't owe me anything."

"Oh, I do, son. More than you know."

Robinson stood at the Medica window in the new clothes Pastor had provided him. He stared at the love of his life motionless on the other side. In the fading afternoon light, she almost looked peaceful.

"Friday, I know I promised we'd never be apart again," Robinson said softly, "but this is something I have to do. I just wanted to say, if you wake up and I'm not here, please don't be afraid. And don't hate me." Robinson felt his lip tremble and gritted his teeth. "Leaving you and our child is the hardest thing I'll do, but I know you'd do the same. That's what being an Aserra is really about, isn't it? Not the training or the fighting, but the willingness to sacrifice everything for those you love. Someone very important tried to teach me that once, but I didn't understand it then. Now, I do. I love you, *Yolareinai-esa-tu-shin-zhi-ma-coctera-wal-pan-bayamasay-fri*. And I will see you soon."

Robinson kissed his fingers and held them up before turning and walking away. He never looked back because he knew Friday wouldn't have either.

Pastor was waiting outside next to the roan Wapasha had given him.

"She's a good horse," Robinson said.

"She won't be happy about her change of diet—or locale—but she's well trained. She'll serve you well. I only wish I was coming with you."

"I didn't want to ask."

"The oath prevents me from leaving the city. And even if I didn't take the oath, I'm not sure I could handle it. The losses are too painful and the gains are even worse."

"Ah, you'd only get in my way anyway."

Pastor's head snapped up, but when he saw Robinson grin, he shook his head.

"Then I don't feel so bad about this."

Robinson's brow knitted in confusion. Then Pastor looked over his shoulder. Robinson turned and felt his chest tighten as the mute sister approached on a horse of her own. She rode with her bow across her back and never once looked at Robinson after she arrived.

"Four weeks," Pastor said.

"More than enough time," Robinson replied.

Pastor watched Robinson whistle loudly before Scout passed by overhead. Robinson nudged his horse to follow. The mute sister glanced once more at Pastor before following, her silence conveying more than enough words.

Pastor stood in place until they disappeared over the first rise.

"Why do I feel like I've just done something terrible?" Pastor said.

"Because you're sentimental," Lysa answered, not bothering to ask him how he'd heard her approach. "It's one of the things people like about you."

Pastor grunted, but said nothing.

"Don't look so glum. We needed the boy to convince *the body* the dangers of the second strain were real. And he succeeded."

"But if he fails in this task?"

"Then our point is made and finally we'll be allowed to act."

"It's not right, Lysa. People aren't pawns to be sacrificed. Those two deserve better than that. They're better than us."

"Well, if they're as good as you say, they'll succeed. Though that would only lead to a different sort of tragedy."

"What do you mean?"

"Imagine, going through all that only to return and find your lover passed."

"She might survive. It's only a month."

"William," Lysa said, as if talking to a child. "She won't last the week. I fear her illness is about to take a heartbreaking turn. Are you coming?"

After what he'd just heard, Pastor found it hard to speak. He cleared his throat and smiled instead. "Of course," he said.

Chapter Thirty-Eight
Waiting in the Groves

The return journey to Saah's farm went smoothly, save for two incidents. The first came two days after they'd left the valley outside the City of Glass. They travelled south until they came across the 18 Freeway and then turned east until they arrived at the town of Mission. The attack came quickly and on horseback, but the enemy's bows and arrows were no match for the explosive projectile Viktor launched at them from a grounded tube. When four Indians and their mounts were eviscerated in a moment, the fight went out of the others and they turned heel and ran.

The second attack came eight days later, after a mind numbingly dreary and hot ride east on highway 20 in the former state of Nebraska, which offered a level expanse of featureless corn and soybean fields and not much else. The wild crops with the occasional river trawl meant they needed less time for hunting, which was a boon to both men but hell on the alpha, who snarled and gnashed at the bars of its cage so often the planks beneath its feet turned black from blood.

The alpha had set both men on edge as its restless frenzy gave them little time to sleep. Somewhere mid-state, however, the beast's demeanor suddenly changed, and it lay down at the bottom of its cage and only rose when Saah returned with fresh game. Otherwise, it sat and watched the men. Saah saw intelligence in the creature's eyes and knew it was waiting for them to make a mistake. It would only need one.

The second attack came from a surprising source, a wild pack of dogs. The company was a motley assemblage of lean hounds intermixed with a handful of wolves. They came at night. The first warning came in the form of a low growl from the alpha that stirred Saah and Viktor from their slumbers. Then, the night exploded with thrashing howls as the wild grass bucked all around them. Viktor stoked the fire as Saah scanned the field with his rifle, only to have the mongrels emerge and encircle them. For the first time in a long time, Saah felt fearful. Then the alpha howled, and the mob halted.

The leader of the flea-ridden curs, a silver and black wolf with gnarled ears, strode several paces in and bared its teeth. But when the alpha slammed against the bars and snarled, the wolf leaped back and fled. Its flock faltered in confusion before they too turned and disappeared back into the grass.

Neither man could shake the incident from their minds. For Saah, the alpha had displayed nature's order in its purest form. It stemmed from dominance. And true dominance could only come from one place: dread. The citizens of Isle Prime had feared Saah, but they did not dread him. That had been his mistake. It was one he would not make again.

Viktor's contemplation of the incident was less self-serving. For months before their departure, he'd been stymied by two things: his ability to control humans in the same way he controlled the afflicted, and his inability to control subjects in their most frenzied, primal state. The alpha's actions now had him thinking in different directions for both. Viktor knew the Master would want to rebuild his pack as soon as possible. He would need time to get it right.

They arrived at the farm at sundown, fifteen days after leaving the City of Glass. The gate was open, the barn door swaying in the breeze. Flesh and gore littered the grounds around the field. Afflicted flesh.

When Viktor saw this, he leaped off his mount and ran for the barn, crying out inside. Saah entered to see that only a handful of Viktor's augmented Renders remained alive. The rest had been fed to the beast of the field.

"Who would do this?" Viktor asked.

Saah knew. He found the man inside his own home, asleep on Saah's bed surrounded by empty bottles of corn alcohol all around him. The man pleaded as Saah dragged him outside.

"W-we didn't think you was coming back," the man said. "Please, Master. We was only having fun."

"If it's fun you want," Saah said, "then you shall have it."

Saah started to drag the man toward the field when Viktor called out.

"I could use him for my experiments."

When the man's eyes widened in horror, Saah relented.

As Viktor's surgery on the man commenced, Saah took the remaining six packmates on a hunting trip to gather more Renders. They set traps within a ten-mile radius, and those garnered sixteen living subjects. A few short hunting excursions rounded up another five. Viktor had implanted them all with control devices and weapons by the following day.

"What about her?" Saah nodded to the alpha. The mechanism implanted at the rear of its head blinked, but the dog's eyes hadn't changed.

"I can't understand it," Viktor said. "She is still resisting the implant even though her amygdala is no different on any Canidae I've developed before."

"Ah, but this one *is* different. Unique. She has been an alpha since the day she was born."

"Even more reason to put her down. You'll never break her."

"All beasts heel to the lash eventually, Viktor. Even nature's perfect killing machine. From now on, she is only fed by my hand. Understand?"

Viktor said he did. Saah took a step closer to the cage. The alpha's growl was low.

"You will be my fiercest champion," Saah said to the alpha. "The omega to *my* alpha."

The alpha growled again but lowered its head to the floor in pain.

"How progresses my army?" Saah asked.

"I lost two on the table," Viktor said. "Twenty-five others should be fit to travel within a week."

"It's not enough. I need one hundred, at least."

"Let me show you something," Viktor said, rising and heading toward the back room.

When Saah entered the room, he found the man sitting in irons chained to the floor. Dried blood covered his face and shirt. His hair had been shaved.

A control device had been implanted just above his forehead.

"Well?" Saah asked.

"Watch," Viktor said.

He raised the pipes to his lips and blew a flat note. The man looked up but remained sitting.

"That's it?" Saah asked. "Is that all he does?"

"The note only alerts him that a command is forthcoming. The subject will respond to any order that follows."

"Do it again," Saah said. Viktor blew the note. "Stand up," Saah said to the man.

The man stood. Viktor smiled and blew another note. Saah pulled a knife from his waistline.

"Take this and kill yourself," he said.

The man took the knife and raised it to his throat.

"Stop," Saah said, but the man didn't stop. His body fell to the ground once he was done.

"The subject will only follow one command per note," Viktor said. "Apologies."

"You've perfected the process."

Viktor shrugged. "Herd mentality. I saw how the alpha established dominance over that pack of canines and knew if I could identify the part of the brain that governed those instincts, I could replicate the process and assume total control."

"You've done well," Saah said. "If only that underground facility was closer, I would have my army tomorrow."

"You're forgetting something, Master," Viktor said. Saah raised an eyebrow. "While that place is several hundred miles away, there is a small town only twenty miles from here. There's no need to wait 'til tomorrow. You can have your army today."

Chapter Thirty-Nine
Tracks

The roan nickered, and its pace lessened as it caught the scent of the small stream ahead. Robinson allowed it to turn from the path so it could sate its thirst. The mute sister followed, and both dismounted their creaking saddles to fill their water reserves and wash the sweat and chafe from their skin. It was their fourth day on the road.

"Let me know if you see Scout," Robinson said as he walked behind the underbrush. The mute sister made no reply. It'd been like that the entire time. Him leading, her a length or two behind. Still, the gap between them was as wide as a canyon. Though she couldn't speak, she had other ways to communicate. The fact that she didn't use them made the silence even more taxing.

There was little question the mute sister blamed Robinson for her brother's death. He couldn't say why. Maybe it was because Robinson had led them to the small village where her brother ultimately died. Or perhaps it was because he'd left to pursue his own affairs rather than stay through the winter and help with the homesteaders' defense. If Pastor was right, his presence wouldn't have mattered anyway. The village was overrun in the dead of night and few escaped. Given Robinson's disdain for retreating, odds are he would have died too. He suspected the mute sister knew this, but like all people, she needed someone to blame for the cruel vagaries life inflicted.

The one bright spot of the trip so far had been Scout. The drone had looked and sounded like every hummingbird Robinson had ever seen, and yet it replied to commands as Pastor had said it would. When Robinson asked each morning if it could track Saah, it chirped once. When he asked if there was any danger each night Scout chirped twice. Robinson wasn't sure what powered the bird. It never rested. Still, when it wasn't under orders, it remained close to Robinson and warbled oscine songs that pleased him.

For the first few days, Robinson worried over Scout's fragility. Several times he'd seen larger birds of prey—hawks and a falcon—give her chase. Scout outran them all but once. The exception came when Robinson and the mute sister were watering the horses. A red-tailed hawk swooped in above Scout, but the bird didn't run. Instead, she turned and assaulted her attacker with her dagger-like beak that left the hawk bloody and screeching in retreat.

Robinson didn't worry about Scout again.

Despite the added security, Robinson and the mute sister still split up the watch duties. Both had traveled on the road too long to put complete faith in an inanimate object. Robinson took the first shift as the mute sister would wrap herself up in one of Pastor's concealment sleeping bags and almost immediately blend in with the terrain around her. When they slept in grass, the bag would take on a green sheen. In dry cornfields, it would turn brusque and yellow. Even the fire failed to reflect off the material.

Robinson was impressed with it.

For his part, sleep was elusive. Robinson had been through enough experiences to know the abject necessity of sleep. Doing without it quickly hampered the mind and sapped the body of resources essential to survive. And yet every time he closed his eyes, he saw Friday motionless in the Medica. At least in Sweethome he could operate under the conviction that her insentience was medically induced. In the City of Glass, it was her own body that had shut down and was failing. Friday's life now relied solely on him.

Friday *and* their child.

He knew little of babies and less of childbirth. In New London, those duties had always fallen to midwives and governesses. Though Tannis and Tallis had grown up in his shadow, their mother and Vareen had cared for them. He remembered the crying, the feedings, and the noxious cloth diapers, but he had no experience with the soothing, the caring, and the loving a child truly needed. And how could he begin to imagine those things now when he wasn't certain the baby would even be born? Or if it was, but as a monster?

The supplies Pastor had given them contained enough sustenance for a six-week trip. Despite that, Robinson felt something was missing. It wasn't the caloric intake or the lack of nutrients—those things were perfectly calibrated for him and the mute sister. It was the taste. It was bland. Robinson remembered how much Pastor enjoyed food while on the road. Something about providing it yourself made it taste better.

After seven days of eating the pasty provisions, Robinson had had enough. He longed for something different. He wondered if the mute sister was feeling the same itch.

"Any desire to do some hunting today?" he asked.

For the first time, the mute sister looked at him and nodded. As she reached for her bow, Robinson tilted his head to the sky and whistled for Scout. He was surprised when the mute sister touched him and shook her head.

"Want to do it the old-fashioned way, huh?" Robinson asked. "All right."

It was midday, and a slight breeze came in from the north. They set off downwind and worked their way back toward the river they knew was a quarter mile to the north. After a quarter turn, Robinson stumbled upon some small tracks and pointed them out to the mute sister. She shook her head and pinched her nose. *Skunk.* Definitely didn't want that on the menu.

They kept going, moving through the dry brush until they saw a rocky outcropping at the foot of a grassy field. As they moved closer, however, Robinson noticed a small dark burrow under the vegetation. Given its size and location, there was little question it was the den of a prairie rattler.

The mute sister drew Robinson's attention and then signaled that she was going around the left side of the outcropping while he went to the right. He had a sense of déjà vu, remembering how they used to hunt together. There was no urgency to their actions, no communications or signals needed. And yet they moved in unison, eyes on a common goal. A goal that resonated in the lower part of every person's brain. To hunt. To feed. Nothing built the bond between people better.

Sweat slid down Robinson's cheek as he crouched in the low grass. His head moved slowly from right to left until he saw it. The animal stood sixty meters away chewing on a shrub. At first he thought it was an antelope. Then he saw the white fur on its rump and the lateral horns. *Pronghorn.* That was its name.

Robinson reached for the bow at his back before remembering he'd left his at the City of Glass. Though he itched to use the newfangled pistol, it seemed an unfair advantage. Instead, he pulled his sling from the loops of his new trousers. He was about to slip a rock into the sling when something moved in his peripheral vision. The mute sister. She'd already notched her bow and was settling in for a shot. The competitor in Robinson urged him to fire first, but he saw the stern look of concentration on his companion's face and knew she needed this far more than he did.

The pronghorn's head tilted up as the mute sister rose. For a fraction of a second, the two locked eyes. Then the string went *twang.* The pronghorn jerked and fell.

Robinson reached the kill site first, and as expected, the arrow had found its mark. A short spurt of blood pumped from its punctured heart before going still. He held up the wand Pastor had given him to ensure the pronghorn was affliction free.

"Thought you'd be out of practice," Robinson said when the mute sister closed. Only she wasn't looking at him. She was looking down.

"What is it?" Robinson asked.

The mute sister pointed to a trail at her feet and a pair of fresh boot tracks.

"Are these from last night?" Robinson asked.

The mute sister shook her head, pointed toward the sun and tapped her wrist twice.

Two hours before noon.

She pointed west, to the highway they'd spent all morning traveling down. Her point was clear. Someone had stood there to watch their approach. The footsteps led back to the east, presumably toward the river.

Was it chance that someone had happened upon them? Robinson wasn't sure, but he hoped that was the case. The alternative meant someone had been waiting for them, and that made Robinson very nervous.

Chapter Forty
Allegiances

Pastor had always felt like an outsider in the City of Glass. On this day, he might have easily passed for one of its citizens, meandering through the vibrant streets, head down, lost in contemplation. With the sun casting the scarred half of his face in shadow, one might have thought him an artist deliberating his latest sculpture or a scientist meditating the plausibility of astral projection. But he wasn't. The truth was, he'd had trouble sleeping the past few days, and the stark reality of his situation was only now washing over him. He had betrayed a friend. It wasn't something he set out to do. But he had done so in the name of duty. And now he was wondering if he could live with the decision.

Pastor liked the boy. Crusoe reminded him of the man he once envisioned himself to be. Strong willed and stubborn. Principled but impetuous. Someone capable of navigating both the treacherous roads of the world and the dark depths of its people—all while maintaining a compass reading of true north. Pastor hadn't been that man in nearly two centuries.

On the surface, the City of Glass did more than deliver on the promise of utopia. It was, for all intents and purposes, the crowning glory of mankind. Grander than the Parthenon or the Colosseum. More beautiful than the canals of Venice, more striking than the Pyramids of Giza. It was aesthetically flawless even in its ever-changing form, the extant culmination of human endeavors. But underneath, its heart beat to a different pulse, one of pride and indifference.

In truth, he'd grown to loathe the place even though he knew he'd never leave it.

It was at that moment Pastor saw a familiar face moving through the crowd.

"Gesta!" he called out.

The curly-haired man looked in his twenties, but Pastor knew him to be several years older than him.

"I'm running late," Gesta said, frowning as Pastor fell in beside him. "What is it?"

"Have you heard any news?"

"About? Ah. You know as much as I do. Your young friend is on his way to … Arkansas, isn't it?"

"*Missouri*. I thought perhaps Lysa had one of her birds following him."

Gesta chuffed. "I think you overestimate her interest in the youth. Besides, as far as I know, the only person to send drones beyond the border is you."

"Drones were available before the pandemic. I was operating within my guidelines."

"Semantics. Lysa was kind enough to agree to let your pale companion accompany the boy, and you took advantage of her goodwill. The girl should have been enough."

"The girl is mute. That's the only reason Lysa signed off on it. Because even if she's captured by all the mysterious *boogeymen* out there, she wouldn't be able to blab our secrets."

Gesta ground to a halt. "I grow tired of your sarcasm. And, as usual, you miss the point. These comings and goings have *the body* on edge. Your infatuation with the outside threatens the prosperity we've enjoyed here for over two hundred years. One would think, given the many ways you've benefited from that prosperity, that you'd at least be inclined to cede to the oath you made."

"How have I not?"

"I really don't have time for this," Gesta said as he continued walking. Pastor rushed to keep up with him again.

"You act as if it was my decision to send *the eight*. Need I remind you—"

"Please, no. *The eight* was one of the worst decisions to come out of *the body* in some time. Many of us saw the writing on the wall before the wagons were hitched, but some voices only carry so far. The point is, you carry on as if you're still out there, searching for answers when we have all we need."

"What answers?"

Gesta looked around as if he'd said too much. *Even he isn't beyond paranoia*, Pastor thought.

"Talk to me, Gesta," Pastor said, pulling him into an alcove. "What do you mean?"

"It means you've done your part, and we've done ours. Now, we must all continue to serve the city and the lands beyond. Trust that *the body* has made the right decisions for us all."

"A decision has been made? What decision?"

Gesta cursed. "I have to go."

Gesta tried to slip by Pastor, but he pulled him back.

"*The body* was in closed session all day yesterday, but only a few of the masters were present. Did Lysa lead the meeting?"

"You know I can't answer that."

Pastor drew close. "You're forgetting, *Brian*, who it was that taught you poker all those years ago. You've already given me the answer. Now, tell me what decision was made."

"I can't. I've been sworn to secrecy."

Pastor jabbed a finger into Gesta's chest. "Don't think for a second I couldn't beat it out of you. Even as old and decrepit as this body is, I'm still capable of taking a punk like you to the woodshed. And *your* oath would do nothing to prevent it."

"And the birds would be on you in an instant. Then who would look after your precious forest?"

For a second, Pastor wanted to punch him anyway. Then he stepped back. As Gesta straightened his shirt, Pastor saw uncertainty in his eyes.

"Doesn't it make you weary?" Pastor asked.

"What?"

"All of it," Pastor said, waving his hands around. "The city, the people.

The sky so perfectly blue day in and day out. I can't be the only one who misses the clouds."

"I miss the rain," Gesta said. "At night I used to listen to it bounce off the gutters outside my window. That splash on the wet cement could always put me to sleep."

"Would you go back if you could?"

Gesta shook his head. "No. Because the rain covered up sounds I'd rather not remember."

"We all felt pain then," Pastor said. "But at least we felt something."

Gesta locked eyes with him.

"Please," Pastor asked. "For old time's sake. Tell me what she's done."

Gesta sighed heavily. He looked out into the city until he caught sight of something.

"See for yourself," he said, nodding in that direction.

Pastor looked out and saw Lysa crossing the main square, heading for the Genesi. He stepped out and followed.

A short time later, Pastor had secured a place in an empty cubicle on the sixteenth floor. He looked across the void to the cubicle Lysa had entered, but his view was blocked by an obfuscating field. He could only see shadows hovering over something dark and oblong.

After half an hour, the door finally opened and Lysa walked out with Gesta and several other masters. It took him a second to understand why she was meeting with men and women of those disciplines. And then it hit him, and his legs went weak. He knew what they were planning to do.

Later that night, Pastor sat in the Medica, watching Friday's chest rise and fall. He'd never seen the girl up close, but he found it oddly comforting that she looked exactly as Robinson had described. Fierce and beautiful. Exactly the type of woman he would have wished for the lad.

For his own part, Pastor had never felt more drained. Even that fateful day long ago when word of the spreading virus with the images of the dead first splashed across the TV screens as chaos spread across the globe, he was the only one that watched in silence. He had explained his non-reaction as shock, but he knew better. The truth was he had no family or friends before, so he'd been apathetic to what followed. Today he felt worse. Because now he had someone to care about, and the oath was keeping him from doing what he knew was right.

Sitting there, listening to the buzz of the life support equipment keeping this remarkable girl alive, he felt unworthy in her presence. And he felt worse because he hoped she never realized her deepest wish—to see Robinson again. *Let the boy die out there,* Pastor said to the higher power he'd renounced so many times, *and I'll make it up to him. Let his journey end painlessly for what I do now.*

"Medica?" he called, tilting his head upward.

"Yes?" A smooth, female voice answered.

"Prepare nano-sweep on subject one and her fetus. Removal of all virulent agents is authorized. Cellular repair and reconstruction is also authorized."

"DNA mapping is complete," the voice said. "Molecular assemblers are now active."

"Commence."

Chapter Forty-One
Lost in the Night

Instincts were an expression of innate biological influences. Every species had them. Determining the difference between instinct and reflex begins by asking two simple questions: is the behavior *automatic* and is it *irresistible?* In the case of the mute sister, who looked over her shoulder for the twentieth time, the answer to both was yes.

They were being followed. Had been for at least twenty miles. And yet neither she nor *he* had seen anyone. For someone so adept at tracking, that single fact was maddening.

He had even sent out his mechanical bird three times to search behind them. But each time the bird came back and communicated that it had found nothing. She didn't understand technology, though she no longer feared it as she once had. It was a tool like any other. In the right hands, it could function properly. In the wrong hands, it could be useless or even a danger.

They had ridden without rest since finding the boot tracks six hours before. Only once in that time did he ask if she was sure they were being followed. She had nodded curtly, expecting to see skepticism in his eyes. There was none. For all his faults, he did not doubt her. Once, she might have taken pride in that. Now, there was only pain.

He.

Crusoe. Even the name felt foul in her mind. As if it, like the plague, might contaminate her just by thinking of it.

Crusoe. He was to blame for everything that had happened.

And the sad part was he had no idea why.

Back when they'd first met, when Crusoe had first helped them escape a band of marauders, her brother had viewed Crusoe with skepticism and ire. After all, he'd injected himself into a kinship that neither wanted nor needed him. She had watched her brother in those early days, felt his tension and anger at everything Crusoe did. His skill with his axes, his gift for navigating the old roads, his talent for the hunt. But the thing that angered her brother most was his bond with Pastor. It had usurped his own so quickly. Pastor would have never admitted it, but Crusoe filled a need her brother could not—one of true companionship and friendship. Their banter filled the hills with sharp arguments and booming laughter, each like a dagger strike to her brother's heart.

Before reaching the farmers, she thought her brother might break them from the party. Then, the attack came and everything changed.

It came down to the blonde farmer girl with blue eyes. She, like her people, had seen the strength in Crusoe's actions and sought to honor it. Hold it. On the morning of Crusoe's departure, the girl stood at the end of the field, watching him leave with tears in her eyes. The mute brother couldn't understand how someone could leave such a mark so quickly.

In the coming days, he began to change. Those traits with which he'd once held competent, he soon embraced. Where before he'd been a loner, he now assumed a seat next to Pastor at the table of leaders. When it came to decisions of defense, his *voice* was consulted and heard. He organized the training. He got his sister involved with the townswomen. And slowly, surely, the blonde-haired girl turned her eyes to him.

"It's passing fancy, nothing more," Pastor had said to the mute sister in private, and she hoped he was right. "But even if it becomes more, they're too different to make it work. Her world is not easy, but until yesterday, it's never been hard. See the way she watches him? She sees what she wants to—the young man's build, his quiet strength. She doesn't know a bear sleeps inside him."

She used her hands to ask Pastor *the* question.

"Love?" Pastor interpreted. "It would make things difficult. That it in itself is both its blessing and its curse." The mute sister knew nothing of love, so his words were confusing. "I know it's hard, but don't begrudge him this," Pastor added. "Calm days like these seldom last. There is always a storm around the corner. And when it comes, the bear will wake, and she will either grow fearful of him or fall victim to him. You'll see."

Only now, with so many months passed, did she see Pastor was right. Each night when she laid down her head, she wished for her brother and that he'd had more of those silent days.

"Could be the heat," Robinson said.

The mute sister's head snapped up. Robinson could see her mind was on something else. He nodded to the bird perched on his knee and stroked its head and mantle.

"Pastor said Scout had thermal vision. Like snakes. They mark predator and prey by fluctuations in temperature. But out here, under these conditions, the air is probably hotter than whomever is following us."

The mute sister's brow knitted as she pointed two fingers down and then ahead.

"That's different. Saah's party is on mounts. Mounts leave heavy tracks, waste. And they've made no effort to hide their tracks, unlike whoever's behind us. Don't worry. I'll send Scout up again after the sun goes down. If it doesn't rain."

Cassa lifted the glasses to his eyes and watched Crusoe and the girl dismount at the foot of the single-treed hill. So predictable. It was the only high ground in three-hundred-square meters, and they reached it just before sundown. They took it just as Cassa had expected them to do.

Spotting the pair had been pure luck. Cassa had left the Badlands two weeks before and ridden hard for seven of those days before coming down with some type of infection, likely from drinking contaminated water from an old well. It'd taken him two days to recover from the fever and another two before he gained his feet. That's when he saw the pair.

At first, he thought it was a hallucination. But he soon began to believe the Gods were rewarding him for his loyalty. After another day, it also became clear where they were going. He had a decision to make. Take them then or wait until they got closer to the Master's farm. Both choices had pros and cons. If he took them early, he could play with them for a while. Watch Crusoe suffer. The idea appealed to him. At the same time, he knew keeping two prisoners would mean a lot of work and little sleep. He decided to wait.

Somewhere along the way, Cassa had been spotted. He watched Crusoe release his bird, which flew in wide circular arcs, presumably looking for him. Cassa could have shot it down, but he decided to ride ahead of them instead, cutting a wide berth through the plains at night until he resumed the road several miles in front of them.

There, he waited and bided his time.

The opportunity came two nights later when clouds filled the horizon and a gentle rain began to fall. Crusoe had propped up a tent underneath the single tree on the hill. There would be no releasing the bird tonight.

Crusoe stood watch the early part of the evening. Hours later, the girl took over. That's when Cassa made his move. He slipped quickly through the tawny corn until he reached the base of the hill. He looked around for the girl. She was nowhere in sight. He approached the tent carefully and pulled back the flap. He heard Crusoe wake. His words came quickly, "What's wrong?" He got nothing more out. Cassa brought the club down with a muffled thud.

The girl was gone, not that it mattered. Cassa had decided to kill her anyway. Now, he had the prize he'd been seeking for nearly a year. As he pulled Crusoe from the tent, all Cassa could think was how happy this would make the Master.

The mute sister pushed quietly through the bracken to find the noise she'd heard hadn't been caused by a human intruder, but a hairy one. The opossum hissed defensively from its warren. She saw why. Her pouch was distended, her teats visible even in the darkness. She was days away from giving birth. She eased away.

She was halfway back to the tent when she heard a noise, high and pitched. At first, she thought it was the wind. Then, it came again and she realized what it was. She was running full speed with her blade in her hand by the time she ascended the hill, chest thumping and filled with dread. She pulled the open tent flap back, trying to ignore the shrieks and calls of the bird as it screeched from within its cage.

Crusoe was gone. She felt something sticky on her hand. Blood, smeared across the tent flap.

The mute sister spun in the rain looking for tracks. She thought she saw what looked like drag marks in the mud and followed after them. They led down the hill to the cornfield fifty meters away. As soon as she slipped inside, however, she realized it was too dark to see anything.

Chest heaving, she turned and turned, but there was nothing she could do. Crusoe was gone, and she was alone.

Chapter Forty-Two
A Walk Among the Trees

She stirred from fathoms deep. Submerged in perfect night, settled heavy in the warmth of the Goddess's bosom. She was at peace. And yet something called to her. Not a voice, but another kind of warmth. It pulled her back toward the cold, toward the light. At first, she fought it. Gradually, she gave in and swam until she opened her eyes.

"You're awake," the man said, looming over her.

He was alone. Face scarred, eye milky. He was a stranger, yet there was something familiar about him. Then she remembered.

"Crusoe," she uttered, voice scratchy as if she'd swallowed a fish bone.

"Yes," the man said, not unkindly. "They call me Pastor."

She swallowed. "Where is he?"

"He's running an errand. You've been through quite an ordeal. Can you sit up?"

Impossible, she thought. And then he reached out and it was easier than she expected. She was in a room surrounded by machines. Unlike Sweethome, these looked like starlight.

"Where am I?" Friday asked.

"You are in the Medica in the City of Glass, in the Badlands of what was once South Dakota. My home."

She remembered. Her hands moved swiftly to her swollen belly.

"Your child is fine," Pastor assured her.

Friday looked at her arms, pulled back the gossamer fabric to see her legs. They were clean of all blight.

"You healed me?" she asked.

Pastor chuckled. "Me? No. The machines did. I merely gave the order."

"How?"

"Nanotechnology. It's a process by which very small robots scour your body for things that should not be there. Then they simply pull them apart and voila."

"And you're certain our child is healed?"

"As certain as I can be. I'm no scientist or doctor. But this," he patted the twinkling lights above her, "isn't your average juicer either. If it says you're *organic*, you are. Are you hungry? Thirsty? I can get you anything you want. Within reason."

"I want up," Friday said.

Pastor laughed. "Up it is."

Once Pastor had fetched Friday clothes, they walked through the streets of the city. Friday was again mesmerized by the sites around her, though she noticed some of the citizens gawked while others looked at her with hostility.

"I am not welcome here," Friday said.

"Don't worry about them. They just haven't seen anyone pregnant in a long time."

"I had not noticed before. There are no children. Why is this?"

"It's ... complicated."

"How? First, you find a mate. Then—"

Pastor laughed again, this time drawing odd stares from those around him.

"I'm familiar with the process, trust me. Though a little out of practice."

Friday eyed him again and asked, "Where exactly is Crusoe?"

Pastor looked around before smiling. "Let's take a walk outside the city."

After passing through the gates, they entered the great forest on a well-trodden path. Almost immediately, Friday felt her tension ease away. The chirping of birds and smell of wet earth were like a boon. Friday reached out to touch the leaves as she passed.

"Robinson left the city a little over two weeks ago," Pastor said once the city fell from view. "He went after the one you call Saah."

Pastor saw Friday react and reached out to her. "It's too late to find him even if you wanted to. And he *chose* to go."

"Alone?"

"No. The one he calls the mute sister went with him."

Friday was only slightly relieved. Though Crusoe had said the girl was strong and good with a bow, she was also prone to reacting emotionally rather than instinctually.

"Why would he do this? We've been evading this man for nearly a year."

"We were told the virus Saah infected you with came in a vial. One of two?"

Friday nodded.

"*They* want the second vial. Unfortunately, traveling beyond the borders of the city is forbidden, so they made an agreement. They would heal you and your child. In return, Robinson would retrieve the second strain of the virus."

"Why? What do they want with it?"

Pastor hesitated. "To study it, I suppose. By the time you arrived, yours had mutated several generations. The fear is this strain is far more dangerous than its predecessor."

"Why not destroy it?"

"*That*, my dear, is a very good question."

Friday studied him. She could sense there was something he wasn't telling her. "Even if Crusoe finds Saah, he has men and Renders. Two cannot hope to defeat so many."

"Normally, I'd agree with you. But I just so happened to sneak a few things out of their armory for him. While they might not guarantee victory, they will help even the odds."

"And you say he left two weeks ago?"

Pastor nodded.

"When is he expected back?"

"Not for another two weeks at the earliest."

Friday's eyes fell to her belly.

"Don't worry. With a little luck, he'll be here for the birth of your child."

"Crusoe doesn't believe in luck, and neither do I. He survives because the Goddess favors him. You should pray this continues."

"*I* should pray? Why?"

"Because if any harm comes to him, I will burn your city to the ground with you in it."

Pastor wanted to laugh, but he saw her sincerity. "I see now why he fought so hard to find you."

They continued up the trail, both weary, but unwilling to turn back. Both had so much to say.

"Crusoe said when he left you, you were near the Atlantica?"

"Yes," Pastor answered. "At the beginning of winter."

"So when did you come here?"

"Early spring, I think."

Pastor grunted as he started up a steep incline.

"Fortunate you were so quick to find it. It took us much longer."

Pastor glanced back briefly. "Maybe your Goddess favors me too."

Was he mocking her? She wasn't sure.

"I would like to ask you a question."

"By all means, do. I haven't had someone as beautiful as you to talk to in a very long time."

Friday ignored the compliment. "You wear the clothes of the city. You know the paths of its forest. You use its machines freely. You call them 'my people' in one breath, then say '*their armory*' with another."

"You're quite observant, Friday, but that's not a question."

"Who are you?" Friday asked.

Pastor reached the top of the rise, overlooking a field of golden grass beyond. He took a heavy breath and stopped to wipe the sweat from his brow. "I don't know," he said at last. "I thought I did once. Out there with your husband. It's strange how in the middle of all that chaos, a person can find clarity on some of the simpler things."

"It's not strange at all," Friday said. "Your people live behind glass where they cannot touch. In towers where they can only see. Here, life is anything but *simple*."

"You don't know what they're capable of. Of all the things they can do."

"Then why are you here and not among them? Why have you not healed this," she reached out and touched the scar on his cheek. He froze at the touch of her hand. "I think it is the same reason you left these on me," Friday pulled up her sleeve revealing one of a hundred scars that remained on her body. "They are the roadmap of a life lived well."

Pastor didn't argue but neither would he look at her.

"You are afraid of something. What is it?"

Pastor was about to open his mouth when he saw a shadow flit by overhead. Was it one of Lysa's *birds*?

"Missing lunch," he said eventually. And then he smiled again. "I know of an apple tree just up ahead. Honey Crisp. I'll let you have one if you promise to keep it to yourself."

He winked at her and continued walking. Friday hesitated before following.

Chapter Forty-Three
What Waits in the Shadows

The beast smelled like rotting meat. At least where Robinson's head lay, bouncing over the side of the lumbering brute, its dense, matted hair clumped with dirt, sweat, and blood. His rider had bound Robinson to the saddle, legs hanging off one side, head and arms off the other. The ropes cut into his wrists and ankles, leaving them both bloody. Several times an hour he arched his back as much as possible, trying to get the blood out of his head and extremities. A few moments of relief lead to prickling waves of pain. Worst of all, the man refused to give him water.

The masked assailant ran alongside his bison, using some type of flute to compel it forward whenever it tried to rest. He dragged behind him an old fabric tarp carrying something heavy and round.

By the end of the first day, every part of Robinson was sore. Midway through the second, his arms and legs had gone numb. He tried to gnash through the cloth stuffed in his mouth. It only left his mouth bloody and raw.

The one positive was he was still headed to Saah. Only now, it was as a prisoner. His hope of slipping in to steal the vial unannounced was gone. What would Saah do when he saw him? Would he kill him immediately? He doubted it. The man he knew—the Tier that once usurped a kingdom—reveled in his cruelty. More likely he would torture him first. The thought brought dread, but Robinson had suffered through similar horrors before.

The physical thrashing by Trog in the caves. Joule's psychological torment underground. To save Friday and their child, he would need to steel himself for the time to come.

Oddly enough, Robinson spent much of his time thinking of the mute sister. Pastor had assigned her to protect Robinson, and within a week, he'd been taken right out from under her watch. Doubtlessly, she would blame herself. She would also pursue them. But would she be able to track them on her own? She had no way to command Scout. Not without a voice. And Robinson had seen no sign of the bird. He assumed she was still in her cage, patiently awaiting his return.

Day bled into night, and the trek seemed to have no end. Early one evening, Robinson woke to find them on the crest of a fertile basin where a farm sat nestled in a grove of trees, smoke rising lazily from a modest farmhouse. A large barn sat in the center of a dirt field some meters away. The long, painful ride had come to an end. A new one was about to begin.

The bison's lumbering came to a stop. Then Robinson's captor cut his bonds, and he fell to the ground, nearly passing out from the agony of muscles that had knotted in place.

The man in the mask rang a bell, and Robinson thought he felt the earth move. Then a shadowed figure appeared at the barn and blew a note on pipes similar to the one the masked figure carried. His kidnapper hauled Robinson to his feet and dragged him across the field and to the barn.

"Well," the shadowed figure said. "I must say, I am impressed, Cassa. I know the Master will be too."

Robinson recognized the voice. He squinted. "Mr. Dandy?"

Viktor raised the lamp, revealing his fair face.

"It's Viktor now," he said. "How are you, Mr. Crusoe? I must say, you look frightfully less well than you did when we last parted. Of course, you were in the midst of one mighty kerfuffle then too. I'm happy to see you survived."

"What are you doing here?" Robinson asked.

Viktor smiled. "Come in and I'll show you."

Cassa tied his bison to a rail near a trough before pulling Robinson into the barn.

Once inside, Robinson's hands were shackled, and he was kicked to the floor. Then Cassa dumped Robinson's weapons on a table laden with an array of ancient, disassembled equipment before reaching for a pitcher full of water.

"Would you prefer to wash first?" Viktor asked Cassa. The masked man ignored him and drank.

Three lamps illuminated the barn, which was bisected by a large set of sliding, reinforced doors. Robinson looked around, noticing several motionless bodies in a pen nearby. It was obvious they had been experimented on.

"My apologies for the unsavory aroma," Viktor said. "You see, I was not expecting company." He pulled a pocket watch from his waist and flipped it open. "Feeding time is in a few hours. I do hope you can put up with the effluvia until then."

Robinson didn't know who or what would be fed, so he asked, "What are you doing here? What is all this?"

"This is my laboratory," Viktor said, chuckling. "Sounds so theatrical, doesn't it?" His smile quickly faded. "But I feel it's an important distinction to make. These days so little effort is made in the name of advancement. Within these walls, we test the boundaries of science. And by *we*, I mean *me*, of course."

"What kind of science requires live victims?" Robinson asked, stretching to get some feeling back into his extremities.

"Oh, I don't know. Every form since man first stood on two legs? I'll spare you the recriminations of naiveté. The truth is I've had nothing but *non compos mentis* to converse with these past few weeks, and it's been taxing. Of course, there's been the Master, but these days he's…" Viktor felt Cassa's eyes on him, so he said, "*preoccupied.*"

"I seem to remember you had a penchant for the tinkering arts. You were a reader as well, if I'm not mistaken. Tell me, did you ever read *Frankenstein* by Mary Shelley? It was a nod to Zeus's creation of Titan. No? Pity. There are some interesting parallels I'd love to discuss. The important thing is *I've done it.*"

"Done what?"

Viktor leaned in giddily. "Beaten God." He laughed. Then the barn door opened and Saah appeared.

"Are you talking about me again?" Saah said.

"N-no, Master," Viktor said. "Merely prattling. Look who's returned."

Saah emerged out of the dark, his focus on Cassa.

"Welcome back, my son. It's good to see you. I take it you were successful in your study of the city?"

Cassa nodded.

"He was successful at more than that, Master," Viktor said. "He brought you a gift."

Saah turned and saw Robinson on the floor. At first, he had no reaction. Then, a joyous smile lit his face. "Robinson Crusoe. How are you, young ser? You look like you've had quite the journey."

"Tier Saah," Robinson said.

"I see you've recovered some of your manners. Though, you were never the paragon of courtesy to begin with, were you? For the record, I no longer go by Tier or Regent. These days, I am simply called Master. Though for an old friend like you, Vardan is good."

If Saah's civility confused Robinson, he was determined not to let it show.

Saah turned to Cassa. "You relieved him of his weapons?"

Cassa nodded to the weapons on Viktor's desk.

"Good," Saah said. "You look tired, friend. Go clean up and get some rest. You've done well."

Cassa nodded. He glanced at Robinson before he left.

"Good lad," Saah said. "Would have made a fine IronFist. Did he abuse you?"

Robinson shook his head. "He was the paragon of courtesy."

Saah smiled again. "And your girl?"

At first, Robinson thought he meant the mute sister, then he realized he was talking about Friday.

"My *wife* is fine. Thank you for asking."

"*Wife* you say? And a child on the way. Bully for you. You must always appreciate the good things in life when you can. You'll never know how long they'll last."

Saah crossed to the desk and slid Robinson's pistol from its holster. "Impressive. Did the people from the city give you this?"

"Yes."

"It doesn't fire bullets?"

"Sound."

Saah aimed it at the back door.

"You can't fire it. It's coded to me."

"Really?" Saah said. He aimed the gun on Robinson, but Robinson showed no fear. Saah handed the gun to Viktor and said, "Find out how it works."

After, Saah knelt close to Robinson as if he was studying him. Robinson considered making a move then, but he noticed a two-pronged device in the man's hands.

"I pursued you for over a year. Wanting vengeance so badly I could taste it in the air. And yet, no matter how close my dogs of war got, you always managed to stay just out of reach. I confess, it nearly drove me mad. But fate, it seems, had something else in store for us."

Saah removed a piece of paper from his pocket and unfolded it on the ground in front of Robinson. It was an old map of the military base that would become the City of Glass.

"Where did you get that?" Robinson asked.

Saah smiled. "From a friend of yours. She extends her greetings, *Bobby Boy*."

"Joule," Robinson whispered, shocked. "You met her."

"*Met*. Interesting way to put it. You have a way of making enemies, Robinson. Though I confess, I wasn't an initial fan of her program to begin with either. The first thing she did upon my arrival was dump me in cold storage for what I assumed would be a very long rest. But fate has a curious way of interceding in these things. It almost makes one believe the Gods of old are real. Imagine my surprise when I awoke a short while later and was tasked with bringing you back to her."

"And what did she offer in return?"

"My freedom, to start. Though I readily admit it was the army of potential servants on ice that sealed the deal."

Robinson looked at the gore in the pen. "Bad luck for them."

"Oh, these aren't from that offering. These are of the local variety. See, as good as Joule's proposition was, it paled in comparison to what she, and by extension you, led me to instead."

He tapped the paper at Robinson's feet.

"The City of Glass," Robinson said, understanding.

"Was it everything you imagined? All that knowledge and power in one place?"

Robinson considered what he'd seen there. He couldn't deny it.

"I knew it!" Saah laughed. "Once again, providence proves a cunning temptress. For most of my life I've dared to ask the question, *what cost greatness*? How ironic that it is you who taught me the answer. *Sacrifice*. That's the price of any significant endeavor. And the bigger the sacrifice, the bigger the prize. You see, Robinson, I am willing to give up the one thing my heart most desires, killing you, for control of that City. But to do that, I need you to tell me how to get inside. What are their capabilities? What are their defenses? Tell me everything."

"You're mad," Robinson said, "if you think I'd ever help you."

"Oh, but you will," Saah said. "You see, I haven't forgotten what happened that day at the Clutch. The look on your face when I activated the FENIX only to see it explode in the sky. It wasn't relief. It was *surprise*. You thought I'd succeeded, which meant you believed the activation code you gave me was real. Tell me I'm wrong."

Robinson couldn't. Saah had stumbled onto his greatest shame, and now he was lording it over him.

"I imagine it's a hard burden to shoulder. And I do wonder what your father would think if he knew his son was willing to set fire to the world all for the love of a single savage girl?"

"At least my actions were for something. Jaras died for nothing."

Robinson expected Saah to hit him. Instead, he reached out and touched Robinson's cheek, revealing a green vial hanging around his neck as he did.

"Jaras died because of you," Saah said softly. "As did Tessa and my wife. But I am willing to put all that aside in exchange for your help. In return, I give you my solemn word—on the souls of my family—I will set you and your savage *wife* free."

Robinson could see Saah meant it.

"Even if I could help you, their defenses are too good. To get past them, you'd need a real army."

Saah chuckled before nodding to Viktor. "Show him."

Viktor walked to the large doors at the rear of the barn and slid them open. Out of the blackness, an odor of human sweat and waste rolled out along with the sound of shuffling. Robinson felt anxiety boiling in his belly. Saah prodded him up with his weapon.

"Go on," Saah said. "See for yourself."

Viktor held a lamp aloft as Robinson plodded forward. He had seen barbarism before at the hands of the Bone Flayers and Renders. This was far worse. Filling the room were scores of people huddled together in the rankest of conditions. Men, women, and children. Their clothes torn, their flesh rent, their faces vacant, but their eyes fixed in unimaginable terror. That's when Robinson realized, these people were aware of their surroundings but completely controlled by the devices implanted in their heads.

"Here is my army," Saah said as he stepped next to him. "A legion of conscripts, bound to a singular will. Relieved of volition. Incapable of fear. Fodder for the great battle to come."

"What have you done?" Robinson gasped.

"I have become Charlemagne. Alexander. Khan. I am Vishnu, the Destroyer of Worlds."

Saah put his own pipes to his lips and blew a clear note.

"Rise, my children! Rise and let me hear your voice! Let the old world and the new know what waits in the shadows!"

Robinson watched in horror as the group rose to their feet and began to howl, bay, scream, and cry. Saah laughed with delight. Even Mr. Dandy was mesmerized. Robinson covered his ears, afraid the sound might drive him to madness.

He turned to look away and that's when he saw it. One living thing not caught in the Master's thrall. It sat on the floor of a small cage near the barn doors. It too had a blunt mechanism sewn into its skull. Yet this creature's eyes were aware. There was pain there, surely. But also sentience. And hate. Robinson knew those eyes well.

He would recognize the alpha anywhere.

Chapter Forty-Four
The Vial

Robinson lay on the floor of his cage, head pounding, unable to sleep. He was surrounded by Saah's monstrous army, listening to the murmurs and whimpers of those poor beings trapped inside their own flesh.

Across the barn, the alpha paced in her cage. She had remained focused on Robinson since they'd first locked eyes. For once, Robinson didn't begrudge the attention. She was the one thing that took his mind off the tortured souls nearby.

Throughout the day, Cassa continued to shuffle prisoners in from some other location. They were frightened, wounded, and confused, but none of them had any idea of what awaited them inside that barn. One by one, Viktor performed his ghastly surgeries, sawing open skulls and implanting mechanisms in their brains without anesthesia. Through it all, Viktor remained indifferent to the screams. Robinson didn't know what was worse, those cries or the silence that followed when those devices were turned on.

The brutality didn't stop there. Viktor also implanted armaments in his victims. The smaller ones bore crossbows or had gasoline-fueled projectiles sewn into their skin. The larger ones were fitted with rifle barrels and pneumatic projectiles with explosive tips. A few were even fitted with flame throwers.

The speed with which Viktor worked was mind boggling. He seemed to operate on little sleep, yet he was mechanical in his precision. Only a couple of the control units didn't take. All were done away with except the alpha.

"Why keep it alive?" Robinson asked.

It took Viktor a moment to realize he was being spoken to. He looked up from his equipment, which he'd been cleaning after a full day of operations.

"Pardon?" Viktor said.

"The dog. Clearly your device didn't take. Why haven't you gotten rid of it?"

Viktor set down his tools and screwed the cap on a large, rusty can of acetone before placing it back on a shelf. Then he leaned back in his chair and scratched his beard.

"The Master forbids it. It's odd. The canine brain is so rudimentary when compared to the human brain. It should work and yet it doesn't. The Master thinks it's because the dog's will is stronger. Personally, I suspect he keeps it around because he wants to break it himself."

"He's mad, you know," Robinson said.

"Without question," Viktor said.

"Why do you help him?"

Viktor rubbed his scalp wearily. "Do you remember the picture house? Back in Cowboytown?"

"Three colors of celluloid, you said. Magic on a screen."

Viktor smiled fondly at the memory. "The first time we showed one, everyone in town turned out to watch. You can't imagine the look on their faces when that reel started to play. Such wonder and amazement. I'll never forget it. Nor the way they looked at me afterward, as if I was a wizard that had conjured it from the ether."

"Don't tell me you're doing this to be admired."

"Do you see anyone here to impress?"

"Then I still don't get it. What's in this for you?"

"I grew up among the river clans. As a young boy, I was bought and sold many times. I won't bore you with the unpleasantries, only to say I learned from a very early age that if you have nothing to offer, you are truly worthless. I couldn't fight or lead, but I did have an uncanny knack for deciphering the ways of the ancients and the tools they left behind. Because of that, I have value."

"*Value*," Robinson repeated. "And what does that earn you? Luxuries?"

"You're still thinking like an aristocrat. Remember where we are."

North America. The Forbidden Continent. Robinson suddenly understood.

"Security," Robinson said.

"I thought I'd found it with Boss. Then you and your principles came along and ruined everything. When the Master found me, I assumed it was only a matter of time before we'd meet our end. But then I saw that despite his unsettled nature, he had a vision and an ability to spur people into action. Have I had to do some dreadful things since then? Yes. I'm not proud of that, but one does what one must to survive."

"You're a coward," Robinson said.

"Unquestionably," Viktor said, yawning. "Though as I recall, you've done some pretty horrendous things yourself. My hands might be dirty, but yours are far from clean."

"Not like this. *This*," Robinson said, indicating the mutilated people, "is an abomination."

Viktor snorted. "*This* is no different than anywhere else. It's the world we live in. I've done what it takes to persist. You will too."

Robinson saw there was no getting through to him. He groaned, and a whine came from across the room. The alpha was still watching him.

"That dog hasn't taken its eyes off you since you arrived here," Viktor said. "If I was a betting man, I'd wager you two have some history. Too bad for it the Master has plans for you tomorrow."

Tomorrow. Saah had promised to give Robinson time to consider his offer. Clearly, that was up. When the morning came and he refused to tell Saah what he wanted to know … Robinson pulled at his shackles, but there was no give. His situation was bleak. Then he heard something go *tap-tap-tap*. He looked around but saw nothing. It came again. *tap-tap-tap*. The alpha looked up. Robinson did too. He felt hope flood into him as Scout inched across the beam overhead.

The mute sister had waited until the sentries rode over the eastern hill before taking them both out with arrows. After hiding their bodies and collecting the horses, she made her way to the fringes of the farm where mist hovered over the open field. She whistled low, and Scout gave a reply from the barn's rooftop. But when she tried to cross the field, Scout flew in, chirping fretfully. The mute sister halted and looked curiously at the earth. Scout hadn't wanted her to cross it. She picked up a rock and tossed it into the field. The ground shook, and the rock disappeared. She paused to consider what to do next.

Robinson stretched his legs and shook them from cramping up. He was still sore from his ride and knew he might need to move quickly.

When Scout reappeared, Robinson glanced up to the loft. Viktor slept on a small cot, a device in one of his hands. Robinson didn't know if it was an alarm or a set of pipes to rouse Saah's army. He would need to proceed quickly and quietly. He locked eyes with Scout and nodded toward the ring of keys that hung on a hook across the barn.

"Bring me the keys," he whispered.

Scout's wings thrummed as she flew across the barn and slipped the keys from the hook. Then she returned and dropped them in Robinson's lap. The noise caused Viktor to mumble, but he did not wake.

Robinson squirmed until the keys fell onto the dirt. Then he turned until his fingers grasped them. The alpha growled. Robinson shushed her. To his surprise, the alpha lowered its head and continued to watch.

Robinson struggled to fit the proper key into the lock when he felt a hand on his shoulder. His body tensed. He turned to see the mute sister. His relief was immediate. After she freed him, he crept to Viktor's desk to retrieve his weapons. The gun belt was there with his axe and sling. The pistol was not. He hadn't seen Viktor with it and wondered where it could be.

The mute sister tapped him on the shoulder and pointed to two black, spherical halves of a device split open. He nodded, having seen it before. It was one of the drone orbs. The masked figure had brought it back with him so Viktor could study it.

Robinson considered dealing with Viktor first, but he was afraid scaling the rickety wooden stairs might rouse the man, and he'd set an alarm off before Robinson got to him. He whispered to the mute sister instead, "Saah first."

As they crept past the alpha, she moaned, plaintively. Robinson had never heard the dog sound weak. *Even she doesn't deserve this*, Robinson thought. He decided to return once he'd retrieved the vial and put the dog out of its misery.

Outside the barn, the mute sister held up her hand before shooting an arrow to the far end of the field where the beast quickly claimed it.

Robinson and the mute sister pulled up just outside the farmhouse. He inquired about the sentries. The mute sister held up seven fingers, snapping three down.

"That leaves four," Robinson said. "Was one of them riding a bison or wearing a mask?" The mute sister shook her head. "That one's the captain. Saah's inside here. He has the vial around his neck. I'll head in and retrieve it while you keep watch. If you spot anyone approaching, tap on the glass."

The mute sister nodded before giving her knife to Robinson. At the same time, Scout chirped atop a nearby tree limb. She too was awaiting orders.

"I haven't forgotten you, girl. Once we're done here, we'll need to get out of the valley as quickly as possible. Find us the best route, will you?"

Scout chirped twice and flew off.

"Be right back," Robinson said.

He entered through the kitchen where the smell of fresh bread assailed his senses and made his stomach grumble. In the parlor, a low lamp illuminated a room with an antique table. Splayed out across it was the map of the old South Dakota military base. Lying on top of it was Robinson's pistol. He reached for it carefully and slipped it into his gun belt.

The old wooden floors creaked as Robinson crept down the hallway. A narrow curtain of moonlight spilled in from a transom window at the end of the hall. Two of three doors were open, revealing empty rooms with old, made beds that seemed to have been transported from back in time.

The last door was closed, but Robinson could hear light snoring inside. He opened it quietly and saw a lone figure sleeping on the bed inside. It was Saah. He was lying under a single blanket, his mouth slightly ajar. The vial shimmered on the chain around his neck. An old scratched stein smelling of mead sat on the bedside table.

As Robinson stepped close, the floorboards groaned, and Saah opened his eyes.

"Who's there?" he mumbled.

Robinson slid his axe out and was preparing for the killing strike when Saah spoke again.

"Jaras?" His voice was slurred and heavy with sleep.

Robinson felt a flutter in his chest. He refused to pity the man after all he'd done. It didn't matter that Saah was unarmed. It didn't matter that he wasn't a threat. Even the sight of his vulnerable eyes searching the darkness for a loved one who'd never return wasn't enough to earn him a reprieve. So, why was Robinson hesitating? He had killed men before. He had done so without hesitation or guilt. Yet something was staying his hand. He could see the vial around Saah's neck. One swipe of the axe and he would claim it and his revenge. The price had been set. The oldest of compacts. A life for a life. But that wasn't the whole cost, was it? He thought of the simple boy he'd been before he fled to this place. The happy days he'd spent laughing and running in the woods, playing with Tannis, Tallis, and Slink. He would never be that innocent again. But his children could if he learned to put the hate he'd learned here aside. Those marks on his soul might never truly disappear, but if he was willing to choose a better path—one of decency and virtue— they might fade enough that they didn't stain others. It was only then that his mother's parting words came to mind. "You are far too young to bear this burden, but someone must. Knowing the choice is yours gives me comfort." To save his humanity, Robinson lowered his axe.

"Jaras? Is that you?" Saah asked again.

This time, Robinson answered. "Yes, father. It's me. No need to worry. Go back to sleep now."

Saah sighed and his eyes closed. Robinson lifted the axe, but Saah spoke again.

"I was dreaming about the time you broke your arm at the Pate. You were rushed to the healer's house where your mother set it. Do you remember?"

Robinson did. He had been there that day. He and Slink had carried Jaras home.

"I remember," he said.

"I dreamed I broke something too, only she couldn't find it. My bones had gone soft as meal, and I couldn't move. Then Tessa came in wearing the white and healed me with her touch. Do you think she likes it at the healing house?"

Robinson's arm shook. Then it fell to his side.

"I'm sure she loves it."

Saah nodded, and he took another heavy breath. "I would like to see her again."

Robinson's chest had gone tight. Every part of him—every instinct he'd cultivated since arriving on this continent—said *kill this man*, but for some reason he couldn't. He could only think of his mother at that moment and what she might think of him slaughtering an unarmed man.

"Soon enough," Robinson said. "Rest now, father. You have a busy day ahead."

Saah murmured and closed his eyes. Robinson pulled Saah's blanket up to his chin and was surprised when he patted his hand. Little did he know it contained the vial, which Robinson had just taken. It was what he'd come for. Part anyway. He thought of Friday. She would view this tiny mercy as a foolish weakness. But he was who he was.

When Robinson exited the farmhouse, he told the mute sister it was done. Scout chirped from the branch, but Robinson couldn't leave yet.

"We can't leave those people inside the barn," he said.

After the mute sister grudgingly parted with a third arrow to draw the thing beneath the soil away, Robinson slipped back into the barn and retrieved the big can of acetone before pouring it around the barn. He was just about to light it on fire when Scout shrieked wildly at the door. The mute sister looked out and dropped to a knee just as an arrow struck above her.

Viktor bolted up from his cot as the mute sister began firing arrows back toward her assailant. Robinson had no time to think. He leaped for the ladder instead, scrambling to reach Viktor before he raised the pipes to his lips. He was too late. The shrill note rang through the barn, and instantly Saah's army of augmented settlers came alive, storming the sliding doors as their murmuring wails broke the night.

Cassa wasn't shocked the girl evaded his arrow. He knew Crusoe's lover was one of the mountain warriors and very skilled, but her bow work had only been marginal. What he didn't expect was for her to charge him, her blade coming fast enough to force him backward. It took a moment to get her timing down. He was about to counterattack when the girl unexpectedly stepped out into the moonlight. His world fell away.

In the barn, Viktor screamed hysterically as Robinson charged him. Robinson shouted for the pipes, but the Master's army was all Viktor had left. He refused to lose them now. As he scrambled back, his boot struck the leg of his cot and he tumbled over it, knocking the table lamp off as he and it fell to the pen below. He felt the lamp break underneath him and smelled the acetone a moment before everything burst into flames.

The mute sister didn't know why the masked figure wasn't fighting back. She'd felt the lactic acid building up in her own muscles and knew her movements had slowed, and yet the man did nothing but parry her blade again and again.

When the pipes blew inside the barn, she knew it was only a matter of time before more help came. She heard the roar of animals, followed by a *whoosh* before smoke began pouring out. Crusoe still hadn't emerged.

The sentry came from the south, the hooves of his horse shuddering in the mud as his crossbow came up. Without cover, she readied herself for the strike when the masked figure suddenly stepped in front of her. The bolt released and punched him in the chest, catapulting him back into her as they both fell. While falling back, the masked figure fired his own weapon, killing the sentry.

The mute sister shoved the man off her, his mask dropping to the dirt in the process. She grasped around for her blade but couldn't find it. Her eyes had gotten splashed by the spray of blood when the man had been hit. She couldn't understand why he'd saved her. Then he rolled over. Half the man's face and skull had been ravaged by fire, yet she would recognize the eyes of her brother anywhere.

She opened her mouth and bellowed an inhuman scream.

Chapter Forty-Five
Behind the Mask

Saah was half drunk and half asleep when he stumbled out of the farmhouse. He couldn't believe his eyes. Black smoke was billowing out of the barn and already flames were licking the roof. In front of the barn he saw Cassa lying next to what appeared to be a girl, yet he wasn't moving. *Why isn't he moving?* Saah yelled his name twice. Cassa never moved.

From inside the barn came a powerful jolt as something rammed the rear doors. Over the roar of the flames, Saah could hear his army trying to escape. Three of his men appeared out of the eastern fields, sprinting toward the barn.

"No!" Saah screamed. "Wait!"

He fumbled for his pipes too late. A giant tentacle burst out from the earth and snatched one of the men and his mount. He screamed as he was lifted high in the air and thrust back down toward the rising maw in the dirt. The other men kept running.

"The rear door!" Saah yelled. "Release my army before it burns!"

Inside the front half of the barn, Robinson threw a woolen blanket over Viktor to staunch the flames. The moment he pulled it back, he knew the man was dead. The smell of burning flesh seared his nostrils. He tore the pipes from his throat and scuttled away.

The barn quickly filled with smoke. Robinson ran for the open door, but a burning beam fell, barring his way. Behind him, he heard the army pounding on the sliding doors. The metal hinges started to buckle. He blinked back tears, coughing, looking for any way out. The loft was already a raging inferno. Near his heels, the alpha slammed against her cage, clawing at the wooden floor and growling as the flames moved in.

Her actions gave him an idea. He pulled his pistol. What had Pastor said? *The blue chamber fires a sonic blast equivalent to a running kick to the chest.* If there was no door, he would make one.

Robinson thumbed the blue button, aimed at the side of the barn, and pulled the trigger. A cocoon of soundless energy burst from the pistol, the recoil jerking Robinson's hand as the wooden slats of the barn cracked in a four-foot circle. They didn't give. Robinson pulled the trigger twice more. This time, the slats burst open to the outside.

Robinson lurched toward the hole but wavered and fell to his knees. He was coughing raggedly, and his vision started to blur. *Not now*, he thought. *Not yet.* He scrambled toward the door, felt a cool channel of air, and breathed deeply. He was about to stagger out when he heard the alpha rattle her cage again. He looked back and saw the desperation in her eyes. Then she looked at him and whined. It was a foreign sound coming from her.

All the pain she had caused him. All the attempts on his life. He swore he'd put the dog out of her misery, but even he couldn't allow her to burn to death.

Robinson aimed the pistol toward the alpha and thumbed the second button.

The green chamber fires a blast with twice the velocity and impact of a normal forty-five caliber pistol.

Robinson felt his throat tighten. At the last second, he shifted his aim. The jolt ran through his arm a scintilla before the sonic blast struck the pen's lock. He leaped outside without waiting to see if the alpha made it out alive.

Saah grabbed a shovel from the garden, tossing it to the men at the barn's rear doors. The fire was now raging on the opposite side. Saah could hear the screams of his army as they slammed into the doors again and again.

The shovel wielder smashed the lock again and again. The sound came before a rumble of earth as another giant tentacle burst upward and snatched the shovel wielder off his feet, pulling him high into the air. Saah blew a frantic signal for the creature to relent. The thing either couldn't hear the notes over the roaring fire or was already seized by bloodlust. The man screamed once before disappearing down a gyre of razor-sharp teeth.

Saah grabbed the shovel himself and struck the lock. It broke, and the doors swung open as his army spilled forth like a crushing tide. Saah blew his pipes again, but at least a dozen of his warriors were already aflame. While some obeyed his commands to make for the groves, at least half their numbers spilled into the field. Most were retching smoke when tentacles took hold of them. Saah was afraid he was about to lose everything.

Through the smoke, Saah saw a figure limping away from the barn and knew without a doubt it was Robinson Crusoe. Only he could cause this much destruction. He blew a tone, commanding his creatures to kill before pointing out the boy.

On the western side of the barn, Robinson limped to the mute sister only to find her huddled over the man named Cassa, who lay in the dirt, a bolt sticking out of his chest. He was about to pull her up when he saw the man's exposed face. He couldn't have been more stunned. All that time it had been the mute brother hunting Robinson and Friday by Saah's side. He struggled to grasp why, then it struck him. They must have both thought the other was dead. It was the cruelest irony.

Blood bubbled around the wound. It had punctured his lung. Still, when Saah's call for death rang out, Robinson didn't hesitate.

"Get the horses!" he shouted. "It's the only way to save him!"

It was this second order that spurred the mute sister into action. She scrambled to her feet and ran through the gates.

Scout flapped her wings wildly as Saah's army lumbered towards him. Robinson's pistol barked, the sonic blast hitting the lead augmented human and catapulting him backward. Robinson waited a half-second for the gun to recharge and then fired again. *There's too many*, he thought. *It's only a matter of time.*

The mute brother tugged Robinson's sleeve. When he looked down, the injured youth was using his good arm to point to the center of the field where the tentacled creature lived.

Robinson understood. He aimed and fired. Soil and gore kicked skyward as the creature howled, its tentacles lopping around, mowing down bodies. Robinson continued to fire. This time the blast took off a tentacle. The beast howled. This time, the rumble of earth nearly knocked everyone off their feet as the creature used every tentacle to propel itself out of the earth.

It had been too dark in the house to see the beast clearly. Robinson had gotten only a glimpse of that many-mouthed demon, but its abhorrence paled into comparison to the thing he saw rise in front of him. Its body was hoary and shapeless, mutating with each lumbering movement as if it had no bones. Robinson couldn't see any eyes, but it had a mouth—one horrifyingly enormous orifice filled with at least three layers of gore-filled teeth. The flames behind it made it look like a demon from Hell.

Robinson watched in disbelief as the creature swooped up people two at a time, gnashing them into pieces before tossing the rest away. A shrill note broke him from his trance as Saah, at the opposite end of the field, pointed in Robinson's direction.

As the creature lumbered toward them, the earth shook, as did Robinson's hands as he depressed the red button on the pistol, having little idea what was about to happen.

And the red? Robinson had asked Pastor.

Let's just say if you have to topple any buildings, his friend had replied with a smirk, it will give you your start.

Robinson pulled the trigger and felt the pistol vibrate before it fired like a cannon, the recoil kicking the pistol back into his face and bloodying his lip. Unfortunately, the blast hit one of Saah's fleeing soldiers, turning his body into one unsightly spray of mist.

The creature roared as it picked up speed. Robinson tried to fire again, but the readout was slower this time—nearly two seconds. His target had crossed half the field before Robinson fired a second blast. This time the shot missed high and to the left, shredding several of the trees in the grove beyond.

A frantic Scout flew at the creature in hopes of distracting it. It bought Robinson half a second at most. He fought back the rising bile in his throat and wished he had time to dry his hands, but the mute brother was mumbling something as the beast closed the distance in several earth-shaking steps, its hideous maw opening wide and roaring—

BOOM!

The third shot sent tremors up Robinson's arm, and it immediately went numb, yet his aim was true. The sonic blast hit the creature in its amorphous core. At once it was there—a tangible mass of power and force—and then in an instant it disintegrated into a shockwave of flying viscera that coated everything in sight.

Robinson heard the rush of hooves over Saah's furious shrieks. By the time the mute sister reined up with the three horses, Robinson already had her brother on his feet and was propelling him up into the saddle. A few ranging soldiers closed in, but by the time they reached the gate, Robinson and the twins were gone.

Chapter Forty-Six
Value

"You purposely cleansed the girl despite explicit orders to the contrary," Lysa said. "How do you explain yourself?"

Pastor looked over the faces of the half-dozen masters that filled the antiquarian room of the Hall of Literature and thought, *So this is your coterie. You, Virgil, Lopamudra, Bryce, and the others.*

"The virus was mutating," Pastor said. "Even in containment, it had reached the point where, had we waited any longer, the nanobots' effectiveness would be called into question."

"It wasn't your decision to make," someone else said.

"We have a deal with Robinson," Pastor said.

"In exchange for the second strain of the EBU-GENC2 virus," Lysa added. "Has he delivered it?"

"He will," Pastor replied.

"You say that, but you have no evidence he's succeeded. Or if he is even alive."

"I don't need evidence. I know the boy well."

Lysa grunted.

"The fact remains," Mathias, the once German industrialist said, "you swore the oath and you have violated it."

"The oath states we cannot aid or effect change upon those outside the city. The girl is inside, is she not?"

"For now," Virgil said.

"Then I've done nothing but help us keep our word."

"And if your friend doesn't return?" Lopamudra, the lithe Indian asked.

Pastor shrugged. "Well, I imagine Engineering could always use another apprentice."

"*That* savage among my discipline?" Lopamudra scoffed. "Ridiculous."

"That *savage* is smarter and cleverer than half the masters here. She could teach all of you a thing or two."

"Enough," Lysa said. "You disappoint me, William. For two hundred years, we've protected you, let you live among us, and this is how you thank us."

"Oh, get off your high horse, *Lysa*. You've always needed me to do your dirty work. And you forget I knew you back when you were a snooty, nineteen-year-old rich kid whose only talent was using single-syllable words on social media. And suddenly you think you're God."

"There is no God," Lysa said. "Or if there was, He has been replaced."

Pastor shook his head. He could have continued with this farce but didn't see the point. These masters believed they were heading into uncharted territory, where they alone might expand the boundaries of human existence. What they failed to understand was that the new roads were the same as the old ones. Only the traveler and the scenery changed. Knowledge and skill could take you far, but in the end, the same DNA that prompted our creation also ensured its destruction.

"He'll need to be disciplined," Mathias said.

"And he will," Lysa said. "But not in front of *the body*. Not yet anyway. There's still dirty work to be done." Pastor looked up, concerned. "It seems your trip to the Medica was more successful than you intended. Your savage girl's water just broke."

Pastor took off running.

Friday's shout's reached Pastor's ears the moment he turned into the Medica hallway.

"Get away!" she shouted.

Pastor entered the room to see Friday on a bed, struggling with two medical masters. One of her arms had been bound to the bed. They were struggling to bind the other.

"What is this?" Pastor bellowed.

"She refuses to let us deliver the baby," one of the masters said.

"Not with those!" Friday screamed, pointing to the robotic arms maneuvering above.

The female master lost hold of Friday's wrist, and Friday cracked her in the face and sent her sprawling to the floor. Friday then grabbed the second master by the hair, pulling the robotic arm and its scalpel toward his jugular.

"Free me," she growled.

Pastor laughed. "You'd better do as she says."

The man freed Friday's wrist, and she shoved him away. She tried to rise but was seized by contractions.

"You two," Pastor said to the masters, "Go."

They didn't have to be told twice. They fled out of the room.

"Can't … have baby in … here," Friday growled as she tried to rise again.

Pastor put a gentle hand on her shoulder.

"But you will. With me. No machines, I promise."

Friday locked eyes with him and lay back.

"The important thing now is to breathe. Big, deep breaths."

Friday did as she was told, and after a few more seconds, the contractions relented.

"Better?" he asked.

"Than what?" Friday spat. "Being stabbed from within?"

Pastor laughed again. Then he looked up at the three-dimensional hologram above him.

"Let's see. Your vitals look good. Blood pressure is a little high, but that's to be expected. Ninety percent effacement, and the baby is in a good position."

"You have done this before?"

"I did many things in my youth." Pastor walked to a machine, raised his hands, and said, "Cleanse and wrap, please." A stream of nanobots poured out and cleaned his hands before applying a clear protective coat of gel. He walked back to Friday and touched her belly.

"My parents were Gypsies—*Romani*—but we almost always called ourselves travelers. We used to travel the country, going from town to town, doing odd jobs, running the occasional scam."

"Scam?"

"Uh, con games. Deceptive agreements. They were not very nice, but they taught me a lot about the world and the nature of people. *Our* nature was reclusive. We rarely interacted with society. We never went to school or to doctors. That is how I learned this."

Pastor watched the vitals as Friday went through another series of contractions.

"Have you ever see…?" Friday said, but couldn't finish.

"A stillborn delivery? Yes. Among other things. But they are rare. And they won't happen under my watch."

"What if my child is born sick?"

"Then I'll do everything I can to heal it as I healed you."

Friday nodded, her eyes watering. "Crusoe should be here."

"I know. But he'll be back soon enough. Now, the contractions are getting close. If you want something to reduce the pain, we'll need to use it now."

"No. Pain teaches us the value of life. And nothing has more value than this."

Pastor shook his head. "You are a remarkable woman, Friday. I hope you know that. Are you ready?"

The birthing would take another two hours. By the time it was done, Friday would hold a healthy, nine-pound baby in her arms.

"Congratulations," Pastor said, exhausted and elated. "You have a healthy baby girl."

Friday smiled, for once oblivious to her tears.

"Have you thought of a name?"

Friday shook her head.

"Perhaps we could come up with a few options before Robinson—"

The door whisked open suddenly, and Gesta appeared with three men in tow.

"I'm sorry about this," Gesta said.

"About what?" Pastor asked. "What are they doing here?"

"Lysa wants the baby," Gesta said.

He nodded to the others. Pastor stepped forward to stop them only to get punched in the stomach and drop to the floor. Friday screamed and clawed at the men until one of them touched her with an object, and she went limp. The last thing she saw was her baby being taken away.

Chapter Forty-Seven
Silent Sorrow

The vial.

Saah had seen it around Robinson's neck just before he rode away. The idea that this boy—this insignificant worm—could continue to take from him without reparations was beyond infuriating. Now, the farm lay in ruins. The field was littered with the carnage of his fallen warriors. Even his beloved pet guardian had been killed. But the loss that hurt most was Viktor. The man had been with him since the beginning of his crusade. He hadn't liked him exactly—he was a terrible companion with his flippant remarks and cowardice—but he was polite and clever and had a mind for deliciously awful things. His creativity would be sorely missed.

If there was any silver lining to Viktor's death, it was that he had delivered everything needed to take the City of Glass. The ordinance he'd manufactured for the augmented had fortunately been stored away from the main barn. And despite the turmoil of the previous night, the surviving warriors had almost all responded to his call once things calmed down. Thirty-six of them had perished in the fire or fields, leaving ninety-two to his command.

As he left the groves to head west once more, Saah looked back at his farmhouse and knew he would never see it again. No matter. A little over seven hundred miles away sat his next home, and it was fit for a king. He prayed the ninety-two marching at his side would be enough to take it.

They'd ridden for a day-and-a-half straight, only stopping long enough to let the horses rest and graze. Robinson had managed to remove the bolt from the mute brother's chest and cauterize the wound, but infection had set in despite their every precaution. Using the glasses and wand Pastor had given him, Robinson had sought out the only available remedies—garlic and purple coneflower—which he used to make a poultice to fight the bacteria. Even it was proving ineffective. Fever had set in the second morning. He had become lethargic.

"He's lost a lot of blood," Robinson said to the mute sister privately. "And the pace we're keeping isn't doing him any favors. Plus, his infection is worsening."

The girl gestured of tall buildings with her hands.

Robinson shook his head. "Even if we rode day and night, it would take six days to reach it. He doesn't have six days. He needs rest."

The girl grit her teeth and pointed at him.

"I'm not a healer," he said. She pointed at him again, then at the herbs. "I know as much as you."

Anger lit the girl's face. She poked him hard in the chest and then the head. She gestured in the direction they were headed and then cupped a hand under her breast as if holding her swollen belly. She pointed to his heart before pointing to her brother and then her own.

Robinson understood. Her brother was all she had. But any help Robinson could provide would only mean delaying his return. Friday was still ill. Every second he was away from her and their child was another second the virus could mutate and kill them both.

And yet he couldn't bear the thought of leaving more wounded in his wake. It was already a tally with too many casualties.

"Scout," Robinson called. The bird landed on his shoulder and chirped. "You saw Saah and his army leave the farm last night. How many hours would you estimate they are behind us?"

Scout chirped fourteen times.

"Are they moving at our pace or faster?"

Scout chirped once.

Robinson took out his glasses and said, "show me a map of this area."

Inside Robinson's glasses, a holographic map appeared.

"Expand to fifty miles."

The image did.

"Expand to one hundred miles."

The image did.

"Lincoln City, Nebraska. How far away are we?"

A prompt in the glasses read: *approximately sixty miles.*

Robinson slipped off the glasses.

"Sixty miles. It's likely to have a hospital big enough to have survived with the materials we need for a blood transfusion. Since you're twins, matching shouldn't be a problem. It's out of our way, but I'm willing to try it if you are."

The mute sister reached out and touched his arm tenderly before nodding once.

"Get ready then," he said. The girl ran off. Robinson turned to Scout. "Scout, I need you to plot us the easiest course to Lincoln City. No distractions. No surprises. Can you do that, girl?" Scout chirped once. "Then get going."

Scout took to flight.

The ride took a day and a half. During daylight hours, Robinson used Scout to navigate their path. At night when they rested, he directed her to fly back and monitor Saah's progression. He had no idea how fast she could fly, yet she always managed to return by morning. The reports, however, were not as welcome. Despite leading an army of close to one hundred, Saah was slowly gaining on them. Robinson knew Saah would drive his army hard. What he didn't expect was his willingness to risk their numbers to catch them.

Lincoln City's hospital was in a bad state. Still, Robinson managed to find the materials capable of transfusing the mute sister's blood into her brother. There was still risk. While Robinson had boiled all the materials first, the inability to process the blood would mean a greater risk of adverse reactions, including sepsis. Yet within minutes of the transfusion, the mute brother's color returned, and he even managed to eat and drink on his own.

For a few days afterward, they made good time. Then, the mute brother's

wounds darkened again. Infection had set in too deep. The mute sister begged Robinson to perform another transfusion, but she was still weak from the first time. Even if she could survive the loss of blood, it would only buy her brother a day or two. In the end, the mute brother decided for them when he pulled the medical supplies from their pack and tossed them in the dirt.

Later that day, Scout found a small pond near a grove of Cottonwood where Robinson and the mute sister helped her brother down and set him against one of the trees where he could look out over the water and watch the sunset. Robinson led the horses away while the siblings spoke their silent language together. The communication reminded him of Tannis and Tallis. They too had their own language. One of words, sighs, grunts, and facial expressions. Were all twins the same? He suspected so.

When Robinson returned, he found the mute sister had built a fire. In the dimming light, her brother looked wan. Robinson was about to excuse himself again when the mute sister beckoned him over. She signaled that her brother wanted to hear Robinson.

"You want me to talk?" Robinson asked.

The mute brother shook his head carefully. This time, his sister touched her heart, then her lips before waggling her fingers in the air.

Robinson understood. The mute brother wanted to hear a song. Robinson felt his throat tighten but fought back his emotions. He didn't want the boy to mistake tears for pity.

"We didn't sing where I come from. Songs were illegal for most of my life." He wondered if that had changed. "But Friday used to hum a tune when we walked. I'm not sure she was even aware of it or what it's about. But if you like, I'll sing it for you."

Robinson started slowly, his voice tentative, but as the first verse elapsed, his breath became deeper, and the melody started to flow from him. He'd lied when he said he didn't know what the song was about. Friday had told him, and even if she hadn't, he would have understood by the profundity of emotion that accompanied it. It was a song of loss. And of remembrance. Of those that have gone but are not forgotten. It was an ideal song for that time and place. The mute siblings must have thought so too because the one time

Robinson glanced at them, both had tears in their eyes. So, he continued, repeating it again and again as the sun continued to fall. His words carried over the water and the mute sister's sobs when her brother breathed his last.

Chapter Forty-Eight
Treachery

Saah found the pack horse lying dead in a ditch just inside the Badlands, maggots having already laid siege to its mouth and eyes.

The Crusoe boy is scared, Saah thought. At least with Cassa, Crusoe had taken the time to bury his body.

Good. Let him run. This time, there will be nowhere to hide.

Saah had pushed his army hard over the twelve days, and as a result, eight of his warriors had dropped dead along with three of their mounts. A few more teetered on the brink, but the effort had been worth it. He now stood within a short march of the City of Glass. One day more, and it would be his.

Saah had an unselfish reason for trying to catch Crusoe before he reached the city. He wanted the first thing the inhabitants to see was the boy's head mounted at the front of his vanguard. They had sent him after all. He knew it was true. No other reason could have convinced the boy to abandon his young lover. Maybe they'd blackmailed him or promised him riches beyond measure. It didn't matter. What was important was that they refused to do the task themselves. That told him they were cowards. And cowards could always be defeated. So, what if Crusoe survived a little longer? Soon the city would fall and Robinson with it.

"We will quarter here for the night," Saah said to the last of his men. "Let my army feast on this steed before they rest."

"One dead horse ain't enough to feed 'em all, Master," one of his few living men said.

"Then they shall have yours too. Come morning, I want their armaments ready. And pay careful attention who you give these to." He patted two bulging saddlebags hanging on his horse. "Viktor crafted these with great care before his demise. Only my healthiest warriors shall bear them."

As Saah's men set to task, he looked to the vacant sky in the distance, knowing it was illusion but admiring it all the same.

"Today the skies glow," Saah said to himself. "Tomorrow they shall bleed."

Three miles away, Robinson and the mute sister pushed their spent horses through the steppes of the pass that lead to the City of Glass. A familiar *whir* echoed over the sands as a half-dozen drones appeared from nowhere and fanned out in front of them.

The mute sister was almost too exhausted to lift her head. Robinson took the vial from around his neck and held it up into the sky. After a moment, the drones parted, and Robinson pushed his horse on.

Lysa was waiting for him at the City gates, looking the same as when he had left. He wondered if she could say the same about him.

"Pastor said you were resilient," Lysa said. She held out her hand. "May I?"

"Friday first," Robinson said. "Where is she?"

"Inside. Along with your daughter."

Robinson's world shifted off its axis.

"My daughter?" Robinson gasped. "Is she…?"

"A fair, healthy child, resting comfortably," Lysa said. "Now, if you please?"

She held out her hand again and Robinson removed the vial from his neck and handed it to her. She passed it carefully to Gesta. "Verify it's the second strain."

As Gesta ran off, Lysa turned back to Robinson.

"You are a remarkable young man. Our probability masters put the success of your task at less than five percent, and they are seldom wrong. There was a time not long ago we might have found a place for you among us if only to study you and learn from your experiences."

"Like you did with Pastor?" Robinson asked.

Lysa smiled. "Oh, no. William was a failed experiment from the start. A remnant of a lesser time when the farce of social order outweighed true reason. He's had his uses though. He delivered us you."

Something in her words rankled Robinson. He felt like a punchline was coming, but he hadn't heard the joke.

"So, now I've delivered what I've promised. I'd like to see my family now."

"Do you know what the true irony of the City of Glass is? Glass is fragile. It's not meant to last forever. For two centuries, we've safeguarded history here as if it was a precious thing to be coddled and studied. Only recently have we realized everything in nature—every civilization, every species, every forest—must be denude so the fallow earth can bring life again. This time, however, man won't be forced to crawl from the muck from whence he came. This time, they will rise from the tabula rasa of our experiences, and they shall thrive."

"What are you saying?"

Lysa smiled as if talking to a child.

"I'm saying that you have played a pivotal role in the history to come. It's a shame no one will be around to remember it."

Robinson came to a sickening realization.

"You're not going to destroy the virus," he said. "You're going to use it."

"It is indeed far more virulent than the first strain. Not that you would know, given how it lay dormant in your lover. But with a few modifications, its full potency will be unleashed and—unlike its flawed sibling—it will only target humans. And it will expunge them completely."

"But that's genocide."

"When you live as long as I have, words like genocide lose their power. I watched seven billion die in the first plague. What's a few million more to get things right?"

Robinson didn't notice the drones sinking in from above until the mute sister started. Then he spun and saw a half-dozen men surrounding them. The mute sister reached for her blade only to be hit by some kind of charge from the drone. Robinson raised his hands, and both were bound.

312

"You can't do this. There are people out there. Good people. Families. They can get it right this time if only you'd give them a chance!"

"It's choice, not chance, that determines one's destiny. I'd tell you to remember that, but I don't think you'll be needing it where you're headed."

Lysa nodded, and the men started to haul the pair off.

"Wait," Robinson said. "There's something you should know. The man I told you about, Saah—"

"Has followed you here. We're aware. At this very moment, he has set up camp just outside the perimeter of the valley and will attack at dawn. When he does, he, his two men, and eighty-four of his abominations will be dealt with once and for all."

"It won't be that easy. He has weapons."

"Sticks and stones before the cavalry."

"You don't know him like I do," Robinson shouted as he was pulled away. "The man is cunning! He'll have a plan!"

"As will we."

They were taken to a holding area, a small windowless room behind an energy screen. Robinson reached to help the girl up when she was thrown in behind him.

"Let me," a voice said. Pastor emerged from the shadows. Robinson glared at him as they helped her to a bunk.

"Was it a drone?" Pastor asked. Robinson nodded. "Fifty thousand volts. I've felt it once myself. Not a thing I'd like to repeat. She'll be all right."

"You lied to me," Robinson said.

Pastor looked as if he wanted to speak, but couldn't. He saw the anger in Robinson's eyes. It was the hurt that troubled him worse.

"I did what I had to do to keep you safe."

"Does this look safe to you?"

"Yes. You're both alive after all."

"For now. You have no idea what we went through out there. What *she* went through. We found her brother. He was one of Saah's men."

Was. Pastor looked at the mute sister and saw she was crying.

"Dear child. I'm so sorry."

"Sorry isn't good enough," Robinson said. "Where's Friday? Lysa said she gave birth."

At this, Pastor smiled faintly. "I delivered her myself. You forget after a time what it's like to hold them. She's a wisp of a thing but pretty as a flower. She has Friday's nose and your eyes." And then Pastor's face turned grim. "Lysa took the baby."

"What?" Robinson said. "Why?"

"She and the others have been preparing something for a while. It has to do with genetics. She thinks the child is special. Conceived naturally, but cleansed and perfected with nanotechnology before birth. I believe she plans to study her."

Robinson couldn't contain his anger. He roared as he rushed the invisible field, slamming it with his fists over and over until Pastor finally pulled him off.

"Why didn't you stop her?" Robinson sobbed.

"I tried," Pastor said. "I wish I could explain everything…" He grimaced in pain. "Did you retrieve the virus? Does Lysa have it?"

"Yes. And you know what she plans to do with it, don't you?"

Pastor nodded. Robinson thought the man looked older than he'd ever seen him.

"How could you agree to that? How could you make me a party to it?"

"I didn't have a choice. I'm a prisoner to this madness just like you. Only I've been here much longer."

The thing that had been bothering Robinson resurfaced.

"When we first came here, Lysa said they hadn't had a visitor in thirteen years, yet you arrived less than a year before. And just now, she said you were a 'failed experiment from the start.' What 'start' is she talking about?"

"Haven't you figured it out yet?"

Robinson's eyes lit. "You've been here before."

Pastor stood, unsure he was capable of unburdening himself of the truth, but knowing it was time just the same.

"I was born in Pittsburgh, Pennsylvania, in the year 1979. Oldest of eleven children. My father was a career hustler and criminal who spent more time in bars and prisons than at home. My mother worked three jobs a day just to make ends meet. When I turned fourteen, I quit school so I could work too. For a while, that was my life. Then I felt the call of the road. In those days, it was much safer to bounce around, though the color of my skin gave me some trouble. I traveled from coast to coast. I lived and loved. And I worked. As a fisherman in Seattle. A basketball coach in Minnesota. A *pastor* in Florida. Sometime after my twenty-sixth birthday, I took an odd job driving people from a small, deserted airport to a retired military base hidden in the mountains. The same base that now rests under these very towers.

"One snowy night I was delivering yet another *great mind* here when news of the pandemic hit. Three hundred of the world's best and brightest watched the lights blink out on TV, and there was nothing they could do. A handful took their own lives, others left. The rest closed the door, sealed the latches, and set about to ensure man would never stumble again. What you see now is the fruit of those labors."

"You're over two hundred years old?"

"Genetic enhancement. It was one of their primary goals. To sustain life. I wonder if they knew back then where it would take them."

"So everyone here is...."

"Equally old, yes. But like all things in life, immortality comes at a cost. DNA accession therapy once a year. The inability to bear children. For Lysa and her ilk, a small sum to pay. For someone like me, an outsider lucky enough to get swept up in their tide? The perfect leash."

"But when we first met, you were outside."

"They called us the eight. It was a plan not without controversy. The masters had noticed mankind's resurgence, so they sent eight of us out across the country to assess whether people had learned from their mistakes and whether we might finally open the doors and use all the knowledge we'd acquired to extend our idea of happiness."

"And what happened?" Robinson asked, though he knew the answer.

"Seven of us never returned. And I, having sworn the oath, told them the truth once I did. Mankind hadn't changed. I spoke of the brutality I had witnessed. The cruelty and evil. It had quite the impact. Unfortunately, what they didn't hear were the stories of bravery, compassion, and joy. As I said in the forest that day, it's why I wanted them so desperately to meet you." Pastor sighed wearily. "Now, I think it would have been better had I not returned at all."

"But you would have died without the therapy."

"At least my conscience would be clean."

Robinson thought of his own selfish acts. *Were these better or worse?*

"Why didn't you tell me all this back then? And please don't say the oath."

Pastor rubbed his face wearily. "The oath is more than just a promise."

"Lysa said the irony of the City of Glass is that it is fragile, and she's right, but not in the way she meant. From the day I arrived here, I saw the towers and the technological advances. But you know what I didn't see? Smiles. Joy. Peace. The man I met in the forest that day—with his great booming laugh and his love of wine and stories? That man was alive, unlike the one standing before me. Sure, in here you can riddle out life's secrets. But it's only out there you can live them. To me, that's utopia."

Pastor looked up at him and nodded. "And that's why you're the smartest one here."

Suddenly, the building shook with the sound of a detonation far away.

"What was that?" Robinson asked.

"I don't know," Pastor answered before several loud *thrums* passed overhead. "But those I recognize. Lysa's birds."

"Saah's not waiting for morning to attack. He's coming now," Robinson said as he leaped to the window calling, "Guard!" One of the city's men appeared outside the barrier. "Tell Lysa I have information about this attack. Now!"

As the guard ran off, Robinson hoped it wasn't too late.

Chapter Forty-Nine
Peacekeeper

"Status report," Lysa said as she walked into the Vista Room, a rotund atop the north tower that doubled as a command center. Holographic images of the city and the exterior valley filled the air in front of them. "Are we under attack?"

"I'm not certain," the martial master said. "It appears the enemy discharged something into the sky."

"*Something?*" Lysa snapped. "Was it a weapon or not?"

"If it is, it never purged the dissimulation barrier. Perhaps it malfunctioned. I've sent drones out for a look."

"What about the remote sensors?"

"Data coming back is inconclusive. It's like something is interfering with their instrumentation."

Lysa felt a nervous sensation run up her spine as she remembered the boy's warning.

"How long until the birds are in range?" Lysa asked.

"I should have visual and spectral readings momentarily."

Gesta swept in. "What's happening? Are they advancing?"

"We're assessing that now," Lysa said. "Why aren't you with Veracruz and the others?"

"They've called for a gathering of *the body*."

Lysa shook her head. "Leave it to that bunch to clambake with barbarians at the gate."

"Are we in danger?" Gesta asked.

"Of course not. But they don't need to know that. A little dose of fear might be just what the doctor ordered to wake the *ordo senatorius* up."

"Before I forget, the savage boy wants to speak with you. He says he has information you might need about the man out there."

"That *man* is about to be dead. And the boy isn't far behind him." Lysa turned back to the martial master. "Status."

"Drones coming into range now," the martial master said.

Cameras from the drones appeared side by side in a hologram HUD, revealing empty desert with a cloud in front of them.

"What is that?" Gesta said.

"I'm not sure," the martial master replied. "Sensors are still having trouble purging it. Trying thermographic and photo-acoustic imaging now."

The screen remained fuzzy.

"Well? Why can't we see through it?"

"It appears to be repelling our sensors. The drones are almost in range."

Lysa opened her mouth to veto the idea, but turned to Gesta instead. "Get the boy."

As Gesta left, the holographic HUD showed the drones cross into the cloud. A warning on the first drone rang out. Visuals went blank soon after and the words "system failure" flashed across the screen as the drone plummeted out of the sky.

"Losing number one!" the martial master shouted.

"Recall the other," Lysa said.

Too late. The instrumentation failure echoed its predecessor across the hologram HUD.

"Number two is down," the martial master said.

"Fire the acoustic cannons," Lysa barked.

"Targeting won't be able to lock—"

"Go manual!"

As the martial master scrambled to adjust, Gesta reentered the room with Robinson, Pastor, and one of the guards.

"Saah isn't waiting for morning," Robinson said. "He's attacking now."

"Really? If the sum of your insight consists of stating the obvious then your presence here is not needed."

Pastor saw the cloud on the monitor. "What is that?"

"A magnetic cloud apparently," Lysa said. "And if this lunatic thinks he can hide behind it, he is sorely mistaken."

"Manual targeting online. Sighting now," the martial master said.

"It's a ruse," Robinson said.

"What?" Lysa said.

"Vardan Saah may be mad, but he's also very shrewd. He's not one to act without thinking through all the angles. Every action has a purpose. Every move designed to elicit a response."

"So?"

"So, if Saah threw a target up, he wants you to hit it."

"Then who am I to disappoint him? Fire."

Four thunderous blasts shook the tower as longitudinal waves of energy broke the sound barrier fractions of a second before they hit the cloud, dispersing it instantly, revealing a barren field beneath.

Lysa gaped. "What happened? Were they eradicated?"

"If they were," the martial master said. "There would be debris, residue. It's like … they've vanished."

Robinson suddenly came to a terrible resolution. "Saah had blueprints of here that Joule gave him. I saw them at the farm."

"I assure you the city has never used any blueprints."

"Not the city," Robinson said. "The base from before." He turned to Pastor. "Didn't you say some of it survived?"

A horrifying realization set in the room.

"Bring up the subterranean map," Lysa said nervously. "Everything that still exists."

The martial master repeated the command aloud, and a three-dimensional map appeared on screen.

"Rotate it over our topography," Lysa ordered.

The tension grew thick as the map fell into place, revealing a long, slim corridor that ran out away from the city, lining up with Saah's army's previous location.

Gasps ran through the room.

"That's a ventilation shaft from one of the old missile silos," Pastor said.

"We have no defenses down there," the martial master said. "If they reach the central conduit—"

"Send in more birds," Lysa ordered.

"What about the Exodus Vault?" Gesta said. "It's underground."

"It was constructed independently. The only entrance is through the Adytum. It's secure."

"I have to warn *the body*," Gesta said, rushing for the door.

"Wait!" Lysa called, but he was already gone. She turned back to the hologram HUDS, several of which showed the drones' POV as they moved through the dark, timeworn corridors.

"You should pull the drones back," Robinson said. "There's no room for them to maneuver down there. If they get into the close quarters combat—"

"Be quiet," Lysa said.

"I'm telling you, Saah did his homework. He knows you own the sky. That's why he's taken the fight underground. Unless you want to lose more of your resources—"

"I said stop talking! The birds have kept the peace here for over a hundred years. Rooting a few rats from the sewer will be no different."

Robinson's guard grasped his arm firmly. He looked at Pastor and shook his head.

The drones continued down the corridor, each agonizing second longer than the last.

"Maybe we were mistaken," the martial master said. "Maybe they retreated—"

At that very moment, the drones turned a corner and ran into a wall of screaming, howling flesh. Blinding drone fire filled the screen as the howls of the augmented echoed through the corridor. Flashes of light and concussive blasts preceded a leaping form bringing down a cudgel. In an instant, the first drone went down, followed quickly by the second as both POVs went dark. The "system failure" warning flashed again in the air.

The room was silent. Robinson thought he could hear his own heartbeat.

"That's three hundred yards from the central conduit," Pastor said. "If we're lucky, we have two minutes before they purge the city, Lysa. You need to evacuate now."

"Where?" Lysa said, dazed. "There's nowhere to go."

Pastor stepped forward. "Send them to the Exodus Vault. It can protect everyone until we come up with a plan." She shook her head, frozen. "Lysa! You need to act now."

Lysa nodded. "You're right." She turned to the martial master. "Activate Peacekeeper."

"No!" Pastor shouted. "You can't!" He took a step in her direction only to cry out in pain and collapse.

Robinson dropped to his side. "What is it? What have you done to him?"

"I've done nothing," Lysa said. "It's the oath." She nodded to the martial master.

The man ran his hands over the hologram HUD, and a warning flashed across the screen. A disembodied voice spoke.

Peacekeeper has been activated. Countdown, ten minutes.

"What's Peacekeeper?" Robinson said.

Lysa's eyes narrowed, her lips curling upward. "Tabula Rasa."

Robinson moved instantly, slamming his guard in the throat and stripping his weapon away. Lysa charged him, but Robinson swung the weapon butt into her face, knocking her unconscious. The martial master stood to halt only when the weapon stopped inches from his face. A tense second, then another explosion rocked the building. The martial master looked at the emerging hologram HUD. A flood of the augmented were streaming out of a smoldering hole in the ground, killing people at random as they fled.

"The enemy's in the central courtyard," the martial master said, sitting. "Birds incoming."

The HUD zoomed in as Saah appeared, pulling one of the special augmented with him. The man raised his hand, and a mortar shot high into the sky and detonated into a familiar dense cloud. The incoming drones began to fall from the sky.

Saah grinned, and his eyes seemed to find one of the cameras as if he knew who was watching.

"Cry havoc," his voice rang through the speakers, "and let slip the dogs of war!"

As the spate of monsters spilled from the earth, people fled. They leaped onto rises only to watch horrified as the floating tiles malfunctioned in the mysterious clouds. They plummeted to the streets, those unlucky enough to survive the drop were descended upon by the augmented.

"Sound the alarm," Robinson said as he raced for the door. "Get everyone to that vault now!"

The martial master did as he was told.

Robinson ran back to the security room. After freeing the mute sister, he retrieved their weapons, activating Scout with a verbal command. Pastor appeared, blood running down his nose.

"Where are you going?" Pastor asked.

"To get Friday and my daughter. Are you okay?"

Pastor nodded. "Follow me."

The trio ran down the hall with Scout flying overhead. They mounted three rises to traverse the gap between towers. Weapon fire and screams rang through the atrium. A group of City Guards appeared far below, rushing out the main door of the Adytum. All around them the disembodied voice continued its countdown, *Nine minutes until Peacekeeper launch.*

"What's Peacekeeper?" Robinson shouted across the void.

"An intercontinental missile from our time, enhanced to disperse an airborne version of the second strain of EBU-GENC into the atmosphere."

"They're really going to go through with it?"

"It was inevitable."

"Can we stop it?"

Pastor struggled for a moment and then shook his head. "I can't, no."

Robinson nodded, but he caught an odd look coming from the mute sister.

At the Medica, the standing guard saw their approach and reached for his weapon. He was out before he hit the ground.

Robinson ripped curtains from their moorings, locating Friday behind the third. He'd imagined finding her a million different ways. Gaunt. Diseased. Frail. She was none of those things. She was only herself, beautiful as the newborn day. He tore at her bonds, and before the second snapped open, she drew him into her arms.

"They have our daughter," Friday said once he pulled away.

"I know. We'll find her." After freeing Friday, Robinson turned to Pastor. "Do you know where she's being held?"

Pastor shook his head. "The system will no longer recognize me."

The disembodied voice sounded, *Eight minutes until Peacekeeper launch.*

"Scout," Robinson said to the bird. "Find our daughter."

Scout chirped and flew off. The group followed her.

Scout led them to that floor's exterior platform, which looked over the streets below. The iridescent avenues now ran red with blood, the screams of victims crawling up the towers. Saah's bloodlust was in full bloom. His pipes blew, and his army cut down the innocent wherever they were found. The alarm had sent the crowd rushing for the Adytum, only to find armed assailants waiting outside.

The air above was clotted with that mysterious cloud, keeping the drones on the outskirts of the battle. A few managed to pick off the augmented, but for every shot fired at one of Saah's, the host turned *en mass*, launching bolts, pistol shots, and short-range missiles. The result was a rapidly dwindling air force that, once fallen, would signal the end of the inhabitants for good.

"We need to get across," Robinson shouted. Scout chirped from the opposite tower, two levels below. "I don't think we can use the rises though. Not with that cloud still in the air."

"There is no other way," Friday said as she leaped onto the rise and leaned away. Robinson shouted her name, but it was no use. The mute sister looked at her.

"Well? Go. I'll cover you from here."

The mute sister also leaped onto one of the rises, following Friday.

Pastor shook his head. "Two centuries, and women haven't changed a bit."

Robinson grunted. After the women reached Scout's platform, the mute sister slipped a bolt into her bow and signaled. Pastor was already halfway across when Robinson stepped onto his rise and it surged out into the open air. He felt a stiff breeze carrying smoke and something else. He was trying to avoid the cloud when he heard a shout below.

Saah had seen him. Robinson felt his stomach tighten as Saah raised his pipes and blew. Immediately, a half-dozen augmented began targeting him from below. Bolts zipped by as did a great plume of fire from a flamethrower. Robinson veered to avoid the column while returning fire with the pistol's green button. The sonic blast struck the augmented with the fuel tank, and he exploded into flames, taking out a handful of companions. Unfortunately, the recoil sent Robinson staggering back. He heard Friday shout and felt a moment of vertigo, but the rise miraculously righted beneath him.

Saah watched Crusoe's acrobatics from below with his usual chagrin. He still chaffed over the decision not to kill the boy when he was in his possession. He would not make that mistake twice. He again slipped the pipes between his lips and blew two notes. The first activated stimulant injections in every member of his army. He heard the beasts gasp as their systems flooded with adrenaline while simultaneously numbing them to pain. Most would die later from the dose, but by then, his objective would have either been won or lost. His second note activated the berserker response Viktor had created. Immediately snarls and screams ran through the throng as rage consumed them. Now, they would kill indiscriminately until they were killed or the last of their energy was exhausted.

Robinson saw the transformation come over Saah's army and knew it was bad. Then, movement came from his left as two augmented with mechanical pistons fused into their legs squatted and leaped two stories into the air, straight at him. The first held a bloody chain with razor wire whipping from the end. He was about to swing it at Robinson when an arrow struck the creature in the chest and sent him tumbling back to the ground.

The second grasped onto the balcony edge moments after Robinson had landed. He stepped on the creature's fingers and watched him fall.

In the streets, the city inhabitants continued running for the main Adytum. Saah blew his pipes and pointed after them. "The feast awaits, my children! Finish them! Finish them all!"

The augmented horde bellowed as they charged the building together. Saah turned to his last two men. "You two, come with me."

In the northern tower of glass, Scout led a dizzying path through several winding corridors.

"I know where she's going," Pastor gasped at the rear. "Lysa's quarters are down here."

They spilled into a lavish suite. One small lamp battled shadows with a holographic image that flashed warnings on the wall. The silence in the room cut into Robinson's marrow. Then he saw Friday go still near the back of the room, her head tilted down over a bassinette.

"Friday?" he called, his voice low and tremulous.

On opposite sides of the room, Pastor and the mute sister turned.

Slowly, Friday reached down and picked something up. Robinson's life swung on a pendulum waiting for the rise or fall. Then Friday turned with a bundle of cloth in her arms. Her eyes welled. Robinson stepped toward her, unable to stop as she peeled back the blanket, revealing two brilliant gray eyes and the pinkest of lips. Their daughter cooed, and something resembling a laugh spilled out of Robinson along with hot tears running down his cheeks.

"Your daughter," Friday said.

Robinson's lips parted, but he was too choked up to manage any words. Instead, he stepped forward to embrace his family.

Pastor sighed deeply. And even though the proximity to so much happiness hurt her, the mute sister smiled. How could she not?

A disembodied voice purged the darkness. *Five minutes until Peacekeeper launch.*

Robinson turned to Pastor. "How do we stop the launch?"

The lines on Pastor's forehead darkened. "I can't tell you."

"*Can't* or *won't?*"

The question hurt Pastor as much as anything in his life. Still, he couldn't look away from his young friend.

"Where is the missile housed?"

Pastor opened his mouth only to wince. He was shaking his head when a shadow broke for the door. The mute sister moved quickly and grabbed a trembling woman, pulling her into the light. She must have been caring for the baby. She looked terrified.

"I can take you to the missile if you promise not to hurt me," she said.

"Lead the way," Robinson said.

Chapter Fifty
The Oath

Gesta was shouting for the crowd to stay as the masters flooded the Hall of History, trying to reach the only entrance to the Exodus Vault. The giant titanium doors had been peeled back, but the crowd had grown too frenzied. The entrance was bottlenecked, the horde now pushing and shoving to get inside.

People were trampled, others fought their fellow inhabitants to get inside. Gesta had climbed atop a platform near the wall to address the crowd, but his calls for order had fallen on deaf ears. The masters had spent two hundred years in harmonious safety. Now that the barbarians had purged the gates, they didn't know how else to act.

For a brief second, it looked like order might be restored when a chorus of shrieks sounded at the back of the room and a wave of augmented broke through the outer hall, vaulting into the air, using blunt and projectile weapons to cut masters down.

The crowd surged forward, once again screaming in terror as the clamor of battle overtook them. A detonation sent people and body parts flying. Snarls of the augmented echoed through the chamber as, one by one, the guards fell.

Gesta tried to maintain order, but as the body count rose, he knew it was too late. The end of the city was at hand. He estimated a thousand masters had made it into the Exodus Vault. A third of their numbers. Too little, but more than enough. It now fell to him to ensure the true purpose of the Exodus Vault, and the second generation they fashioned there, endured.

Gesta nodded to the master manning the other side of the gate. The man plucked a shimmering ball from his belt and tossed it into the crowd. A second later, it detonated, sending out a wave of kinetic energy that cleared the entranceway. Then Gesta and the man leaped down and activated the doors. Standing at the threshold, they watched as those toppled souls realized what was happening and surged forward once again. They were too late. The last thing Gesta heard before the darkness closed in was the shouts of agony from those about to die.

The governess led them through the empty streets. Robinson recognized where they were headed. The entrance to the Genesi remained hidden, yet active. Once inside, Robinson saw the staggered tiers were now protected by shimmering barriers to safeguard them from the object at the building's core. Two concentric doors in the floor had opened, and a colossal rocket had risen a dozen feet upward, gas steaming from various vents as lights strobed in time with the countdown. *Four minutes remaining.*

"This is the Peacekeeper?" Robinson asked.

The governess nodded, and when he asked her how to disarm it, she looked at Pastor.

"Do it," Robinson said, but Pastor refused to move.

"He can't," a voice said.

Lysa stepped from the shadows, an old pistol, no doubt claimed from one of the dead augmented, in her hands.

"I tried to tell you, the oath is more than a verbal pledge. It's been hardwired into his very DNA. Impossible to defy or even speak about. One of our more brilliant achievements."

The mute sister reached for her bow, but before she could free it, Lysa fired. A crimson stain blotted the mute sister's stomach as she was propelled to the floor with a grunt.

"I'd prefer witnesses over martyrs for this, but ultimately it won't make much difference, will it?"

"Why are you doing this?" Robinson asked.

"I thought we've been over that."

"You can't honestly believe destroying the human race is the answer to solving the world's woes."

"No species has a greater or more calamitous effect on this planet than us. This, despite our presence here, representing a mere wink in the expanse of time. We've poisoned the soil, the oceans, and the very air we breathe. We've driven untold numbers of species to extinction with millions more on the precipice. All for our own hunger and insatiable greed. Those of us lucky enough to have survived the pandemic had hoped it might cleanse us of these instincts, but look out that door, and you will say they have not only survived—they have also worsened. We can no longer risk our fate or the fate of this planet on our fickle nature."

Robinson saw Friday glance at the mute sister's bow, which had slid to her feet, an arrow still nocked. Robinson shook his head subtly. *Would she dare attempt that with their baby in her arms?*

"Beneath our very feet lies the *Exodus Vault*. An indestructible structure capable of housing and sustaining the populous of this city *in omne tempus*. Contained within its walls is ten thousand variants of a new human DNA, culled from our very own. Wholly perfect and without the instinct for chaos and destruction. It is humanity 2.0, you might say. And whether they rise today or in a thousand tomorrows, they will realize what we could not—a paradise worthy of our conception."

"There's still no guarantee the variants will succeed," Pastor said. "The same instinct that causes strife is what drove us from the muck."

Lysa smiled. "I don't expect you to understand, William."

"It's you who's confused. You remember what we used to say about glass houses?"

You've always loved the old days more, and that love blinded you to the possibility of a better future."

The disembodied voice echoed, "*Three minutes until Peacekeeper launch.*"

"A possibility," Robinson repeated. "Then you admit there's a chance this could fail. And you're still willing to kill all of us on some vague probability?"

"I am. Unlike you, I am willing to sacrifice my life for what I know to be right."

Robinson paled.

"Did you think I couldn't hear you out there in the forest? My birds are everywhere. Twice before you said you've had a choice like this one. And twice you chose to preserve yourself and the thing you loved the most. I'll give you a third choice now." She turned the gun on Friday and their child. "Your life and the lives of those you love for the abort code."

Robinson looked at Friday. She nodded without hesitation, but as Robinson looked at their child, he found himself struggling to make the same call.

Lysa shook her head, reveling in his shame. "And that is why you fail."

She pointed the pistol at him, finger tickling the trigger. Then Scout screeched a warning a fraction of a second before a bolt burst through Lysa's chest.

Saah screamed as he and his two men swarmed the room. "No one kills the boy but me!"

Robinson immediately pulled his pistol and fired three green rounds. One of Saah's men crumbled to the floor. Friday fell to the ground as Pastor leaped for the mute sister's bow, firing the nocked bolt at Saah, narrowly missing him by inches.

Friday crawled backward, cradling her baby as she pulled the mute sister into a small lee. Though weak, the girl lifted her hand. Even as she lay dying, the mute sister was offering to protect their child. Friday gently settled the baby into her arms before scrambling across the floor for Lysa's pistol.

Robinson's sonic blast rebounded off the invisible barrier, striking a ventilation pipe that exploded and sent hot steam belching forward, scorching Saah's face. At the same time, Friday moved with the speed and surety that only one of the Aserra could. She wove through the gunfire of Saah's last man, slipping under another vent of gas before sighting the man with the pistol, pulling the trigger, and watching him fall.

"Force him out of the ring!" Pastor screamed, as he struggled to approach the Peacekeeper controls. Each step felt as if he was being torn apart from the inside.

Robinson and Saah continued to trade fire. Robinson ran around the venting gas, hoping to get behind Saah, when he tripped and landed hard on the floor. He looked up to find Saah's bolt trained on him. Saah beamed, reveling in the moment. He pulled the trigger only to watch the bolt bounce off the barrier Pastor had managed to raise between them.

"No!" Saah screamed as he pounded the barrier to no avail. Robinson stood and locked eyes with him before turning away.

Two minutes until Peacekeeper launch, the voice said.

Robinson ran back to Friday, who held their daughter once again.

"We're fine," Friday said. "Destroy it, and let us go from this place."

Robinson toggled the red button on his pistol and turned to shoot the control module, but he stopped when he saw Pastor standing there pointing Lysa's gun at him.

"I'm s-sorry," Pastor said. "I can't help myself—"

"Pastor, this is me. Your friend. We have to stop the countdown."

"I know," Pastor growled, as his hand shook, but the gun wouldn't lower. "But I can't fight it!"

The building rumbled as mounting mechanisms released from the missile, and the floor started to vibrate.

"The oath. It's too strong!" Pastor said. "You have to run!"

"I can't," Robinson said. "Not anymore. Pastor, look at me. Can you see me? Can you see your friend? Just a few years ago I was a spoiled boy living a life of luxury in a home I didn't appreciate with a love I hadn't earned. I was oblivious to everything but the comforts around me. And yet I was safe and happy. And I could have lived that way forever. But life had other plans. Since then, I've gone through a thousand kinds of misery—misery that would destroy most people. But I wouldn't change it. Because I know who I am. As do you. Please, put the gun down."

Pastor tried to fight the voice in his head, but it was impossible. The harder he pushed, the harder *it* pushed back. He felt blood run from his nose. His hands shook.

"I-I can't," he pleaded. "It's too strong!"

"I know," Robinson said. "Lysa was right about one thing. There's too much pain in this world. And we've had more than our fair share. But we've also shared in the beauty of the road and our friendship. We are more than trees in the forest. We're the canopy that gives everything else life. It took me a long time to understand that." He looked to Friday and saw the tears splashing down her stoic face. She knew it had to come to this. "I love this woman more than I have ever loved anything in my life, but, I'm willing to die by her side if it means others will live."

One minute until Peacekeeper launch, the voice echoed.

"Put down the leash, my friend. You can choose."

Pastor's finger tickled the trigger, and he grimaced. It was all too much. In a flash, he turned the gun toward his chest and pulled the trigger.

Robinson cried out and ran to his friend as he fell. He lifted his head into his chest as his life blood spilled across the floor.

"Forgive me," Pastor said.

"There is nothing to forgive. How do I stop the launch?"

"Lysa's hand," Pastor mumbled.

Robinson turned to Friday. "Drag her over here."

Friday grabbed Robinson's axe and cut off Lysa's hand instead. She set it atop the control module, and the countdown halted. Friday closed her eyes and hugged her daughter tight.

"The trees I showed you," Pastor said.

"The sequoias. I remember."

"Did you know they are dependent on fire? It clears out the soil, allows the cones to open and the seeds to germinate. That is why fire is important to the forest. Its job is not to destroy but to cleanse."

"I'm not sure I understand," Robinson said.

Pastor smiled as his eyes grew heavy. "We aren't the trees or the seeds. We are the fire that helps the forest live."

And finally, Robinson understood.

"Then I'm proud to have done so by your side."

Pastor coughed, blood trickling from his mouth. He struggled to raise his voice. "Self-destruction sequence—initiate."

The disembodied voice answered, *Two minutes until Peacekeeper self-destruct.*

Robinson started to rise, but Pastor grabbed his arm again.

"Have one last surprise for you. A gift from someone you love. Made during my DC exploration. Scout will take you there."

Robinson wanted to say more, but he didn't have the time. Instead, he simply said, "Goodbye, my friend."

Pastor's eyes fluttered, and then he was gone.

When Robinson stood, he saw Friday kneeling next to the mute sister. From the black bile pooling from her belly, he knew she had scant time to live.

"She wants to stay," Friday said.

Robinson crossed to the girl and took her hand.

"Are you sure?" he asked.

The mute sister nodded, and her lips parted. Robinson leaned down and listened. Then he nodded and smiled.

"Go then. Your brother awaits you, and I wish you both fair travels. I'm sure whatever forest you end up in next, your voices will be like honey."

The mute sister smiled, and then Scout chirped.

"Lead the way," Robinson said.

Scout led them out through the barrier. Saah was gone. Robinson and Friday followed Scout to one of the upper tier bays. Robinson was stunned at what he found. It was a flyer from his homeland. Friday saw how it moved him.

"It must have been my mother's. We never found it."

As the countdown continued, they loaded into the flyer. Robinson powered the engines as they strapped in and the anti-gravity came online. The ship bucked once as it thrummed out over the missile and then rose through the open roof and sped away.

The ship landed in the valley, its engines powering down. Robinson opened the door and walked out into the desert plains, turning back toward the City of Glass, which now shimmered openly from afar. A few black snakes of smoke curled around the towers, but they didn't detract from its beauty. A second later, a blinding light lit the horizon, followed by the echo of a tremendous blast. Robinson turned away for a second but looked back in time to watch the towers fall. So much knowledge. So much power. Gone in an instant.

As the city burned, Friday's eyes stayed on Crusoe. She wondered if this would be the incident that broke him. Some warriors did once the big battle was over. But when he turned back, she saw the weary smile she'd come to love, and she knew he'd be all right. He held up their waterskins, and Scout led him to a nearby brook. The baby cooed and pursed her lips. Friday knew she was hungry. She sat down in one of the flyer chairs to feed her child, never seeing the bloody hand push the exterior panel to close the door.

After Robinson filled the second water skin, he stood and felt Scout settle onto his shoulder and chirp. He knew Pastor had come to care for the bird, and now he did too. He leaned toward the bird and was surprised when its beak nuzzled his nose.

The gunshot tore into Scout with an explosion of feathers. Robinson spun to find Saah standing in front of the flyer, Lysa's smoking pistol in his hand. He was a bloody mess. Half his face was blackened. Eyes wild. And yet his lips curled in their familiar cruel smile. *The flyer jolted as it rose. That must have been Saah leaping onto the skids.*

Friday pounded on the flyer's glass, but there was nothing to be done. Saah had him, and this time there was nowhere to run.

"Do you believe in fate, Ser Crusoe?" Saah asked.

Robinson was about to answer when he heard a familiar noise in the brush to his left.

"Yes," he said. "Yes, I do."

Saah raised the pistol again and Robinson slipped two fingers into his mouth and whistled. It wasn't identical to the note he'd heard come from Saah's pipes so often, but it was close enough. As the alpha sprang out of the darkness, Saah saw it and let out a shout. It was too late. The beast tore into its target with a ferocity Robinson had never seen before. Saah's cries lasted for only a few seconds, only to be swallowed by the night.

When the alpha turned, it seemed surprised that Robinson hadn't moved. It took two steps toward him and bared her teeth. Robinson shook his head.

"Enough," he said.

The alpha remained there for a few seconds, eyes locked to the prey it had hunted for so long. A chill wind blew in, carrying with it the smell of smoke and dust. Then something passed between the two, and the alpha turned and bounded off into the night.

Epilogue
From the Ashes

The flyer cruised over the great Atlantica, which rolled with lazy waves and the occasional spray, lighting the dappled water with the cobalt sky above. Friday had never seen anything so large or lovely.

The fuel cell readouts that once doomed Robinson remained constantly full. Whatever Pastor had done to the ship, he'd provided it with an energy source far beyond its previous capabilities. Once Robinson got home, he knew he'd be eager to peel back the curtain for a look underneath. He had other things to concentrate on first.

"Can you fix it?" Friday asked.

Robinson looked at Scout, lying dormant in his lap. The bullet had opened one side of her chest, severing gears and wires, but the CPU appeared intact.

"I don't know," he said. "Her workings are so advanced, but I'd like to try. She deserves that much."

He looked at Friday, finally able to ask the question he'd been holding inside.

"Have you chosen a name?"

Friday looked at their sleeping daughter and nodded.

"Were she to grow in the shadow of the mountains, her actions would choose her name, as I am named, 'the reed that does not bend to the wind.'"

"That's appropriate," Robinson said.

Friday elbowed him.

"But this child will grow up in your land and so she must have a name worthy of it. What is your mother's name?"

Robinson didn't want to get his hopes up. "Annabess," he said at last.

Friday smiled. "Annabess Fenix Crusoe. The healer who rises from the ashes."

Robinson reached for her hand and squeezed it.

A moment later, a telemetry warning announced land approaching. As Robinson sat up straight in his chair, his daughter opened her eyes. The sun was bright in the sky, and water dappled the window, but she didn't turn away.

Dear Reader

Thanks for embarking on this journey with me. It's been a remarkable couple of years and I've enjoyed every arduous step of it. I really appreciate those passionate fans who waited patiently (and not so patiently) between books. Your emails, posts, and tweets helped keep me going.

I've always envisioned Robinson Crusoe's story as a single trilogy, but if you'd like to see more, feel free to drop by my website, Facebook, or Twitter and let me know.

Also, please consider signing up for my spam-free "Newsletter"— an email alert you will <u>only</u> receive when I have something new in the works. Your email and personal info will remain completely confidential.

Sign Up at:
http://erikjamesrobinson.com

Acknowledgements

Writing this first trilogy, I had the good fortune to work with some exceptional people, but none more significant than my editor Jessica Holland. Every time I leapt, she leaped, but together we managed to create something special. I am deeply grateful for her friendship and exceptional talent.

And thanks to Ric Morelli for being reader *numero uno* and keeping the compass due north.

I also appreciate the invaluable insight and support of John L. Monk, Mike "he-who-writes-and-lives-by-a-dozen-names," Celia Aaron, Donna Rich, Jason and Marina from Polgarus Studio, and the wonderful group of family, friends, and readers that have taken this journey into the forbidden kingdom with me. I'm glad we all made it out unscathed.

Lastly, thanks to my wife and children for allowing me to live the life I've always dreamed of. Heaven doesn't always resemble Iowa.

Made in United States
North Haven, CT
16 January 2023

31117865R00207